PRAISE FOR JONIS AGEE'S SHORT FICTION

Taking the Wall

Agee's absorbing new collection of short stories, *Taking the Wall*, is set in the world of auto racing, but it's really about those times in life when we have to switch gears. . . . Much of the power in Agee's short fiction lies in what's left unsaid. . . . By writing just enough and nothing more, Agee forces us to imagine the rest. . . . spare, muscular short stories.

—*The New York Times*

Car racing is somewhere below wrestling and fishing for me, but I was very, very moved by these stories about race car families and their aspirations and heartbreaks. This is universal stuff, and any writer who can compare motor oil to honey deserves our attention.

—Carl Lennertz, Book Sense 76, *Bookselling This Week*

A .38 Special and a Broken Heart

A .38 Special and a Broken Heart is short-short sto deserves to be read, read again and passed to eve down the road.

Death figures in Agee's tales, but so does forgiveness; despair and the burden of family share these wide open spaces with fragile hope and moments of kindness. Agee's fans—and readers who appreciate the immediacy of good short-shorts—will find much to relish here. —*Booklist*

Bend This Heart

The title of Jonis Agee's new collection of short stories, *Bend This Heart*, is instructive, an invitation to make someone feel, not to break a heart but to bend it—to change its shape, to turn it in a different direction, to subdue it—to make a heart work.

These are 23 love stories, though the phrase needs qualification. They are the clear-eyed reports of someone who sees things as they are, not as she would wish them to be. . . . Keenly alive with language, [making] both the heart and the mind work. —*The New York Times Book Review*

Pretend We've Never Met

Some authors tell stories that have happened but have not been told before. Agee writes stories that have to be told before they can be true. The characters could not come to life, and what happens to them could not have happened until Agee told the stories: Someone loses a paring knife that sprouts, grows into a tough tree, the fruit of which is paring knives. And once Agee has told this story, it becomes more genuine than if it had really happened. —*Minneapolis Star Tribune*

ACTS OF LOVE ON INDIGO ROAD

Acts of Love
on Indigo Road

NEW & SELECTED STORIES

by Jonis Agee

COFFEE HOUSE PRESS

2003

COPYRIGHT © 2003 by Jonis Agee
COVER PHOTOGRAPH © Peter G. Beeson
COVER & BOOK DESIGN by Linda Koutsky
AUTHOR PHOTOGRAPH © Richard Gray

Coffee House Press books are available to the trade through our primary distributor, Consortium Book Sales & Distribution, 1045 Westgate Drive, Saint Paul, MN 55114. For personal orders, catalogs, or other information, write to: Coffee House Press, 27 North Fourth Street, Suite 400, Minneapolis, MN 55401.

Coffee House Press is a nonprofit literary publishing house. Support from private foundations, corporate giving programs, government programs, and generous individuals help make the publication of our books possible. We gratefully acknowledge their support in detail on the last page of this book.

Library of Congress CIP Information

FIRST EDITION | FIRST PRINTING
1   3   5   7   9   10   8   6   4   2

PRINTED IN CANADA

ACKNOWLEDGMENTS

Thanks to my daughter Brenda, my sisters Jackie and Cindy, for believing in life and love, for being brave. Thanks to my friends Heid Erdrich, Leslie Miller, Tom Redshaw, Jim Cihlar, Bill Reichard, Greg Hewett, Tony Hainault, for continuing to save a place for me at the table, no matter how far from home I manage to roam. And to Lon Otto, the oldest and best writing friend I have in the world. And to Allan Kornblum, publisher and printer extraordinaire, who has made these books of stories possible.

Some stories from *Acts of Love on Indigo Road* were previously published. "The God of Gestures" and "Once the Dogs Are Sleeping" in *Orchid Literary Review,* Vol. 1, 2002; "Binding the Devil" and "Here We Are" in *Natural Bridge,* No. 8, Fall 2002; "Earl" in *Road Work,* Backwaters Press, 2003; "This is For Chet" and "Cleveland Pinkney" in *Descant,* 2003; "Indigo Road" in *Orchid Literary Reveiw,* Vol. 2, 2003.

For Brent spencer, who taught me how to love again.
And for Sharon Warner, who keeps a wide heart open.

~Contents~

"Drop by drop in sleep upon the heart
Falls the Laborious memory of pain,
Against one's will comes wisdom;
The grace of the gods is forced on us."
—Aeschylus, *Agamemnon*

❖ ❖

NEW STORIES

~Acts of Love on Indigo Road~

❖ ❖

❖ ❖

The God of Gestures

Somewhere in the middle of my last marriage I stopped believing in psychology. He was doing things like, well, you know the drill. We all have the list. But it's because of him that I was the only person at my tenth high school reunion who had dated someone on *America's Most Wanted*.

I met Darwin, his last name's not important, at the Lancaster County Fair, right after the Crying Man, as I called my husband then, had moved in with the fifth grade Girl Scout leader. There had been a flurry of camping and s'mores all spring at the county park where he worked until the fine Sunday morning when he appeared in the doorway in his rumpled ranger outfit and made the announcement with tears flowing down his face. I always hated the crying—it was like he'd stolen something that was personally mine, like my tampax or my purse. I got so I couldn't cry even if I wanted to, and when we argued or a sad scene came on the TV, I had to brace myself against him.

"She likes it when I cry," he'd said, his eyes blinking furiously. "I still love you, but—"

Sometimes you just don't have an answer. So I packed the warped plastic colander, the rusty iron skillet, a dented aluminum saucepan as his share of the kitchen, two threadbare towels I used to dry the old dog with before it died, and a set of stained sheets I'd had since high school. He took his own pillow, of course, battered gray, dense with must and mold.

"Good luck!" I called after his startled face, feeling cheated. Those tears were my private property.

It was another I-Love-You-But Day, and I couldn't stay home trying to plug the holes that had sprung in my life.

I spent the morning at the County Fair, paying strict attention to the dairy cow judging, watching kids corral pigs and comb out sheep and dress them in coats like they were giant Barbie dolls. The local TV station had set up a broadcast booth, and I grew to like the weatherman because his clothes were cheap—polyester tie and shirt from JCPenney—and he stumbled over the names of states like they had hidden vowels. But the anchorwoman was disturbing. When she looked down, the whites rolled out and you could see more of the human eyeball than seemed decent. Bad eye job. Her whole face seemed frozen, only her mouth flexing, like a puppet head. Botox injections. Her brown Jackie Kennedy wig sat slightly askew, as if tilted by the wind. With big Lana Turner sunglasses, she'd be perfect on the afterdeck of the Andrea Doria. Well, we were all sinking ships here, I guess.

I tried not to think of the Crying Man and his Scout leader, rocking in each other's arms, tears soaking the bed as I ate foot-longs slathered in cruel mustard, deflating cotton candy that left a blue rind around my mouth, cones of Tom Thumb donuts swallowed whole, too much hot grease and sugar to be chewed. I wanted the food to stack up in my stomach, to compact and turn hard, because that thing Brother Bob talked about at church was swelling up inside me, dissolving the world like acid—compassion, caring for others, helping—I wanted my old anger to stay calcified, solid. I didn't want to have to explain or understand anything anymore.

"T'aint no thang but a chicken wing, so put it on the platter like it just don't matter." The man held up an air rifle attached by a chain to a plywood ledge other shooters lined along, sighting down the barrels on the battered metal ducks bobbing by at the end of the booth.

"Here, try one for free." He put the gun in my hands and I stared. He was teeth-picking greasy, a tribal tattoo writhing from his wrist to his elbow. Two of his thick fingers were bent stiff and immobile. He was not my type, maybe I should just shoot him, I thought.

"Aim at that target there—" He pointed at a wall of discouraged balloons deflating dustily in the heat above the metal ducks. I shot from the hip and slapped the gun down. There was a dull pop and he snatched a small turquoise plush ball from under the counter and dropped it in front of me.

"Be the ball and kiss the baby," he urged, cocking the gun and handing it back to me.

I shot from the hip again without aiming and another balloon wheezed to death. He snatched back the ball and put a small plush gray shark in front of me, cocked the gun, and nodded toward the board. I closed my eyes for this one. It didn't matter, the balloon swallowed the BB and gurgled flat. The shark disappeared, and a slightly larger pastel striped snake appeared. He cocked, I shot. Other people joined in, all around me were the clangs of pumping and the thuds of shot hitting the ducks, the board, the wooden booth walls. It was as if some crazy magic had taken hold of the place. Nobody missed. Plush toys were flying through the air.

When it was over, he'd run out of toys and ammunition. The customers shrugged and sauntered away, arms full of booty. I had traded all my winnings for a huge turquoise dog, big enough for me to sit in its lap.

"You owe me twenty bucks." He had come under the counter and was standing close enough for me to smell tobacco and sweat on the black T-shirt and blue jeans he'd been wearing for too many days.

"Why's that?" I asked, pulling a floppy dog ear against my stomach.

"You never paid—" He gestured toward the guns.

"You said it was free." I wrapped an arm around the big plush head, the faint chemical fiber smell seemed clean compared to the rest of the midway.

"First one only," he said with a grin. I was wrong—his teeth were surprisingly clean and white.

I thought about the Crying Man and how my heart was a piece of soggy cardboard in my chest, wet and chewed and spit-out looking. Tears filled my eyes so suddenly, I had to bend down and pretend to take a piece of dirt off the dog's back to let them fall to the pounded grass at our feet.

"Hey, I was only kidding—look, come on." He took my arm and pulled me up, hefted the dog on his back and led us across the midway, to the livestock barns where we found a bench in the shade to sit and watch the two-horse hitch competition.

The tears wouldn't go away, though, despite my snuffling and wiping with my T-shirt, but he pretended like he wasn't seeing them, and kept up commentary on the merits of this or that wagon, driver, team, handling, laughing when two wagons almost collided. He didn't seem to find one thing sad.

His name was Darwin, and he'd been working for a feeder lot in Ogallala and got sick of manure and cows and came east to Greenville. He was a good carpenter, he said, raising his hand with two stiff fingers as evidence. He kept brushing the front of his thick dark hair off his forehead so it stuck up and bent slightly forward, while the rest was pulled back in a short ponytail.

I told him that I taught sixth grade in town, and that my husband had left that morning to pursue his career in scouting. I didn't explain. I was as tired of explaining as I was understanding and sympathizing. I still had that solid-as-concrete thing in my middle, and wanted to hang on to it. Too many modifiers, conditional clauses, I said, and he looked puzzled.

"My ex told me I had two minds—" Darwin said, watching me expectantly, his dark brown eyes crinkled. "One's lost and the other's out looking for it." He chuckled and shook his head like the joke wasn't on him.

He stuck to me the whole day, avoiding the midway, except for the rides furthest away. It wasn't until three nights later that he confessed. He was just filling in for the regular guy who got sick and he was supposed to turn the profits over at the end of the day, it was all rigged anyway, but when he saw me—I put my hand over his mouth, trapped him with a leg, and got him going again. We were in the Lighter-Than-Air Society those days, I just wanted simple sentences, doer, done. No adjectives or adverbs, no subordinate clauses, no case histories which began in "remember," the moment you met, and ended in "but."

Darwin. "When his IQ reaches 30, he should sell," his sister said on *America's Most Wanted* that night. The family was sorry, but they couldn't take it seriously. His father said, "Wherever he is, he's depriving a village somewhere of an idiot." In his defense, his mother said she knew he couldn't have staged the robbery and shooting of the monks because "It takes him two hours to watch *60 Minutes*." You get the idea.

I think he was looking for a place to settle when I told him at the end of the summer that it wasn't going to work. School was starting and I needed to be alone. The Crying Man was calling again, his tear-clogged voice muffling the ends of his words. Camping season was coming to an end, and he faced a long cold winter picking up park trash from beer blasts and dogs in the garbage.

"The only thing keeping me alive is I'm so darn afraid of death," he finally confessed, and I had to start seeing him again. I still had my dead parents in To-Go boxes at the cemetery for the day I'd take them back home to Missouri, but they were never gonna be gone either.

I was driving Darwin to the train station when he saw the billboard announcing: Monks, Yes! 1-877-Me-A-Monk. He made me circle the block so he could write the number down.

"You're not even Catholic," I said. He looked startled, the way a dog does when you give it a new command, and for a minute I wasn't sure if he knew what a Catholic was. "Like your sister-in-law's family," I reminded him. But he lifted his butt and shoved the slip of paper in his jeans pocket. I had no idea what he intended to do, and I doubt he did either. It seemed that Darwin was a lily of the field, and the rest of us were just weeds grasping for purchase, knocking down anything in our way.

We said good-bye, his smiling face slipping away as the train pulled out and he tapped on the window shouting words he could've just mouthed. But I knew what he meant, and so did all the people around him too. It wasn't until I got home and discovered my watch, engagement ring, and an expired credit card gone that I laughed with him.

So the Crying Man moved back in, faithful again, though I still didn't speak to the Girl Scout leader when I saw her in the hallways at school. And once in a while Darwin would send a postcard, in his childish scrawl, usually of an animal or an amusement park, as if those held the tenderest moments in a person's life. I showed them to the turquoise dog when we were alone after school was out.

Then, one night a year later, we turned on the TV and there was Darwin's face. He looked creased and angry for the first time, older, more bitter, and the sheer sadness of that made me break down and cry, my husband's arms around me, though I have never said a word about the time I spent with another man. You see, I may not believe in psychology anymore, but I've learned something about sympathy. So when he asked why the tears, they concerned him more than his own suddenly, because they came in such a huge wailing rush, I could not stop to breathe even and he was pounding me on the back saying what's wrong, what's wrong, like I refused to do all those years he cried, and I could only shake my head. Darwin had finally entered the grief-filled waters that flooded the world.

The Presence of Absence

It was like blind bowling, Johny Toronto thought. And then they were chased by a funeral all the way across Kansas, the ten-year-old van with the magnetic signs saying *Hypnosis and Other Stage Shows* stuck on the blue sides just keeping ahead of the hearse and cars maintaining a stately 65 m.p.h. By the time they reached the Nebraska border, the engine had a knock deep within its chambers that threatened to shoot up through the floor, possibly taking his foot flattened on the gas pedal in the process. He turned to his niece, a girl as skinny as he was, chewing the end of her hair like gum and staring at the rolling green hills as if they'd just been to the second coming. Johny was going to say something, but changed his mind. She wouldn't answer anyway, and since the argument about the radio, they'd been living on silence for the past four hours.

Her pink-and-white flowered dress had slid all the way up her skinny thighs and twisted so it became only layers of wrinkles. That'd look nice on stage, he was about to remark, but she glanced at him and he stopped himself. God knows what possessed him to listen to his sister two days before and agree to take Cecelia on the Midwest swing. She could be his assistant, his sister had begged, the cigarette in her trembling fingers sending spirals of smoke up toward red-rimmed eyes that had squinted at him in that painful reminder way. Her husband had just been blown up at a fireworks show in the county park, and she was busy farming out the kids like they were a cash crop anybody'd be a fool not to grab at.

Johny wondered if the kid had seen the funeral procession behind them for the past three hundred miles, but had decided hours ago that talking was pretty useless. When they'd stopped for gas at the Texas border, she left for the bathroom and came back with pop and a half-pound bag of M&M's peanuts which was the only food she consumed the entire way. Fine, he thought, don't offer me any.

He opened and shut his mouth again at the thought of how good they'd taste, but she had the top twisted closed, and the candies trapped in the triangle of her lap and legs folded up on the seat. She glanced at him, spit out the hair end and began to work on the nail of her little finger. He'd already tried to suggest that assistants needed nice nails, but she'd acted deaf or stupid. Maybe she was both. He'd end up paying for nails. Nice long ones with glitter that showed up in the spots.

Cecelia used her sharp little teeth to clip the nail down and moved on to the next one, giving him a G.H.-look. Go straight to hell, it said.

I didn't kill your daddy, he scowled back. It was the 100-Shot Titanium Salute with Tail.

"He promised he was gonna caulk the house," his sister Denise kept saying. "Just give him August and a good caulk gun and he'd go crazy. Now—"

That's when Johny had held up his hands and agreed to take the oldest girl on the road. He glanced at the time. Five o'clock and they had to be on stage by eight. Farm folks went to bed early, the supper club had warned him on the phone. Keno parlor or no, they were in and out with their money. He glanced at Cecelia's wrinkled dress again. It was too much to think that they'd have an iron in the dressing room. Hell, they'd be changing in the bathrooms or the back of the van. Sleeping by the side of the road if they didn't make enough for a motel. Hell, he'd have to give her the costume Marie left when she'd met the preacher in Waco and run off to God and a double-wide. But she'd been a plump girl, round and fluffy as a laying hen. The spangled dress would look like it was still hanging in the closet on this kid.

"I feel kilt." He almost jumped at her words, the first she'd spoken since they'd left Texas. He slowed the van.

"You gonna throw up?" He signaled the turn onto the shoulder although there was absolutely no one around. When he shifted into park, the engine relaxed to a steady ping.

She looked straight ahead out the windshield, her eyes locked on the green rows of corn on either side of them, the patched pavement stretching into the distance.

"You don't need you a young trainee," the waitress in Wichita had remarked, her eyes clearly disbelieving his story about the girl being his daughter. She'd been right though. He couldn't imagine how Cecelia was going to work the crowd, get the retired farmers and angry young men trying to make gas money in the Denton Keno Parlor to come up and be hypnotized. Women were easier, but you couldn't make them do the goofy things that brought the big tips and laughs. Not any more when every thought a man had was a criminal.

"You gonna be sick?" he asked again.

This time she shook her head. She had the same limp brown hair they all had—too fine to curl or cut right, it ended up shaggy. Anyone could see the resemblance between the two of them, her small sharp nose and chin same as his, he didn't know why that waitress had a question in her eyes.

Cecelia took a deep breath and let it out in little spurts and hiccups like she might be going to cry.

"Scared about the show?"

She glared at him this time, a look full of pure animal hate that sharpened the muddy brown eyes, like a vicious dog on a chain. It set him back.

"I ain't your daughter," she said through gritted teeth. "You're just some old bum, driving around in your old junker." Her fist flashed out and hit the radio, knocking it loose from the big hole in the dash he'd repaired with duct tape after the thieves had stolen the original unit. The radio sputtered on with weak static, then whined into silence.

"Look at this thing—" She unleashed a long skinny leg and kicked the blue dash, setting off a cloud of dust and cracking the dried-out vinyl. She pounded the door and the window handle popped off.

This wasn't good, Johny thought, reaching down to the floor and being met by a flurry of feet and fists.

"Get off me!" she screamed.

He plastered himself against the driver's side, too scared to speak as she suddenly calmed, jerked down the visor and stared at her face in the cloudy mirror.

"I need lipstick, eye shadow, mascara, foundation, blush . . ." The list went on, and he nodded dumbly. "You better get going," she said.

They stopped at Wal-Mart in Crete and wound their way over blacktop roads into Denton, population 161, while Cecelia transformed herself in the round vanity mirror she'd had him buy. He hadn't even asked what all the stuff in the cart was, just handed over the two hundred-dollar bills he kept tucked in a secret pocket of his billfold for emergencies and carried out the big plastic bag.

"Go get set up," she ordered as soon as he stopped in front of the Denton Supper Club and Keno Parlor. Usually he took this time to calm himself, put his powers together for the evening. You couldn't just go in and hypnotize people, you had to have confidence and magnetism. Right then he'd have trouble putting gas in cars, let alone convincing people to be part of a stage show. He got out and went inside.

The manager was nice enough. The place was pretty bare bones, a small pole barn next to the Legion hall which was at least wood. Both of them offering Keno so losers could spread their luck.

When he came out, he didn't see her in the van, and he panicked that she'd taken off or been kidnapped. Then across the street he saw her skinny legs sticking out of a gold-and-brown snakeskin print minidress, a thing so slimy and cheap it looked worse than anything, even a motel bedspread. On her feet were black four-inch block-soled sandals that made her lift her legs like a show horse or a person caught in quicksand as she clumped around the concrete statues of the Denton Stone Works next to the Squeegee Gas 'N Go. The one-story store was surrounded by naked and semi-clad figures from antiquity—girls whose tendrils of hair were twined with flowers, dresses draping to expose a breast while they held baskets of more flowers; naked men with horns growing out of their heads and water spouting from their open mouths; huge funeral urns and small children playing around them; stone carts pulled by stone goats, horses, and dogs; cats curled in stone contentment; giant chickens, deer, ducks; a gray pig the size of a cow—it was so confusing to the eye he felt a little turned around.

He hurried across the wide street lined with pickups and dusty sedans parked at an angle. Even before he reached her, he could hear the clatter of the black and gold glitter plastic bangles she now wore.

She was standing in front of the largest statue in the yard, a life-sized ape glaring like King Kong as it leaned forward, hairy stone back humped, the knuckles of his hands almost touching the gravel.

"I need this," she said with a nod. "I really do."

She turned toward him, and he felt like an M-80 had lodged in his heart. She was a stranger, utterly not his own, and utterly frightening. He couldn't even look at her face, so foreign was it, so painfully separate as she held out the white price tag that said eight hundred ninety-five dollars.

"This is what I want," the voice soothing in a way that told him he'd do anything she said.

The Creek

It's because our creek doesn't need a name, Pa says. Muddy, no count, flushing the dirt from the cow barn, the hog pen, down into the depths of the lower meadow, flooding us in the spring. We moved down here to get away from people, Pa says, naming just reminds me.

So it's my private business when I call it Salt Creek though the water has more dirt than anything. Or Bother Creek after the Appaloosa stud lies down to roll the flies and me off his back. I kick his belly and jerk his mouth bloody until he stands again, rolling his white blue eyes with his ears flat and teeth snapping the air beside my head. You, you get up here, I yank a sucker off the cottonwood almost toppling into the water, and shake it at him. He snorts and grabs the stick with a wicked snap of teeth. I let him have it, he has to win sometimes too. I nudge him in the ribs with my bare heels when he cow-kicks as I swing onto the dripping back. Lucky I've left Pa's saddle at the barn. He'd pitch both of us out for breaking the tree.

Where you going, Blue? my little sister asks when I come out of the trees, the stud muddy to his knees from scrambling up the bank. Lindsey is picking bush beans for Ma, one eye on the dirt between the rows where the snakes like to rest on hot days. She waves the snake-poking stick at me and the stud and he half rears, pretending to be afraid. Lindsey is wearing my overalls and Pa's tall rubber mud boots to fend off the snakes and bugs. Grandpa's old straw hat hangs loose over her ears, and she has to keep pushing the brim up as she bends for the beans.

Can I come? She lets the tin bean bucket drop and it rolls to its side. The answering rattle from the green shade of the next row makes her yelp and startle toward us. The stud snorts and paws, stretching his long neck toward the sound. I can feel the angry swell of his belly and chest and have to fight him. Lindsey stops by my foot, holding the bare ankle with her wet muddy hand. We listen but the cicadas and hoppers are buzzing like mad, and the birds calling and running around the woods and field.

Throw your stick at it, I say. No, here, give it to me. And she hands it up, the stud rolling his eye and flicking his ears at us. He doesn't flinch when I walk him around the edge of the bean patch, up the next row. The snake is a young timber rattler, red and black ladder-back, speckled white and black on its sides. It's trying to look more pissed off than puzzled when I wave the stick and yell. The stud starts pawing again and I have to hold him tight or he'll go after it. He hates snakes.

Despite my yelling and the stud's giant shadow over it, the snake doesn't budge until I throw the stick. It whirls and strikes at the stick as it lands with a clunk in the dirt. The rattler's too young and dumb not to try to bite the stick and almost gets its fangs stuck but manages to pull back, reorganize, give me a quick angry look, then slide down the row, the newly forming rattles the last thing we see before the green shadows swallow it.

Don't use that stick again, I tell my sister. It's soaked with poison now. Lindsey looks like that's about the last thing she intends to do, and finally I have to slide off the stud, pick the stick up by the very end and fling it into the woods, then go and get her another snake stick before she's willing to go back to work on the beans. I even pick the bucket up, pull a baby toad out and hand it to her. She squeals and drops the toad, rubbing her hands together to dislodge the imaginary wart juice.

Don't tell Ma about this, I say.

The snake? She looks over her shoulder at the next row of beans gleaming hot green in the sun, the long beans dangling like slender fingers.

Any of it, I say. She's got enough to do.

Can I go with you? she asks again. Those blue eyes are full of scared tears but I can't tell her where I'm going. I want to but I can't so I grab a piece of the stud's mane and swing up again.

Just bang the pail with the stick and sing real loud, the snakes will run for the creek, I say.

Her little shoulders slump and she looks down at the pail, shaking the beans to see if there's enough. Of course it's not even half full.

Mom's canning today, isn't she? I say. Lindsey nods her head. Better get a move on then, I say.

I'm scared, she says, her shoulders starting to hunch against the crying that's moving up from her stomach.

So I push the stud on down the row, pivot at the end and head back, going up and down the whole vegetable patch, singing and whooping. Even the orange and yellow butterflies bust loose and cloud off.

There, I pull up beside her, you won't even see a daddy longlegs in there now. Scared the bugs to death and put the fear of God in every snake this side of Crete. Now go on, get, before Pa comes down here to check on things.

She glances up and frowns. We both know what Pa's visit could mean, and as I thread my way along the edge of the woods again, following the line to the road, Lindsey is picking as fast as she can, the snake stick left in the dirt behind her. I'm the big brother and I should help, but it's her job and she has to learn or it'll be harder and harder on her. All us kids have had to learn that lesson.

Finally where the pasture and woods curve back toward the west, we climb down the gully, cross the creek, and scramble up the other side, bursting out onto the dirt road that leads up to the old house and barn where Pa first settled. Hot sweat soaks the insides of my legs, up my crotch where the jeans rasp, and I keep thinking about getting in the water tank up there, soaking the wet hair stink and creek mud off if I have time.

Come on, I lean over the stud's neck and squeeze him with my calves. He leaps forward, instantly running flat out, body a long hard muscle as we sail up the hill, down the hill, up the next, the trees of the lane in the distance coming closer and closer as if we're pulling it toward us on a string. At the tree-lined lane, he breaks into a trot, shaking his head, splattering my legs with lather. I reach down and slap the hot soapy neck, wiping my fingers on the wet white mane.

Here, I say when we reach the stock tank next to the barn. The windmill has been pumping non-stop for a week, and the cattle have bunched in the lattice of shade it makes. Some of them are so hot they just stand there with their noses in the water, as if too tired to drink, and too tired to move. The muddy ground is deeply pocked from hooves in the spillage. The stud quickly bullies his way in, kicking and snapping and shoving as the cows lunge and stumble out of his way until he's pushed all of them off. Then he sticks his nose in and takes a long drink before I can haul his head up. He fights me for a minute, but finally I get him turned facing toward the house until his breathing slows down to normal.

I'm hot too, I tell him. He shakes all over like a dog trying to fling off water, then he looks over his shoulder, eyeing the tank and my foot like he's deciding whether it's worth it to pull me off so he can get to the water faster. Then he shakes his head, flapping the wet mane, and drops his head to nuzzle the patch of dandelions at his feet. I let him have the rein and he pulls the yellow heads off, tonguing them delicately to the back of his mouth where he can chew around the bit.

When he's cooled down, we fight the cattle away again and I turn the stud loose while I strip off my jeans and shirt and climb in the tank. The stud sticks his head in and shovels water at me until I splash him back. We play around like that until he rears up and his forelegs almost come down in the tank.

Go on, get out of here! I yell and slap his face and neck until he shoves my chest with his nose and walks over to a good clear patch of dirt, lowers himself and rolls over and over. When he's done, he raises himself to his haunches, gives me that wall-eyed look, rolling his whites wildly, and stands up with a long dusty shake. Noticing some cows bunched in the slice of shade from the barn, he herds them down the hill into the larger part of the pasture, following close enough to nip their butts. Pa would kill me if he saw that.

The stud was my idea. We should cut him before he gets ornery, Pa tried to argue me out of it since I saved up and bought him at auction three years ago. Don't need no stud around here, he'd say. Appies are the worst, he'd warn. You'll never be able to trust him.

I kept my mouth shut though I wanted to say, Who ever said anything about trust?

You're cutting him before winter, Pa said last week. I mean it. He's too old for this nonsense. Then he'd added, I'm too old for this nonsense. The stud had broken through the fence and jumped Pa's favorite roping horse. He'd done the same thing when Lindsey's little mare came in heat and sored up the mare's back so Lindsey was on foot. He'd been banished to the lower creek pasture for the past week, with Pa's pissed off longhorn bull between him and the other horses.

You should do it before it gets cold, Pa said this morning. Give him time to calm down before spring.

With the stud eating quietly, I lie back in the water, letting the clumps of green scum we've broken loose from the sides of the metal tank eddy across my stomach as my legs spread and the water flows over and around me, making me feel more than naked. She'll be late if she comes at all. That's how it is. I don't even bother looking at the house, she won't be there yet. I know that.

There's a special quiet about the homestead, something deeper beneath the hiss and rustle of the wind in the cottonwoods and cedars, the clank and click of tin roofing and loose boards, the blue jays arguing in the old lilac bushes, somewhere below the drone of insects there's a silence. Maybe it's just us missing from here, I decide, maybe the sound right after we're done, the open mouth when there's nothing left to say, the dark hole of disappearance we become at the end of things.

I get up and climb out, wipe myself with my shirt, then push my arms through the holes of the missing sleeves. The stud in the pasture looks up at me.

You know where I'll be, I call to him, and his ears flick back and forth before he sighs and drops his head to eat. His pasture's getting too low, I told Pa this morning.

Cut him, Pa said. Then he can be with the others.

Is that a flicker of white in the window frame of the house? I step into the damp jeans that stick and pull the hair on my legs all the way up. Hurrying to climb through the wire fence, my arm catches on a barb but I don't feel it until the warm blood starts weeping from the long gouge. I wipe it on my jeans and walk faster and faster until I'm running up the two-inch-thick wooden steps, sturdy after everything else is falling down. Pa and his steps, you need a good strong entrance, he says.

Yes, Pa, yes, I sweep her into my arms, full and white her dress, the blood of my arm making a circle around her as I pick her up and carry her to the other room, to the shuck-filled mattress that crackles around us as I bloody her dress with my kisses, my hands and more until we are both in the quiet again.

I've ruined your dress, I say, plucking at the darkening blood we're lying on.

You've hurt yourself, she says. Does it hurt? She touches the edge of the cut, and I want it to hurt more for her. I squeeze the gouge, pressing the sealing blood until it bubbles again. When it coats her finger red, she stares at it, then touches it to her lips, then to mine. The tip of her tongue tastes my blood, then she pulls me down to her and we taste it together, salty, bitter, the blood. I've ruined your dress, I want to say, what should we do now?

It's a long time before I see her again. My arm swells up and yellow pus runs in long streams, then red streaks appear and the doctor threatens to cut it off and I'm so full of fever and pain I can't stop seeing Pa lifting the ax and coming for me. I won't let him near me for two weeks. When they cut it open to let it drain, I can't stop myself from calling for her, over and over, until Pa relents and lets the doctor give me morphine. You don't have to pay for it, the doctor keeps telling Pa. It's mercy, he says. You're killing him.

I remember Lindsey in a white dress and it's the end of summer, and the wind is blowing the heat off the land, and she's safe beside me. Don't get blood on you, I say. She pats my hand, keeping her eyes off the draining wound while she waves the flies off with the cardboard cover she's ripped off her storybook.

Don't let Pa touch the stud, I tell her. Come get me if—

Shhh, she says.

I know I thought of the old house, the girl, how she tried to wash the blood out in the tank, and finally left at dark. She never told me where she lived. Close by, she'd say. Her name—what's your favorite flower, she asked. Iris, I told her. Iris, she said, my name's Iris.

It's November before I make it back there again. We're in an early winter, and the fields are snowed down already. Cattle fighting the icy crust for dried grass. I haven't wanted to go out. This is really the first time, you understand, after I saw the Appy in the big pasture with the other horses.

You should have told me, I said. Lindsey shook her head and stared at the beans on her plate. Pa?

I told you all along. Then you were laid up—He gestured with his knife toward the healing arm that is withered and paler than the other. I've lost so much weight my jeans barely stay up and my shirts hang on me like I'm wearing another man's clothes.

The Appy trudges over dutifully and I give him the apple I've stolen from the winter barrel in the dugout storeroom of the storm cellar. He nudges me with his chin, but his eye stays calm. He isn't on his toes prancing either. So I sling Pa's saddle on, knowing I can't swing up with the weak arm and heavy coat. I never seem to be warm enough these days.

Pa's eyes looked like they were nervous when he told me to go on up and drive the cattle into the hay yard. But I think that was just me. Everything looks different now. I drop my head and make the horse walk into the wind up and down the two hills, feet carefully testing the icy road, grunting when they start to slip. I give him what reassurance I can, resting my bad arm on the horn, patting him with the good hand.

There's a giant cottonwood down at the top of the lane, and we can barely edge awkwardly around its shattered trunk. I pause. The yellow flesh glistening starkly against the dark wet bark and white lane. Must have happened in the wind last night, when the cold came roaring down from the north snatching off tree limbs and frosting over all the windows of the house. The Appy's thick hair stands on end like millions of white and black needles, and he's shivering just standing there.

Come on, I say, and nudge him forward. We plod down the lane, wading in drifted snow that nothing has disturbed yet. I open the hay yard down by the creek and drive the cattle in so they have water and shelter and food. They're so hungry they circle a huge stack and begin tearing away at it. I glance down the bank at the creek to make sure it's still running. The water's as muddy as ever, but it's better than eating snow. It won't freeze unless the cold holds for a long time. Too many springs feeding it. Spring Creek.

The door to the house is blown open, a small pile of snow wedging the entrance. I shove it out with my boot, glancing back to make sure the App will stay tied to the post of the broken apart fence. His back is already turned and hunched against the wind, head down, eyes blinking away the ice on his lashes. I haven't loosened the girth. Don't mean to be here long. Just to see—

The mattress is a blanket now, the coat, it's a man's coat, worn threadbare, feet bare in the summer, sheathed in thin black shoes now caked with ice. Her face blue-white and perfect. The fingers of her hand reaching out, white and hard, for me.

When the sheriff comes, he tells us that she was a runaway from the Lutheran Home for Girls two miles away. They had hoped she'd made it to safety when the cold came last night. She'd been gone three days. I don't say anything. Nothing at all. Not for the whole long winter.

The first warm night of spring when the wind's blowing fragrant from the south, I put Pa's saddle on the App and ride away. Bitter Creek, I tell people I meet, I'm from Bitter Creek.

Easy Montgomery

I thought about killing that dog.

Then I tied him to the front bumper of my car and slowly chased him instead, the rope taut between us. Me steering with my knees and drinking beer, while he ran ahead following the true lines of Indigo Road, maybe believing he was actually pulling the car like a sled.

I had enough satisfaction just thinking I was chasing him those nights—the moonlight blanketing his black coat with silver and his breath panting small frozen clouds the prow of the car broke through. He was silent, his breathing absorbed by the engine knocking into the cold night around us, and the roaring my own craziness made in my ears.

Where Is Ed Abboud?

Serena is having a come-to-Jesus meeting with the front yard while from the concrete apron of the front porch Dr. Laura's self-righteous radio whine chastises people with really bad judgment. Like the mother who has just called in to see if it's OK to let her five-year-old daughter play with the molester two doors down.

"I know he's on parole," the caller says in a hesitant voice, "but he's so nice."

Dr. Laura is the fourth-grade teacher kids fear—the one who knows what the dirt on a person's hands really is. Serena's waiting to hear her husband Ed's voice calling in, or even maybe her sister Candy who ran off with him last week. One of them should be calling asking how to make it up to her, how to get their stuff back.

When Candy's boyfriend tried to burn her clothes in a pile in their driveway, she'd moved in with Serena and Ed. "Just a few days till I get on my feet," she'd promised. "This is pretty nice for a used house."

Candy's boyfriend had a new double-wide. Serena's house is a small pink box with a garage of equal size squatting at the dead end of a single street development next to a dry creek on the edge of Greenville. Nobody knows where the water went, and the creek lost its name after it lost the water. Maybe her husband Ed went there too, the place where the lost water got to, the place where the call-ins hide after Dr. Laura has her say. Maybe there's no way to retrieve something once it's gone. Serena yanks out the whole row of floppy pink petunias and tosses them in a heap.

The grass is turning yellow around the edges of the big pile of gravel and sand she's been hauling up from the dry creek bed for the past week, and the new cactus are starting to lean and shrivel in their black plastic pots. Zero Landscaping. Put nothing in, get nothing out.

"Sweet dreams," her husband had whispered her to sleep that night. Sometime around dawn she'd heard the swish swish of Ed's in-ground sprinklers hitting the house siding, but hadn't missed his long body next to her. It wasn't until later that she remembered the watering schedule—Sunday was a skip day.

She'd been so pleased that her husband had pitched in and helped put Candy back on her feet. She hadn't minded when they'd run to the grocery and come home laughing with a twelve-pack of beer. Now, of course, Dr. Laura makes it clear that she was just being stupid, weak. She rakes the gravel six inches thick across the little front yard, carefully covering the lush, green grass, the black sprinkler heads with their solitary screw eye and slit mouth, witnesses she doesn't need.

The cactus raise their stiff little arms in alarm and stick her hands as she plants them along the front of the house. Ed's petunias looking smashed in their wilted heap.

"Cactus only need to be watered every two weeks unless it rains," the Earl May clerk had promised.

Serena presses the gravel close to the spiny bases and stands, leaning on the rake while Dr. Laura chides a woman who wants to move across the country to shack up with her boyfriend. Serena shakes her head. Didn't anyone ever learn anything? She thinks of the nights she went to bed at ten, leaving her husband and sister drinking beer at the kitchen table, still laughing at the same joke.

"You knew," Dr. Laura tells a man calling to complain about his girlfriend. "You knew what she was doing, didn't you?"

Did he? Did he really know? How does he know if he really knew?

That night a cricket clambers over the gravel and lodges itself in the dusty corner outside her window, chirping a warning into her sleep. At dawn the sprinklers spurt on, a couple managing to push their heads to the top of the gravel, producing a sickly gargling instead of the fine, clean spray sweeping against the house like shirtsleeves brushing her screens. A thief breaking in, or already leaving, her life tucked safely under an arm.

The Waiting

 It wasn't such a big noise, more a muffled thump like a body falling out of bed at night. A bad dream that sends it sprawling. And that's how we found them. Some parts whole, untouched, like faces pensive as sleeping children when you go to tuck them in, but we're done with that in our little prairie town. Our children born and moved on, trying to forget us or sending notes glued to the top of retirement home brochures, places whose new yellow brick rests as low and flat as hands on a table. There's nothing to worry about here, they try to assure us, nothing hidden. We file those in the cardboard box with our children's drawings, school papers, clippings they send us when they move up the ladder. We hardly recognize them in their suits and fresh haircuts so we place them sadly away in the dark brittle folds of paper. All they are now. A confident voice on the phone shouting the distance down to our age which they see us wearing like deafness.

We went right out there at dawn, of course, as soon as one of the retired farmers coming into town for coffee noticed them. The plane separated into parts burrowing into Pearson's old wet spring cornfield. Someone said it looked like a snake shedding its skin, and another said like when you smash a spider or beetle, how the parts come off and scatter but you can still tell what it is. That was the way we talked to gather ourselves as we stood there realizing that the weight of them might somehow belong on our shoulders now. We were waiting for the authorities on that little ridge above the field pooled with standing water at the low south end by the cottonwoods where the wire fence has rusted off the posts. There are always people in authority who arrive at the scene and organize you, get you started, tell you what to look for. But by the time the sun was situated firmly above us, nobody had come, so we started down there ourselves. We'd been aching to. It looked from the ridge like someone's laundry had been spilt and dragged, and we had that urge you get to put things right.

No matter what you hear, nothing is the same. That's what we said to each other later. They were curiously shorn, bloodless I mean. Fairly clean except for the dirt. Someone wondered if we shouldn't wait as we got closer and saw it, but we went on about our business. A woman's hand, fingers relaxed and bent, wearing a milky opal ring, that was my first, and I picked it up and eased my fingers between hers and held her for a moment. Impulse, maybe, I rubbed the smear of dirt from the back with spit as if it were my own and placed it in my pocket, keeping my hand clasped to warm her.

People backed their pickups and cars down the ridge and we took the blankets and garbage bags and settled into it for real. I sank ankle-deep in the mud but my galoshes saved me as I collected from my little area. We were so used to working together that we moved across the field like mowers in the old days, a line that broke and wove as someone collected enough to be taken back to the vehicles that couldn't follow us for the deep mud. It was the same way we set up our Arbor Day and Veterans Day parades and strung the town with decorations for holidays like Christmas and Flag Day and took care of the cemetery on Memorial Day. So few of us now, we each have work to do, even the old grade school teacher, Miss Moss. Once in a while the blackbirds would cry from the cottonwood grove the plane barely missed taking down, or the breeze would ruffle the torn metal, but we were quiet. I kept touching the outside of my wool coat, patting the hand in my pocket to let her know I was there.

Things we hadn't thought of: the shoes and handbags, the sheer bulk of suitcases and paper, paper everywhere and we collected every single piece, chasing some of it half a mile. Not easy on legs like ours. Newspapers, glossy magazine pictures, pages of books, letters, bills, receipts, notebooks and tablets, plain white sheets full of numbers and reports that spewed from blown-up briefcases, photos, names and addresses. We kept thinking in the back of our minds that the authorities would be arriving soon and we wanted to do our part. You don't leave a thing like that just sitting there. I found two arms which didn't match, but I brought them together anyway, thinking that they might have held hands once, or wanted to if they had been in different circumstances.

They looked relieved when I laid them in the car trunk on the quilt from the guest bed, joining the pair of brown oxfords, stained and torn sneakers, and tan raincoat wrapped around something my husband had placed there. He was always thoughtful of everyone he met, and while his children mistook it for weakness, I recognized it for what it was.

We worked hard all day, rubbing our shoulders and arms and backs when we paused for the coffee and sandwiches Louis's café sent over. It wasn't such a big plane, and all told, not that many people, fifteen or so, but we wanted to make sure we got them all. That field would be overgrown in another month and animals would move in there at night when we left. The crows were already collecting in the cottonwood groove, tipping their heads at us when someone found a bright bit of jewelry or metal. I kept her hand safely in my pocket until we were done, then I slipped the ring from her finger. No luck for her, it seemed to say.

And we were waiting for the authorities to come the way they do on television with big lights and special trucks and yellow rubber caution suits. At the end of the day, we put them all in the old high school gymnasium, careful to avoid the places where the roof leaked. Most of their things too. I think even then some of the others kept things the way I did, because we couldn't bear to be parted. If the authorities had come like they were supposed to, I would've given it to them.

We waited all the next day while the smell sprouted heavy and sweet in the dark room. Then we collected them carefully, wrapping each assembled with the right number of parts as best we could in good linen tablecloths, quilts, or lace curtains, and hauled them in Guttman's Feed Mill truck to the cemetery. As we lifted them out and let them down into the holes, they gave off little puffs of corn meal dust which we took as a good sign. Afterwards, we went to the church to sing "Amazing Grace" and "What a Friend We Have in Jesus" and "Rock of Ages," pray some, and go to the fellowship basement room for coffee like we always do. But I think we all felt that same green regret. Like clothes left for years on the same hanger, we've known each other so long we just naturally take the same shape of things. So we all began to drift back to the gymnasium, to pick up a few particular things to take home.

Our children were gone, moved away, gradually forgetting us here. We didn't look at each other with surprise when the white hair appeared at the forehead, and the walk slowed and crooked. After the minister died, nobody else came to take the All Faiths Christian Church so we did without. Usually on a Sunday morning somebody would get up and say something they remembered that was good or interesting after we'd sung a few hymns. We kept choir practice on Wednesday nights because we'd been doing it for so long it didn't make sense to stop now. And we were anxious that things our people left behind in the gymnasium have someplace to belong while we all waited.

There were names on some items and we took the ones that seemed to fit or gave them new ones after a while, names they should've had. My husband kept the tan raincoat after he put what it had held in the state flag he'd gotten when the Rotary chapter closed but didn't call it anything after we laid it on the guest bed with the opal ring, a lady's red leather glove, a letter from a sister with small, neat handwriting like we were taught in school, the yellow dress, black high heels with a scrape across the toe I polished away, a tube of pink lipstick, a blue plastic hairbrush, a sample bottle of green mouthwash, a muddy toothbrush I never could get clean, and a big white man's handkerchief I bleached the dinge out of. There were other pieces, but as you would expect, it was certain ones that kept our attention. I didn't ask what had been held in the coat. I've learned to trust my husband over the years, he is so tenderhearted. Maybe it was a baby, but I could not know that and stay the same, so I had never looked. The ring and the lady's glove seemed lonely there, the dried leather fingers cupping up for something, so I put fresh snapdragons in her palm one day, then after that daisies and a rose and flowering white clover from the yard. All summer she held flowers and I began to dry some for winter too. When the next-door neighbor inquired, I told her they were doing well, comfortable in our extra little room. And we began to share stories of our people, how their dreams and wishes seemed to be spreading from their belongings into our houses, and how we worked to keep them well. We stayed so busy those summer months, we felt our town growing again, pushing itself like a full stomach back from the table. Having spent the night in the dreams of others, my husband and I met at the breakfast table, touching hands as hot as fresh toast. Soon, our yards were as full of flowers as the old days when our children were young and there was love to keep servicing, when what was good spilled out of the doors and windows and kept everything green and growing.

Then one Wednesday evening right around Thanksgiving at choir practice, my next-door neighbor took a pale-blue man's work shirt from her purse and draped it across the back of the pew beside her. The next week, there were three pairs of shoes, the shirt with a yellow-and-white polka-dot tie loosely knotted at the throat, a maroon silk dress, a cornflower-and-pink figured long skirt, and a plump naked doll without the head, its twin arms reaching out to the dark oak pew in front of it. The next week the doll had a new yellow organdy dress on, and I brought the glove with me for the first time. She was holding the last of the daylilies, the tips of her fingers dusted orange with pollen, and she was wearing the opal ring. Next to her sat a neat brown purse with a shoulder strap. She wasn't that old, you see. An opal ring was something a young woman would wear and laugh about, while an older woman would know better. It gave me comfort to have her there, and afterwards we all talked about our people, relating stories of their lives, shyly at first, then more boldly, as if we'd been living with secrets we couldn't not share. We gave them places around the tables, their own wooden folding chairs, and respected their silences as well as the stories they had to tell us.

Everything got easier then. When Mr. Adam passed on a week before Christmas, we were feeling so good, we decided to keep what was left on the shelves of his Corner Hardware and run it on the honor system. It was just us and we already knew the one or two who might steal. I think that's when we stopped waiting for the authorities to come and went ahead and hauled the plane parts to the big gully and dumped them in to stop the erosion. It wouldn't work of course. That gully had been there since before the town got started and it had eaten everything else we'd dumped: cars, tractors, barrels, dead animals, tin cans and bottles, furniture, appliances, ruined barns and houses, billboards and highway signs, books, clothes, mattresses and springs, asphalt, gravel, chunks of cement. They all collapsed, rusted, disintegrated, and disappeared and the gully remained the same, maybe even a little deeper. It didn't surprise us that the plane made no difference either. It had all but disappeared by the big January thaw.

When the first anniversary drew near the next spring, we decided to invite everyone to church for a service. It was to be in the evening, and we were to wait up all night long, in a kind of vigil, with candles though most of us weren't Catholic, until dawn when someone would climb the tower and ring the bell that hadn't sounded since the minister died. My husband climbed up a few days earlier and cleaned out the sparrow nests so we'd get a good clear sound. We wanted our people to see that we weren't taking them for granted just because the authorities weren't coming. They were ours now, and we intended to do the best we could for them. So we all brought what food and drink we could from home, and I decorated the pews with the last of my dried flowers. I thought she'd understand and spring was here, the tulip heads fairly bursting and as soon as they did, she'd have fresh flowers again, I assured her. Toward evening my husband brought our people since I'd been at the church all afternoon getting ready. He laid the raincoat next to where he was to sit, and arranged the others along the pew so they had enough room. I stood in the back, making sure the flowers didn't get brushed into and fall apart on the floor, they were after all, dried, and by the time everyone was settled down, the church was full, something we hadn't seen since before the children grew and left. I think that night we all felt that swelling of pride that comes when you see a good thing done as we sang and prayed and shared the new people's stories and concerns. How they missed their loved ones, their children, how they worried about jobs and debts left unfinished, unpaid, how they wanted something more out of life than what they got. They had grown hurt and sad along with the resignation of the past year, and all night long we did our best to comfort them now that they had come home to us.

The Land You Claim

 Sometimes, the most dangerous land to claim is that of your fathers, so we came down out of the Tennessee mountains, quickly crossing the valleys, running from the wide-open sky. We wore our eyes on our knees in the deep grass, low and open, the sky pressing around us, drooping and draped like a sheet shook fresh from the sun, softened by a good green wind. It rushed down among the trees into this little clearing after us. Now I sit on the porch of my cabin and wait in the shadow on my skin for that big hissing to shake the cedar limbs and rattle the bushes like a flock of passing blackbirds.

Here above the rising lake, I watch the wind come down to drink, brushing a circle in the water like a horse nosing aside the bits of leaves, twigs, loosened plants tugged and washed free of their moorings, sudsing these waters brown. Why is the water dark, little Carolyn asked, black like rusty blood? Is it the bodies they left behind?

I know. Now I see she does too. I went down to the hollow before they came. Alone I took the mules and pulled the gravestones up the hill. Pushed them into the quarry hole at night when no one would be watching. The turquoise water as dead as those slabs took them with a splash, a gulp, a disappearance into its bottomlessness. One hundred and fifty feet of rope never reached bottom. Now I know. In the cave on this side of the hill, deep inside, there is ice frozen in blue and lavender puddles.

This flooding is for the lake, they said, you'll finally have electricity. Progress, they announced, like a second coming would hike itself up and tiptoe on the roofs of houses and barns, arms wide open, bright electrical eyes flashing welcome, welcome. I know better. Last winter was cold, that bitter cold that snaps things in two when you touch them. The hoe blade when I tried to chop the ice out of the trough for the mules and cow. It took till March for the blade to thaw loose of the chunk I chopped out with the ax. That ax is a true metal, brought down from the mountains, carried into Kentucky and then up here into the Missouri Ozarks where we could breathe again. We don't thrive without hills, and the effort it takes. Kidwells go to ruin on the plains, we've always known that. Little Carolyn could chase the oak leaf shadows all afternoon, or have lunch in the little graveyard below before I pulled the stones down. Talking with the spirits, she had the nearly perfect companionship of the dead. When she found what I'd done, the tears filled her eyes and she turned from me. I'd as soon she struck me. I couldn't explain it was to save them. No Kidwell ever thrived out of the hills.

Because the men came for the cemeteries. It was the decent thing to do, people over in Lynn Creek kept saying as the mules hauled and the men lifted and the soaked, rotting wood fell apart in their arms, sloshing bones, half-eaten flesh, and wild matted hair to the ground. I didn't know Carolyn was gone that day I drove us to town in the wagon for supplies. The shelves in Tibbets's store were already getting bare as people moved out. They'd left the dead for the last as if that were the final say. Without them, the town, the land didn't exist anymore. They gave it over that easy to the water. I tore down the notice at the foot of my road and nobody ever came to replace it.

The candy sticks in Tibbets's were fly-specked, the potatoes sprouted with tired little red eyes, and the flour had dark specks of weevils, but I took it all. And the last hundred-gallon drum of kerosene. Stopping at the creek I washed the candy for her, scrubbed it clean so the red and white stripes shown again and the smell of peppermint stayed on my fingertips for days. I thought she was at the schoolyard playing on the swing like she would other times, but she wasn't. Nobody to speak of on the main road. Half the folks already gone, relocating on the money they were offered. Seemed odd, the empty stores and houses not bothering to close their doors, board up their windows. A stray dog sniffing up the peeling blue steps across the way with nobody there to stop him. I watched as he pushed his ornery brown head through the small hole in the screen door and looked around. I'd half a mind to throw something at him when I noticed a commotion from the cemetery beside the Methodist church there at the end of the road. I walked, the wet sticks of candy clutched in my hand, past the mules tied in front of the store drowsing in the hot sun, bothering only to flick a big ear at a fly, or wrinkle a shoulder.

Her mouth was open, her face red struggling for breath that as soon as it could would find just the right howling note. You could see it there, trapped in her bulging little chest as she watched the corpse burst out and splash putrefaction onto the men who turned away as if they'd been sprayed with lye. I threw the candy down, clapped one hand over her mouth, and scooped her up with the other. Put her in amongst the supplies, her head resting on the gunny sack of half-sprouted potatoes as I jerked the mules awake, whipped them trotting past the cemetery and on up the road. Don't know if she watched the whole time, but I'd like to think she didn't, to think I saved her that at least.

That's when I made up my mind. The dead belong where they are. After little Carolyn'd gone home again, I went and pulled down the stones as I said. Some of the graves were sunk, you know, but I didn't fill them in. They had their own reasons for things. I had mine. Nobody could know how Carolyn would turn out, years later, in the sandhills of Nebraska. Like I said, Kidwells need shelter from the sky.

They never came for our cemetery. I heard that one of the men took the stones from any empty graves they found and laid them in his yard for a path, the writing side down. Another took three and made steps to his porch. I have nothing to say to these men.

They never came and the rest left. A month later I went down to the town and it was empty. Big bob wire fence blocking the road it took but a minute to clip through. I carry my ax and nippers with me these days. They were so busy putting up notices and fences, never occurred to them to ask who they were keeping out. I never went in but a few places. Jarman's was too empty. A blank form waiting to be put to use, even the thin layer of dust on the window sills seemed a contrivance. She'd cleaned before she left. Dogs hadn't bothered with this place. Copeland's was half full of broken furniture, cracked dishes, shredded curtains and clothes that were rags. I picked through and found a pair of good thick woolen trousers with a burst knee I could use. And a couple of mason jars without their lids. A nice chipped china bowl with little blue flowers and an old doll with a cracked face Carolyn could use for play. I half wished she was there to help me, but she was in school again and only sent down to her great-uncle when she was getting so in her mother's hair.

At Tibbets's store, I found two half-melted white candles, an old box of matches, a rusty pie tin I could clean up, and a short length of chain nailed to its heavy wooden spool. Tibbets probably got tired of loading stuff by then, or the boys he'd hired. Back deep on a shelf behind the counter I found five shotgun shells. At the feed store, I shoveled up as much loose shelled corn as I could find and contrived to fill two gunny sacks. My corn patch was gone before I got it in, and the mules needed more than the grass hay I could give them this winter. The hay meadow was soaked, water to the tips day before yesterday. Something wasteful about not taking in the hay of a summer. Even if you're leaving, it seems wrong.

The Methodist church was missing its bell and stained glass window they'd saved so long for. And the crosses, both outside and in when I stepped onto the good oak plank floor my people had helped lay seventy-five years before. They'd picked up the pews, gold maple and who could blame them, and the altar of course, and the choir benches. The windows were open for some reason, and I went around and closed them carefully, not wanting to look down at the rain-spoiled floor. Then I noticed the sparrows flying in confused circles, landing on the beams where their nests dripped grass and string, and taking off again. I opened the windows. In some way the emptiness still held a feeling that made my bowels contract, and I turned and walked out again. That church and I had a history we never spoke of, but stopping in the road to look back, I wondered if she had.

She was just a girl, and I still a boy, but we were first cousins and therein was the wrongness of it. We splashed in Lynn Creek, we watched the soldiers go off and come back, and one day we noticed each other and the rest of the days were breathless with wishing heat. That summer I chopped at weeds so hard my hands broke new blisters on the hoe's bloody handle, and still I didn't feel them until she wiped the blood off and wrapped each one in the scarf she tore in half before she let me touch her. Then my hands slid in their silk gloves, and my fingertips cracked with work and dirt caught at the thin skin of her breasts where I could see the blue veins just beneath the blue-white surface. I hadn't realized she was so delicately alive until that moment and it made me suddenly careful and clumsy, the way you have to be when you lift a newborn kitten with its mewling eyes shut. Her nipples were little pebbles I took in my mouth and sucked for the way they quenched my thirst, and her belly this strong place I pushed my hand down. Not here, she whispered. We met in the field behind her mother's house, her father dead from the war, and his mother moved in to help teach school and music. There was a thick plank back door to the church and she knew where the key was on top of the frame. We held hands bumping up the three narrow dark stairs and burst out into the colored moonlight flooding the carpet in front of the altar. Groaning, I pulled her to me and down. I lived for years on the body's memory, her hands where only mine had been before. At dawn we looked up to see the feet of the crucified Christ above us dripping blood frozen in gold painted lead, and there must have been something about it that cursed us. Though I didn't realize it at the time, of course.

I finished with the town that day, pulling what I could from its emptiness, leaving the houses like ghosts with vacant looks on their faces, the water inching its way down the road toward them. Within two months their glass windows caught the restless shimmer of rising water and I could hear the moaning as swelling wood burst nails, then the joints crying loose, and the heavy grunt as mud caved in the basements. For days and weeks now it has been like watching a whole fleet of boats going down as houses tremble and tip or simply sink.

The animals have begun to flee too, those that can. Those that can't drift along the edges on their backs, thick swollen chunks with legs that stick up to the sky, like something obscene. Wild pigs, deer, a stray cow, coyotes, dogs, cats, once in a while a mule or horse. All things big enough to get out of the way, but somehow stranded in the midst of their dreaming on a disappearing island. At night I begin to see their struggles in my dreams, their panic as the water spreads so far there is no longer anyplace to swim toward and they give up, their legs straightening, bodies sinking until the eyes close and the tip of the nose blows at the water one last time and lets go.

Little Carolyn never visits anymore. No one does. So I sit on the porch and watch the snakes as they begin to rise up the hill. Their migration is slow, their expressions bewildered as they slither, stop, look around, tasting the air with their tongues, and slowly shiver forward another foot or two, sliding under the leaves and fallen branches like soldiers moving on a key position held by the enemy. But I never think of them as the enemy, though they come forward like men on their elbows, inching their bodies in long spasms. Sometimes I catch a

glimpse of a green tree snake when the dogwood branch suddenly star-
tles into motion. I don't mind how their rustle adds another tone to the
water swelling inch by inch up the hill behind them.

How living things talk even afterwards, gurgling and whispering
beneath the surface, swallowing other sounds of birds in the brush,
pigs and deer, while the trees seem to cease as if they've been shot
through the heart and stand there propped up in some punishing effigy.
It reminds me of the way first the Union soldiers, then the guerrillas,
propped the enemy dead against fence posts in the hay meadow below
us, strung their arms in wide embrace, the slack jaws gaping with flies
laying eggs which hatched by late afternoon in the rich moist soil of the
tongue. The eyes solid as boiled eggs fed blowflies and beetles until the
crows came curious as aunts walking gingerly along the fence wire and
boards up onto the hand, a peck to try the flesh of the arm, to clean the
beak with two quick swipes like a carving knife on the back of a china
plate, then on up the woolen sleeve to the shoulder to peer at the head
flung back in a permanent stare at the white hot sky, to look closer and
closer, black oily head jerking from side to side as it neared the eye and
finally gave it that first tentative stab, jerking back as the flies clouded
up, cocking the head toward the commotion above as the turkey vul-
tures rode down the air and settled on the tree limbs and ground. They
made short work of it, the face flesh, tugging the cords of sinew from
the neck, the chest entered through the dark dried holes, tearing the
flesh ragged until in the days to come the shirt and pants slowly emptied, as if the flesh had itself turned liquid and seeped out and away.
First time I saw the bones stained pink and fleshy, I stopped looking,
turned my face away toward the hill, the quarry where the granite was
cut and sheered like hard loaves of old bread.

That was when I began my work. The other stonecutters gone. My
older brother and father. Into the hills of Kentucky, joined up, then shot
and floated facedown in the river for miles until someone pulled them
out and sent their effects home. I put up their stones and then my
mother's, joining the others who came down out of the Tennessee
mountains. After that, the soldiers from the fence, my younger brother
the day he shot at a passing patrol from the woods, and finally my
cousin's husband the day he came to find me and make me stop.

I don't know how high the water will come. How long I'll wait.
There's the mules to think of and the cow. My hunting dog's been gone

for two years now, but with all the game driven up here from the lake, I don't need her. I don't want to take any more of life than I have to. Not even then when Carolyn's grandmother and I could not stop. As useless as trying to put this water back. All a person can do in the face of such force is try to save something small, something that can be carried into a future such as this one has turned out. I saw that as soon as the sun came up that morning in the church, helping her dress, my rough hands leaving slivers of blood on her blue cotton skirt. And later after she married him, and again after I buried him below here with the others. See, I cannot unclaim these people. I am a man with nothing to show for himself but this, and only the dead to bear witness to what acts of love can do to the world. Thus I cannot join them down in the hollow, and I cannot leave them behind. She would not have it. Sometimes, you see, the most dangerous land to claim is your own.

The Tire Man

I thought my flesh was a good disguise, but Ray found me anyway. Not so much that he'd put his arm around me like one of those television wives, but those are only the Winston Cup drivers. "Sunday Specials" I call the slim, pretty women who kiss their husbands climbing out of cars in the winner's circle, or sometimes say good-bye before the long afternoon of racing. Women comfortable in their beautiful living rooms when the TV crew comes to tape the at-home special. "Women without Worries" I call them, ignoring the tiny pinched lies at the corners of their mouths and eyes. "My Day Is Coming" those lines say: a husband airlifted to the nearest hospital, his blood spilling in the dark helmet, flesh charred to the seat of the crashed car. Nothing I have to face.

I will never be on television. Ray found me, but that does not mean we don't, the two of us, understand what the straining seams of these jeans mean.

My body.

It accumulates around me like dust in the corners, under the bed. I have to get down there on my hands and knees like a big fat dog and wrestle the vacuum cleaner wand—wand, my ass—dirty household magic turning all the princesses back into Cinderellas.

He has principles, the one who found me. He doesn't try to shuck my shell to find some missing meat. He knows I'm in here.

Sometimes Ray sleeps with his head nestled in the pudding of my lap, his fingertips, on the verge of sliding between my legs, waiting politely like strangers at the gate. He may have found me, but he knows better than to think he owns me, or that I owe him anything.

And that's his downfall, I think as I take the throw rugs off the floors of our three rooms outside to the concrete apron. He doesn't mean to drag the track dirt in here, but I spend every Tuesday morning like this—rain or shine—shaking the heavy rag carpets one after another, feeling my loose breasts rise hopefully as I lift my arms and then flop back as I lower them. Like twin rabbits they squirm and struggle in the baggy shirt, 3XL from the men's department at Target.

The music Ray likes on the light rock station la-las from the open door. He's already gone to work at dawn, preferring to fix his own coffee and soft cold bread from the fridge spread with peanut butter and grape jelly like a kid would eat. I used to offer to get up, but he prefers to see my puddle of flesh curdled and thick, the way I release across the top of the bed once his board-hard body is taken away. He checks my sleep several times before he leaves, as if it's a present he's given me and he wants to make sure it's liked. Through slits in my eyes, I watch his big front teeth take bites of sandwich followed by sips of coffee with that saucer-empty face. A kid winning a goldfish in a plastic bag of water at the county fair coin toss wears that expression. I've seen it across from the Methodist Dining Hall where we serve Protestant pie and lots of gravy. Usually I am sleeping and dreaming, though, one the same as the other for me.

There were nights naked in the shallow water of the Platte River in those early days in Nebraska before we started following the dirt track wonders. August when the water was syrup-thick and warm as melted butter, we'd splash and crash around alone there in the moonlight until we finally lay down, believing the warm muddy water would keep me safe as he sloshed in and out, always pulling away at the last moment when my fat thighs tried to lock him down and my back buoyed up. But the brown water took what he spilled on my chest and sometimes when he's working late at the track or the garage these nights, I think about going back there and maybe finding those half-human fish soaking away the hot nights, waiting patiently for someone to come claim them.

We're in Prophetstown now. Illinois. Our life has become "a lie in progress," I tell Ray, "it could be true any minute but it probably won't be." He blinks and threatens his lower lip with the front tooth turned like a hatchet. It's caught me bloody more than once. I could work, I tell him, and he blinks faster like the thing in his eye is getting bigger and busier. The way it did in Amarillo when we stopped at that place offering a free seventy-two-ounce steak to anyone who could eat it in an hour. Technically, it was smaller than that since nobody had taken them up on it in a while. Technically, I left the fifty-cent-sized chunk of fat. They'd never seen a woman go all the way through it. Cowboys tried, but with their little waists and butts, it's just dreaming to think they could compete with a woman my size. I ordered their special strawberry pie with whipped cream afterwards just to show off. Sick as a dog for a week, but by then we were well on our way through Oklahoma with a long stop in the Missouri Ozarks to see if he could get a job to stick to him.

That's where he got drunk on the case of beer he was paid for changing tires on the second-place car that one night and didn't come home. Well, didn't come in the house. At dawn I found him passed out with his face pressed in the gravel driveway dribbling a grin like he was in bed with me. I wanted to leave him there, but you know, a person doesn't. I wasn't raised that way, so I lifted and dragged him staggering into the house and took his clothes off and let him down easy into the bed. He's not the type to get sick on a person, so I knew he could be trusted. When I went out to the truck, I found the can of red paint. We got fired, of course. If it's not one thing, it's another.

On our way out of town, he drove by the track and showed how he'd painted "I Lov U Vonnie" on the railroad bridge over the entrance to enter the speedway.

"Ray, honey, you're in the attic crawl space of fame," I told him as we hit the interstate headed for Illinois.

"I could take that engine rebuilding course off the television," he offered, but I don't have the heart to listen so I don't. Ray's trapped in the future, so I try to take care of everything leading up to where he is. It's me that says let's stop when we do. Me who saw the sign for Prophetstown on the interstate and made us pull off. With any kind of luck, this would be the place it should be. Ray was already busy in his new mind career that day, working on Dale Jarrett's 88 UPS Ford, rebuilding the engines every week between races. Sometimes even the morning of qualifying. He'd go as far as a dream would let him. Call people on the phone and act like old friends. Half the time it worked, too. He's not hustling, you see, he truly believes himself.

The best he can hope for is being the tire man. Maybe the spring man. Not the engine man. Never the engine man. Ray can't read. I don't tell him this, he's forgotten it like always. In the old days it didn't matter, but they have computers now. Things are way beyond Ray. Even spark plugs and pistons.

Tonight I take his hands in mine and let him feel how soft my flesh is, how I keep it carefully with lotion and just the right foods. Ray needs something gentle for his head and heart. He has not been a bad man, has not done less than try. So I smooth the deep scrape on his index finger from the stud that sheared while he was changing rear tires for that spoiled brat racing on his dad's car dealership money. I use my own hard nails to clean the rim of dirt from his splayed and broken ones. I soak his hands in a moisturizing soap and afterwards blot them dry and rub my own witch hazel hand cream mixture with long soothing strokes into those thick callused fingers and palms. I treat each finger as if it is my own special one, the very best I have. These hands have no finesse, no finicky touches in them, they can only handle big tires and me.

You see, that's when I realize that to love faithfully is a terrible gift, and I remember how shaky the letters on the railroad overpass were, how unsure of their own right to be there, under his hand, the red paint escaping the crooked words in long streaks like a heart trying to flee its own body.

Winter Dreaming

It wasn't more than a dream. Not at first. Then Percival got his hand caught in the corn picker and Fritty said he wouldn't have enough after the stump healed, not more than those thick fleshy hooks of two fingers could be recognized, like a sweet potato caught in a hard freeze, then thawed out. I didn't have a notion to say this to Percival, not with him saving so thoroughly to go and all. I mean when the winter clamps hard enough to snap the teeth off a rake, and the whole world gets that tired slump of gray and brown, you don't go around telling anyone they can't have a dream or two in front of the fire.

The ad came on TV regular as those rerun car races every Saturday and Sunday, and then late at night sometimes during the week. Percival and I did enjoy watching, once his folks were tucked down like kids we were going to have someday. That's what we promised each other and you know I believed us then, I did. Like I said, winter dreaming. The hand didn't bother me much, I mean it wasn't exactly a picture, but Percival was very sensitive at first, or maybe later, too, and that would be my fault, I suspect, not perceiving it after a while. I'd bathe him while he kept it wrapped in a JCPenney bag over the side of the tub. And I like to think he felt something when my hands dragged slow over his skin, working the dirt out from under his good fingernails, sometimes shaving his beard off so the black flecks floated like gunpowder on the gray soap-scummed surface of the bathwater. When he stood up, balancing himself with his good hand gripping the edge of the tub, I had to be careful to wipe off that black whisker line. Percival was by nature a dark man, so it wasn't easy sometimes, getting him as clean as I liked.

Afterwards, we lay in the fresh ironed sheets, I had time to do that then, run them through his Mama's mangle, careful not to let it take my arm with the hot smooth rollers. One is enough in a family, I'd scold, then catch myself in case Percival or the folks could hear me in the basement. Wasn't much of a basement, only a dugout with a rocked-over floor, but it was dry and Percival had rigged the electrical so I could work on the clothes. Keeping our things clean and wrinkle free had become an obsession of mine after I moved in here and his Ma showed me the mangle and the big ironing board. It seemed natural, and I was next in line for the sewing machine too until Percival's sister, Antoinette, came down from the hills and took it with her one time. I can't begrudge her though, with five little ones and that husband. Ray is not a bad one, not outright, he's just not very ambitious. Not like Percival.

When I try to picture Roy Hill now, I can't. I can't find that smiling face full of drag racing experience he'd be willing to share with Percival anytime we could get enough money and time. I can't.

Fritty said it was normal. What was happening to us.

I wonder.

Ma passed on the first day of the new year. Like a piece of wood slipping under water, too logged to float, she disappeared. I took the oatmeal in like always to spoon-feed her, and she was just lying there next to Pa, her mouth open, her wash-blue eyes big and solid as marbles, those old china ones. Pa was staring at the chipped plaster wall, like always, watching TV that wasn't there. We'd taken it out a year ago, after Ma complained. It hadn't made a bit of difference to Pa.

So Antoinette and Ray come down, without the kids they dropped off at his relatives, and we buried Ma on the hillside with the rest of the family. Ray had to do the digging with Percival's hand still tender, and you could hear the two of them out there arguing about the size of the hole. Ray not being ambitious, after all. But finally we had it to do, we did it, and it was done.

And then we set down to some eating, and I must confess some liquoring too. Percival had been working at his tears all day, and finally, around dark, the men had staggered out to hay those bellering cattle and slop the hogs, while Antoinette and I tried to straighten up the dishes. In the middle of it all I remembered Pa and went into their room off the kitchen there, and found him staring at the wall, his eyes fixed like Ma's but when I put my finger on his wrist, the blood was thumping along as if nothing in the world had happened, so I turned on the light by the bed and tucked him in and brought him his supper which he still managed to feed himself if I let him take the time.

Antoinette was leaning over the sink when I came back. Her thick shoulders and humped back shivering like the old board bridge at the bottom of the hill when a truck passes over it. I touched her back lightly, the way I did the old horse when he finally let me catch him after our usual chase through the woods, prepared to pull my hand away. She sniffed and I stepped close enough to see the streaks like tiny silver roads over and down the lumps of her full face. Antoinette was doing dishes so she couldn't reach up and brush at them so they each one hung there on her chin, each drop full of its own possibility and pain. I reached for her face and she shied and I knew something I didn't want to know. She used her arm to wipe her own face then and I pretended I was only going to rub the steam from the little window so I could see what those men were doing out there under the yard light.

We don't get so much snow here, but a skimming had fallen after we went inside from burying Ma, and those two men were slipping around and grabbing for the lightpole to keep from going down. I worried about Percival's hand, but the bandage had been off for a week, and it was pretty pink and brand-new looking in a terrible proud way. He put it in an old boot sock whenever we were going to town or having folks over, just till he got used to it. Like the other thing we were waiting on. Watching them out there, I couldn't tell if they were joking around or fighting, and I worried for the hand which was suddenly naked and cold for all I knew from the way Percival was waving it at Ray, who kept trying to grab it and hold it still, which is what it seemed like, though I couldn't be sure.

I wanted to go out there and call them in, like boys who'd played long enough before bedtime, but Antoinette was rattling her hands in the cooling dishwater, the soap too little too late it looked like, and sobbing now, letting out a lot of grief that hadn't had much place to go until Ma. I went to patting her on the big shoulder like that horse out in those woods, getting her used to me and my little comfort, like that horse who needed to be reminded each time I went there trying to give him a handful of sugar from my pocket, so I could bring him back for Percival to work on his hooves while I curried and tugged the ticks out of his mane and tail. I wished there was something I could do for her like that, but sorrow makes us so useless and I felt those tears in my own eyes but I bit them back because it wasn't my place. Not yet.

Ma had a little money she'd been saving, O'Dowd at the bank said the next time we went to town. It wasn't much, but she'd set aside what she could from the eggs and the vegetables and sometimes the ironing she did for other people, summer folks who come to our region to escape the heat and noise. Well, where else could they get sheets and pillowcases done like that. I hadn't it in me to take up where she left off, with the old folks bedridden and Percival needing help with the outside work, but seeing her little account that day did make me pause and wonder.

I was for leaving it in there, just in case, but Percival wanted it home, he said. He wouldn't look me in the eye. He'd changed since his hand.

O'Dowd shrugged and gave it over.

That money worried me. I mean, it worried me. Every night, while Percival was checking on the animals and shutting things up before we went to bed, I looked to see that it was there, tucked in an old sock of Pa's in the pine dresser drawer where Ma had always stored her good wedding linen nobody ever used except the night they got themselves married. I even took to mistrusting my eyes, and him, and unfolding the bills and counting. $546.78. In bed it lay there like a plank between us, that money, as if it were a tiny living thing crying out for help from that dresser drawer across the room. And I couldn't get its voice out of my head when Percival rolled over and laid his good hand and arm across my chest and started fiddling around. Sometimes he'd go on with it, pretending I wasn't acting like I was, sometimes he'd sigh and roll away, holding his hurt hand tight against his chest like a baby child he needed to protect. I'd wait till he was asleep and get up and go to the window and sit on the dresser, looking out across the fields all laid to sleep too, silvery and dead in the moonlight as cold and white as skim milk out of the spring house at home when I was a girl and growing up down on the flatland by the river. I sat up there to keep it safe and quiet, the money, and I sat up there to watch the way the deer came down out of the woody hills behind us, hungry, looking for anything that corn picker might have dropped last fall. I had it in my mind that they might find those missing fingers, and I don't know what, maybe I intended to stop them, maybe I didn't. Maybe I wanted something to carry them away, those pieces of him, carry them away where he couldn't find them again.

After that money came, we kept our habit of watching car races on the TV. It had always been our pleasure, getting the chores done in time, arranging our days around them, but it wasn't the same anymore. Percival got up during the commercial for Roy Hill's Drag Racing School and fussed around in the kitchen or went to check on Pa. It didn't mean what I thought it did, though, because the brochure and catalogue had come and gone. Disappeared, like they were something a person like me, a woman, shouldn't be forced to put her eyes on. I looked for them, but I didn't have my whole heart in it, so of course I didn't find them. Maybe he threw them out, I decided one day in March when the weather broke for good. I opened the windows in Pa's room and let the air flow through to take that beddy old man smell out with it, and he didn't even blink when a chickadee flew in by mistake and it took me half the morning with a big pan and lid to catch it. I tried not to cause any damage, but it didn't fly right off when I turned it loose in the grass. By then it was too late to help it so I turned my back and went inside and down to the basement where the cool winter air was going to store itself in the clay walls and rocky floor.

I ironed sheets and pillows and shirts all afternoon, even things I'd done before, I emptied that dresser and took them down by the armful, stacking them on an old chair, going over each piece, making the folds crisp and perfect. Even the wedding sheets, bleached so many times, the little embroidered flowers were pale gray against the white. I loved the way the heat climbed my arms and flushed my face that afternoon. I loved the sweat that clung to my hair and dampened the back of my neck like a promise. Once I thought I heard someone walking around overhead, and I called out Percival's name, but it stopped, and I forgot it, ironing and ironing and ironing.

He didn't mean it the way a person might take it. Leaving. I knew that.

The money wasn't the first thing I looked for, but I did look. It was there, but it was right on the top of the dresser, spread out in a fan, the coins holding it like rings on a hand.

Pa and I still watch the racing, side by side on the bed in the folk's room, where I moved the TV back to. I couldn't stand to think of him staring at that wall alone anymore. I keep thinking we'll see Percival, driving the way he wanted to, beating the other car off the line, smoking, screaming engines as they skid down the track. I watch each face carefully in case. Every once in a while I put a finger to Pa's big wrist and feel the thump thump of his heart, and watch the little blue vein on the top of his hand lift. He has such big hands, each thick finger so perfectly strong it reminds me of Percival. The old Percival, the way he was when I first saw him all promise and days to come, tossing the hay bales down from the wagon in the barnyard of my family's flatland farm. Percival with two good hands holding me against the gritty sweat of his bare chest, his skin red and bumpy from the hay.

Oh my dear dear man, I whisper in the dark, after I've tucked Pa in and shut off the TV and climbed the stairs to the half-ceiling room I sleep in now, where Percival and Antoinette slept as kids. I have a pallet on the floor there and a little window I keep open so I can hear Percival rumbling across the planks of the bridge and coming up our road the night he finally comes home from his dream.

This Is for Chet

Because last night he saves me from hanging. At least I've come to believe that it was his hand released the thick braided leather lash of the bullwhip I'd jammed between the spindles of the stair railing. Maybe his voice in some fashion overriding my own as I hung there briefly, too drunk to feel the bite of the stiff, badly cured leather into the skin of my neck. There isn't even a red mark this morning, so maybe it's true that I was just playing. Just writing it for one of my characters to say.

From the first night here six months ago, as tired as I was after a day at the computer answering my on-line writers, I thought I heard him climbing the stairs, continuing past the second floor where my room is, up the steps to the attic. A couple of weeks later, I followed him up there and found the piece of wood tucked between the joists at the top of the stairs, the same reddish brown of the unfinished wall. Four feet tall and an inch thick, the board is plain and flat except for the odd orange shape slashing down the center. I didn't want to bring it downstairs. There was something about the figure in the wood that looked like an eye or part of an elongated face, brutal though, more brutal than you could accept. But then I thought of Chet leading me there and brought it along, putting it in the room next to the blue linoleum-topped table with the scaled and flaking white legs my computer sits on.

Setting, setting, setting, I tell my internet writers. Having the board there, leaning against the wall in the corner, makes me come to a kind of attention, military in nature, you might say. *But I want my story to apply to anywhere,* my writer from Iowa replies.

A few days later I opened the booklet on Kaiser Motor Sports I found in a kitchen drawer when I first moved in, and there he was, Chet and the crew standing around in the garage at some racetrack. Just behind them, leaning against the red metal toolbox as big as a dresser on wheels, was the piece of wood with the face staring straight out at me. In the picture there was a pair of eye hooks on the top. When I looked more closely at the board, I found the holes. Then I thought about ordering a brochure like the Kaiser Motor Sports one for my business, too, but remembered that I didn't really like seeing my name and address in print.

No one coming to the house ever asked about the board, almost as if it was invisible to anyone else, although I know that's not true because I actually pointed it out several times. No one else seemed much interested. They wouldn't even speculate about its use. But then, they weren't much interested in anything here. It was as if we'd all come to this little island to die. That's what I think. But it's not an island, it only feels like it. Michigan, surrounded by water on three sides, shaped like a thumb stuck up the ass of the watery world, I could tell them. The Upper Peninsula should break and run while it has a chance.

Chet creaks the picture on the wall beside my bed on nights I'm too full of opinions like this. *OK,* I tell him, *all right,* as I lie in bed thinking of rules for my writers who expect new input every few days. *No more than three lines of dialogue at a time,* I decided one night while Chet blinked the lamp beside the bed a couple of times. He likes the attention, so I quit speaking to him when he does things like this. *And give three different qualities to every character to make them memorable. People think in threes, remember in threes,* I add as if I have scientific authority. *Three kings. Twelve days of Christmas: three times four.* Although I've only written a couple of stories myself, these seem like sensible things to say.

The woman from Friendship, Arkansas, who's writing for children, shows up for the first time in months, saying, *I'm having trouble with this chicken—*

Use your own judgment, I tell her.

I was in the basement yesterday, putting in a month of laundry, color by color, fighting cobwebs and looking sharp for two-inch centipedes that treat my house like a country club, the way they stroll through the living room, pausing in front of my chair while I'm watching TV. They're right, of course. I'm the last to interfere with their progress as long as they stay out of my bed. My ex used to farm silverfish in his pillow. It was so old, for all I know, he brought them with him when he moved in, infesting an entire neighborhood with his East-Coast strain. You don't know. I used to chase them off the bed before I climbed in. He didn't even notice.

Avoid the middle ground, I advise the on-liners, *there's no risk there, no danger, nothing happens.*

But I don't want to upset people, the college girl from Long Island says. *I want to make them laugh.* She writes about dorm life and students getting goofy drunk and stoned all the time. *Show this stuff to your mother,* I want to write back, *watch her laugh.*

So the laundry started choking and chugging in the murky water and I did my monthly check on the windows in the basement rooms. I had to push at the cobwebs crisscrossing the doorways, and try to shake my hands free of any rampant spiders though the sticky strands didn't release until I wiped them quickly against my shorts and T-shirt. I switched on light after light until I reached the far room with the shelves and workbench. Chet's relatives had cleared them for my arrival, and I was curious every time I came down here about why they left the half-used can of WD-40, the solid gray roll of duct tape, the small curls of wire, the nearly new sponge sitting hard and yellow in the brown dusk, the four fat colored bulbs for a string of Christmas tree lights, and the small cardboard box with the folded flaps. I hesitated, picked it up and held it away from me as I headed upstairs again.

In my understanding of the world, people's lives always ended up in boxes like these. And when the hereafter looks in, it's this jumble of divorced, discontent, discontinued items, as black and resistant as what was in this box. Years ago, I bought several small clear plastic boxes three and four inches high and a couple of inches to a side, and in these I put all my debris. I wanted it to be easy for people to throw it out, a convenient one-handed gesture after they'd puzzled over the buttons, pennies, lone earrings, pebbles, shells, beads, pins, and seeds. I knew where each one of those came from. In a way, I gave them birth and sense, and someday they'd die too, collapsing, world after world into the garbage bag. I liked that. Taking something with you when you go. I tell my on-line writing students, *each character should have an object or objects associated with them.*

Is that in addition to the three characteristics you mentioned earlier? my Presbyterian minister from Vermont writes. He's very careful to follow the rules, I've noticed. His characters have the same trouble and keep having to learn terrible lessons. The Baptist from Omaha is much more forgiving. Everybody in his stories gets to come to Jesus after a little mistake or two, especially at Christmastime. My nun from St. Paul is writing a murder mystery with a stolen box of letters and no mention of religion at all.

It wasn't easy to know what to do with Chet's box. It was his, of course, and maybe he meant it as I would mean it. But maybe not. Downstairs the washer was groaning and harrumphing like an old man, and the dryer's light thumping threatened to ease its way off the cement platform to follow the aluminum lint-lined tube of exhausted air out across the room. Nothing escaped in this house, though. The tube fit its mouth over a white plastic bowl of water where it exhaled fuzz like an animal too tired to drink. *What about the carbon monoxide?* I asked Chet's relatives, *there's no outside vent.* They just looked at me like maybe I wasn't the right person for the house. See, I'd had to talk them into it in the first place. I had no idea why a person with money, good credit, and a job running writing workshops on-line could not be allowed to purchase any house she could afford as long as it was for sale. But they were reluctant. I had to write them a big, lying letter. Everyone said I was so lucky.

Yeah, right.

Who the hell else would move here on purpose? Less than a block away, the racetrack's so close you can smell burning rubber, and you can hardly spend a summer day without hearing some kind of racket over there.

That wasn't why I got to the end of my rope last night, however, if that's what you're thinking. I've gotten used to all the noise. When the train shakes the house at two A.M. and blows its whistle to clear the intersections one after another like dominos falling before its bright roaring light, I feel good and taken care of.

I put the box on the dining room table with the pine-veneer-chemically-protected top. You see, when one of my students writes a story like this with a person who sits around meditating about her life, I yell at them, *don't let your character think so much, make her do something for a change.* I say it in a nice way, naturally, because I need their money in my account every month or this is not going to work, moving to Michigan. Why *that* place, people asked when I packed up and left. *Because there is not one thing you can imagine about it,* I told them. *It barely exists. What few writers are using it, can barely lift it onto the page. It's not even a state of mind. Look how Hemingway had to move away. Even their one major city is vanishing. Beirut on the bay. Detroit makes Windsor, Ontario, look like Paris, France.*

I didn't answer what they failed to ask, why I wanted to make myself disappear, why I had to take up less space now. Get smaller and smaller. Now I'm only a name on the internet with a business. Not even my real name. And I don't have a phone with a listed number. Every month I get fewer and fewer bills. Everything's paid through the bank now so I don't have to answer questions they don't ask. Even when they come to visit.

But I suppose last night is something that has to be addressed at some point.

The laundry was done. I'd responded to three crackpot ideas from that idiot in Wyoming. Aliens and hairy butts. He probably has a sheep for a girlfriend, but he likes to pay, so I do it, take him seriously every couple of days and charge his ass double if he gets too far out of line. I mean, people should pay for offending you or wasting your time, don't you think? It's when he writes this stuff to me, and some of the others too that make me laugh out loud, or cry if it's just terribly terribly sad and you can see it's true about their own life even though they pretend it's fiction, it's those times I wish there was somebody here, leaning over my shoulder, the hand there so I can feel the weight of it, pushing me down into the chair, the press of fingers on my collarbone, like they're hanging on to something, and I point to the screen and they agree. Some days that's all it comes down to, a whispering breath of agreement like the dryer below me hushing hushing hushing as it floods the rooms above with poison gas.

Nothing dies here. Not Chet. Not me. I don't think I could die if I wanted to. Dilution. The wooden handle of the bullwhip would've held between those two stair spindles on the landing, and the leather, though brittle, wouldn't have snapped. I can tell you that much. It has to be something else.

Chet was a jack man. I learned that reading about Kaiser Motor Sports and watching TV racing. A long-time tire man who moved from Goodyear development to the team. *An artist in the pit,* they called him. *The jack man's the quarterback of the pit crew,* the race announcer tells me during a rain delay. And Kaiser's still competing, I discovered one

Sunday a month ago. The drivers dressed in green and red and yellow, like Christmas elves rushing around the sleigh when it pulled into the pit. I thought of the board in the other room and stayed put, watching the men skate around the car, sliding the jack under one side, whipping tires off, slamming them on and punching the five lug nuts in place with the air gun. It was like kids dancing below the stage on MTV, some crazy out-of-sync thing that comes together just as the lead singer throws himself into their suddenly uplifted arms. The car blasted off on smoking tires, spilling the last fuel through the air in a bright golden rope behind it.

August. Now there's a disappointing month. One to let you down. Starts out hot and full of itself and goes soft and cool by the end. Like a football team folding in the fourth. Or a driver without the guts for those last three laps when everything's on the line, three wide into those corners and the wall breathing closer and closer and closer and closer as I opened Chet's box from the basement. I shook the hard, dark pebbles out on the table where they stumbled out and rolled. A few round, most lopsided. I recognized the rubber from the tires that scatters along the banks of the racetrack like black marbles the cars have to skate through. In the pit, the crews scrubbed them off grills and windshields as best they could. On the track under caution, the drivers wove the cars back and forth trying to scrape the pieces of rubber off the tires.

They looked like bits of black licorice, shiny and sweaty, but when I ran my fingertips over them, they were cold and hard. *Chet?* I called and he creaked from the living room.

Yesterday was Saturday, you see, and all afternoon through my open windows I listened to the Busch Grand National being run at Michigan International Speedway just over the hill from my house as I watched it on TV. There were nine cautions, wreck after wreck, lone cars and cars that took three or four others with them, cars flying up and flipping over like magnificent sailfish, then landing in a rolling ball flinging pieces down the track or coming to a stop against the wall. After each wreck, the screen went still waiting for the window net to come down and the hand to shoot out waving that the driver is OK. About half of the cars managed to get taped and riveted back together enough to continue running though they were many, many laps down now. Like old dogs, they limped around the track favoring one side, hoods blown off, fenders missing, tires exposed and raw looking, rear ends crumpled, flaps of metal dangling. But no one died. Drivers were whisked off in ambulances, examined, and released. They reappeared with sprained ankles, broken fingers, and bruises, to smile and talk about next week's race somewhere else. On the dining room table in the next room, I imagined the rubber slowly melting onto the heat of the pine veneer, attaching itself for the coming disaster around the next corner. I'd probably survive and have to walk away, but maybe what looked like triumph to the witnesses would be another form of failure for me.

See, again it's the kind of thing I tell my on-line writers not to do: making the character pitiful, without hope. *Everyone has hope,* I tell them. *Everyone has desire. What do your characters desire? What will they do to get it? What stands in their way?*

Aliens, the guy from Wyoming writes me.

You do have a sheep for a girlfriend, don't you? I almost write back.

And don't give me a bunch of alcoholic, drug addicted, suicidal depressives. That's the bottom line. I have to be especially firm with the twenty-something from L.A.

"Happy Hour" they call the last hour of running the cars the day before the Winston Cup Race. Last chance to get the setup right on the engine and chassis for this particular track and weather. Drivers and teams wearing anxious looks were momentarily rude to the TV commentators shoving mikes in the car windows early Saturday evening. It made me nervous so I built the first gin and tonic. A medium-sized one that grew into a large glass. It was so hot and all afternoon the toxic dryer air had been pumping up through the heat grates. I needed another drink, I realized as soon as I finished the first, using Real Lime instead of fresh juice, which gave it a bitter underbite that reminded me I was drinking.

I didn't drink all evening, only long enough to get the sun safely down, the dryer hauled to a stop, the clean clothes upstairs without actually putting them away. The stairs seemed extra steep now, and I hung on for dear life going back down. I was in one of those moods I especially didn't like to let my writers use. In my study, I picked up the carved wooden nut with the tiny hinge that opened to reveal a Santa Claus pinned inside with his arms and legs jingling loose from tiny wires. This was not a happy Santa. His mouth was a straight black line in his pink and white face, and his eyes were upturned like Christ's on the cross. In fact, Santa's arms were out at his sides, elbows bent, mittened palms up like Jesus too. OK, it'd be the ex who gave me this in some big symbolic gesture if I were telling the on-liners how to write, but in truth, it was a gift from an old boyfriend, someone who had stuck around for years, faithfully sending me a tiny gift each Christmas though now it is only to a P.O. box. I have no idea why he continues. I've never asked him, nor did I intend to. Usually I sent him something in return, though I hesitated to make it personal in case his wife worried. Probably when he died, there would be a box of these presents, unwrapped but unused in the back of a closet.

You have to tie up loose ends, I tell the writer from Mississippi, *sew the threads together.* They're willing to listen to anything, I realized a long time ago. Even though their own lives put all of my advice to the lie, they listen and write, listen and write. It's discouraging.

Suddenly with the peculiar clarity of enough gin, I decided to purify the house of Chet and his damn restless walking. He was dead. Time for him to go. I lit the stalk of silvery sage I'd yanked up from the roadside in Custer State Park, South Dakota, two summers ago when I was looking for the last desperate place to vanish to. I moved from room to room, holding it in front of me like a miniature torch, trying to catch the ash and sparks from the smoldering weed in my hand. *Good-bye Chet, rest well, good-bye,* I chanted out loud, happy no one was here to see how ridiculous I felt. But I had to do this, you understand. I couldn't just leave him around the way his relatives did when they moved on.

I got all the way to the attic, skipping the darkest corners of the eaves, but wafting some of the smoke their way in case he was waiting there, crouched, absorbed almost into the splintery wood where the roof meets the walls. By the time I was done, there were black worms of ash marking my trail and the house smelled like I'd been smoking pot. But it was empty for the first time since I'd moved in. Really empty. The kind of good-bye empty you get when you move all the furniture out from your place on Indigo Road, load it up, and go back for that last look around before you drive off. And I guess that was the first time I understood what I'd done to myself. I was all alone, you see. Really alone. The racetrack over the hill was silent, it was too early for the train, and even the refrigerator had stumbled to a momentary halt. There was nothing holding me here anymore. I didn't want anything. I wasn't even depressed as I slid the thick yellow pine whip handle in between the oak spindles on the second floor and tiptoed on the middle stair with the rawhide cinched around my neck.

This is the part I am especially condemning of with my writers. *Death is not a good solution to your character's problems. You have to come up with something better than that*, I urge them. *Use your imagination.*

But it's only today that I realize the big thing I forgot to tell them— *no ghosts, no deus ex machina. Nobody gets saved by the supernatural. Get rid of all that cornball stuff.*

❖ ❖

The Burning

 It wasn't the permit that took your power—not the phone calls tracking you to the local fire station so many miles away that the corn field, woods, and house would be ash by the time the strong young men in their nearly new 4x4s arrived.

"Don't burn today or any day the wind is over fifteen miles per hour, only brush, follow the rules, read front and back, have this on you at all times."

So when the ATV comes busting over the hill, you think of the yellow sheet on the kitchen table, one hundred yards away, but aim your hose, the water pouring weakly at the flaming fringe of dried grass that outlines the fire, as long and as tall as a fire truck. You started it with gasoline, newspaper, and matches that kept going out until you dared to step close enough for the explosion to burst the skin off your face, should it come. That's when you discovered how fire teaches you like love to step into a wicked embrace.

When the man pretending to be searching for the neighbor's two dogs arrives—labs with names—too much detail for a lie, you want to tell him, it doesn't add up. They got lost yesterday, but you're here today checking our fire. You insist on more detail, cruelly curious to see how far he can go before the lie makes him too restless and he has to take off across your back pasture. You see you're going to hell, and this fire you keep trying to get closer to is proof.

He doesn't ask about the melted plastic puddle that was Mr. Coffee, or the glass windows that found a heat to turn them into sand. There is so much love in that brush pile—sheetrock walls and mattresses, a porcelain toilet you expect to spew orange flames but which disappears instead. Have you said how slow you are at grasping the way fire takes us on, reshapes our thoughts?

Some trees disappear wholly into corrugated ash while others get tossed aside, edged to the perimeter in a gray economy. When you toss them back, they fail to burn. Even now, two days later, they're waiting like unpopped kernels, virginal boys at their first gym dance, but nothing so trivial, so fraught with the commonplace, because the fire takes away that particular privilege. Everything bursts into flames or fails. It's the rule of love. Almost nothing but the oddness of ash recalls the past.

In places the fire was so hard it stiffened your hair straight on end. Burned your face and arms, threatened to take the wet from your eyes. You see, there's some truth here—how what burns you up also takes feeling with it. You moved closer and closer to the fire, your hose wetting the air between you, the grass and mud, so you could step up and grab smoldering branches and boards, toss them into the deeper flames, wondering if the ash were hot enough to melt your sneaker soles, the hose, or steam the water loose.

The others stay away, curious and a little frightened of the dish towel wrapped around your face, the ashy look around your eyes. They recognize a person who is taking too many risks and turn their backs. So you are alone, the fire beating the air with heat and smoke, the gray yellow of plastics.

At first it's just two rabbits that dart away in opposite directions, like the getaway plan of amateur thieves. Then a fat raccoon galloping down the hill as if expecting pursuit. You look carefully, no smoke. Later, and you want to be mistaken here, a vole or field mouse that runs into the flames. And later, raking the ash, what might be a garter snake, but must be something metal or rubber, you reason, because by the time the flames have disappeared, the fire becomes intellectual property, reasoning itself out of the acts it has committed, and giving shape to ashes is how we spend the rest of our lives.

You don't remember any sound, though you believe there must have been the usual language of fire—but the roar of light in your eyes took it all away, like love, you keep insisting, like love you can't hear the words in the razzle-dazzle display. He tells you everything about his life and later it gets reported again—the feelings and other words burned off, away.

"You didn't really believe that?" they say. You feel like that snake, a spring uncoiled in lava, frozen in stone. You get that dry, burned tongue, but water only tastes bad. Like love, you tell them, like love.

Indigo Road

I knew I was dying and going to hell, is that plain enough? I'd come down to Indigo Road to see the children. I'm not a nosy woman, but I'm curious, and while I knew better than to try to breathe life into a dead rooster, I had something to say.

The place looked better than I left it—they'd planted everything you could eat, even flowers, nasturtiums and marigolds and bachelor's buttons. The summer has that mass of color and urge that just spills across the land here, disciplined by lines, furrows of corn and beans, barbed wire and blacktop. If I could have stood it.

They were all on the porch, like I'd called ahead, but I was just on the wing then, running hard ahead of the tether. My children were the shapes of dreams, cloudy beyond the small reach of my skin. I pulled over and got out before someone could stop me. How good I am to you, I almost said.

The dust kept settling on the hood of the car, a nice white little Honda with a jacked-up engine the kid at the Squeegee Stop parked out front. A little small, but when you're in a hurry, you don't try things on for size. I had the gun tucked in my purse swung over my shoulder, the weight bumping my hipbone as I walked. You could tell from the expression on their faces that I was on a carpet of disturbing wrong all the way to their door.

I just wanted to see—I said, and mouths opened in little Os of incomprehension. The kids had bare feet, toes like dusty tubers, ankles and calves bitten bloody, arms dirty-tan, with the golden hairs prickling in the heat. Their faces, bothered in the noise of their wings, but I'm getting ahead of myself.

I just wanted to see—I said again. Everybody who was hurt, killed, or whatever—

There was nowhere to sit, so I stood, my hand in the purse, the metal cool to the touch. They still weren't talking, and the birds silently sailed into the picture window and dropped without a sound. No one moved. Butterflies collapsed into the flowers, and while I watched, insects ate the bachelor's buttons to the ground, then took the roots too. We had time on our hands.

It's the way we are in our family, we marry forever and die alone. But they hadn't missed me, I could tell from their faces. The dust kept settling, on the bleached white hair of the children, the faint green dress of my sister, the pilot-blue shirt and pants of the man.

I'm all poured out, I said, trying to bind their anxiety and waiting for the youngest to stretch his arms toward me.

Sometimes it's this silence I can't wait in, sometimes it's the noise of their wings flattening the world until the moon lies on its side like an old egg, and I take the gun out again.

This time I was wearing the wedding dress, Brother Billy was waiting inside, and all I had to do was walk up the porch and tug the screen door open on its squeaky hinges. I'd turn to the man and tell him to soap the frame so the swollen wood slid in this heat. The dog would wag its tail, brushing the dress with a swish of mud I wouldn't see until later when I let it drop down my slim hips, spilling like milk around my feet. And the children.

You never get over being crippled by sin, I said, but the dust sifted down, and the faces didn't change. We're all crippled by sin, I said, sliding the gun out of the purse.

All they can do is shoot and kill you, hallelujah, you been saved, I said. The baby's fingers twitched and I thought he was going to call out for me as I lifted the gun. It's grief that finally takes the weight from our souls and scrubs us clean again. Grief, I said. But this time I waited until the preacher was calling from the parlor, and the sirens were crying for me down Indigo Road.

How Good I Am to You

The weather had finally broken and there would be stars in the sky, but it was serial killer night at the bar. Psycho Sunday. Issues people. At least it wasn't a full moon or a holiday. When Frank came on shift at seven, the sun was spreading its margarine light across the parking lot, firing up the windows of all the beat-up cars and pickups. A husband-and-wife team of drunks were leaning on the open doors of their bumperless black Bronco glaring at the orange-red oozing out of the west.

"It's the sunset, you son-of-a-bitch." The wife took a long, nearly fatal drag off a cigarette, stared at the glowing stump and tossed it to the ground, grinding it for longer than necessary under the rubber toe of her sneaker while she coughed and waved a hand in front of her face. The husband rubbed his face and looked at his hands as if surprised they were his.

The license plate said South Dakota. They were new in town and Frank was glad they were already drunk enough to go home.

"I'm not joining in this jamboree." The husband struggled toward the seat, climbing the Bronco like a stepladder.

Frank paused, in case he'd have to help them. He wondered who'd served them. They should've been cut off hours ago. If Salter was in the patrol car, the bar'd be cited again, and the insurance was going to drop them. They'd had their last warning after the shooting in December when two deer hunters squared off with rifles and blew the beer cooler to pieces.

It was game day too and he dreaded the score. If the Vikings won, all the drunks would stay around and celebrate until they got in fights with the psychos. If the team lost, they'd drink themselves stupid watching the recap while the phone rang off the wall, then leave a dollar tip and stagger home to fight with their families while the psychos fed on the bad feelings they left behind.

The Bronco fired up, the mufflerless engine roaring, then edged out of its parking place. Maybe Salter wouldn't stop them, maybe they'd make it home safely, the husband peering like a gerbil over the rim of the steering wheel, while the wife braced against the high seat, her face in frozen shock at the speed as they drifted down the blacktop at twenty miles per hour. Salter didn't mind the drunks as much if they went slow, what he hated was the speeders wrapping themselves up in trees and poles and livestock trucks.

With his hand on the door, the scent of beer and smoke wreathing the building like a sacred mist, Frank took one last look at the outside because in eight hours, at 4 A.M. when he'd be finished cleaning the glasses, hauling the bottles and cans out, counting the registers and the day bar and waitress bags, and checking the doors, it would all be different. He'd be the one giddy with exhaustion and the drinks he'd pour for himself as soon as the last customer was safely out the door and the lights could come up for good and the jukebox was finally silent. He wanted to remember the way the cottonwoods across the road shook their round leaves like gold and silver coins in the falling light, and the last swoop of the swallows feeding on mosquitoes and gnats that clouded up out of the ditch weeds and marsh as if the hands of light had disturbed them. A great blue heron drifted just over the trees into the marsh, "sky-pokes" he and his cousins had called them as boys using the big awkward forms when the urge for death rose up in their hearts and they pointed their rifles for the easy kill. This one must have a nest nearby. They were optimistic birds, never quite believing the bullet that took them in flight, continuing the big leisurely flapping of wings with a trail of blood streaming down their breast as they descended to earth. Frank took a deep breath of the spiced wood and marsh-scented air that still overrode the bar stink, and opened the door.

Inside the TVs were already on the evening baseball game from the West Coast with the sound turned off and badly spelled captions rolling across the bottom, and the regulars were lined up waiting for the action their drinks paid for. Out back a freight train roared by sending the liquor bottles on the shelf behind the bar clanking against each other, and shaking the jukebox CD off its song. Trains were supposed to be

doing thirty-five through town, which would mean they were just starting to build again by the time they got to the bar out here. He knew
this one hadn't slowed to much below sixty the whole way. Frank nodded at the regulars, avoided looking at the others, and made his way
toward the back. From the mood, he could tell that the Vikings had
probably lost.

In the bathroom, washing up, he noticed that the Jesus Man had
been around today pasting heart stamps on the mirror, the towel dis-
penser, over the urinal, and on the back of the stall door: JESUS loves
you, Be a JESUS fan, REPENT! USA Revelations: 17, 18. He'd have to
get Rafael in there with solvent before they got too deep into the
night. No point stirring up this kind of trouble on a Sunday. Place
could use a quick scrub too. The floor was littered with wet towels,
pieces of T.P., and cigarette butts. Rafael would jump at the chance to
douse it with the Pine-Sol he liked to use full-strength, no matter
how Frank explained the notion of dilution. Drunks couldn't hang
around long enough to mess things up in there after Rafael had
cleaned—the ammonia stink was too strong—so maybe he was right
after all.

Frank gave a last look at himself in the mirror, his narrow, clean
shaved face just below the heart-filled prayer: Lord Jesus, I Know I'm A
Sinner, Please Forgive Me. . . . It went on. He inspected his eyes. Clear
and tired brown. He made the light jump up in them with a smile for a
moment, then let them settle back. The jagged scar on his cheek from
splintered glass the time the drunk kid heaved a bottle at him was
angry red. He remembered the blood dripping off his chin, and how
good his knuckles felt cracking against the bottle thrower's nose.
They'd told him to keep the scar out of the sun for a year, but it was
the middle of summer and anytime he got a day off he had to be outside or he'd go nuts. He pushed his brown hair off his forehead and
inspected the hairline. Definitely headed north. When he had time
again, God knew when, he'd make an appointment and ask the doctor
about that stuff they sold.

He pulled at the bottom of the black T-shirt with the Harry's Bar
logo on the pocket. It kept shrinking in the dryer, either that or his little belly was getting bigger. He didn't want to think about it. OK,
troops—one last glance in the mirror, turn on the smile, and off to war.

"She's got the slow dwindles," Ralph said. "One of those slow dealies you can live forever on. Like Ali. Only his wife's lucky, she finally shut up. Flora hasn't taken a breath between words in thirty years." He was a small, stocky man with short arms, skinny legs, and a large balding head. Frank was nodding sympathetically while he filled a pitcher of Leinie's. Ralph and his buddy Harold liked to sit by the tap so they could catch Frank up on the gossip and jokes while he served.

"Frank, you going to that Jell-O-rama deal they're having at the Legion Hall Wednesday night?" Harold had once sat on the town council and still felt he had to take part in civic activities.

"Jell-O-rama?" Frank poured a glass of foam off the pitcher and kept filling it. Have to get Rafael downstairs to check the line, see if it was time to change kegs. Where was Rafael?

"Every family brings Jell-O." Harold sipped his beer. "They get pretty wild too—Coca-Cola Jell-O, vodka—what have you. Plus the usuals. I like the shredded carrots in lime myself, but Marjorie has something else planned. Can't see why. I tell her I like the carrots in it and she goes and makes another kind. Can't see why. You going?"

Frank shrugged and smiled. Harold nodded. Frank slid the full pitcher and four glasses to Michelle, the pretty, dark-haired waitress from the community college. Only problem was she already had two kids by different dads and no end in sight.

"I hate Jell-O," Ralph said. "Can't stand the stuff. It's like boiled okra—just plain slimy."

Frank moved down the bar, checking drink levels, emptying ashtrays along the way. A punk in baggy green cargo pants hanging off his ass and a long-sleeved tan shirt buttoned at the throat climbed on a stool. Drumming a quarter on the bar he flipped his chin at the bottles of liquor.

"You got any Goldschläger or Jäg?"

Frank wanted to shake his head, but instead he ID-ed him and got the Jägermeister out of the cooler. "Five dollars." He put the full shot and water back on napkins in front of the kid.

"You're shittin' me." He slid the quarter across the bar and it bounced at Frank's feet.

"Five dollars." Frank looked toward the kitchen in case Rafael was taking a break with the cook.

The kid grabbed the shot and tossed it back. Grinning, he slid the glass toward Frank again. "Hit me again." Then he added, "Put it on my tab."

Frank hesitated. "Back in a minute." He headed for the kitchen at the end of the bar. If the kid was going to stiff him, he'd rather it was a five-dollar tab than a fifty. He'd priced the shots high enough so the kid would leave after one, but it wasn't working.

The cook and his helper were dumping bags of french fries into the deep fryer baskets.

"What's this?" Frank waved at the five smoking fryers.

"Guy just dropped off a huge order for wings and fries." Flaco stepped back and lowered a basket into hot grease. "Looked like a little gang-banger."

"You seen Rafael?"

Flaco shook his head and frowned. Rafael was his nephew he'd brought up from Mexico. The boy at Flaco's side was his son, Jack, formerly Joaquín. They'd been able to get green cards ten years ago and were now on the verge of opening their own restaurant in town. Harry was going to be out of luck when that happened.

"You know that kid out there?" Frank asked Jack who just shook his head with a sideways glance at his father.

Frank took a deep breath of greasy air and watched the two men, so alike except that the father had deep acne scars like a mask across his nose and cheeks while the son had a smooth, sullen face and his short black hair was bleached blond in front. Where was Rafael?

"We're out of both fries and wings now," Flaco called after him.

More of Harry's poor planning.

"It's the wood that fails in a stone house," Monroe was saying over his seven and seven. He'd drink all night long and walk straight as a new two-by-four out the door at closing.

"I know it," Roy says. "When my ex only gave me an entry level miter saw that last Christmas we were married, I could see the writing on the wall." Roy's son had tried to hang himself in the garage that Christmas afternoon, and Roy had just barely managed to get him down and call 911. Now the brain-damaged kid sat around in the basement watching TV twenty-four-seven, growing fatter by the week. Every Sunday Roy came in for a night off while his ex-in-laws sat with his son. Roy never complained about his son though. He drank his Crown Royal and Coke and talked to Monroe.

"Can I get my drink?" The gang-banger tapped another quarter on the bar.

Frank grabbed a clean glass, poured it sloppy full, and set it down hard so it wet the napkin. The kid's lips split apart, baring his upper teeth with the sharpened incisors. This time he let the quarter drop into the ooze on the napkin after he knocked off the shot.

"How're you back-slidden Christians doing?" Sterling put one big ham on the stool, then levered his butt up so bags of flesh hung off each side. Frank poured the glass of gin with a twist of lemon and scooped a glass of ice with soda water. Sterling nodded at him and took a sip, closed his eyes and took a long drink.

"Got a new M.D.I.—million dollar idea—for you. Food Chain Theme Park where birds of prey eat reptiles and reptiles eat mice, and mice eat—you get the idea." He put the glass down and rubbed his hands together, looking up and down the bar for the basket of popcorn that usually appeared about now.

"Popper's busted. We got potato chips," Frank said.

"French fries. Fries and wings. Lots of hot sauce on the wings." The tip of his pink tongue appeared to glow in the shadows of the room. "Double, no, make it a triple order so I can share with the boys here." He lifted his glass to the two men staring at the TV set.

Frank tapped in the order, ignoring the message that shot back to remind him they were out of fries and wings.

Sterling had started coming to Harry's two years ago with his girl-friend while his wife spent the summer in Europe and the winter in Arizona. In the spring and fall, she traveled to the Twin Cities or Chicago to see friends. Sterling, who almost never had more conjugal duties than he could stand, finally took up with one of the opinion takers for his small, very exclusive polling business. Then she too began to travel. Now he was trying to date one of the teachers at the college who wasn't sure she wanted to be the girlfriend to replace the girlfriend to replace the wife.

Sterling looked around at the rowdy group of twenty-somethings in the corner on their third pitcher and already knocking glasses around. "How's it going tonight?"

Frank shrugged. "It's Sunday." Sterling nodded. He'd been here the night Frank had been cut and had slammed his huge fist into the chest of the attacker, dropping him to the floor for breath, which surprised everyone.

"Where's Rafael?"

Frank shook his head. "He should be on the door backing Donnie up." Donnie was an ex-football jock with a blown-out knee who chatted up the girls while he pretended to study their IDs because he could barely read. Rafael was almost as big, packing muscle where Donnie was turning soft, and he could read in three languages.

A man in a dark-blue wool coat edged around the bouncer and girls, and scooted to the end of the bar. Although his face gleamed with sweat, and his long gray hair separated in greasy, wet strands around his face, he only unbuttoned the front of the coat, revealing three layers of shirts. The ragged cuffs of long underwear fringed his wrists as he leaned his arms on the bar and looked hungrily at the bottles of liquor. The stench had reached Frank by that time. It was a head-numbing combination of filthy clothes, rotting gums, sweat, and something so acrid it made the eyes smart. He tried to cough it away, but found the stink sucking into his throat instead. It was L.C. and Donnie was supposed to stop him before he came all the way in, but he'd been too busy.

As Frank drew closer, L.C. pulled a wad of limp dollars from his coat and pointed at the end bottle of cheap scotch. Frank poured a glass full, forgoing the water and ice on the side, and watched as L.C. drank it straight down. They went through the ritual twice more, before Frank put the bottle away and produced the glass of ice and water for L.C. to drink more slowly. Then suddenly Michelle was bumping into the bar, twisting away from the hands of a twenty-something in a backwards baseball cap and purple Viking football shirt who'd decided to dance with the waitress. Turning to shove him off, she backed into L.C., spilling his water down the front of his shirts. With a roar, he leapt off the stool, brushing his clothes frantically as if he were on fire. His high-pitched wail shut the bar noise down. Frank flung the gate up and started rubbing at the soaked shirts with a dry towel, trying not to touch L.C. with his hands.

"Donnie, get him out of here!" he yelled. "Here, take the towel, L.C., take the towel. It's dry, see, it's dry. Now take the towel. Donnie!" Where the hell was Rafael, he knew that L.C. got his drinks in the alcove of the doorway where it was safe and he didn't stink up the place.

The twenty-something had retreated to the back table, nudging his buddies and laughing with the girls who were too dumb to know better.

Michelle had disappeared into the bathroom which she'd fill with pot smoke and a heavy dose of air freshener before she came back.

"Can we get another pitcher?" One of the boys yelled in the lull between songs. Somebody had played the entire 70s disco album for the fourth time, and Frank's head was beginning to throb with the beat of "Dancing Girl."

"Frank," Flaco was standing at the end of the bar near the gang-banger who had now been joined by a friend dressed identically except for the addition of a gold chain thick enough to use on his tires in winter. They'd tied blue bandanas around their foreheads. Flaco was making a point of ignoring them as he beckoned to Frank.

"I told you we're out of fries now," Flaco said. They were just inside the kitchen door, and Jack, formerly Joaquín, was shaking the hot fries into styrofoam take-out boxes lined along the long counter already half full of wings.

"Give me three of those," Frank said.

Flaco shook his head and Jack looked up, smiling.

"I mean it. I'm the manager and I need three of those boxes."

"I'm in charge back here, Frank, you know that." Flaco crossed his arms. "It's first come, first serve here."

Jack started down the line of boxes, putting two containers of hot sauce and packets of ketchup in each one. He was still smiling.

"Take it up with Harry then," Frank said. "Right now, I can fire your ass unless you give me three of those boxes."

Flaco glanced at his son who just smiled and shook his head as he went down the line, closing and taping each box shut.

"Kitchen's closed," Frank said. "Take off."

Flaco untied his apron and threw it on the floor in front of Frank while Jack carefully taped the last box and started stacking them in large brown bags. His father touched his arm, but he shrugged him off and continued his work.

"Get him out of here, Flaco, I mean it." Frank could hear the noise level rising in the room behind him. He had to get back out there. Jack threw the last box down on the counter, splitting the bottom and spilling greasy red sauce on the white Formica surface. "And where the hell is Rafael?" Frank yelled at the retreating men. "He's fired if he doesn't get his ass out there now."

Leaving the split box on the counter, Frank carried the bags out and put them on the bar. He took out three of the boxes and put them in front of Sterling, then slid the bags over to the punks.

"Ran out of food," he said.

"What about those—" The first gang-banger tilted his head toward the three boxes Sterling was just opening. "Dude came in after me." There was a whininess in the punk's voice, as if he'd gotten the smallest piece of cake at a birthday party.

"Here's your ticket." Frank put the bill in front of the kids and turned to cash out some customers for Michelle.

"You son-of-a-bitch, you're gonna be sorry! My dad's rich—I can buy your ass—I can—" As soon as the kid reached behind him, Donnie was there, pushing his arm up the middle of his back until the punk bent forward, his face kissing the wet surface of the bar.

"You packing, you little piece of shit?" Donnie reached down and pulled the gun out of the pants while the other punk sidled away. Donnie flipped it open and laughed. "It's not even loaded! What a jerk-off—" He gave the kid's arm a last yank and pushed his head down on the bar once more before he let him go, sliding the gun to Frank who stored it beneath the bar with the other weapons they'd confiscated the past month.

"Pay your bill and get the hell out of here," Frank said. The punk pulled out a platinum Visa card and Frank had to smile. "This daddy's too?"

"Me and my friends are never coming back here!" the kid yelled as Donnie shoved him out the door. The guys in the corner laughed and stomped their feet.

"Food order too," Michelle said as she put an empty pitcher on the bar and waited expectantly for him to put it in the computer. Another of Harry's innovations which cost Frank extra time.

"Kitchen's closed." It was taking Frank twice as long to refill the pitchers. Rafael needed to get down there. "You seen Rafael?" He was running low on ice too.

Michelle looked toward the kitchen, her face flushed red enough to be seen in the dark room.

"Michelle?"

"Maybe earlier—"

"Did you get him stoned or something?" Frank gave up on the foam and lifted the pitcher onto her tray.

She turned quickly enough that the pitcher tilted and she just managed to save it. Was he going to have to fire her too?

He started the trip down the bar again, stopping to clean up around Sterling and Monroe and Roy. Ralph and Harold had moved on to army stories and politics, while these guys were on parents and children.

"We had neighbors who used to dress their kids like dead relatives for Halloween. Nobody ever knew what they were supposed to be—kids turned into rotten bastards when they grew up." Roy never had a happy story.

Monroe mostly kept quiet, drinking and eating as much as he could while the other men spent their time talking, but now he piped up. "My daddy only gave me three pieces of advice: If you lie and get caught, lie some more. Never kiss and tell. And always keep your fishing equipment in the car." He stuffed the last french fry in his mouth and emptied his glass. Frank refilled it with seven and seven.

"I remember one time mother got so mad because father refused to buy her new dishes, she served us dinner on pie tins instead of plates. You should've seen the expression on his face when his roast beef came out in an old pie tin." Sterling touched his empty glass with his forefinger and Frank took it for a refill.

Down the bar a man and a woman were arguing about where the King of the Gypsies' house was. She said it was in town, the place with those stunted, dying shrubs outlining the perimeter and the three old Cadillacs rusting in the driveway.

"They always go for the Caddies," she said, "that's how you know." Frank checked their drinks and emptied the ashtray which was brimming with smoking butts.

The disco music went on for a fifth time, and he made a mental note to tell the jukebox man to dump the CD or he'd be finding a new way of "Staying Alive, Staying Alive."

An old couple at the table nearest the bar got up and sat at the stools emptied by the punks. When Frank got there, she was asking, "Where are we?"

"Somewhere between hell and Philadelphia," the old man replied. They were dressed in matching khakis and polo shirts, and their white hair was cut the same length, above the ears, with hers a little poofier in front. Their faces seemed to share the same baggy wrinkles and blue eyes.

"My sister Agnes," the old man pointed his thumb to her as she turned around and stared at the room. He dropped his voice. "A little

Alzheimer's these days. Just bring her a Coke and tell her it's got rum in it. I need a vodka tonic in a tall glass."

"Are we naked yet?" Agnes turned and smiled flirtatiously at Frank.

"Working on it," he said. "Rum and Coke, drink up." He carefully put the glass in the middle of the napkin and watched while she tasted it. She smacked her lips. "Sweet. Do you have ice cream?"

Frank glanced at the old man, who shrugged. The bar kept a gallon of vanilla for specialty drinks. Frank made the vodka and tonic, apologizing for the lemon instead of the lime twist. Harry again. Then he dug out the ice cream and served the woman who looked puzzled for a moment, until the old man told her to eat her dessert.

"It's what the dead want done that's important," Roy was saying as Frank started down the bar for the last time.

"Are we immortal yet?" Sterling asked.

"Just about," Frank said. "Any minute now."

The Suicide Who Came to Visit

As far as he could tell, Bobby Diamondback's mother had Belated Meter Maid Syndrome—every time she visited she tried to kill herself. And it was usually after nine o'clock at night when the emergency rooms were beginning to fill up with bloody knife wounds, bar fighters with their own police escort, and sick kids. Really sick kids—small, very small, and burning red with fever, their little cantaloupe heads rolling around dangerously, tiny arms and legs limp, helpless—really, really, sick kids. It made Bobby furious to be sitting there while his mother was having her stomach pumped, followed by the long, boring interviews with the social workers and some pathetic shrink they'd drag in from doing something productive like watching TV or wrangling with their own family. But still, it was better than having to sit there watching those little tiny kids trying to die in their parents' arms.

Only they didn't die. Bobby knew that. He hadn't, and he had the crown jewel Jesus of all mothers to remind him of it.

"Men just want you to die," she'd said tonight. He should've known what was next, but it was too early in the visit. So he'd thought it was safe to run out, grab a beer at Billy's with Marie, his girlfriend who would never ever come around his mother again after the last visit. He was going to pick up take-out Thai food, he told Mom, great new place. She was going to love it.

One look at her face reminded him she never loved anything, and that had made him frown. She knew exactly what he was up to.

"No," she said, crossing her arms. He noticed the pelt of long, mannish hairs for the thousandth time and wondered why she didn't shave them or get electrolysis like Marie had on her little mustache.

"No what? Thai food, Mom, you'll like it—" Truth was she wouldn't, but Bobby couldn't think of anything else.

"You need a spinal boner," Marie announced as soon as he showed up, half an hour late.

The beer had been sitting so long it was flat. He deserved that, her face told him. He nodded.

"You need to come to the party, Bobby, your mother—"

Bobby held up a hand. For the past year they'd gotten along fine because of the agreement not to talk about his mom, no point changing it now.

"You don't have it like that—" She shoved the half-full bowl of stale popcorn at him, and it knocked into the flat beer, slopping it on the table.

"Honey, Marie, you know—" He mopped at the beer with his napkin until the waitress plopped a rag down as she walked by. He really didn't want to touch the gray, smelly bar rag.

"Here—" Marie swabbed the red Formica impatiently, and set his glass down so hard it slopped again, but she ignored it.

"She's leaving in a couple of days, honey—then I told you we'd go on out to Las Vegas with the rest of the bar like we planned. Honest, Marie. Her being here doesn't change a thing." He felt proud of the little speech, almost convincing himself despite the glare that cut lines along the sides of her mouth, pulling the full lips down so she looked ever-so-slightly like his mother, just ever-ever-so-slightly. As soon as she smiled again, he'd forget all about it—if she'd just smile. Her brown eyes seemed to darken as they pinned him against the wooden back of the seat, straight as a church pew. It was like she held a rake under his chin and was pushing, his throat closing against the metal teeth. He took a quick gulp of beer and pulled his gaze away.

Other couples were laughing and playing pool like it was just a regular Tuesday night. The bartender was ignoring them. People kept away from him when his mother was in town. He was going to have to get her to leave by Friday so he could board the charter with Marie, like he'd just promised. He drank again, pretending he didn't hear her long patriotic red and blue nails with the white stars drumming the table. Fourth of July design. He'd bet on those nails in a contest with a paint scraper, they were so hard. Marie knew nails, had her own little shop, and Bobby loved the long red arcs they left on his arms and chest the next morning. Like tattoos almost, which he couldn't have, because of his mother. She'd jump off a bridge if he did that. She'd already told him so.

He let himself glance quickly at Marie, squinting his eyes into tough, lazy slits, the way she liked. With a name like his, you should be a lot worse character, she'd told him right off the bat. Then she'd made him buy all black clothes and grow his black hair long and sweep it back with the gel products he sold. Actually, his sales had improved, and he'd gotten a twenty-dollar bump in his base pay at Hansen's Beauty. His mother had taken one look and demanded to meet the girl. That was a bad one—Mom had used the quart of vodka with the pills and actually almost killed herself while Bobby'd stayed in front of Marie's house kissing instead of coming right back. They'd kept her for three days in the hospital running enough charcoal through her stomach to hold a barbecue.

"Have you told her she has to go by Friday?" Marie asked.

Bobby hesitated. He had muttered it, but his mom didn't seem to hear. He was pretty sure she hadn't heard because she told him she wanted to go to the zoo on Saturday.

"You're up the creek with nothing to paddle with but your dick, Bobby, and that ain't gonna get you too far—" Marie slammed the table with her fist, stood, tried to push the bolted-down table against him, and strode up to the bar, taking an empty stool between two guys when there were plenty of others vacant on both sides.

"You just be ready." He threw a ten on the bar in front of her and left, his heart bumping furiously in his throat and ears. He wanted to go back and pound the living crap out of someone, but then he'd be one of those guys in the emergency room later tonight.

The Thai food wasn't ready. It never was. The little room was crowded with diners and half a dozen people waiting furiously for take-out. He thought about calling his mother, but he was still too pissed from seeing Marie. Mom would hear the tone and think it was for her.

By the time he pulled into his driveway, he had given up all hope. He almost left the food in the car so he'd have something to eat while he waited, but he didn't. He picked up the hot, greasy bags, they always overfilled the containers, and walked through the grass gone to seed. He kept meaning to get the mower fixed. The stalks were heavy with dew and wet his pants halfway to his knees and sopped the short black boots that pinched his toes.

On the porch, he paused long enough to sniff the front of his black nylon shirt. It reeked of smoke and beer, she'd know. He thought of taking it off and throwing it in the bushes, but what would his excuse be then? He pushed his long hair back even though it was glued in place with gel, and wished he had a James Dean comb in his back pocket so he could pretend indifference when Mom hit the ceiling.

Soon as he stepped inside the house he knew. She'd cranked up the window air conditioner and left him a little trail of clothes, jewelry, and old photos she carried in her suitcase. The note was sitting on the scratched old mahogany dining table she'd inherited from her mother and insisted he take when he rented the house. There was the usual scrawl—she usually waited until she was dropping off the little cliff into unconsciousness to write. It began, "We're all going to hell, right?"

He was tempted, really, really tempted to tiptoe out this time, to pretend he was still picking up Thai food or having a beer with Marie or the car got pissed and flattened itself so he couldn't make it back in time. Maybe he'd spend the night with Marie like they did when Mom wasn't visiting, maybe he'd drive her to a motel on the outskirts of town for a change, have dirty sex in dirty sheets for the days remaining until they climbed up the stairs of the charter to Vegas. He'd tell her it was time to make good on the ring, his grandmother's ring he'd stolen last time his mother had draped his house with her things, and he'd been so mad, he picked up the diamond and sapphire ring and put it in his pocket, later saying someone must have come in and stolen it, and now he'd give it to Marie and they'd get married, because that was one thing his mother and Marie agreed on, jewelry tells the tale, and he'd whisk her off to the Elvis chapel and have their picture taken and he'd mail it to his mom as proof, and that's when he stopped, picked up the phone, and punched in 911.

Once the Dogs Are Sleeping

"Soon as I get my life out of Public Storage," he said to the deputy taking him to the front door. He'd just been let out of the overcrowded Spate County lockup because he was the only one *not* doing meth in jail, the sheriff said.

Jimmy Cavalier was grateful. He'd come to this pass from having shit-for-shit, as his brother said. Two hundred parking tickets set a record in their little southeast Oklahoma town, and Jimmy wasn't so sure why he couldn't be proud, except they'd taken the car—and all his stuff was in Public Storage next to a couple of guys cooking meth and living in their unit.

On the sidewalk he looked both ways down the street, but no brother and no car. Impound lot. He stuck his hands in his jeans pockets, feeling the two quarters and three dollars. His brother probably hadn't heard he was out yet.

"Need a ride?" The maroon van's side door slid open.

"Lawyer just bailed us out," the red-bearded guy in the front passenger seat said.

Jimmy peered inside. It was the two guys from the storage unit next to his.

"They took my car," he said, climbing into the dark interior and settling in the burgundy velour captain's chair with the ripped seat behind the driver.

"Yeah, well—" Beard waved his cigarette at the two-story granite courthouse. "The day of the dog is coming."

The manager's office at Public Storage was locked up like always and the place looked like a drive-in movie in the daylight—weeds poking up through cracks in the cement drive, wind-blown wrappers from the McDonald's down the street caught at the edges of the long row of battered white metal buildings. When the van stopped in front of their two units, a plastic Coke bottle tumbled at their feet, paused, and bumped under the van.

For a minute the three men stood awkwardly in front of their locked units, the driver lifting his baseball hat, smoothing his bald head and thin, dry fringe, then replacing the blue hat firmly in the middle of his head, squaring the red bill so the Salt Dogs logo was bisecting his nose.

"Well—" Jimmy stuck his hand out to Red Beard, then Hat, and the men turned to their respective doors which opened and clanked up like on his girlfriend's garage. Inside, he pulled the black beanbag chair to the open front, disentangled the little antique sewing box that had been his mother's and set it next to the chair, found the eleven-inch black-and-white TV in the bottom of a collapsing garbage bag of clothes, and set it on the sewing box before realizing his girlfriend's kid had chewed the cord in two. OK, that had bothered him, but he hadn't said a word. She was wrong. Definitely. Collapsing in the beanbag that burped a few beans and separated under his weight until he could feel the concrete under his butt, he argued it out with his girlfriend again.

All he'd said, well, the last straw deal, was him waving his arms at the walls and furniture, curtains, chairs, books, dishes, towels, every goddamn thing relating to cars and car racing. Winston Cup, Busch, IRL, Formula One, Cart, he had to put a pillow over his head at night to stop the drone of undigested facts and numbers after they made love which was the by-God only thing to shut it down. He worked as hard as he could to make it last so he could really enjoy the long panting silence until she was calling his name like he was in the lead at the Brickyard 400.

He remembered they'd fought about Billy the baby who'd painted the screen of the new TV set with Elmer's Glue while Jimmy was on the phone trying to line up a job with his brother. When he felt he'd had enough blame, he waved his arms at the living room and said, "Well, you live in a goddamn theme park."

Next thing he knew, and really it was, he was in his car carrying another cardboard box and suitcase of his stuff to the Public Storage. He looked across the vacant red dirt lot where the MORE STORAGE UNITS COMING SOON sign had been half-knocked apart by wind and faded to pale, unreadable pastels by the sun. He had the sinking feeling that nothing was coming. His girlfriend hadn't accepted his call from jail, and his brother wasn't looking for him. When the dogs got loose, he guessed, they got real loose.

He got up and went to the doorway of the unit next door where a red velvet couch stood on end towering over the two men fussing like his old maid aunts over the stinking contents of a saucepan on the stove they'd hooked up to the utility pole behind the units.

He couldn't tell if they were cooking drugs or food so he went back to his beanbag chair, wondering just how many men were living here, waiting until the dogs went back to sleep.

Carl Millennium

 "When I'm talking to you about your case, I cannot think about your case." Carl Millennium has a larva face, like it has been slightly under a rock. When he stares back at me with this perfectly satisfied expression, it's as if he's just solved the final equation for the time-space continuum I've been working on. So I let him have his little moment and sit quietly for a while in the smoke-choked office where even the gray and lavender pin-striped wallpaper is shellacked with dull yellow like the whites of Carl's eyes.

The flies stagger like errant black stars burning out above us, and Carl's phone rings impatiently for a long, long time. But I'm a patient man, spending nights at my own expense with the homemade tele-scope on the roof of my garage, and sleeping away the useless days. There's always a genius about Carl's silence, much like deep space, full of unseen comets, phalanxes of stars, as if he's drunk on both the cig-arette smoke and the facts of my case.

Finally Carl lumbers out of his chair and goes to the wall of scarred blond cabinets behind him. I'm already groaning as I get out of my chair, careful to keep the weight off my bad ankle which is the whole reason for being here in the first place. It jabs with pain that feels like a piece of glass is gnawing at the tendon.

Carl stops shoving gallon jugs around on the head-high shelf and looks at me. We're both average height.

"He left a tooth in there, I can still feel it," I say.

Carl nods and pulls out two gallon jugs. I groan again and limp over to take the green one. It's the all-purpose power drink that tastes like spinach soaked in coffee. Carl has to be brewing this stuff in his garage.

"What's that—" I lift the jug and nod toward the milky one in his hand.

"Bone densifier," Carl says.

His voice isn't so much gravelly from the cigarettes as browned, deepened, and smoothed, like his wrinkleless sixty-year-old face. The face of a man who sleeps well at night.

"Have you filed yet?" I ask.

He stares toward the ceiling, letting the words balloon and drift toward him in slow motion. He lifts the jug and nudges me over to my chair again.

"I mean, the longer we wait—"

He doesn't bother to look at me. Just settles the jug tilting on the mound of papers growing from the surface of his desk.

"Carl!" the voice squawks as the door opens. "This dog has got to go—I mean it!"

The black and white speckled terrier that flayed my ankle open a month ago trots in. The dog eyes me suspiciously and begins the deep, rolling growl that sounds like an old man gargling at the sink. I rub my ankle. The dog's tooth is still in here, no matter what the doctors say.

"I'm not running a kennel!" The young woman, named Doray, stamps her short red boot and the dog flicks his eyes at her thick ankles.

"I wouldn't do that—" I lift my bad foot. "Wily son-of-a-bitch'll surprise you."

Doray glares at the dog like she'd as soon punt him and holds out the rope leash. The dog barks and Carl goes over to the cabinets again, pulls out a styrofoam bowl. That's when I notice the pillow and quilt on the lower shelf just above the balled socks. Is Carl living in his office?

He pours the milky "bone densifier" in the bowl, sets it on the floor, and waves to Doray, who half-drags the growling dog over.

The dog hesitates, then slurps thirstily. When the bowl's empty, he lies down on his side and starts snoring with little sucking breaths.

"Not sure I want any of that—" I say, thinking of my nightly vigils.

"Not charging you full price," Carl says and begins searching the mass of papers for his receipt book. Doray snorts and leans over the desk, her hands shuffling papers like a card shark.

She's wearing a pair of jeans so tight, I can count the three rolls bulging over her belt. Her pink stretch nylon top squeezes her breasts almost flat. The short red boots have fringe down the sides that snap every time her foot jerks. Doray, Carl's niece on his brother's side, is stuck here in Nebraska. She has disgraced herself in too many towns to be able to go home again.

She tosses the receipt book at Carl, then nudges the dog with her foot.

"Carl," she says, her eyes wide with surprise. "Carl, look at the dog—" She uses the sharp point of her boot to lift its middle and the head rolls drunkenly. "It's dead, Carl, the dog is dead."

He leans over in his chair and inspects the diminished heap of fur lying in a shawl of spreading wet.

"Carl?" Doray squats down and glares into the bowl, then stands up.

He picks up the jug, uncaps it, and sniffs. "Oh," he says.

"What is that stuff?" I ask.

He turns it around and around, searching the narrow white hand-printed label.

"Well, the dog's dead." Doray's boots are tapping again, the fringe jumping alive. "What about his case?" Her thin lips and frown say I'm part of the problem around here.

"Cleaner, the All-Purpose Elixir," Carl says. But for the first time there's doubt on his face, riding perilously without lines or wrinkles to cling to on the boneless structure.

"That dog was our case," he says with a shake of his head.

"I'm not paying then." I wave toward the receipt book he's paused over and lift the jug of Vita Drink.

Doray's head jerks toward me. She's pulled her thin brown hair back in a tiny ponytail held by a dingy rag of lace.

Carl has been selling me VitaLife products in exchange for legal advice. Some complicated financial scheme I can't begin to sort out, but he was there the afternoon I dragged my foot with the dog attached through his door. He even drove me to the hospital and helped the E.R. doc pry the jaws apart. A lot of service you expect to pay for. I just won-der—it's been a month and the lost-dog posters blaring from the utility poles and grocery store bulletin board are starting to show some wear and tear.

"Can't file now." Doray puts her hands on her hips and cautiously toes the dead dog's head as if he might still spring up and sink his teeth into the red leather.

Carl and Doray look at me next—it's my move. Kepler wanted to map the mind of God, but he never met Carl Millennium. I stand, using the jug of Vita Drink to balance against the chair as I pivot on my good foot toward the door. Have to get that tooth out somehow.

"You got satisfaction," Carl calls after me. "That has to be worth something. Peace of mind—"

My ankle stabs me as if that dog is gnawing the bone, like a cosmic question my telescope refuses to answer, no matter how deeply into the heavens I probe.

The Man in the Closet

Pain is a leaky vessel, that's what I tell the man living in my closet. He rattles the hangers, just a little so I won't be frightened, just to know he's listening, paying attention. At first I was frightened by the doors that kept cracking open enough to watch me sleep, bathe, walk the house in the middle of the night. Then I settled down. *We get used to everything*, I tell him. *Are you considering buying your own home?* That's one of the things I ask him periodically, to help identify the available space for him.

I've never asked him the usual *how did you get here* questions. It seems beside the point when he hands me the clothes in the morning, takes them back at night. But don't get me wrong, he's not some neurotic neat freak. He lets my closet order remain about the same, pretty much on the verge of extinction. Except for the cowboy boots I keep in military rows in case they decide to bolt for a night on the town, dancing, the way we used to until my husband found a lighter partner, someone he could twirl on the edge of church and work, someone with a big family that liked each other, that hadn't each one of them installed motion detector lights on the perimeter of their houses to keep people out.

I call my ex for Easter to see if he's risen yet. *My pride*, he mutters, *I'm losing a lot of pride these days. Why is it that makes me mad*, I wonder to the man in the closet as I walk the corridors of my house, inspecting the rooms like barracks someone else is responsible for, pausing as always to straighten the borders of the towels in the bathroom, surveying their center on the rod with a practiced squint. I don't accuse the man in the closet of off-kiltering the towels, but it makes me wonder. Sometimes I can feel the stirred air of a person who has just left the room I enter, and there isn't a closet or bedroom door in the house he'll keep shut. I don't ask him if he has that kind of pride that makes you up and leave after eight years of cold cereal looks and oversleeping. He's just trying to help, I know that.

Are you married yet? I ask the man who delivers our taxes. He won't look me in the eye but glances instead at the door behind me, as if that is the cream he's going to put on the conversation if I keep pushing it.

It's good to have someone to watch over you, I tell people who don't know I mean the man in the closet. Good to have the hot breath joining yours at night when the dreams take you down, flatten you, and throw you back up like an unwanted fish from the ocean. Good to open your eyes in the twilight room and feel he has been there at the foot of the bed, that the shadow leaving is his, for another room, asking you to follow like Columbus fingering the flat lines of his horizon for the hole where the curve leaks out when you arrive. I didn't hire him, you know, I only decided to let him stay. He makes a rim around the cup of my living here, he keeps me from rancid behavior, puts my research into pain on a nine-tenths program so he can save me from the last installment in the loan called my life.

Should I establish a bank account in your name, I ask, pedaling my recumbent bike steadily in place on the floor before his favorite closet. The door is open enough to see the stacks of T-shirts erupting, the paper bags overfull and tilting like buildings in a bad earthquake. This is the pretend closet, the one I don't use, only pretend to use because I had to fill up all the empty space one day. It wasn't easy figuring out how to spread myself so thin, looping scarves like road-flattened snakes over the wooden pole, stranding a white gauzy outfit like an abandoned wedding dress among the wire racks purchased to fill with things even the wind wouldn't pick up. I prop a mirror in there in case someone wants to watch herself, and keep sliding the doors shut all day long. It's the closet I don't want him to know about, not really. I mean, truth be told, it's the emptiness that scares me, the emptiness I can't do without.

Take the others, I've assured him. *I don't mind sharing the one in the old master bedroom, it's full of things that might interest you, keep you busy and warm, like a good life. Don't bother with this other one, the one that can't make up its mind, the one where nothing stands up, where nothing takes on character or meaning. This isn't a closet of any use. It's better let alone, better stayed out of. You go ahead, look in there. No comfort, see. The mirror is cheap, shiny new, but the leaning lies, makes you look longer or shorter, not nearly who you really are.*

There's only the belts pinned on the wall like trophies. And those two scarves long enough for a good strangling, the price tags still dangling, and that white outfit accusing me. Don't bother with this one, I urge him. It's cold in here. Nothing warms it, even in summer it's basement-cool, doesn't that tell you something?

He doesn't listen. This is the closet I find him in most now. Waiting, hands ready to receive and pay out what I need, what I believe I need when the sky darkens just after dawn and clouds move over the room with a rumbling wet breeze. I've been saving this one, I admit to the bare trees waiting for spring, I know I'm just asking for it, but it's the last one, and I want to make it the best, the very best I can, a permanent mailing address. *You understand,* I tell the neighborhood, lightless and burdened with sleep.

In my dreams I am traveling, places I don't recognize, lands that don't even exist, I suspect, and when I'm at home, the walls are always torn off the house, repairs haven't been made, closets full and useless, and the man never around, not in my dreams, he's only here when I'm awake, and I take that as a sign, a contract with the future that says *you don't own all the options available on this model, have a nice day, thank you, thank you.*

The sun comes up blood-brown like a peach pit stuck in the blue ridge across the river, Columbus opening a closet, handing our future back to be hung up until the sweat and smell of smoke disappears, until it's time to move on to a new emptiness. The pink flares the heavy bottoms of clouds, then goes out like a badly set fire. *Which is it,* I ask the man in the closet, *which way does the lock turn, which box has safety deposited in it, which heart did you come out of?*

The October Horse

 I was sleeping my way to Nebraska, and everything I resisted stood in my way—the cattle like ghosts in the unplowed cornfields, my sister Carren's phone call, a break in the fall heat that brought the cold mouth of winter down from Canada. I always imagined winter lived up there somewhere, that it only retreated to wait in some icy village, peasants scurrying to keep him, because it was bad luck to give poor hospitality, and the winter life was all they knew. There was a lot of time to think of such things trying to get to Nebraska.

The trees along Indigo Road to our family farm had flamed up in gold and orange and died back brown, but held on longer than usual. The ice-skimmed ponds looked opaque as steam rose up and flowed across the pastures. Ducks clogged the edges with their drowsy muttering, stretching their long, dark green and black necks toward the sun.

The pair of shaggy white-and-brown dogs trotted and sniffed and trotted along the ditch beside the road, ignoring the car and my arm hung out banging the door for their attention. "Come, Buster, Sally, come on," I called and they acted as if they'd never heard those words in their whole lives, less than a mile from home. They were off-duty, on their own time, they didn't owe me a thing.

The horses were already out, grazing in the frosty grass, their backs steaming in the cool air. They looked up at the sound of my tires on the gravel, their faces grave and curious, watching me drive slowly past them. Where was he? Was he still here?

Carren wasn't my sister, we were only related by blood, so it was surprising that she called and that I would come. But in family, they sew your eyes shut during training like you're young falcons, so you always come blindly home to the call of the bone.

Dicus was already walking back from doing barn chores as I pulled in, and he only glared and kept going, as if my car were an insult. He was long-legged and hunchbacked in his stained tan Carhartts and the shaggy brown hair hung at his neck like a ruff on a dog. He had strange malamute ice-blue eyes and a wide-lipped mouth. In our family his name was always followed with an apology.

He shut both doors behind him so I had to knock, and it took a few minutes before he decided to let me in. Although the back porch was filled with mud and junk, the kitchen was spotless. Even Dicus had left his boots on the rubber tray at the door and was padding around in gray wool boot socks as he got his breakfast ready. He didn't offer coffee or a chair so I stood.

"She's in there—" He waved his thumb at the living room. His jaw was working overtime, chewing the fact of me finally showing up as he swabbed at the clean gray counter with a new green sponge.

"What'd you do to her?" I held onto the back of the wooden chair, prepared to take the stand I'd been making all the way across Iowa.

He waved his hand and lifted his coffee cup, cleaning the bottom, then the counter, then the bottom again before setting it down.

"Dicus?" In our family, people's lives ended badly. He just kept scrubbing what was clean and I finally gave up, edging past the table and chairs, thankful for the refrigerator that finally came between us by the doorway. The sizzling smell of bacon made my stomach lean back like a hand catching the door frame. Why didn't his wife feed him at home?

Carren was on the unfolded hide-a-bed, scrunched up trying to avoid the metal bar bisecting the middle. Her face was rumpled and gray as the old sheets, and she was shivering under the thin cotton summer blanket. The old pink-and-yellow floral comforter from our childhood bed lay on the floor out of her reach.

"Here," I said, unfurling the comforter so it settled evenly across her. She grabbed the edge with a bandaged hand and pulled it up to her chin.

"What happened?" I pointed to her hand.

"That's nothing." She closed her eyes and shifted to her side, grimacing with pain. I sat down on the edge of the bed. She opened her eyes.

"My feet are cold," she said. I found her white terry cloth socks and pulled them on, noticing the green and purple bruises splotching her legs.

"Sleeping with socks on gives me nightmares," she said, "and Dicus wouldn't turn on the furnace."

"You're all beat-up." I started to lift the comforter to look at the rest of her, but she shook her head. "What happened?"

"She tried to kill me." Her voice dropped to a whisper and she rolled her eyes toward the kitchen. "His wife, Dicus's wife tried to kill me." Her eyes blazed for a moment at the memory, then quieted again.

"You didn't—"

Carren gave a slight shake of her head followed by a spasm of pain. "I never—"

I stared at her. Then she was the only one. Her white blonde hair was cropped boy-short, but her face was so tan and freckled, she looked years older than she was. The rest of us kept our brown hair and clear skin and plain brown eyes, like we were wedded to our regularity. She was the baby and bleached her hair as soon as she found the bottle of peroxide we used on the palomino's tail for shows.

"Here—" Dicus put a plate of food and a cup of orange juice on the glass-topped coffee table next to the bed. He didn't even look at me as he dropped the silverware on the bed beside her.

"Chester's lame again," he said. "And Flo got cast in her stall last night. I called the vet, but he's on an emergency colic surgery."

Carren put the bandaged hand on my arm. "My sister can handle things."

Dicus looked at me, those china-plate eyes expressionless as snow, which made you forget about the rest of his face.

"How's Michael?" I asked. Dicus shook his head and looked down at Carren whose face jerked as she caught a sob.

"Michael's—" I started to get up, but she held onto my arm.

"Put down," Dicus said. "Accident—" He waved his hand over my sister. "Got a horse to shoe. You meet the vet." He turned and left.

Carren pulled a tissue from under her pillow and blew weakly, then crumpled it in her hand.

"What happened? You said you needed help—what's going on, Carren? God, he was my horse—" I grabbed her wrist and squeezed until she jerked it away.

"I told you!" she said in a loud whisper. "His wife tried to kill me! She swerved her car into me on purpose while I was cantering down the road a week ago. Michael broke his leg, and I'm bruised head to foot from getting caught under him when he went down, OK?"

"Why you? God—"

She slowly rolled onto her back again, took a breath, and rolled toward the food. "Could you—?" She pointed at the plate of scrambled eggs, bacon, and toast. After a few bites, she gave me the plate to finish. Despite losing Michael, I was starving.

"What'd Bobby and Harry say?"

"Bobby's his best friend, he always takes his side, and Harry, what could he say? He works for Dicus's wife's family. So much for our brothers. Everyone's real sorry, and they all believe it was an accident."

"Doesn't she know you haven't slept with him?"

"Hey, he's slept with every woman in this family for thirty years. She probably figured it was a pretty good guess." Carren pouted for a moment. "Except it wasn't."

"Maybe she's pissed that you turned him down."

She looked at me with a peculiar expression, then said, "You think this is funny? They're going to have to redo my neck surgery again, graft it with cadaver bone this time." She shivered. "Dead person's bone."

We sat there for a while until she dozed off, the day brightening outside, then going gray as clouds moved in and the room grew noticeably colder. I got up and checked the thermostat, then turned the furnace on and went outside.

The long sheltering roof of the prairie-style house led naturally to the new three-stall garage and then to the stable and indoor arena added onto the old two-story red barn. Carren's horse business had been doing so well, there was a new six-horse trailer parked to the side of the barn, and a matching red one-ton dually truck in the driveway. I wondered again at the luck of it all—her going with Dad when he left. Leaving me and the boys who were almost out of the house anyway and our older sister who wouldn't part with her mother even though she'd been sleeping with Dicus. When it all came out and Dad up and died from the blood pressure that had been pounding his heart to mush for years, Carren got the farm and I got a savings bond and a used car full of secondhand smoke. It wasn't long before I moved in here to help with the horses and Dicus came back to work as if nothing had happened. He always showed up for work, you couldn't fault the man for that.

There were heavy-bellied snow clouds moving toward us, and the day was sinking into a deeper gray. The wind started to pick at the oak and maple leaves stubbornly clinging to the trees, and the horses in the pasture stopped and pricked up their ears as if they could already hear the storm that was going to make their world a white distance in a few hours. I thought about Michael out there, his long body trotting fluidly along the crest of the hill, breaking into a gallop for the charge across the valley to the gate when he heard me calling. I thought for a moment that I could see him, then blinked and realized it was another horse entirely—that useless thing Carren had picked up at auction and kept to prove a point that could never be proved—that she could train anything.

"Are you a pro, or is this just all for your own amazement?" I asked at the start of year two on the hopeless horse project when she finally got him to canter once around the indoor arena without rearing. Dicus had told me to lay off, and I thought they were doing it then.

"I am not dead," I had told him. "You cannot keep treating me this way." He'd been mad because I told his wife about him and Mom, him and my older sister, him and me. I guess she'd run out of patience waiting for Carren to join the ranks.

The vet's van pulled in just as I was opening the office door. Gary Bonner was a Vietnam vet who got flashbacks every time there was a loud noise, and Dicus's hammer banging on the anvil as he shaped shoes wasn't going to help. I hurried inside and told him to bring the horses out for the vet, then ran back. Dicus muttered something, but brought the first horse out. He'd changed out of his Carhartts and was wearing his jeans, leather shoeing apron, and a denim shirt over a red long underwear shirt.

"You can only see what you know," Gary said as the horse limped up and down the aisle in front of him. I remembered that Gary went around telling women he couldn't have a relationship because of paranormal experiences. "You quick him?"

The question pissed Dicus off, so he only shrugged. I looked at the shoes worn at the toes and overgrown on the sides. "No, he's due for a shoeing now."

As I helped set up the portable x-ray machine, Gary said how sorry he was about my horse and sister. When I didn't say anything, he said, "The horse running away from something?"

Not unless you count being chased by a car. Why was she on Michael at all? He was retired. I was paying my sister to let him eat grass all day.

We positioned the horse's hoof on a block of wood and snapped the pictures, then pulled the shoe and took some more pictures at different angles.

"My guess is navicular. I'll put him on some Bute and Warfarin, see if that helps. Won't nerve him until we have to," Gary said. "Where's the other one?"

Dicus brought the mare out, and she was pretty banged up and sore from being wedged against the wall in her stall and having to break the boards through to the next stall before she could get herself turned around to stand up.

An hour and a half later, the vet left us with two hundred dollars of drugs and a big bill for x-rays coming in the mail.

"I don't know how she's making any money," I said.

"Who said she is?" Dicus said.

I followed him back to the office, which looked like it hadn't been cleaned in a couple of months. A layer of dust coated the red leather couch and easy chairs, and gritted underfoot on the parquet floor. The papers and bills on the desk wore their own fine coating. I went to the pop machine in the corner, but it was empty, the plug pulled out of the wall.

"What's going on here?" I asked.

Dicus settled onto the couch, lifting his dirty rubber boots onto the leather arm.

"Did you do my sister?" I asked.

"Listen, on our first date I ended up having to talk her out of suicide. That was also the last date." He folded his arms and stared out the window where the first white flakes were drifting against the gray. "You're taking the road backwards, like always."

"And you didn't used to be bitter." I went to the couch and stood over him, searching that face, those blue-white eyes and long body for something I left hidden there all those years ago. Maybe it was the same thing I kept looking for in other men, sorting them like cards as I drove to Nebraska. Anymore it was a reflex, brush the teeth, gas the car, have sex with the Quik Stop cashier in the break room while he watches the security monitors over my shoulder, do the trucker eyeing me at the rest stop, the college kid trying to sign me up for MPIRG for environmental action, the new dentist, the dog trainer, the homeless vet camping in the park across the street, and lately the jazz horn player who shot up in my bathroom before he let me give him a blow job while he crooned "I'm living my life faster than the speed of pain."

If you don't ask, you won't ever get anything, I realized after Dicus. You see, we all asked him. He didn't have to lift a finger. He was the Hand-Me-Down-Man.

"So why did your wife try to kill my sister?" I sat beside him, half-on, half-off the slippery leather so I had to brace my arm across his stomach. When he didn't answer, I leaned my face close to his, staring into his eyes until he opened his mouth to me.

As the freak storm wailed outside the barn, the horses in the pasture huddled with their tails to the wind, heads down, shaking against the ice freezing in long shards on their hides, and the dogs that had been gone too long whimpered and scratched the office door and finally curled and buried their heads. While our naked bodies cooled in the twilight, I remembered a story from years ago, how people used to believe that coupling horses sprang from earthquakes, and that in the fall, you must sacrifice the October Horse.

Was

 I told the first three I still was, but after that I never bothered when the question came up. It wasn't out of any need to protect myself, I tell my friend Maris one night on the phone, it was to ease it for them. Those first three were, and in some sense, because of my lie, they still are.

The first was a boy named Pat who was nearly as overwrought as I was those nights of desperate kissing and nakedness. We were illicit in everything we did, sneaking out on his best friend who was my boyfriend at the time, a fraternity rat with a hardtop convertible whose lid sucked itself neatly back into the trunk. Otherwise he was a nerd and it was clear to everyone that the only reason he could go out with girls was the car and the fraternity. He was after all dating someone in high school, which meant a fifty-mile drive Friday night after classes. He was simply another fling with cars, as far as I was concerned. The driver was relatively unimportant. Later it would be someone with a Corvette Stingray, the hottest car in town. The guy didn't have a clue and I didn't do it with him either, in case you're wondering. In fact I never did it with any boy who owned his own car. There was just that amount of contrariness in me, I guess. Or maybe it seemed like the boys with cars felt they deserved you, all of you, and the boys without knew enough to be grateful you'd even go out with them. And it was that gratefulness that made me so protective.

My folks were fishing up north and it was a crazy time in our little house that summer. Every day we waited for them to pull in the driveway because they did that—they always lied about when they were coming home so they could catch my brother and me at something, while my older sister just drifted along in some cloudy weather state she'd invented as a kid in front of the mirror in our bedroom where she'd be mouthing the words to the soap opera on the radio at herself. "Portia Faces Life." She must have thought that mirror was life, not just herself staring back at this maniac in bright red lipstick and blue eye shadow though she was still as much a kid as I was. So Sis wasn't much of a problem. My brother was busy ordering liquor and beer deliveries from the store on the outskirts of town, having the oldest boy in his group meet the delivery truck in the front yard with ready cash and an extra five to keep the driver's mouth shut. Generally they weren't too destructive and each morning we'd all crawl out of bed to clean up the damage before anything else.

Pat and I figured it out pretty quickly—how much more comfortable beds were than the sofa or the seat of his parents' car when he could borrow it. Mostly he arrived on a bike after the grocery store where he shelved and sacked groceries closed. He wasn't on any fast track, except for me. There was this real sweet way he had of doing everything in the world to please me, and for the first time in my life, I let down and appreciated it. After all, he had nothing to gain, he already knew he wasn't going anywhere.

It was almost dawn. We were in my narrow bed; they called it a "Hollywood Bed" because it had no headboard, only a mattress on a metal frame. I never made that connection either. Pat and I had our clothes pretty much off and it was hot enough to make our skin slide around nice and easy, and he asked, nice and polite. Not too much begging the way boys did that made me say no. And I wanted to. I'd graduated a week before and I knew he couldn't go back to the locker room at gym class so I'd never have to hear the whispers rustle up the hall ahead and behind me as I walked. I thought it'd be more painful, and more something, something more. But there it was and the moment he wiggled a little it was over and we both lay there soaked and almost satisfied.

I only had to pretend a little, and maybe that's how the lie got started. I was one then, this was the first time, and I tried to act like girls I'd read about in dirty books who were, so he'd *think* I was. See, I wasn't very good at this, the writing wasn't very clear, but I did my best and told him it hurt a little bit, and he was too sweet to look for blood the next morning.

It was that darn Rabbit, my horse. I remember the twilight runaway gallop which was almost his worst gait, after the trot, and the sudden jarring pain as I slammed into the saddle. I didn't dare tell my father or mother why I could barely walk, because injuries only irritated them. So I climbed into bed and prayed to God that I hadn't ruined something I'd have to confess to and woke up perfectly fine. It happened a couple of years earlier, and I didn't think about it again until that dawn holding Pat like a young boy with his head nestled on my stomach while he slept, his breath making dewy little spots on my skin. Stroking his hair, I knew I'd leave him, he'd done about all he could for me. He couldn't heal this little thing that felt torn up inside me, not the sexual way, it was something else entirely. Now I had nothing that made me any different from anyone else, and I suppose that's what led to the next one.

When Abbott called a few weeks later, I was flattered and worried. Had Pat told someone, had the word spread so quickly? I knew how this happened to girls, I'd taken my share of their reputation with those fatal words "she does it" to the next person down the line, as if it made me bigger and better that she did and I didn't. Later I would come to see this time as the stupid days of my life.

Abbott was scientific in his approach. He'd read everything he could, now he needed a human specimen to experiment on. If he hadn't been so straightforward, I wouldn't have gone. I was curious, too. Maybe without the blur of feelings, it would give up the thing I'd felt was promised in those books and stories. So you see how the lie came about. As always, he asked. He'd already confessed he was, and somehow I felt the experiment would be tainted, the way we learned about in high school lab classes, if I wasn't, too. All the properties in a pure state. And I could tell, he needed it that way. He had this blank, unfelt thing in his eyes, like a dog that wanted things to work out real bad, and I couldn't deny that, could you? That's what I asked my friend Maris one night. She cleared her throat and said she guessed not.

This time we lay on a blanket on a concrete shelf under a bridge of an uncompleted interstate in the middle of the corn and alfalfa fields outside town. We took sips of whiskey from an old peanut butter jar, and he laid the condom and Vaseline and handkerchief out in the moonlight like instruments he was going to operate with. He knew what to do above the waist and maybe that's why it finally worked. I don't know what I would've done if I'd had to take on the whole job. Then as we each pulled our jeans and underpants off, he asked me again. When I saw the size of him, the anxious lean to it, I had to lie. It was what I could contribute. I think it was better for him and he was certainly considerate because of it later, so much so it started getting on my nerves. I was breaking it off with Pat and he kept crying like a girl and poking and scratching his arms with the sharp end of the pin on the back of his grocery store name tag. So when Abbott started reading Freud and calling me, it was all I could do not to tell him the truth and give him Pat's phone number.

Then there was Jack. I'd had my eye on him for a long time, ever since he kicked my horse Rabbit in the belly with his pointed-toe cowboy boot to make him understand he wasn't the boss anymore. Rabbit straightened up after that, learned three good gaits and never ran away with anyone anymore. I thought that was pretty fair since he'd been the one to get it, what these boys were all after, and I'd probably had to lie because of him.

Jack was big and strong all over. He was the strongest boy I'd ever known. He had muscles everywhere, even his blunt-fingered hands. But there was something else, a gentleness that let my horse Rabbit know he could nuzzle him and get a head rub, because Jack never held back anything physical he could do for another creature. And it never occurred to Jack he'd need a car, he had horses and strong legs of his own. But he took his mother's car and drove us out into the country night after hot August night when I taught him how to make out, how to take off my shirt and make my breasts burn with fullness and desire. I was almost begging him the night he took my shorts off, and asked me if I was safe or in the middle of my cycle. The others never knew enough to ask, but there was this animal information in Jack that knew women and mares so I lied and spread my legs for him. He mounted and tore me apart he was so big and hard. I bit and scratched and cried for real. And afterwards, when he asked the question, was I, I could truthfully say, yes, yes I was.

The House That Jane Built

JANE'S CLOSET

There were always a lot of historical figures in there. I mean Audie Murphy hiding from the bad guys in the cave, dark and leading you from room to room, each one furnished with a portion of his soul. There was the room of antique toys, a train whose cars were cast in gold that I remember him picking up and rubbing. Not for the appreciation of the precious metal, but for the toy he'd always liked. I tried to hint that people would be after the gold, but he was blank on that score. Audie was a small man with a boy hidden beneath the thoughtful face and efficient body. He knew things, like how to fool your pursuers and how to hide a woman and a child and a horse in a cave that unfolded like an accordion house going on and on forever.

Such was the plenty of Jane's closet. There were whole cities uncompleted because of forfeiture, collapsing economies, poor planning. Once I met a man in her closet who had just such experience. He stood beside the crevasse bridged with concrete tongues and explained where every structure was to have gone. After the concrete was poured, the money evaporated, so there were only these three arcs across empty space and a lot of half-walled basements and sidewalks. It made me wonder if maybe he should have started on something else first.

You saw things in Jane's closet. Looking up over the small one-story houses, you would notice a missile headed into the middle of your neighborhood, and realize it was another military mistake, some accident by the hop-heads running the switches at the silo a hundred miles north of Indigo Road. Jane may claim a lot of things about herself, but she was a Midwestern girl through and through, so we all prayed and focused and the missile shot around the corners of houses, up the sidewalks past bicycles and wading pools, seeking some target we kept out of sight until finally it darted upward and exploded far far overhead, leaving only the fallout to worry about. Such was the cost of immediate dreaming, we assured her as she left town.

Her closet wasn't home to the kinds of sexual concerns that took over later either. Not that I know of. As I said, it was more of an historical site, someplace for early settlers and attic memories. I never knew Jane to like basements. She said they were male by nature and no self-respecting woman would rent a basement apartment or purposely move a studio or study down there. Naturally, her closet was well above ground, a place of dreaming and regret, but nothing allowed to make you forget yourself as she saw happening below ground. What do they need with all that darkness, she used to ask, thrusting aside the hangers and clothes she carted everywhere. She couldn't bring herself to throw anything away once it had gone through an experience of her skin. She said those things carried time and she intended to keep them on file as if they were pages of a diary which of course she wouldn't bother keeping. She was always one for the ordinary. She laughed at the busy scribbling of men around her, tapped her fingernails unrhythmically on the black tabletops through coffee house poetry readings. Jane hated to explain, and being a Midwesterner, she hated explanations. You could trust the sky, your furniture, and some of the relatives, she'd say.

But back behind the clothes, there was the rest of the closet, as I've said, and that was the part of Jane not many people got to know. Sure, she got some attention. We all did. We were young and free, what do you expect? People always ask, what did she look like? I don't like to talk about that, I say, and they tend to let it go at that. Jane disappeared in that closet, like a dream she transported from place to place on her back. She was an old peddler of households and goods we abandon in the face of the advancing army. I think she saw herself in years to come having a kind of plenty she could afford to save now and give away later. That's what her closet was filled with—all the undreamed mixing and mingling with the already dreamed. But in other ways she was a woman you would walk right past on the street. There are so many of us everywhere. I've noticed our invisibility making us naked and wished more than once for some of the old clothes, costumes really, Jane kept in her closet. You could say her children made her as common as grass. That'd be about right.

Without that closet, she was nothing, we used to mutter after our visits. We all had a theory, you see. It grows out of envy and longing, a closet that keeps a piece of your life as the price of admission. You go on in there, you'll see, but I'm not telling you what's mine and what's not. She said we all lost that right in the first dark step past the hangers. I think that's why we stopped going after a while, why she ended up so alone and friendless there at the end. And we only felt a little apologetic when we lost track of her. Well, by then, the closet had changed, of course. Or maybe she was trying too hard to empty it or something. It must have been pretty full by that time, I mean after all of her old friends stopped coming around, and those new people, well, the purity only lasts so long. Even she used to say that. There was that hard-nosed Midwesterner about her. It makes a lot of sense to think about her that way, too. A blonde whose face never aged. A body that never grew fat or stooped. Those pale-blue eyes the color of a high, thin sky over the Dakotas.

She gave it away, she used to say, just to have it over with. On the oil-soaked dirt floor of her grandmother's garage, with her young cousins outside banging on the tall wooden doors she'd helped close and lock. It was her older cousin, the dark boy who ignored them all until she turned fourteen and he took her in the cool, dark, oily smell day after day, working her courage up to the first kisses and touching until he pulled her panties off and lay her down on her back, leaning over her, she said, refusing to tell her anything as he did it. At first they watched each other, then he turned his head and closed his eyes as if he had somewhere else to go, and she turned to look at the dark wood wall hung with hundred-year-old rakes, hoes, and shovels her grandfather had brought with him from that poor dirt farm just outside town. It was then, she understood, as he made the small mewling cries and punched through her. It didn't hurt and that made her feel cheated. It was so much less than she'd expected, and she was glad she'd gotten it out of the way for that very reason. The only unusual thing about that whole event was the hand prints she thought she saw grooving the worn gray wood shafts. They glowed deep red and burned like old fires someone had forgotten to put out. I used to look for those old tools every time I went to Jane's closet, but of course, you know, I never found them.

JANE'S CHAIRS

Jane never paid a bill unless she had to, and there were many chairs the dead sat in she refused to get rid of later. A night in her house was a noisy affair and every morning the cushions were hastily reasserted on the sofa she'd salvaged from the dead neighbor who left her dog to the old man and that thing, well, there were dog obituaries he published in every small paper of every town they'd ever lived in and there were plenty since he traveled for a living. Then one morning Jane called me up to come over and see for myself. He'd whitewashed the back of the house, the sidewalk, and the yard, it was white white white and wet. The other dogs tracked it into her yard and around the houses like powdery elf feet but nobody much complained. They were all used to him. It was a joyful time for the dogs who were all let out together and romped around as if they'd gotten a day off from work, white on every paw like they were in a chorus line.

Another time the neighbor ladies came to check on Jane, this was when she was still living in our Midwestern town, you understand. They arrived in Civil War dresses, she said, come on over. They were lending aid if aid was needed. Jane's parents were out of town and she was having a few parties and more than a few drugs. Don't let her kid you on that score. She wasn't so into it herself, but all the boys around her were. They were playing cards and debating whether they should eat the hash or smoke it. The ladies hastened the decision even though all they did was stand in the side yard and make noises about the garden and trash. Her father had rigged this elaborate spinach-washing system to avoid the usual dirt in the sink. He was by nature a small inventive sort of man. He'd never make money, but he'd leave his mark on every place he lived. They were in ordinary houses then, and later too I guess. Small, one-story, with a basement they painted and pretended was a rec room for the kids though it was always damp and cold.

That time we stayed up for days and nights and once I tried to sleep in her parents' bed with Tommy on one side and Byron on the other, but nobody would touch me so I curled up and felt sorry for myself until both boys got up and went away. Then I went downstairs and looked at all the mail. That's how I found out about Jane's brother who was getting thick envelopes from some girl even though he was at the state boys' school in Red Wing at the time and nobody was about to tell her or forward anything. I wasn't even tempted to open them. Jane might have if she wasn't so busy picking up after people in case her parents came home early. They always did and noticed the one out-of-place thing they could get mad about. It's no wonder she left when she did. It wasn't just the pregnancy. I've read that stuff they said about her, and most of it is complete bullsh—, well, you get the drift. People had to see her as we did, standing in the rain, letting the water pour down her face, shivering and laughing because the neighbor's whitewash was flooding into the street, flowing like skim milk down the drains into the sewer. Cars were splashing it all over her, and specks of it landed on their windshields to dry like the arsenic-laced spray her father used on the fruit trees.

That's what happened to her later. In that apartment in New York. Those empty chairs the dead came to sit in at night. Jane never let anything die. On the phone, she'd suddenly make you remember. It wasn't only the people she was close to who used her furniture that way, though. It was the dead she barely knew or never spoke to. Sarah, the girl from Latin and art classes in high school, who one day didn't show up anymore. Jane wept in the hallways, on the landings of the stairs. We had girls' and boys' stairs then. Or the twins who killed themselves, one because the other did. She'd never even met those two boys. People she read about in the paper. Mostly it was suicides and accidentals that caught her eye. The terrible mistakes of the living. A couple of cats unjustly sacrificed when she couldn't afford a vet. She was the only person I ever met who entertained the ordinary dreams of the dead. Every morning she'd wake up from an excursion to another common day. She said it made her appreciate the advantages of travel.

I think that's why she started in on the furniture. It was for them. For her brother J.D. who died in a car wreck after a night of drinking nine months and a week from the day he got out of Red Wing. He was alone, and I used to wonder if that girl was missing him. She never put a return address on those envelopes. J.D. didn't seem inclined to visit, she said when I asked. They'd never been close, well, he'd never been close to anyone. He was sort of out of the picture his whole life. Not that she'd refuse him a seat in the house of the living, but I can't see him bothering with it. No, I think it was all those boys who laid their lives down around us, the names that floated through our conversations and nights like moths that burnt down by morning, scattered on the cement porch. And the girls, who disappeared like used lipsticks rolling under the seats of old cars. Jane understood the terrible cost for just one of us to make it through. She used to look at her kids with a kind of expectation you don't usually find on a mother's face, like she was already measuring them for a chair in her living room.

That's why she never paid the bills until they made her. They were so beside the point by the time she'd fought her way clear of the afterlife.

JANE'S FLOORS

Wishes are the floors of dreams, she used to say, and I've scrubbed them all. She never made beds unless she was changing sheets and that wasn't very regular. I'd come over, and there'd be a child-sized pile of laundry blocking the front hall. She'd push at it with her foot to keep it off the floor heating grate that was prison to all sorts of tiny colored objects that sat on the metal landing just out of finger reach. She had the sort of house where the lights blinked every time the furnace came on. One night she called me because she smelled electrical smoke coming up the floor grates. I didn't have a solution then either.

But most of her emergencies she solved herself. Jane had that can-do domestic attitude. You'd come over, and there'd be the toddler and the dog both wearing men's T-shirts for diapers. Why don't you get that dog fixed, I used to ask, but she was convinced it'd bring in the big bucks once it carried a belly of puppies full term. Jane was the only fertile thing in the house, from what I could tell. Plants took one look and gave up the ghost. Even those darn poinsettias that are supposed to last the holiday season started dropping leaves within hours of landing on her dining room table. She said her mother had the same black thumb. Herbicidal tendencies, she called it. Later I would think about her when American planes were dropping napalm like thick currant jelly all over the palm trees of Vietnam. I don't know that I actually saw it, but I imagined the elephants and buffalos bursting spontaneously into huge bright pears of flame, and wondered if plants self-immolated in Jane's presence. It puts a seriousness on memories that have lived so long in the frivolous part of my mind to think this. Jane, Jane, Jane. The floor of desire and memory where all else burns and burns.

She'd call me at dawn, sometimes, or rather that in-between night and dawn time, three and four A.M. on her knees in the kitchen, scrubbing the floor. If she'd been drinking with a man the night before, the kind of man she knew how to attract, going-to-someday men, we called them. They were always on their way there, so they'd catch you later. If it was one of those, she'd be using the toothbrush or hairbrush to scrub out the pebbled dents of the linoleum. A bad choice, but one that served her perfectly, she often remarked about the white floor. She'd be panting with effort as she sweated out the wine and bleached her hands in the chemical suds. How does it all come down to this, she'd ask, but we both knew there was only one answer to that question. This was probably what drove her to leave Indigo Road for the city. I like to think that she wasn't always intending to go, that like the white floor, it was a mistake that served her perfectly.

Maybe it was the tiny black spots of melted plastic from cigarette ashes, the brown stains of coffee, the slice from the kitchen knife that dropped point first and stood there until she yanked it out where later she spent extra time prying out the hair-thin line of black dirt with a toothpick, and the black scuff marks of dragged heels. Doesn't anyone pick up their feet anymore? she'd ask huffing into the phone.

Jane had a dream that put her to work those nights. She always told it to me with the sloshing bucket of water and harsh breathing to score the words. I never remarked that I'd heard it before. It seemed important to look for the variations, and to keep her from understanding her own repetitive nature. No one needs to hear the truth on their hands and knees at that hour.

Here it is: She has come into enemy territory, and she is hiding while the others do their work, their assignments. The important thing is to keep out of sight, not be caught. She slides under some sheet metal, sometimes the remnant of a house or barn, a pile of debris. She can see out, they can't see her, although there is constant worry that they will. The enemy goes about their work, in the course of which they come closer and closer to her hiding place, even lifting edges of the metal that covers her. But they never see her for some reason. They even have a guard posted on a tower with a gun, but nothing happens. They come in and shift pieces of metal around, get ready for work the next day, stand and sit right next to where she is lying, but never see her. She wonders how long it will be until they do. Tomorrow, they will move the stuff she's hiding under. She doesn't know where the others are, if she is the last one left. She just knows what it means to be found.

So she wakes up and scrubs the kitchen floor. That's how she finds the red crayon mark a foot up the wall, traveling in a line around the room, circling in the private magic of her children. She leaves it alone as long as they don't scribble on the floor.

He asked me for canned goods, she tells me that last time. He gave me a poem with my name at the top of the page, but you know, it was the same poem I heard him read the night before with another woman's name on it. But he needed those canned goods. He was hopping a train in an hour, and had no money. It's not like he asked for money.

I think that's why she took him with her when she left. That and the fact that he took his shoes off at the door, wading through the pile of laundry large enough to lose a child in, and coming to rest his holey socks on her white kitchen floor. He doesn't bathe more than twice a month because it's bad for his skin, she tells me. The dirt protects you. Skin is the largest organ of the body, the land of the soul, he tells her, when I dream, my skin takes me home again.

He had the kind of destiny Jane believed in after she gave up floors. When she got to New York, she wrote that she tore out all the linoleum and found these unfinished boards beneath, full of cracks trapping a hundred years of dirt, and giving off splinters like free advice. Her children cried as she pried slivers out of their hands and feet, but Jane didn't consider it a crisis. I used to imagine them learning to pad their bodies against her floors, wearing shoes on their hands, leaving trails along the walls like wide brown lizards.

It would be nice to think that they accommodated each other, Jane and her man, that she loaded the shelves with canned food and he went barefoot so long his feet were callused with wood, and you could hear his steps banging from room to room. I don't want to believe it was any other way.

The Third Gravitational Pull

Duwayne hasn't been the same since the Southern Pacific took the front end of his Crown Vic right down to the firewall last week. Something about the fatal attraction between his vehicles and train tracks has him spooked—when he was a boy, his mama's pickup had stalled at the same crossing after his father left and they had to be pushed out of the way by Ferdie's John Deere mowing the right of way.

Women just happen to Duwayne and now he really has his hands full. As the preacher up the road says, he's sinning like Peter and praying like Paul. This one, Fiona, is the heart and soul of Mary Kay, pink Buick, pink dress, and now he's painting her house pink. He always ends up doing some building or painting for women at cost or below, sometimes even for free. But it's been pissing rain for a week, and the boards he scraped down are dark with water. He's tried to explain it to her, but this morning like every other one since they met, she calls before eight, taking him out of a bad sleep where the train was bearing down on him. This time he had a carload of dogs. Every dog he ever owned, plus a few he just petted, were jammed in the Crown Vic.

"Meet me at the Mildred Pierce Café," she says. "I'm buying breakfast."

He nods, then mumbles OK before he hangs up the phone. They have dang good coffee at that place, despite the name, and the idea of breakfast offset an awful lot. He just hopes the good cook is on so the grits aren't runny.

But he isn't having much luck because as soon as he sits down across from Fiona, the owner, Nancy, a tall, dark-haired woman with sharp eyes and a mean mouth, comes out of the kitchen and looks around the room.

"Oh my," she says, "it's all my favorite women in one room." She looks right at Duwayne and frowns, as if he's going to ruin her morning instead of the reverse.

"It's all right." Fiona holds up her cup for the scared young waitress who's quickly pouring coffee to stay out of Nancy's way.

But it isn't all right. When the owner cooks breakfast, the food's awful, but he doesn't dare argue. He is a man among women here.

After a couple of refills on the good coffee and some real half-and-half, he leans back expansively in the little straight-back chair that digs into his shoulders. Fiona is looking especially pink today—in flamingo-colored blouse and slacks, her lips and cheeks matching. Even her fluffy blonde hair has a pink cast to it that makes her look like one of those dolls little girls are forever carrying around, undressing and dressing, the ones with pretty, hard-set features.

"Duwayne, I got something to tell you." Fiona leans forward, her pink nails and tiny fingers resting like paws on the black Formica tabletop. "Duwayne, the song of our love is coming to an end. I finally found the man of my dreams—" She pauses. He begins to hear a whistling train roar in his head and has to stop himself from throwing his arms across his face.

"Honey, you always knew you were my Mister-In-Betweener." She settles back in her chair, her eyes reflecting pink from her glowing cheeks, while her lips struggle not to share the joy and relief of revelation. They simply won't turn down, and finally she lets them curl up in a satisfied little smile. "Be happy for me, Sugar!"

"Here's your food." The young waitress plops the plates down quickly, snatching her fingers out of the slopping grits.

"Ketchup?" he asks. "And jelly."

The kid's so scared she keeps bumping into the backs of people's chairs, like a poorly played pinball. He watches her drop the ketchup bottle and cower on the floor. There's an awful lot of turnover here, never the same waitress for more than a few weeks. They're usually girls from the Catholic college and this is their first or second job, and they all seem to look alike—thin, athletic, brown hair, clear skin, little makeup.

"Aren't you going to say anything?" Fiona asks.

"You do much business over at the college?"

She looks confused, but shrugs. "They like store brands more."

He nods and sticks a fork in the part of the dry eggs that isn't scorched brown and eats. The toast is black on the bottom, so he keeps it turned over, using the cherry jelly the scared girl drops, without a word, on the table.

"It's Tyrus DeClure," Fiona announces. "He has that Full Gospel Church? Over on Vine? The Jesus car?" When Duwayne looks puzzled, she adds, "He's painted JESUS! in two-foot-high red letters on the sides of a white Corvair he parks various places around town—to remind people?"

He uses the toast crust to sop up some watery grits. Apparently, when he's done with women, they don't know which country or religion they're in. "Thought you were a Methodist."

That smile again that curves her lips up in the sweetest way imaginable. She used to do that for him. "Honey, it's a real Powerhouse of God place. I go out and sell like crazy after those services."

He wants to ask her if this means he doesn't have to finish painting her house, but the owner is glaring at him from the window cut in the kitchen wall, and he can't risk upsetting Fiona. He'll wait until the rain stops and see where he stands. It's true that while he begins a lot of projects for women, like as not, they don't get finished. Someone always gives up first.

"What got me going last week—" Her fork waves in the air as if signing her name to the best of her luck. "He was talking about science, it's so much in the news these days, you know, scientific this and that—"

Duwayne thinks about how he gave up Cynthia the real estate agent for Fiona the Mary Kay rep.

"—gravitational pull. Attraction. You know what I mean?" Fiona asks and he nods. He'll have to see if Cynthia is still available. She always brought him these apple-pie-flavored things, a cross between a bagel and a muffin and a sweet roll.

"There's three. First is earth, gravity. You know about that."

He met Fiona the day Cynthia was showing her the house he was now supposed to be painting pink. Fiona had asked if he came with the place, and Cynthia had laughed and said she'd write it into the deal. Then Fiona hired him to inspect the property before the closing, and afterwards she kept on calling about this or that little repair until he started going over there on a regular basis.

"See, and he related each of these to Jesus and it made so much sense. The Trinity and stuff like that. The second is celestial—the planets and stars. You can see the God part there, can't you?"

He wonders if Cynthia is still mad about the skylight job he left with the shingles and boards pulled off and the blue plastic tarp nailed over the hole in the ceiling of her bedroom. On clear nights, he'd unfasten the tarp and they'd watch the moon and stars until they fell asleep. Really, she was a great comfort. He can't remember how he got off that track onto Fiona's.

She takes a breather for eating, but he can tell she's building up to something. He wonders if he should call Cynthia at the agency, on her cell phone, her home phone, or her voice mail. Now he remembers how they slipped apart.

"So what's the third one?" he asks.

She pauses, concentrating on the blueberry pancake oozing lavender batter out of the middle. "Something about density, he called it 'weak-force' and 'glue-ons.'" She sounds apologetic. "I didn't quite get that part."

While he picks through the food for edible parts, she digs in her purse and finally pulls out a small white envelope. She hesitates before pushing it across the table at him, swabbing a clump of congealed grits with the edge.

"Thought you might want these," she says.

He puts the fork down, picks up the envelope, and wipes the grits off the edge. Inside are pictures of him. He remembers the night—they had the play thing going that was still possible at that stage of newness. She'd gotten out her cosmetics case to show him what she did, and one thing led to another, and he was naked and she wasn't and they were drinking a lot of sweet wine from the grocery store and she was making up his face. When she was done, he staggered to the bathroom mirror.

What surprised him, and it's still there in the pictures, is how different, and maybe better he looked—the yellow swashes of color over his eyes extending almost to his hairline, the pearlized white above and below, the dark liner enlarging his eyes, the lashes thickened with mascara, his whole face smoothed with foundation, cheekbones highlighted with glitter and blush. The lipstick too—he'd rolled his lips the way he'd seen countless women do in his presence, and the lubricating red tasted like raspberries and another woman. In the large mirror over the sink, he touched himself.

When he returned to the living room, they drank more sweet wine and made love on the floor so his makeup wouldn't smear on the tan velvet sofa cushions. He doesn't quite remember the photo-taking part, but there he is, his head turned defiantly to the camera, a fierce, pouty expression on his face, like an oddly beautiful girl he feels attracted to.

He slips the pictures back in the envelope, and stuffs it in the pocket of his T-shirt.

"I thought you'd want them back." She lays some money on the table and stands up.

He looks down at the food he is going to leave—the kind of breakfast a kid who's trying real hard fixes for his mom. He probably made the same mess when he was young.

The image of the train taking the front end of the car comes back, and with it the surprise on his face in the rearview mirror when the train left the firewall pressing against his feet. In that instant, he'd wanted to say the words out loud that had roared through his mind as the train sheared the front of his car off, but they had followed the rattling cars down the track instead. He remembers only one—*love*—he had wanted to say that word in a sentence to someone, to tell her something, to ask or beg for something, but it had disappeared in the noise and fear of the third gravitational pull.

The World. The Text. The Crime.

"If Mama ain't happy, ain't nobody happy." Al-the-molester burped so long, the people at tables around them stopped talking. Then the scent from other regions spread and Larry Clarion felt like he was doing WWI trench warfare, the way his grandfather used to describe gas attacks. Although it was only pasta primavera and Caesar salad, the food was too rich for Al after two long months in jail, but Larry had wanted to boost his confidence for the cross-examination that afternoon. Now he considered asking for a conviction just to get away from him. With decent food and quick service, the place attracted the downtown business lunches and overflow from the courthouse, and the soft mauve lighting and gray walls were muted enough to calm the psychopathic nerves for an hour. He was about to remind him that they do have jailhouse toothbrushes for that breath, when Al pushed away from the table, throwing his napkin down and knocking over Larry's wineglass.

She was a tall, fierce woman with white hair and a bosom raised and shelved by what must have been an old-fashioned corset, made of steel, because nothing on her whole body moved as she strode across the room toward them. Al's mother. Larry had been careful to keep Al away from his mother who had her own bone to pick, but here she was, cropping up like a thistle in the middle of his cultivated cornfield.

"Like I said—" Al stood, then sat back down, as if to make himself a smaller target.

The button-down-the-front blue cotton dress with the narrow belt looked as new as the day she'd bought it, like it didn't dare drop its store creases though it had to be twenty years out of style.

"Don't think I can't find you," she said. "Now sit up."

Al threw his shoulders back, which just made his chin jut out more. Was it his fault that kids seemed drawn to him because he looked funny, comic, like a friendly giant of some sort? He didn't ask for all those e-mails. Larry knew better, though he hadn't asked directly. He did wonder if it would be crueller to turn Al-the-molester over to his mother than send him back to jail, and that balanced his earlier inclination.

"There are a lot of horses' asses in the world, and not all of them are on horses," she said, slapping both hands down on the table. Larry and Al both jumped.

"I don't know why you're defending him," she said to Larry. He felt himself shriveling, and grabbed the edges of the chair to keep from sliding under the table. Lately he'd been having trouble staying upright. Gravity failing at such regular intervals, he wondered if it were something more cosmic than local.

"One thing's certain, men named after hand tools are no damned good."

Larry had no idea what she was talking about now, but figured it was best to keep quiet. The little restaurant was enjoying the scene, however, people at the other tables openly staring and smiling.

"Your computer's in the car, Al. Maybe they'll let you use it in prison," she said. "I'm taking it to the police." She turned and marched out, sucking the room's silence with her, leaving a hole of noise in her wake.

"I thought you said you weren't on the computer," Larry said.

Al-the-molester shrugged.

Larry stared at him for a moment. "Didn't you get rid of it, like I said to do if for instance a person had been using it to lure, invite, solicit, etc.?"

Al-the-molester nodded and shrugged again, his big, hairy stuffed fingers like a bear's ending in thick, yellow nails that stuck out like claws. At least he'd stopped dressing like a Santa elf in his homemade green tunic and wide black plastic belt—the outfit he'd been wearing the day the police picked him up at work at the video store.

Larry sighed. He'd been counting on the curve of gratitude to pay the rent on his apartment and car and buy a new pair of shoes. What's the luck of a client whose own mother helps lock him up?

Things hadn't been going too well lately. There was that thing at the office last week where he'd gotten down on all fours and barked like a dog longer than he needed to. A husband had called him late at night with some absurd threats because Larry had sniffed Candi, the legal assistant's leg. Larry couldn't even remember why he'd done it, but there had to be some legal point, he knew.

"History is all about bad karma, Al," he began. "You just have to see yourself in the larger ocean of events."

Al's face stood open like a door into a closet of stupid delights, and Larry stopped talking.

What Al and his mother hadn't understood was that when they found him guilty, Al would be led back to jail for a longer stay. So when Larry got back to the office, the phone calls from Al's mother began: Al had taken a bottle of pills in the police van. He was having his stomach pumped. He was on suicide watch. Couldn't Larry get him out so Mom could take him to church for a prayer service. He was going to die in jail, when all he needed was his hands slapped. Larry had wanted to say, ma'am, your son needs more than that slapped, but she continued: It's the Fourth of July, can't he come home for the weekend?

He'd answered *no* and *I'm sorry* to every request, then hung up quietly on her talking. He'd never get paid now, and this made it the fifth case in a row: Two meth manufacturers busted for cooking in the back of a stolen van while they drove around the suburbs of Omaha, a drug dealer who tried to burn down the county courthouse to get rid of the evidence in Wahoo, a DWI with five counts in one month, and Al-the-molester. All guilty, all gone, all broke.

Now Candi, the legal assistant, had left her resignation letter on his desk in big, bold, hand-printed letters he could read as soon as he flipped on the light: I QUIT. MY ATTORNEY WILL BE CALLING YOU.

She'd done that just to piss him off. She knew he didn't have a dime. What'd she want, the leased Ford Escort, his efficiency apartment? Nothing is out of character, he'd tell her when she called, human character is capable of everything.

But he'd better not say anything. Last time they'd had sex on the floor behind his desk, she'd said, "Whenever I need sympathy, you give me advice." His mistake. He'd thought the sex was sympathetic. Her husband worked nights and slapped her a bit when he drank on the weekends. At least that's what she said. Her mother had Alzheimer's and her brother and his wife were hooked on meth. When the kids came to visit their aunt at the office, they stank like burning plastic, and she was constantly borrowing money from him. When he had it. Lately when he couldn't pay Candi at all, he'd started calling her his legal assistant instead of secretary to cheer her up.

The phone rang. It could be any number of bad things, including Al's mama who definitely wasn't happy now, Candi, his landlord, the leasing agent who'd been trying to get the car back for two weeks now, or someone from prison. A case. He let it ring until it stopped.

He looked at the desk, seeing the mahogany finish ruined from his cans of pop and coffee cups for the first time in months. Candi had swept all the papers and pictures of his ex-wife and kids onto the floor so he'd had to wade across folders and briefs and papers overdue for filing just to sit down and read her note. The rest of the office furniture had been taken back on Monday. But he'd fooled them, the desk and chair were his own.

Al's computer, which Larry had lugged up the stairs after the trial, now sat on the very edge of the desk with its wide blank screen pointing toward the door as if it were on the verge of bolting for freedom. The prosecution hadn't wanted it. They had all they needed on Al. Larry was supposed to give it back to Al's mother or something, but when she'd called, he hadn't mentioned it. The computer lease company had repo'd the office system last Friday, leaving him with some disks and a surge protector still plugged into the outlet. He'd rolled onto it a couple of times when Candi and he made love behind the desk, and had long, narrow greenish-yellow bruises on his hip and back for his efforts.

He didn't mean to call up Al's web page. It just seemed to spring into view as soon as he got through the preliminary business. The pictures were cartoonish, simple, friendly, nothing more harmful than a mall Santa Claus with a child on his lap. Larry was frankly surprised. He really hadn't had much time to research this case—too much happening, but he might have been able to use this, to turn the tide that had swelled against Al during the afternoon when his mother came in and sat behind the prosecution and glared at her son, snorting through his testimony, shaking her head, giving every bit of encouragement she could to find him guilty.

"I get hundreds and hundreds of e-mails from kids all over the country saying, 'Hey cool!' And only a few of them are from big nasties!" Al had typed on the bottom of a montage of his tunics in a rainbow of colors, the bottom edges carefully scissored scallops. What had

Al-the-molester actually done? Larry couldn't find evidence of anything even faintly salacious on the site. Sadly amateurish, maybe—there were pasted-up pictures of Al-the-elf outside Santa's North Pole house, Al eating cookies in Mrs. Claus's kitchen, and Al working in Santa's toy shop, superimposed so that he was way out of scale with the diminutive elves of the original picture. Even tracking Al's movements through the internet, Larry couldn't find visits to the more vicious sites he'd been assuming were part of his client's daily bread. But the prosecutor's office had acted like their case was rock-solid, they'd done a real job with Al. He had to be guilty.

Larry leaned back in his chair and stared at Al's moony face wearing an expression of love as it smiled back at him.

It was a nice computer. All the latest stuff. And fast, fast, fast. It even had Quicken so he could do the billing himself, not have to rely on Candi's errant ways, sending out notices when she felt like it, cutting slack for anyone who roused her sympathy. And maybe she wasn't coming back. What about that? But he knew she'd be back. Whoever sees the devil truly, as Machiavelli said, sees him with smaller horns, and not even dark. So Larry Clarion didn't even look around at the blank, white walls, worn maroon carpet splotched darker where sofa, coffee table, and client chairs had sat as he began his labor: deleting files, expunging the web site, erasing all evidence of Al-the-molester from their lives.

Binding the Devil

 Eddie Falconer closed the front door of the Golden Rule Realty and took a long, hard look at the '72 Olds Cutlass at the curb. The black paint had a couple of dings in it these days, more farms on dirt roads for sale now that the tire factory had been bought by the plastic replica company and that Computer Camp, that's what they called it, had opened its doors to every sort of person from around the world. They even had a Bosnian restaurant-billiard hall in town now. Main Street had been dying on its feet, staggering into the next century when all this business hit like it was blown in by a good Kansas wind.

The Hirsh engine roared alive, and the twenty-eight rounds on the odometer stared accusingly as he shifted into reverse. "I know," he muttered. It was a good car—no, a great car—but it belonged in a collector's garage, not on dirt roads with the sound of gravel pinging against the paint. He needed to get something more practical that could take a beating.

Two blocks up Main, Eddie parked in front of Frock's Clean Center.

"Thank God I gave my heart to Jesus thirty-eight years ago," Frock Walz said. Raising his coffee cup in a toast to the car out the window. "I'm tempted, I really am." Frock was the dry cleaning-laundry specialist in Bellefontaine, with a bank of washers and dryers churning out dollars twenty-four-seven, and a daughter, Ivo, with nobody-home-eyes to run them. His wife had up and died when the girl hit high school, which was just as well as it turned out. Even Frock didn't begrudge her that.

Ivo drifted to the coffee pot on the counter and stared out at the car too. Her flat gray-green eyes as vacant as the store windows on Main used to be. She poured a cup of coffee to the brim and let it spill over some, almost as if on purpose, then she swiped at the strands of dirty blonde hair sticking to her hot face and spooned sugar into the overfull cup so it spilled some more. Black ants began to collect along the edges of the spill. Ivo dumped some of the coffee back in the pot and took a sip, then added more sugar, stirring with a finger that seemed oblivious to the heat. Eddie could understand how lucky Frock was to have Jesus in his heart.

"I'll buy that car," Ivo said to the air in the room.

Eddie's heart chunked. Later, he would tell his ex-wife, "You know how I used to say there's some things worse than death? Well, I really think that now."

Ivo was wearing a pair of men's red plaid undershorts, so large the elastic waistband clung to her naked hipbones as if it were going down for the third time, and the too-white thighs sticking out of the holes were so skinny they looked like a man's hand would crush them. On top she wore a red T-shirt cropped just short of her bra, the edges still bearing the violent scissor slashes as if she'd just cut it up that morning. Eddie remembered seeing Ivo running along the blacktop outside town at dawn and dusk, her long pale arms and legs churning awkwardly. She always looked like she was about to trip and tumble, her body made up of spare parts that couldn't be expected to move gracefully—tiny feet stolen from some child, big hands grabbing the air, boy hips and flat butt and then those breasts she must've inherited from her mother, high full saucers that bounced painfully on her chest.

"Honey, I don't think—" Frock said.

"I don't know, my mind's not right," Eddie said.

She drank some of the coffee, then poured in another tablespoon of sugar, spilling enough to make the ants swarm drunkenly. Setting the cup down, she said, "I'll get my purse so we can go for a test drive."

"At the light there's always a tunnel," Frock said, and Eddie could see the apology in his eyes. "She's got the money."

Eddie shook his head, refusing to look at the car again. This place smelled of hot bleach and soap bound up with cottony dryer lint, plus the stream of dry cleaning chemicals that flowed in from the next room, but generally stuck to themselves in the hot, humid air. One of the reasons he'd never joined the Jesus boys was the Wednesday night Bible meetings there. But he was getting desperate about selling the car, his black beauty, his baby.

"Ready." Ivo appeared with sandals on her feet and a huge black leather shoulder bag that looked heavy enough to split her arm off.

Then she'd need more spare parts. Eddie followed her to the car, intending to drive around town, show her how things worked before she drove, but she beat him to the driver's side, climbed in, and began adjusting the seat. Nobody ever touched the seat. He'd had it in the same place for twenty-five years, and when she pushed it back, there was a rim of brighter beige carpet beneath her legs. Even his ex had known not to touch that seat.

She started slowly, running the gears like she knew something and Eddie nodded as if consenting. He looked in Dub's Barber Shop to see if the usual characters had collected, but it was empty. They coasted by the Gem Theater, closed now.

"That's closed now," Eddie jerked a thumb toward the empty marquee and padlocked doors before he could stop himself.

"I do get out of the house, you know." Ivo pressed on the gas.

"Place was coming apart," Eddie continued as if she hadn't answered. "Just trying to find a seat was a trial, so many of them busted. Screen had holes in it, roof leaked, bugs and mice had a field day."

Ivo gave the big engine a real shove and the car leaped forward. She gripped the wheel tighter and grinned crookedly. The last of Bellefontaine zipped by with Eddie half-hoping the deputy was lurking behind the Quik Sack and Gas which took over when Ideal Motors closed its doors. Now he had to go all the way to Useful to get his cars worked on.

They were rolling along at 80 m.p.h., the big engine stroking smoothly when she used her knee to hold the steering wheel and started digging in the bag. He reached over to hold the car steady, brushing her leg in the process and she jerked back like she was snake bit, glared, and pulled out a pack of cigarettes. She put one to her lips and pushed in the lighter, then retook the wheel.

"No smoking in the car," he said in a small voice. He was losing control of the situation.

She acted like she hadn't heard him and held the glowing lighter to the tip of her cigarette, drawing deeply and filling the car with plumes of smoke. He cracked his window, which only drew more smoke toward him. She smoked hungrily, as if she couldn't get enough fast enough. He wondered how she could smoke and run.

Glancing over at him, she unrolled her window and let the smoke pour out over her. For the first time she grinned. "It's the kind of car makes you have to smoke in." She held up what was left of the cigarette which was burning away quickly. "Organic. Had to give them up though." She pulled out the pristine ashtray, looked at him and quickly stubbed the cigarette on the cuff of her shorts instead, then tossed the butt out the window. She wet her thumb and rubbed the blackened cloth.

They rose up a hill, the engine never changing tempo and coasted down the other side. Woods began to surround the road, and the air in the car cooled and sweetened. Last time he'd been this way was to show a little bitty place in Useful. Converted garage. But he'd made five hundred dollars and given it to his ex to catch up on the alimony. Twenty-five years of marriage and now he was paying for the privilege. The car was their last bone of contention. He'd rather sell it than hand it over and watch her drive it up and down Main Street, the engine dragging in first, until she ground into second. And she'd drive it out to see her folks on that gravel road and pretty soon she'd crack the windshield with a rock like always happened and let it go because it'd just get another one if she fixed the glass. Before long the special-order beige leather seats would be cracked and split too because he wouldn't be around to rub them with the imported cream to keep them soft and pliable.

Ivo slowed and looked around. "Road should be—there—" The car coasted onto the dirt road and Eddie's heart thumped again.

"Go slow!"

This time she listened, downshifting, and the car immediately filled with a bobolink whistling and a woodpecker's persistent thumping on a tree overhanging the road. Red, black, and yellow butterflies flitted in front of the car and bounced off the windshield. A pair of cardinals chased each other in the limbs of trees just ahead of them. Somewhere in the shadows a blue jay squalled like a baby. The damp spice smell grew denser and filled the car, a heavy, heady scent that made him drowsy. He could almost hear the noise of their wings as the butterflies swam the air around them, dipping, curving back, coupling and releasing.

"My boyfriend's been UC-NR," Ivo said. "Unemployed on the couch, no revenue. Dad won't let me use the car to see him. On the weekends I can run out here, but it's too far during the week."

"Why didn't you just buy a car?"

Ivo thought about it. "I don't actually have a license, number one. And number two, I didn't want to—until I saw yours was for sale." Her voice softened and he felt it reach out for him in some obscure way, like a tendril, a hand.

"Here we are—" She pulled up and stopped in front of an ancient shack built of raw split pine logs that must have once been used as someone's hunting cabin. To the right, set a couple of feet off, was a tilting outhouse, the door tied shut with a red bungee cord.

Ivo honked the horn twice, filling the little clearing with the loud noise as she got out with the keys in her hand. She stood beside the car for a moment, then looked back inside. "Come on."

Eddie thought about the spare key he kept in his wallet. He should probably just go on back to town. Somewhere behind the shack, a dog howled and shut up abruptly. Yeah, he should just slide over and peel out of there. Ivo could run back to town, even if it was a weekday. He looked around for the boyfriend's vehicle. There was a rusted-out Jeep with its doors lying tangled in vines that had taken over the interior, walling the windows with green shadows.

"Les?" Ivo tapped her flat palms on the top of the car door frame and scanned the shack and woods around it. "It's just me, Les—" she called and glanced over at him. "And Mr. Falconer. I got his car, come on—" She looked worried now and stepping out from behind the car door, she called again in a higher, more childlike voice, "Les? Les honey? Are you in there, Les?"

"We should go on back—" Eddie said. "I got an appointment." He hoped Les wasn't home. He hated the insides of these hillbilly shacks and just wanted to get back in the car with the too-skinny girl and drift on down the road to Useful, stop and have a burger maybe, talk the way two people can. Now that they'd stopped, he realized it felt good to have someone else drive, someone who had a real gift for it, and Ivo was a natural. Not the kind of woman he'd ever—she was just a girl, his friend's daughter, and come to find out she was hooked up with some out-of-work, no-good hillbilly—

They waited in the silence that had gradually settled around them, as if everything was waiting to see if they stayed or went away again.

Ivo made a sound like a hiccuped whimper. "We have to go see—"

Eddie shook his head, looking down at his black dress shoes and tan trousers. He was at the end of his clean clothes and patience. Frock Walz would owe him dry cleaning for a month, but then Frock would probably blame him for being sucked into a deal like this with another man's daughter. The nearest dry cleaner outside Bellefontaine was twenty miles away.

On the porch, Ivo hesitated, then pushed the door open with her foot, standing to the side like a cop on TV before she could bring herself to look inside. Her boyfriend wasn't on the couch.

"Maybe he got a job," Eddie offered to avoid going further into the dark house belonging to a stranger in the Ozark woods. They were officially trespassing in shotgun territory.

"He's here, I can feel it." Ivo lifted the surprisingly clean pink chenille bedspread on the couch as if he could be lying underneath.

The house was tidy, even the raw pine floor was swept up, and fresh field flowers dripping yellow pollen sat in a pickle jar on the homemade pine plank table. The cheese on the lunch plate had started to sweat and the edges of crackers were falling in the damp heat. Eddie hoped Ivo wouldn't notice, but she was already heading down the narrow hallway. The bedroom and kitchen would be strung in a line behind the first room in this layout. He hesitated before following her back there. She was stopped outside the door, her head leaning against the warped knotty pine that bulged at the top of the frame. Even before she pried the door open, Eddie could hear the smothered giggling.

Les Monroe was a medium-sized man who looked like he'd missed too many meals to ever catch up, and judging from the woman in bed next to him, there was a reason. For a moment Eddie was caught by the familiar dyed-black hair, fleshy shoulders, and double chins, and his heart gave another clunk and shudder that this could happen twice. The terrible injustice of it came over his eyes like a thick red hood— he'd just kill her, that was all there was to do—murder her ass!

Then she turned her face defiantly toward them and it wasn't his ex, but the bartender from Douse's Inn instead. Eddie felt the anger flick its tail and slither out of him just as Ivo's breath whumped out like a thumped cushion.

Les lifted the arm hiding his eyes and grinned at them. He had a full set of teeth to match the round hard bareness of his head. His quick eyes shifted back and forth between the two of them while he adjusted the black sheet over his hips. Even his chest and legs were hairless, Eddie noticed, giving him a boyish quality that seemed odd, almost evil, against the bald head and clever old eyes.

"She's just my weekday woman, dahlin," he drawled. "You still got me on the weekend." He reached over and flicked the switch on the bucking horse lamp, illuminating the black cowboys walking around the edge of the yellowed shade. "See what she brought me?"

"You just smoked yourself right out of smarts," Ivo said. Grabbing the plastic baggie of dark-green leaves off the dresser next to the door, she threw it at the bed, showering the two of them.

"Does this mean I have to do my own wash?" Les called after them, and the bartender laughed outright, followed by a pig-like squeal.

Eddie was so relieved it wasn't his ex that he opened the passenger door for Ivo without thinking. She climbed in and he shut the door. She handed the keys over without a word, crushed in the seat with her spare-parts limbs folded around her like a broken spider. He headed them back down the dirt road, then onto the pavement, feeling the mortal spills of their lives overlapping in the hum of the big engine powering its way up past 100, on through to 110, then 112, and finally 115 where they stopped hearing even the sound of the tires pulling sticky off the hot blacktop, and the pistons' pure oily rise and plunge dissolved into the roar pressing them past the limit of endurance. Suddenly he was glad he hadn't left her to run back to town on her own. If a person just had to go out and try love, Eddie thought as his foot asked for the last quarter inch of power left in the pedal, then you needed a good fast car to bind up the devil.

Cleveland Pinkney

They were in the Bermuda Triangle of relationships now, and Cleveland knew better than to even cross his legs. Instead, he kept his eyes trained right on what she called her *come-on y'alls,* the top halves like brown moons being eclipsed by the pinching pink nylon bra.

"They said you were going places. Me, I just went for a ride," John Connolly sang from the radio strapped to the dashboard of the truck.

"You'll feel so much better than yourself if you just tell me. What can it hurt now? She's dead." Nyla shifted so her short legs stretched across the seat, the toes of her yellow-and-green cowboy boots nudging his thigh like they were thinking of pushing him out altogether. He still wasn't going to talk.

"Whyn't you open your door—get some more air in here," she said.

He fumbled behind his back and tugged the stiff handle up until it gave with a click and the door groaned metal on metal as it cracked open. This was Nyla's truck, and she was in no way going to take care of it. That's why she had him around. Now the squealing door was another piece of weight sinking his ship. That and the timing belt that gave out on this particularly lonely stretch of blacktop halfway up the mountain they weren't even supposed to be on. Angel Fire was ten miles behind, and the ski roads were closed for the summer. They were dead-on stranded, shit-for-brains out of luck. Luckily she didn't seem to care yet.

"And you lay down and got you that child—" Cleveland pointed to the swollen pouch of stomach and she stared at him. Somehow the cracked lens of her glasses made it easier to see her eyes which were rinsed green and squinty in the harsh mountain light. It was partly those eyes prying apart the flaps in his soul that kept him from talking about his wife.

"You better start walking." She waved her hand at the road winding down the mountain behind them, a black path surrounded by tan and orange rock and piñon pines whose resiny breath sweetened the air with spice that cloyed at his nose and throat.

"You're not coming," he said and she nodded as if he'd finally seen the same thing she had. She'd wanted to come up here for some reason, now she'd just as soon stay.

He eased himself out of the truck, letting his stiff legs straighten slowly, then turning around to gaze across the mountain. Leaning his arms on the roof of the black truck, he noticed how quickly the hot metal burned through the long sleeves of his denim shirt. He poked his head back in the truck and looked at the woman on the seat—pregnant and furious. To know her was to want to kill her, and she assured him he was the kind of man made a person feel alone.

She gave him that grimace she called a smile and wiggled her fingers in a wave. "You're gonna tell me about her—" she promised.

He noted the water bottle on the floor but decided against taking it for the walk. She'd need it more.

"I'm going—" He pulled back and looked around at the trees rooted in the thin soil and rocks. If it got too hot, she could go sit under a tree.

"Keep a lookout." He stumbled on the jagged edge of a rock, but kept himself from running down the steep road.

"Wait!" She climbed out of the truck and came toward him, her red hair a brighter flame than the sun burning up her head.

"Nyla—" He spread his arms wide to stop her.

"It's OK." She shook her hands as if to ward off gnats. It was one of her little gestures, the spasm of hands.

The road down was bumpier than they'd realized coming up in the truck. The blacktop was a smear of dark blue slathered onto the mountainside that now seemed to be melting and sinking like icing in the heat.

It took half an hour for Cleve to realize she'd left the water. They had paused so she could rest on a slab of rock. Scraping her damp hair off her face, she twisted its cloud into a long stalk and tried to knot it at the back of her neck, but it sprang loose again.

"You OK?" He stood over her, trying to create shade. She used the tail of his shirt to wipe her face and squinted at him through the broken glasses.

"Oh Cleve, all those other times I thought I was in love? It was just anxiety. This is real—" She scratched her stomach like it was an itchy insect bite.

He could feel the heat working down the back of his neck, across the backs of his hands and wrists. A large crow settled at the top of a small pine with a flapping of wings, then cocked its head and yapped at them, the black feathers glistening like hot oil.

He reached out a hand, and when she took it, he pulled her to her feet. She frowned.

"Hurting?" he said.

She nodded, shook her hands, and ran the tip of her tongue across her lower lip. The first thing he'd ever noticed about her was a green tongue, moss green. She'd never explained and he'd never asked. It'd taken him a while to kiss her with his mouth open.

"We forgot the water," she said. Looking around, she seemed to really notice the heat for the first time.

He took off his shirt and felt the immediate sear of heat as if he were leaning over a barbecue fire. He imagined black grill welts across his back.

"Here—" He tried to wrap the shirt and tie the sleeves in a turban around her head. She pushed him away, but he held the shirt out and she took it, quickly fashioning the head cover.

"You're burning," she said.

He shrugged. It was ball-tightening time, but she didn't need to know that.

She couldn't walk well in the boots, and the road had such a steep incline he had to hold her arm to keep her from stumbling forward.

Next time they stopped, she collapsed against him as soon as they dropped to the ground under a nearby pine.

"Why him?" Cleve asked, his throat closing until he coughed up its dryness.

The glasses sat crooked on her face, and for a moment he wondered if she was asleep or unconscious. "There wasn't room for both of us, honey," she murmured.

"Us?" He tried to ignore the pain of pine needles and stones against his burned back as he stretched out.

"Her and me. You have to let go of grief to love again, Cleve. It was like two bodies trying to wear the same set of clothes. You know?" Her hand flopped on his red stomach, and he closed his teeth against the groan.

They had dozed off, and she was still sleeping when he raised his head and squinted into the hard light bouncing off the shiny hot road and firing pieces of mica and sand. From a nearby rock, a small lizard gazed at him, mouth open, green paper-thin sides flaring and collapsing rapidly. The sky was so white he couldn't stand to look up, but he could see enough to know that she was right. All around them the dead were carelessly sprawling on rocks, hanging in trees, blocking the road to darkness and safety.

Earl

 Earl figured it was a chicken and egg thing—who drove who crazy first. Fact was, both of them were about out of the roost. Reeva believed the Bible from cover to cover, and she believed the cover too. It didn't help that the old preacher had brought on his nephew, who was really that bastard kid of his from down in Greenville. His Mama Dorcas worked at the Warren County Public Works, flagging on the highway crews that tarred and graded roads all summer long, and driving a salt truck in the winter. The preacher had his hands on Dorcas long before she got saved by God and the county, and now her kid was the preacher-in-training, since Reeva's church was so far into Christ's belly, there wasn't a seminary good enough for them.

And he was young and Earl's wife wasn't so old. That was a fact. Not as old as he was, so Earl had decided to have a talk with somebody. That's where the crazy part came. First he packed a lunch, two ears of sweet corn from last night's supper, a chunk of steak, a slab of American cheese, a burrito smothered in pale green sauce from break-fast—now that Reeva had taken to embracing new cultures they were having all kinds of weird stuff first thing in the morning when he could barely look a cup of coffee in the eye, let alone green slime—and five crescent walnut cookies the old Czech lady on the next farm over had made. She always paid him pie or cookies for mowing her lane with the wide sickle bar on the back of his tractor.

Well, he put the food in a plastic bag from the Sun Mart. They had about five hundred now that Reeva was recycling to show she loved all God's creatures too. He just wanted to cycle them all right down to the burn barrel, throw some brush on top, and have a nice fire, but a man learns after fifteen years of a new wife to let a lot of it go. Or do it where she can't see it. He'd gotten rid of so much of her recycling so far the gully by the creek was almost full of bottles, cans, newspapers, cardboard, rags, paint and oil cans, machine parts, pieces of the hog shed he would have burnt in earlier years. Maybe she was right—it was taking care of the erosion, although she thought he was dumping the stuff in the bins off Highway 2 or driving it all the way into town to the Catholic Mission Store. Good thing she avoided Catholics.

After packing his lunch, he carefully scraped all the crumbs off the counter into his hand and dumped them in the sink, waited for the ants to swarm, then turned on the water and rinsed the whole lot down the drain. There. He couldn't kill anything when she was around and the house was wriggling with flies and ants and spiders. He looked around, and caught his reflection in the window to the barnyard. He had to admit it—he was probably too old for what he was about to do. If she were home, she'd stop him.

Reeva was in town having her hair done again. Second time this month. She was a good-looking woman, that big mass of red hair brightened from the bottle, freckled skin that about drove him crazy, orangey brown eyes the color of fox fur. That little scar from her lips to her chin hardly showed at all—even though she said it made her look like a pirate and she'd have it fixed in a moment if he'd give her the money.

Earl wasn't cheap. That wasn't it. He just thought she looked as pretty as a woman needed to look—plenty pretty enough for him. He didn't even like her to wear makeup, and he was secretly pleased when Merle the old preacher said a word or two about it. Now that Merle Jr. was praising her natural beauty, though, it made him regret his stand. Maybe he should encourage makeup and drive her up to the medical school in Omaha to see a surgeon. A man shouldn't take such a hard line he gets knocked over it when the wind shifts on him. That reminded him—even though the heat index was 107° that afternoon, things could change. He'd take a suit jacket and wear his best straw cowboy hat. He wasn't above trying to impress the preacher or his kid, regardless of what the little bastard's birth certificate said. He'd pressed his suit pants too, and polished the toes of his brown cowboy boots so he wouldn't show up looking like an old farmer hunting for his young wife.

On his way back through the living room, he picked up the photo album sitting on the desk by the front door they never used. He was closing the door to the basement when he saw the .12-gauge leaning in the corner of the landing. It was loaded for rabbits and weasels, his current customers at the vegetable garden they figured he planted every year so they could enjoy their summers without having to work too hard for food. He juggled the album, lunch, and jacket and tucked the shotgun in the crook of his arm. It prickled his scalp to walk out the door that way, but he headed directly for the pickup.

The last of the chickens were pecking around the pole beans he'd strung up next to the garage, but most of the crop was finished or had gotten too old and hard. Years ago, with the first wife, he would've picked those and boiled them down to softness with some fatback and onion. Reeva didn't can or freeze or cook from scratch either if she could help it. But Earl kept the custom of the garden and the beans, picking and preparing them in a poor imitation of Opaline's recipes which those darn sisters of hers came and took when he married Reeva. Took the card box, the cookbooks, the department store dress box full of clippings of things she was going to cook. He was too embarrassed to buy his own book, wouldn't know where to start, so he pretended to cook. And ate it, no matter what it tasted like. Fortunately, the vegetables turned out hard or mushy, bland either way. He knew enough not to burn things, though he couldn't get the lumps out of mashed potatoes to save his soul, and he secretly loved the ready-mades with chicken gravy Reeva bought at the Sun Mart when she picked up a whole broiled chicken at the end of her shift. Meanwhile, their chickens were dying of old age and raccoons.

He settled in the truck, the album of their Las Vegas wedding pictures snug against his leg, took a last look around his farm, and thought about the business at hand. He was driving out the lane when he spotted the riding mower with the flat tire, tilted next to the tree line. He should be taking that tire off and getting it in to Ham's Tire for repair. The grass was going to seed around the mower. Nights he dreamed about mowing, that's how much it had taken a hold of his life. When they woke up in the morning, Reeva would relate these complicated dreams about traveling to foreign countries, knowing other languages, being chased by serial killers, and he'd just have the mowing troubles to report. No wonder she was turning her attention to Jesus and other men.

In his current craziness, Earl had begun to think of the deity as another man. He knew it was wrong to be so suspicious, and as he pulled up beside the mailbox, facing the wrong direction on the dirt road, praying the rednecks from a mile on didn't come roaring over the hill and put him in the ditch with their latest twelve-pack of empties he was forever retrieving from the deep weeds, he thought maybe he should turn around and leave it all alone. Then in the mail came the weekly church bulletin with the attached envelope for donations and the father and son picture of Merle and Merle Jr. looking like a skinny-ass Santa and a whippy young elf the way they were smiling, all teeth hungry for Reeva's paycheck which she was now slipping whole, her signature confirming the donation, into the envelope every week. It was her money, he kept repeating to himself, but it did no good. A man and a woman had to agree on major purchases, they promised each other the first year, and he was not purchasing this particular form of salvation for Reeva. Not even God could make him do that. He threw the bills and bulletin on the shotgun and they slid off onto the floor along with the Sun Mart weekly flier whose loss leader was always some kind of beef. They must slaughter half the cattle in Nebraska, Earl figured, but he had mastered the barbecue grill and nothing was better than those T-bones unless Reeva was on her kick about meat, eyeing the steak like a dead baby as he flopped it over and grease sputtered and sparked on the coals. All winter he'd just savor that smell and taste, hauling the grill out as soon as the lawn showed any sign of green at all. So that was another thing.

He made it up the gravel road onto the blacktop with no mishap, turning toward Greenville. It wasn't until he hit the outskirts ten minutes later that he began to have doubts about what he was doing, and when he saw Highway 2 heading south and east, he tugged the steering wheel and coasted smoothly onto its four lanes. Nebraska City, it said, thirty-nine miles, and he thought he'd just go along a little further and then pull off while he figured this thing out.

But the longer he drove, the less he knew. Another sign of his craziness he figured, and when he saw the sign for Saxon's Farm Fresh on Ninety-first, he pulled off the highway toward Cheney. He'd never been this way. Then he turned into the parking lot and got out. What he needed was something he hadn't grown himself—he didn't know what. He looked at the Royal Red Apricots big as tennis balls, felt their soft blushing skins, passed up the smaller strains of apricots, the sweating peaches and plums the tiny fruit flies were busily swarming, and went inside the small pole barn where a young girl, so young her breasts were barely suggestions under the tight blue striped tank top, was heaving on a big butcher knife embedded in a huge, long watermelon. When it broke open, the juices ran pink, he could just tell they were cold and sweet, and the meat was that red ripe it got just before it turned mealy. He watched her wrap a half carefully in plastic, then heft it in both hands and carry it over to an open cooler to sit on top of the whole melons, all of which were impossible in their size, large enough for entire families of parents and kids, cousins and grandparents, uncles, aunts, in-laws, these were picnic and party and family reunion melons—all much too large.

She wrapped the other half, then suddenly looked up at him. She was a very young girl, just on the verge of sullenness and lipstick, already unwilling to smile at any adult. Just as suddenly he wanted to please her—is that for sale, he asked stupidly, grateful when she simply nodded.

You want it? she asked, cradling it like a baby in her arms, unmindful of the wet against her shirt.

Yes, he said and followed her to the makeshift checkout counter.

Can you put it in something so it doesn't drip all over? He paid the two dollars and watched as she hauled out a recycled Sun Mart bag and slid the melon half in. He could have sworn it wouldn't fit, but it did when she lifted and held the two flimsy handles out to him. He'd never trust a plastic bag, so he took the melon into his own arms, cradling it as she had, feeling the deep cold seep into his shirt, calming the heat that had been waiting there all afternoon.

In the truck, he made sure the safety was on the shotgun, and tipped it so the butt rested on the floor and the barrel was wedged against the door, pointing out the back window. He shoved the photo album over so the watermelon could sit beside him, pressing its cold nose against his leg like his dog used to, as he turned around and headed back the way he'd come. He kept seeing himself delivering the melon, so rich and cold, the sweet flesh filling their mouths until they laughed. They'd have it for dinner—they'd eat the whole thing in one sitting, just the two of them, and not once, not once would she glance out the porch window toward the tall rows of corn pressing against the yard fence, her face filled with a kind of longing that hurt to look at. He'd tell her then that gods are just dreams with deadlines, and that he was never going to leave her. And although he knew this wasn't going to work, he had to try because they were both crazy in this heat and the lunch was going rancid and the gun was bouncing dangerously beside him and a man, no, a person, had to feel like they weren't going to be put aside just because they hadn't suffered enough.

❖ ❖

FROM

~Taking the Wall~

❖ ❖

Good to Go

Well, we'd mortgaged everything but the baby, and Donnie tore the rear spoiler half off, lost his downforce, and that was about it. Track came up and smacked him silly. That was the last time we had any money to speak of. Since then it's been working at Wal-Mart and a '78 Olds with a hole in the floor big enough for J.P. to lose a sneaker through. Last time it rained I was ankle deep in water floating down the blacktop to Cedar Rapids. Donnie's too busy welding other people's cars back together to put that piece permanent over the floor. He's the nice guy the neighbors call at suppertime to come fix their mower or disposal. We're making love and somebody needs a spark plug. Same thing when he was racing. Bob there needed to finish high enough to keep his sponsor. Frankie Jr. had the wife's medical bills, and then there was the night Spanus came to look over Owen Brach for the Craftsman Truck Series. Donnie, I said, Donnie we got bills and babies too.

You pay for your mistakes in racing, my stepdad Walter says. You miss the setup and you take the wall. Walter has his own garage and Donnie was working there when we met. It's funny, that's where Mom met Walter too. She'd driven me and a car full of stuff through one whole night to get away from her boyfriend and Versailles, Missouri. Needed gas and an answer for the terrible thumping in the rear end. Walter's Friendly Service squatted on the outskirts of town in possession of twenty acres of abandoned cars and a fairly new, pink and white double-wide mobile home that sat in its own pavilion surrounded by a fence of half-buried tractor trailer tires painted white. Mom always loved their half-moon scallops, and admired a man who would take the time, she said. She's gone, of course. Hers was a restless heart, and even Walter understands how she came to leave with the UPS man right after Donnie showed up. She'd been going away for a while, her eyes shiny with longing of an impossible kind whenever she watched those long legged country singers on CMT. Dwight Yoakam, Alan Jackson, you know the ones. She loved us, Walter and me, with as much as was free inside her, but the rest of her, well, it was always going someplace else, and she was just the wagging tail to its dog.

The UPS man was half-Indian too. That's what she told me the night she left. Walter and Donnie were at the fairgrounds, watching the Demolition Derby that was our town's annual contribution to the Fourth of July. The fireworks would follow and I was getting ready to go out and climb on the roof of the garage to watch. It was my general policy to avoid men wrecking cars on purpose whenever possible. You see, I had that whole twenty acres of torn sheet metal and smashed windows to grow up in. It didn't take a genius to figure out the evolution. That particular family tree don't branch, I'd tell Donnie later.

Mom always seemed to leave places at night. She wasn't a Monday morning, new start kind of person. She waited and waited for her time, and it always came somewhere between eight and ten at night. She'd make all her decisions then, like one of those nocturnal animals whose brain clicked awake as soon as the sun set. I used to wonder what kept her with us as long as she did stay. I helped her pack that night. Maybe that was wrong of me, but I personally wrapped the pressed-glass swan vase she got from her Ozarks grandmother. I was afraid she'd be in such a hurry she'd forget it or not take enough care packing it, and I couldn't bear the picture of her standing there later with the pieces in her hands, knowing she'd lost something precious forever, something she could never ever make up or come back to. She was that kind of person. You wished her well. She had enough desire and longing for all of us, and I was just glad it was her having to drive away from places in the middle of the night, not me. My desire does not have geographical dimensions, I tell Donnie when he suggests we move to the other side of town.

I miss her. Miss how she could make Walter smile and shake his head and turn fast as a pony on a dime and try to chase her down when she teased him in the middle of work. She never minded the grease prints on her blouse and white-blonde hair or the burn his red stubble made around her mouth when they got to the house. Walter's not too sad now, you understand, he's just lost a little bit of air. He's skinnier somehow, like Mom took the fat out of his life. Now he has to live on lean and while that's good in some ways, it's really less than before and neither of us can forget that. I know he wishes I was more like her, that I'd treat Donnie the same way so he could get that lift out of watching us. But like I said, I'm not that kind of person. I leave Donnie to his work, and he leaves me to mine. Mine being J.P., working part-time at Wal-Mart, and keeping track of the salvage business.

It's funny how those twenty acres of cars became my responsibility. As a kid I wanted a horse, begged and pleaded, tried to win one in contests, prayed for some old man to leave me his money anonymously. I knew no woman would do anything that foolish, but I still believed in the crazy goodness of men then. One night at supper Walter put his fork down, finished chewing his Salisbury steak, swallowed, and announced that he too had been thinking hard about my problem, and he thought he'd found a solution. I could have a horse as soon as I cleared enough of those cars away for a pasture. He figured ten acres would be a good start. It was the kind of announcement filled a kid with despair and hope both, tangled impossibly, leaving you sleepless with frantic planning. I was twelve so it still seemed fairly simple to sell or move enough cars for my horse. First, I decided, I'd have to catalog the cars and make a list I could send around. Someone would want those good parts. Later when I came up with the plan to have them hauled away to a place that crushed and recycled metal, Mom gave a gentle shake of her head. Honey, she said, Walter loves those cars, no matter what he said.

And so it was that I came to see that I would have to defeat Walter's love for one of my own, and the unfairness of it struck me for the first time as what it meant to be helpless in the face of your own desire. It had been a year since our bargain, and while I had increased the salvage business by a good amount with my little catalog, the cars never seemed to do more than grow more hollow, piece by piece, until their skeletons rested mossy and black among the weeds that grew higher and higher, and as much as anything they came to resemble untended graves.

What I had ignored was the fact that new cars would be added as out in the world they grew old and died, got wrecked or totaled, and people in them escaped or died. It came to me after a while to look suspiciously at some cars: the black Trans Am that took Buddy Holden's legs, the green and white Chevy pickup that developed a fatal attraction for the Burlington Northern train taking the whole Smithen family with it. By the time I was fourteen, I began to dread spring nights when the high school seniors would scatter their lives like dandelion seeds to the wind in cars that the next day would be hauled through our gates and deposited, sometimes with blood stains still visible on the uphol-stery and the jagged glass of the windshield.

I avoided those cars on my walks then, hated to see the cats tip-toeing across the hoods, leaving dusty little prints, then pausing at the smashed windshield, sniffing the air, and pumping their tails slowly up and down before springing inside. Mice and field rats seemed to like those cars best. It took me a while to get on any sort of basis with those cars. Sometimes it never happened. I'd try to sell their parts fast, cheap, get their lethal hearts out of there. Still do.

There is one car I don't ever advertise though. One I'd never sell a piece of. I'd as soon bury it, but for Walter. Kids come around wanting a rocker panel, a header, a camshaft. I tell them take anything but leave that one up by the fence alone. I keep it close, you see.

Donnie and I might never have gotten together if it hadn't been for Mom's car, the one that drove us into Walter's heart. It was an old Chevy Malibu with the paint worn off to gray and rust eating its way up the doors and down through the roof and hood. The trunk lock was gone from the time we'd lost the key, and the lid was held down by a bungee cord. Walter always threatened to do something about that car, but the best thing he could manage was to keep the engine strong after he'd dropped in a new one when it became clear that we were staying on more or less permanently in the double-wide. The motor came from an old Buick Roadmaster and was really too big for the Malibu, which made it a spicy little car that spun its wheels at every stop sign and lifted its front end if you stepped on the gas too hard. When the muffler got a hole, it sounded like the hottest car in town. Walter didn't believe in new cars, and Mom didn't care. I was the only one interested in something with shine and glitter, I guess, since I'd had to give up on the horse. I needed to satisfy myself somehow, and I still thought it was going to be something with four legs or four wheels. I had no idea it was going to be Donnie until he came to lean over the engine one day while I was checking the oil. He took the dipstick out of my hand and wiped it clean between two fingers he rubbed off on his jeans while he stuck the stick back in and pulled it out again. Squinting in the sunlight at the light new oil, he nodded as if we'd come to some essential agreement and put it back in the hole. I was watching his tan arm with the veins popping and the hair bleached blond, the thick wrist with that bone sticking up and it made my stomach hollow with want.

You keep your engine tight, he said lifting the air filter off and checking the white folds for dirt. Big mother, isn't it? He screwed the wingnut down and jiggled the hoses, running his hands down their lengths for tears. Think I could drive her sometime? He pressed the fan belt for give and nodded with satisfaction. Turn it on, he instructed.

We won money almost from the start, drag racing Mom's car on the blacktop three miles away in the middle of the night. Donnie put on a glass pack muffler, leg pipes, and dual exhausts, then went to work on the engine. Walter watched us out of the corner of his eye, kept Donnie working late as possible, and Mom fell in love with the UPS man.

The first time we did it wasn't in the backseat of the car though. It was in the middle of Heison's oatfield. We'd won a hundred and fifty dollars that night from some guys from Iowa City, and they'd gotten so pissed we'd had to take off and hide. Wasn't hard since we knew every farm and field road in the county, and we'd been necking on most of them. That night the wind was blowing hot with an edge of cool rain we could smell from someplace not too far away, so we flung open the car doors and ran into the middle of the field and lay down making angels in poor Heison's oats. In the morning, he'd think it was deer and threaten to go hunting out of season, but we didn't care. The grain was coming ripe and it smelled nutty and sweet as the wind pushed it around and about us like big heavy waves of hissing water. Donnie undid the only button fastening his shirt, and when I saw that smooth tan chest and stomach, I knew what I was going to do. I sat up and pulled my T-shirt over my head. He shrugged out of his shirt, and the wind moaned in the trees on either side of the field, tossing the sound back and forth over our heads as he lay down on top of me, and I licked the salt sweet sweat on his cheek as sandpapery as a cat's tongue. Then I let him put his thick oil-dark fingers everywhere he wanted.

Afterwards we lay there side by side while the storm came up and lightning struck the cornfield on the other side of the trees, and we could feel the razor jolt ripping along the ground in all directions. We made love again in the muddy oats, naked, our clothes drowned somewhere beside us. At dawn we drove home, and Walter and Mom met us at the door. Donnie moved in that day. It only took ten days to get us married. I was sixteen. Donnie was nineteen. But that isn't the car I'm talking about.

I don't know how we moved from drag racing to oval tracks. Probably the junked racer we got the year J.P. was born. I'd just turned eighteen and was still running the salvage. Donnie and I had our own trailer now. Not a double-wide, but it was enough. We had the twenty acres, the garage, and the office to run around in, and Mom and I spent time together too, so I never felt confined or anything. Some days, I admit, while I was nursing J.P., I'd sit at the kitchen window and look out across my cars and think of them as horses, grazing in the snow there, pawing to get down to last summer's grass, their coats shaggy as sheepdogs. I had bays and blacks mostly, with one or two chestnuts or grays. But mostly I liked the good reliable colors, nothing too fancy, nothing that showed dirt or too much personality. I'd read that the browns were best, that all other horses wanted to be brown, that's why the palominos and whites kept rolling in the dirt. It could be true, I decided, leaning into the tugging weight of J.P. at my nipple. It would be nice to go out there and call and have your horses come galloping up to the fence for a carrot. To be able to pat their warm chests, to bury your face in their thick necks, to feel their hot breath blowing on the back of your head. The cars looked forlorn out there in the winter, the only tracks from the dogs trotting up and down the rows, inspecting the ranks like visiting generals. The deer don't bother coming in the salvage yard. People work less on their cars that time of year too, so it could be peaceful and lonely out there, especially when I was nursing. That winter Mom got a job in town at the drugstore, so she wasn't around much either. That way she could see the UPS man more often, I guess, though I didn't know it at the time.

The racecar showed up on the back of a flatbed from Mason City. "Lady says to tell you she doesn't want to see this thing again," the driver announced and backed the rig through the gates. I had him put it right up front so I could go over it when I had time without having to wade through the deep snow. Donnie could use the tractor to drag it back down with the others later. But that's not what happened. I fell asleep after J.P. was done nursing, and by the time I woke up and got us both bundled for the outdoors, it was well past lunch and Donnie was back from his morning job driving school bus for the kindergartners. He'd found the number two red and black Pontiac and was already inside trying to fix the ignition box. Thank you, oh thank you, thank you, he crawled out the window and kissed me and J.P. enough that I couldn't tell him the truth. And so Donnie came to believe that I'd given him the Christmas present he'd always wanted, and I came to be the biggest liar in the family. At least I was then.

So we went racing, taking Walter with us too when he could find someone to work weekends at the station. Mom was working long hours in town, or so we thought, and we were too busy to notice all the changes that were taking place. Me, I thought it was Dwight Yoakam she was in love with, and what was the harm of that, I'd ask Donnie late at night at the track, snuggling in our truck bed camper, J.P. in his own little bed on top of the flip-down table we ate at.

Once in a while we'd win, but it wasn't anything like the drag racing we'd done. We were broke all the time, borrowing from Mom and Walter, taking extra jobs, the both of us, finding J.P.'s clothes and toys in the secondhand stores, rummage and yard sales. Donnie had that true believer look in his eyes though, and I don't think he noticed how it was going for the baby and me. I'd spend my time trying to rustle up deals on parts off flyers I'd make during the week at home, and trying to line up what Donnie needed for his car too. I took to keeping J.P. on a piece of clothesline tied around his waist and mine. Got dirty looks for that, and some laughs, but it was safety really. We were both about half deaf from the roaring engines. But I remembered what it was like all those years before when I'd wanted a horse more than anything else in the world and how it had seemed like both the easiest and the hardest, most distant thing that could happen, and I could not deny Donnie that one little corner of his dream.

Then we went through a time when everything seemed to click. Walter was helping with the engine and Donnie was driving like Richard Petty. Our life started moving faster, we bought a newer pickup and then a decent used car for me. We went to bigger tracks and got to know some of the other drivers and their families. The crowds started cheering for us once in a while. That lasted a year and a half, with our dreams tumbling out hot and fresh like clothes from the dryer. We would move up, get into newer cars, we'd get a team, we'd find sponsors, and so on. We'd just won at Mason City, and Donnie had decided to spend the Fourth at home because the next month he'd be gone part of every week.

He and Walter wanted to go to our town's annual Demolition Derby and take J.P. He was old enough, they said. I backed out. I was tired, I told them, wanted time to just sit and go over the books on the salvage yard and talk to Mom. And I remember we all looked around at Mom like we'd forgotten she existed, and in a way I guess she had. She'd been disappearing so gradually, we hadn't noticed, not even Walter, though as I say that, I don't believe that part is true. Walter would have noticed. He just might not have been able to say anything. There she was, Mom, with this forced little smile on her thin face and her pale blue eyes so long gone you could tell they weren't seeing any of us sitting around the table of her house. She was already out the door, down the walk, past the heavy tire scallops of her fence, stepping into the UPS man's brand new Camaro, a too-good-to-be-true gold yellow. But I wouldn't see that for several more hours yet. You go ahead, she smiled. I'm fine. We can watch the fireworks from the garage roof and when you come home, we'll have some ice cream and beer.

It's the small lies we come to hold against a person, I've decided. Not that she wouldn't be there when they came home, that she'd leave me to face Walter by myself, but that she promised them ice cream she already knew she didn't have in the freezer. Ice cream and beer, that should've been a tip-off, don't you think? Even her Ozarks hillbilly relatives knew better than to offer up a combination like that. What were we thinking, all of us?

So, like I said, when I came back from checking the books on the salvage yard, which Walter and Pugh did not bother keeping worth a darn, there was Mom packing. Wasn't much to say, really. At least I didn't try to say much. She was the determined one in our family, and she had that restlessness. I was a grown woman with a family of my own to worry about. I thought she'd be back, or that I'd go see her. I thought all kinds of things as I wrapped the glass swan in her underwear three, four times and bedded it safely with her socks on top of her jeans and put her T-shirts on top of that. I wasn't thinking about Walter. Her happiness swept all those thoughts up and away like a good strong wind blowing the house clean again as she opened the door and ran down to meet the yellow Camaro's honking horn. I carried the black nylon bag myself and put it in the trunk when he popped the lid, saw it safely resting on jumper cables next to a lava lamp even I knew was cheesy. His clothes were in a cardboard box. I remember a white athletic sock with a frayed heel hanging over the edge, and I reached to tuck it back in but stopped myself because suddenly I couldn't touch anything of his, as if his things were too nasty in a personal, naked way. I slammed the trunk lid and leaned down to kiss her good-bye, only getting the glance of her ear for she turned away too quickly to laugh at something he said. And by the time she turned back, he was stepping on the gas and spewing gravel from the tires that stung my bare legs as the car burst away, suddenly tearing a hole too big to be closed again.

Walter and Donnie and J.P. drove right by the wreck on their way home, hurrying to tell me about it. How they could still be excited by a wrecked car, I'll never know, but I didn't blame them, not at first. Not until they said it was a new yellow Camaro with the front end so crumpled they had to cut it in half to get the people out, and the rescue squad turned off the blinking lights after they loaded up the bodies. Kids, Walter said, and I couldn't look at him again for a month.

That was the end of our racing luck. I never understood how one thing got in the way of the other, and maybe it didn't, but maybe it did. We dug a hole of debt so deep we about drowned, and now even Walter's working twenty-four-seven to keep the bills at bay. We were all good to go, though in some strange way we didn't realize it, and then she went and took it away. So you know now that the remains of that Camaro are right inside the gate here where I can keep an eye on them. I never unpacked the trunk either, the one part of the car intact. I've left it there, the black nylon bag with the glass swan safely nestled in its dark sleep among her clothes. The UPS man's cardboard box molding and collapsing in the wet years since that dream arrived and took ahold of our lives. Because it's like Walter says, you pay for every mistake.

Over the Point of Cohesion

That was the strange thing. He woke up thinking he'd been right on it going into that corner, so he hadn't braked. But he'd been wrong, stepped on the brakes too late and took the wall. Just like that. But he'd been so sure. Then the long stay in the hospital getting rehab and listening to people congratulate him for his twelfth year and this special award for his retirement and being a good sport so he could stand on the stage in New York with the top ten. Well, standing wasn't exactly right. It took him a whole year just to stagger along with those metal braces, and he'd never stand without the odd bend to his back, swaying him to one side like a tree pushed by the wind. None of that mattered.

He looked up at the waitress pouring the coffee like it was some grand achievement and then went back to scribbling numbers on the napkin. He'd made the drawing of the track at Martinsville, the angles of the corners, written what he remembered of the setup on the car, and began rebuilding the race in his mind. Some days it was the race he'd run. Some days it was the race he was going to run, and some days it was the race he should've run. Those were the hardest days, when he corrected each move, each brake and throttle, each bump at the rear or side of the other cars. But never that corner. He'd gone in right. He knew it. He couldn't believe it hadn't worked out. He'd demanded the printouts from the team in the pit and gotten them. But they didn't show enough, he'd protested, and the men looked away. Twelve years and they couldn't look him in the eye.

"Anything else?"

"What?"

"Anything else for you?"

He looked up at her to see if he could figure out what it was made her need to bother him like this. The waitresses usually left him alone of a morning. They had plenty to do without nagging him. She was plain. Plain brown hair, plain brown eyes, prim little lips with caked pink lipstick her tongue kept finding. By the end of her shift her lips would be chapped. He knew that because he'd had the same problem racing and had to coat his lips with balm before he packed himself into the helmet. He shook his head. "Just leave the pot, OK?"

"Can't. I'll be back." She disappeared and left him alone for so long he began to worry he was going to have to order more coffee. Another thing he could do now. Couldn't afford the nerves or the dehydration before. Now—

He held up his cup finally, and she took her time while he anxiously searched the café. He didn't see anyone he knew, but that was probably because he hadn't made it a point to make friends when he'd moved here eight months ago. He wasn't even sure why he chose this place, but it seemed far enough away that he wouldn't miss what he was missing every moment of his day. Iowa. Nebraska. Kansas. He'd gone down the list of places far enough away from his racetracks to be safe. Kansas. Hays. Out there on the plains, his eye taking in the wheatfields like they were the prime surfaces of newly poured concrete with just enough skin over so the tires didn't shred up like at North Wilksboro. Last race a week ago. Opened in 1949, he'd been there five times himself. Never won. Hardly ever in top ten, hell, top twenty. Hell, it wasn't his deal, the short tracks. Something nagged at him. OK, maybe he wasn't any Rusty Wallace or Richard Petty and that new kid, Gordon, who might be the best of them all. Even Dale Earnhardt couldn't take it away from him, running second at North Wilksboro, bridesmaid to the bride again. That would chap old Dale's ass. But he came back. After his last pileup, Dale came back and raced with a broken collarbone.

She took his cup and poured the coffee and stood there, looking at him. Her eyes weren't so dull brown, he noticed, every once in a while there was a little spark of purple or blue-black like what he saw when he closed his eyes sometimes, like a movie trying to get started, but having trouble with the reel. She kept staring, pot held up like a trophy in both hands. He looked away again, still nobody he knew. Half farmers, half cowboys in their straw hats and boots, spending more time than he'd ever had sitting in the café at the Sunoco. Outside in the parking lot, the bawls of cattle in the long silver stock trucks and the tires whishing on the interstate two blocks away. Every sound carried on the plains where the wind blew almost nonstop and it was like an ocean that sank him deep into sleep every night, that wash of engines and tires. Sometimes the way he'd heard it in his car during a race, only much quieter, safer, under control, rarely the winding engine, the screeching metal on metal.

"What are you?" She gestured with the pot toward the napkins he'd written on.

He had the urge to climb out of the booth and leave, but it wasn't time yet so he shrugged.

"You don't know what you are?" She grinned and looked back at the counter where the manager was talking head to head with a bleached blonde whose body had seen better days. His waitress put the coffeepot down on the table and leaned her fists tiredly on the edge as if to reassure him she wasn't going to claim more than that little bit of space.

"You're new, just move here?" She fingered the drawing of the corner where it happened.

"Been here a while, few months."

"Just learning those things, huh." She tipped her head toward the metal braces on his legs he kept propped up on the bench opposite him. His legs ached almost all the time, and raising them seemed to keep the pain at more of a distance. It'd taken a long time to pry them apart from the metal and engine. Almost too long, the doc said after they'd saved the things. "Saved the legs," he'd announced after surgery. "Don't have to worry about that." His sponsors had sent him flowers, fruit baskets, and farewell checks. There'd been talk of a benefit dinner or concert to help him, but he'd never returned the phone calls. Just moved here, a place he'd found on the interstate, far enough away.

She looked over her shoulder again as the manager slipped out the double glass front doors and turned the corner with the blonde who still had very nice legs. The waitress looked at him and made a scooting gesture with her hands, and he pulled his feet off the bench, hating the clunk each foot made when it hit the tired brown linoleum beneath the table.

"Thanks. Feels good to take a load off. Dennis won't be back for a while. He goes down to this other place. Has his morning coffee there. That's his girlfriend. His ex-wife. They keep at it, gotta give them that." She pushed the thin brown hair off her forehead with the back of her hand and looked around. "That's Frank up there at the end of the counter, he comes in almost every morning on his way to Salina, hauling cattle for some big place out by Colby. He's never been further east than Kansas City, doesn't like anyplace he hasn't been, he says. And Johannes there in the hat with the feather? He was a rodeo cowboy in high school, went on the circuit, got stomped on too hard by a bull in Tulsa, Oklahoma and lost the retina of one eye. Sees fine for farming, but he don't drive so good. Nobody dares say a word. I went to school with him. And that guy there—"

He stopped listening. It was too much like the obituaries. He didn't subscribe to the racing news anymore either. It isn't over till it's over, he kept telling himself. If he could figure out how that corner turned into a slingshot and put his car into that wall, well, then maybe.

"You're hanging onto the wrong things," his wife had said as she packed. She hadn't even taken the bank account, what there was of it, and he'd felt that as a kind of double insult. Hell, she hadn't even slammed the door behind her when the cab honked out front, like in those country songs. But it hadn't been a cab. It was a friend of hers from work. She'd had to hold down a job those last three years to pay the mortgage because he was on such a shoestring, they couldn't keep a house that size and the two cars and all without her paycheck. "Soon as I start winning again," he'd promised her, but after those early years when he was young and full of vinegar, there hadn't been much.

"Head injury?" the waitress asked all of a sudden.

He examined her face to see if she was making fun of him, but she wasn't. "I—" He couldn't say it. He hadn't said it yet, wouldn't till he understood how that car had failed him.

"My brother and cousin died in a car wreck out County Road 4, the year I was up at Chadron State, north of here? Massive head injuries. Closed casket. Mom hated that part. Almost as much as losing Lonnie, I think. Saying good-bye to your loved ones and all that stuff. Very important. You had a car wreck too?"

He nodded.

"Thought so. You're still not used to them leg thingies. And the scars on your arms and face there. I noticed that. Part of my training." She waved at the room. "Not this, I'm saving to go back to school. Mortuary science."

His stomach filled up something nasty. What did she want?

"Lonnie wanted to be a drag racer. He and Jackie were practicing, something went wrong, and they crashed into each other going a hundred and ten. I didn't know that old car of his would go that fast. Guess he'd been working on the engine. Anyways—" She twisted her hands together and back apart.

"Hard business to make a living in. Most people don't make it," he said and shifted his legs in their metal cages to move the aches around.

"How old do you think I am?" she asked suddenly, smiling at him in a way that took the coarse grain out of her skin and made her seem younger than he'd thought.

He shrugged.

"No, take a guess. Really—"

"Thirty, thirty-five?" He'd made a mistake. The light died in her eyes and she pushed back against the burgundy Naugahyde of the booth. "I'm no good at that—I never—"

She looked toward the counter and waved her fingers at him. "Never mind."

It made him feel something, bad maybe, and he didn't like it. "No, look, what's your name? I'm—" He'd been about to give her the name he'd earned his rookie year, Spit, but he didn't want to do that, not now, not yet. "My name's Ricky, Ricky Torrence."

She swallowed, brushed her hair off her face, and looked at him quickly, then at the cuticle she was picking. "Bonnie Jassy." She smiled again. "Bonnie and Lonnie—my parents—"

They sat there uncomfortably for a few moments, then she pulled the napkin with the drawing on it around again, looked at it, and shoved it back at him. "So what's this?"

"Racetrack."

"The rest of this stuff racing too?" Her fingers touched a couple of the other napkins lightly, with enough respect that he nodded. "You a racecar person?"

"Driver."

"What kind?"

"Winston Cup." He wanted to look away when he said it, but he found himself staring at her face which changed again, lighting up as he remembered women's had in the racing days. It still made him feel good, and he pinched the thigh his hand was resting on to punish the thought.

"Lonnie mostly watched the dragsters, funny cars, straight line stuff. So I never got to see you, I guess."

"It doesn't matter."

She looked at the scars on his arms and face where they'd sewn him back together, and he got ready for the questions. "Crashed, huh?"

It always made him feel like he'd committed some big social mistake, a crime even, that he'd messed up enough to earn exile from all human decency by crashing into that wall, the sponsor decals crumpling, then flying pieces in the air, miraculously inflicting only minor injuries in the crowd while he tumbled and turned and torqued down the racetrack, taking out five other cars in the process. The race leaders who were lapping him for the fourth time. Hell, he hadn't even been on the lead lap, he woke up thinking. What was the glory of a crash like his?

"They start you small in school and work up to crash victims. I skipped ahead in the textbook and read that part first."

"Hit the wall going 118 at Martinsville." Suddenly he found himself talking, telling her every detail of the race as if she were just dying to hear it, and he knew he was acting crazy, not letting her into the conversation, holding her attention captive at gunpoint, as his wife used to say, but he couldn't stop himself and she kept nodding and smiling like she understood exactly what he was saying and it was utterly fascinating.

"At Martinsville, you need to be careful of brakes, see. We use carbon-metallic brakes that heat up to a thousand degrees until they're glowing red and sparking. You have to be careful because eventually they can melt the bead that seals the rubber of your tire to the wheel. Some of the teams were starting to use metallic tape to prevent the bead from melting, but we didn't, we didn't think we needed it with the setup on the car and me driving. I wasn't hard on the brakes, most of the time. Hell, I wasn't going fast enough to be hard, I guess." It surprised him saying that.

"So what happened on this corner?" She tapped the drawing.

He took a sip of the cold coffee and made a little face but she ignored him. In fact, she had her chin propped with her two fists and was staring right at him, full force. "What happened?"

He shook his head. "There's this point of cohesion on a corner. You hit it and you don't have to brake so much, you go over it and you have to brake hard. Simple. Somehow the car got loose on me. I thought it was running a little tight and when I got there, it was loose and I was kissing the wall. It made the highlights tape on all the networks, and the year-end film for the awards banquet." He didn't mention the video of the worst wrecks of the decade they were selling on late night TV when they reran old races for the diehard fans. Somehow that embarrassed him.

"Must've been something." She shook her head and looked at the pieces of napkin, letting her eyes slide to the counter again. He pretended not to notice.

"It was. I've been trying to figure out what happened, how it happened. But it doesn't show up in the numbers like it should. Nobody tapped me or nothing. I don't know." He shook his head and the numbers jiggled on the paper in front of him. Sometimes his vision did that.

"Pretty obvious, isn't it, Ricky?" She stood and picked up the coffeepot as the manager came through the glass doors looking around with a critical expression ready to accuse somebody of something.

"How's that?" He felt the bile climbing in his chest. Acid reflux, not your heart, it's strong as an ox, the doctor at the clinic on the other side of downtown had told him last week.

"You made a mistake," she said and spilled a little more coffee into his cup before she left.

"Yeah," he agreed. But it should show up somehow, shouldn't it? What was the point of all that printout business if it didn't tell the story when you needed it? Maybe he'd explain more of the details to Bonnie tomorrow, he decided. Maybe by doing that, he'd find the thing he'd been missing in all that data. Then he stopped himself. Mortuary science? What kind of a job was that? He had to stop himself from calling out the question to the whole room.

❖ ❖

The Level of My Uncertainty

"I bet the whole family can weld." Someone always says something like that. Moving from track to track I've heard it all before. It's true that my wife Myna and three babies help out around the shop between competitions. Well, they aren't babies anymore. Dove is sixteen and she's the biggest help. She can hold a torch with the best of 'em. Tiny Pine, we call him T.P.—he's twelve and he's begging to get started driving on his own, soon as those legs of his grow. And even Cleo, the real baby at seven, is good at crawling into the engine cavity and wiring things that get to hanging loose.

All in all, a man couldn't wish for a better family, and the championship should have been mine, it should've. Everybody said it, not just the wife and kids who wear their pride on their faces and keep their disappoints in their hearts like I've taught 'em.

"A man is lucky to have a beautiful wife." That's the other thing people say about me. They don't know the half of it. With those looks, she can't help but produce a passel of kids I have to worry about taking after her. And they do. That Dove—well, and there's T.P. who's being followed around by every little girl on the lot, especially that clown Frogger's eleven year old who has red hair, for chrissakes, and is already five-eight. She's a giant. Why doesn't she pick on someone her own size? T.P. has life plans, not girl plans. Least that's what we tell each other as we work father and son, ripping torn metal sheets off and riveting new ones on the car each week. Thank goodness Cleo is still a baby, though she has her mama's brown curls and enough of Dove's big brown eyes to put a real scare into me. Dove, well, that will bear some thinking, I decide as I reinforce the gas tank on the '69 Olds I picked up last week from Fred's Salvage outside of Red Oak. The

Olds is a tank, a big Ninety-Eight. Glance can run into me all day and I'll still be steering with my fingertips. They knew how to build 'em back then.

Dove saw that Olds. She thought I was buying it for her, maybe, from the hungry wishing look in her eyes. She's working inside the car right now, tearing out all the accessories. She finds that job more than satisfying and she is good at it to boot. She is the best stripper I know of and she can handle a torch like she's conducting a damn band. For a while there, when she was Tiny's age, she nagged me to let her start driving, but I put her off with one thing or another. Now I have to wonder if I made a mistake.

"There's Rhonda Harmon Smith running top-fuel dragsters," Dove said when she turned fourteen. Then a month ago, right there in the second week of school, she showed up at the garage and announced she was done. Not going back. Staying home to work on the cars with me. I knew what that was all about, but figured I'd let it ride a while. She'd get tired of the old man, but she hasn't.

And then the water man showed up twice last month. That got me to thinking for sure. Both times it was Dove left the shop, wiping her hands on a rag as she went into the office to sign the delivery slip and discuss God knows what because how hard could it be to lift one of those water bottles and set it upside-down in the holder for us? Myna was the mover and shaker behind the water deal. Said the well was tasting funny being so close to where we parked the old, demolished cars. I didn't wrangle. She's a beautiful woman, as I said, and a man learns early with such a wife to have a little give in him. And thinking on it, I began to notice that brake fluid aftertaste too, though you can't be sure in a deal like that.

The water man's driving up now, as I speak, pulling his white and blue truck around and looking in the side mirror to see if Dove is about. Well, I am a perverse son of a bitch, and I often have to stop myself for the general good of things. So I go over and thump on the roof of the car so she can hear me over the screeching and sawing racket she's making inside. She looks up startled, like our bird dog caught with its nose in the trash. It's not an expression I like to see. I tilt my head toward the water man's truck, and she glances that way and puts down the snippers and electric saw. She's getting to be a big girl, I notice as she climbs out and doesn't slam the door because she's busy smoothing herself down the way Myna does when she stands up to go to the bathroom all the way in the back corner of Black Charlie's down in Red Oak on a Thursday night.

I decide to watch. Like I have a choice, right?

She's wearing my old Doobie Brothers tee from the 1980 tour with the tear at the neck and washed so thin, well, you get the idea. I vow to use it to change the oil on the Olds soon as she takes it off. The water man has very strong, thick arms, lifting four bottles onto the dolly and easing them down the ramp while Dove stands there with her hands on her hips. I bet she's grinning. She who won't smile a whole day in the garage with me. Nor a whole long evening with the rest of us watching motor sports or tapes of the Derbies we've done well in. All the way to the championship a week ago. Should've won, like I said. Radiator puncture. What's the luck of that, you ask, but I have my family with me. We travel in that old camper, roasting hot dogs and marshmallows over the barbeque I made from an oil pan and a Chevy grill. Handy as you please.

The water man spends a long time unloading today. Off where I don't dare go and see because she'll know what I'm doing. I work real quiet repacking the bearings on Seidel's car he left this morning, my back just a few feet from the office door which we keep open to hear the phone. Once I missed a chance at an interview with ESPN2 keeping the door shut, so now, you know, a person needs the boost once in a while. It's not easy climbing in those cars every week, getting smashed around all afternoon, hoping to come out with enough money to take the family to a good sit-down dinner that night. It's not all fun and games. That's what I would've told them. They caught me at the track just before the second qualifier at the Championships, and we had a few good words, but it's not the same as being featured. I could use a sponsor, I mean I sponsor myself, of course, the garage, but it's becoming more a team deal now, and I just have the family.

What's taking so long in there? This is the tricky part. A man doesn't want to push on his sixteen-year-old daughter, and Dove has never—she's good with that torch. She can gut an engine faster than you can say Jack Sprat, and she's never—she comes home at night. That water man looks older, a lot I mean.

What does a man have to do?

Last night we were watching a rerun of that last Winston Cup race at Rockingham and Dove starts in about steering boxes, ratios of turning, tire pyrometers and depth gages, and which cars picked up a push and which ones were getting loose. It scared me. I looked over at Myna and she lifted her eyebrows as if to say she didn't know either. We're a Demolition Derby family, I wanted to remind her. We have a tradition here. Not many can say that. But I didn't. I watched Dove's eyes taking in the fancy matched outfits the pit crews were wearing, down to the expensive metallic stripe shoes, and the hustle they used shooting that jackhammer around and changing tires, taping and riveting after someone kissed the wall, squirting fuel into the tanks and letting it splash out without a care in the world as the driver peeled off. Her heart was right there, I could tell, and she wasn't bothering to hide it.

She's laughing some more. I lie down on my creeper, slide under the car, and angle myself so I can see through the open door of the office. Really, I am not trying to spy. But she is my daughter, my only Dove, and she could weld a house in a hurricane if you asked her to.

The water man is drinking water from one of those paper cones they dispense right next to the bottle. Dove is turning the spigot on and off fast enough to catch a drop or two at a time on her finger and licking it and he's watching and they're laughing at nothing. Absolutely nothing that I can see. His dolly is standing there with the empties loaded on. And he's wearing cowboy boots. You'd think his feet would get tired. Mine do. I tried, when I was a younger man and courting a beautiful woman, to wear those boots everywhere, but I had to give it up after I crushed my ankles that time in Omaha. I knew the Chevy was too light. Pure luck I survived as long as I did. Damn Crazy Eddie had a Cadillac big as a hearse. It probably *was* an old hearse, now that I think of it. Took the front end of my Chevy and practically shoved it up my nose. Hurt like the dickens. End of my boots and dancing days. Now Myna has to dance with others while I watch. Early in the evening it's other women she knows, wives and girlfriends from the Sears where she works in Automotive. Well, why not, she could rebuild an engine any time she had a mind to, but she's in sales not service. Later, as things get louder, the men get braver and ask her to dance, with little sideways looks at me. I nod as if to say, you go ahead, go right ahead, but she always goes home with me. I used to drink a little too much those nights, but I don't anymore.

As long as I'm under this thing, might as well change the oil, surprise Seidel, he's too cheap to ask for it. Funny thing about that run last week. When I hauled the car back home, got the radiator patched, and turned it on, the engine froze up solid. No oil.

I pull the oil plug and let it drain out in a thick black ooze. Seidel's lucky he's got an engine left.

What's she doing? He's sitting on the edge of my desk, and she's standing between his legs. That's not right. She's got her hands on the water man's thighs, resting there. That's definitely not right. I push myself out toward the door, but she steps back and he stands before I have a chance. She's shaking her head and picking at her fingernails, looking like a kid being asked to get in the car by a stranger. I'm thinking of going in there, but she turns and gives the spigot of that water bottle a good yank, splashing water out in a wasteful stream. That's not what's worrying me though. The water man touches her long braid, his face not looking like a stranger's. But he's not cruel in the way his fingers stroke the straight thick brown hair she has inherited from me and my people. It stops me. I have seen my own hand at such a gesture with my wife. I know it for what it is. There is longing in this water man as he speaks to my daughter. And there is longing in the hand she reaches out for him, the hand I have seen so ferociously gutting wires and hoses and upholstery all morning long, so that now it is nicked and dirty, but full of its own promise nonetheless.

I wonder if she loosened the nuts on my car's oil pan last Sunday, and made the engine freeze up. I suppose if she drove the screwdriver through the grill herself, draining the water, it is the least I could give her.

My whole family can weld, and we often do, a team making the thick, protective seams on the cars I am wrecking. After Dove, T.P. will be next, then little Cleo the baby who at seven still nestles on my beautiful wife's lap in the shade of the awning I've salvaged and rigged along the side of the camper for my family.

I was running good that day, won the first qualifier, only had minor repairs to make for the second. I suppose it was Dove on the engine, tidying up. I guess I can picture her there, now that I think on it. I was in the zone, that's what everybody was saying. I'm no Dale Jarrett, but I was on the money. Driving into the ring, the Pontiac engine chugging and roaring, a little lift there to the right side where Homer had run into us hard last go, I looked around, ready to take every last one of them down. Before the flag dropped, I saw Dove standing there on the sidelines, arms crossed, not waving like the rest of them. In fact, she wasn't even looking at me, I realize now. Her head was turned, looking directly into the sun at something the other side of her, squinting and frowning. If I could, knowing what I know at this moment, I guess I'd get out of that car and run over to her there on the sidelines. Leave the engine running, sure, just climb out and take a hike over the dirt bank and bales of straw and stand there next to my daughter and see what it is she's seen that is taking her that way, not this.

And then the radiator went.

So I replace the filter and gasket, wipe the plug down and tighten the whole thing. Scoot out and pour the new oil in. One of the real pleasures of life is the butterscotch stream arcing into that hole. I can't even say why, but it makes me feel good to see that every time. I screw the cap on and check the oil level, wiping the old dip off on my coveralls first. The new read is clear and full, and I rub my fingers in the oil just because it's what I do. Like I deserve it. I haven't looked up the whole time, you understand. Not once. I keep my back to them, protecting all of us.

Omaha

We're sitting around waiting for the rain to make up its mind, playing Omaha. Rooster deals the four cards down and we all bet. Henry, the transport driver, is on short call in case the track washes out and Fat Fred is all that's left of the pit crew. The others have gone back to their camper with a two-way in case it clears. They've driven half the night to make the show here in Michigan after putting in a full day at work. So it's the four of us, and I raise it by two, and Rooster puts three cards up in the middle for everyone to bet on. It busts my flush, but lo and behold I start on a damn high straight that looks pretty good. Rooster is the best player, but as the crew chief he'd have to have that kind of cool. Carl, the owner, beeps again, and we all stop and look outside the garage at the dripping sky. The weather has scrubbed the face off things pretty good, and the track shines like Black Beauty for a few minutes, if you don't remember the cracks and bumps that'll send cars into the wall today. If the damn sun ever comes out.

Doc, our driver, is in his motor home like always, sleeping or screwing around with his computer. He has to stay local now, Carl ruled after Daytona when Doc snuck off to town and got himself tattoos of his car number thirty-three in big sunbursts on both shoulders. Hurt him enough in the fire suit that he had trouble making the turns. "That was a dumbass kid thing to do," Carl had yelled. "Well, he *is* a dumbass kid," Rooster had muttered, and we all knew the truth of that. But it was Rooster got Doc on the internet and now all we have to worry about on race days is how pink the kid's eyes are from staying up all night talking to his girlfriend in Romania. We already lug five hundred pounds of weights around in case the kid needs to work out. Got that idea from Mark Martin. Doc's not even thirty, he can live on

HoHo's and ice cream bars and still not have to worry about zipping the jump suit up the middle. Sometimes I wish he'd go with the Jesus boys and spend his free time on his knees. Or get married. Time for Doc to settle down. We've all been saying that. Then maybe he'd be grateful to sit around the garage playing this damn card game he's taught us.

Everybody's in. Rooster deals a single card up for everyone and the betting starts again at a leisurely pace. We're in no big damn hurry. We got chips and Coke and cards. While we're waiting for Fat Fred to make up his mind picking up and setting down his cards fifty times like they might change once they have time to think things through on the table again, we all look out the garage doors. The rain has stopped dripping and now we're waiting for the track to dry. Pretty soon they'll have the trucks and blowers out there. Since we've already gone out and tried to run once, we can't touch the cars. Swaps is sitting there under the cover next to us, and it's like he can't wait to get out there. Sometimes I swear I can feel his headlight decals staring right through my back, trying to grab my lungs in his teeth and force me to let him out of here. You're going soon enough, I tell him in my head. I wouldn't be in any big hurry with Doc at the reins. We're lucky to finish a race, let alone have a car whole enough to drive itself onto the transport. Last week on the way to Pocono, Secretariat broke loose in the carrier and smashed his nose in. Had to replace the radiator just to be safe. Great idea naming these things after racehorses. Doc again. He's a piece of brilliance. Got his name from some radio show, Doctor Science. He's always trying to come up with new ideas for the car, things like using Velcro on the windshield to make it easier to replace. Yeah, that'd be safe. He's not a bad kid.

It'd be nice to have a driver like Rusty Wallace or Daryl Waltrip. Somebody with some smarts could help you when things got rough in qualifying or Happy Hour. He'll learn, Rooster says. But I'm still thinking about that experiment he ran at home with us a month ago. He'd seen it on the Home Improvement Channel, which I don't really believe exists. Taped off five sections of oil-stained cement where we worked on the cars and poured Coke on one part, then bleach and soap and some other chemicals he'd picked up on each of the others. The idea was to see which cleaned best, but he'd managed to get ahold of some kind of acid that spilled over the masking tape lines and interacted with the other things and sent us choking out of there as fast as we could go. There was a hole in the floor when the firefighters got through. Carl held us responsible for that one. Said we should know better than to let the kid play around with toxic materials. I haven't felt the same about Coca-Cola since.

Shoot. Rooster gives us one more card up. Three of us have possible straights showing so mine's worth zip. What the hell is this? Carl the owner buzzes in again. Rooster nods as if Carl can see him, then says, "OK," and tosses in a ten-dollar bill. He clicks off and we all bet. Out of all these cards I have to find two in my hand and three in the middle that add up to something in this game called Omaha. Fat Freddy takes no time at all which is not good. Henry who never talks or does anything but hold the unlit cigarette in his teeth, grimaces and folds. It's up to me. High or High-Low. I've got nothing to speak of, but damn if I'm going to let Rooster or Fat Freddy get away without a run for their money. Behind me the car sighs and creaks.

Everybody's talking about how nice it'd be if NASCAR let us put computers in the cars so Winston Cup would have telemetry like Indy cars. Sure, get some bio-cam on the driver too. Like at Charlotte when the blower hose came off and was spewing hot air in Doc's face for a hundred laps. He was cooking in there, but he never said a word over the radio except during the fourth caution when he said that maybe they could think about putting air conditioning in the cars this summer before it got really hot.

Cars cost a hundred grand now, and we couldn't afford to go racing if the cost went up much more. Besides, shouldn't the driver have to do something?

If I could just go Low, I could maybe take it, but with this damn game, you have to take both High and Low. Rooster ignores Doc's callback for a minute to watch me with those big cow brown eyes behind the wire rim glasses. Reason he's Rooster is the crowing he makes when his team does well. Fast pit, good setup on the car, pole position, or win. It's been a while since any of us heard it though, and his gray hair says he's not getting any younger. The loudspeaker announces that the track's drying now, the front has moved on through. Not expecting another one till dark. Time enough to get the race in. There's ESPN to consider, the television crew pulling the plastic sheets off the cameras as the big blower trucks inch down the track side by side. Pretty soon they'll ask us to pull the cars out, drive around. With the headers pouring 1,200 degrees onto the track when they're starting, and 1,800 degrees when they're full out, the surface dries damn fast.

"OK, OK." I fold the cards face down and shove my chair back a couple of inches so I'm nearer the car. Around the time Doc fires the engine and rolls onto the track he's going to ask us which of the identical thirty-threes he's in, and like always, we're going to say, "it's your favorite, Swaps, the fastest." Then he's going to wait half a lap before he says, "wasn't that what you said last week?"

There'll be lots of green-flag racing today, because at Michigan you can run three wide in places. It's a fast track with easy passing. If Doc's on, he can run 200 m.p.h into turn one and still finish the race. Just has to watch his fuel and turn three. It's one of the places we use the cold air box. But he has to watch going into turn three and letting the car drift up and lean against the wall of air there. Then there's the setup. If the sun comes out, the track changes, and I'll be sticking spring rubbers in and pulling them out all afternoon.

Rooster has a straight flush. Son of a damn gun. He takes our money in one handy swipe and it disappears. Henry leans back and almost tips the chair over, catching his cowboy boot heel against the leg of my chair just in time. He lifts the team hat and resettles it, his cigarette half-damp with spit bounces up and down in his grin. "Another game?" Fat Freddy says, but Rooster shakes his head and glances at the TV set we're using for the Weather Channel. Later we'll move it outside and keep it tuned to the race while we listen to the spotters and the radio. I'm doing the fuel mileage today, so I have all my charts and calculations ready. All week I've tried to explain it to Doc, about running leaner and taller, not using the engine so hard, but making sure he keeps enough fuel in the engine so it doesn't burn up. He's not a bad kid, if the other drivers would leave him alone. It's his rookie year, and they're testing him every step of the way. Can he take it, is he patient, can they put him in the wall every race until he's so sick of it or we're so sick of it he disappears back into dirt tracks?

We all stand up and Henry takes custody of the cards. Fat Freddy trots off to call the pit crew and Rooster walks out to meet Carl coming down from the owners' meeting. I'm the one lifts the cover from Swaps and peers inside the dark to see how he's feeling. Everything smells good in there—oil, paint, and the wet metal scent of new welding.

There's the picture of Einstein with the wild hair on the dash. We'll have to take it off if he ever gets the on-board camera, but for now, it makes the kid happy to think we think there's a connection. The seat looks inviting but I know it's not an invitation I'll ever take. My job is making springs, putting shocks in, taking care of the chassis and engine, fuel and tires. I pat the window frame and notice the attachment on the window net is coming loose. Have to fix that, can't have the kid falling out on his head before he wins his first race for us.

Maybe things are beginning to look up. Last week it was Earnhardt himself, the Intimidator, who said, "I stuck my nose out there, I probably coulda drilled him a couple of times—" But he'd gone on and let Doc run ahead of him a couple of laps until the right rear tire started going down and we tried pulling the kid in, but the rear end tore loose and he spun like a damn ballerina up and away, tapped the wall lightly, then floated down into the grass. He was damn proud of himself saving the car as much as he did, and not taking anyone else with him. For once I had to agree and thank Earnhardt. See, we told each other, there is hope. And that was with only one roof flap working to slow the car so it wouldn't go airborne. Heck, with two working, who knew what was possible. You see, no matter how many times we go over the car, there's always something doesn't work. Look at those Yates engines blowing up for a month until they realized they couldn't just replace the broken or worn parts. Now it's Rusty Wallace's turn. And even with on-board computers, those Indy cars break down. Nothing is completely predictable.

I can hear Doc whistling as he comes in the garage looking new as a kid starting school. His sandy hair is buzz cut like the boys are doing now. No mustache, nothing but that corn-fresh face and the kind of reflexes an astronaut could envy.

"I have an idea—" he starts in, and I nod, bending to find the tools I need for the window net. You see, he's not a bad kid, with his big restless hands touching the car, the tools, the back of the chair Henry was tipping back in. They're like two big pale moths, lunas I believe they're called. This morning there was one as big as the palm of my hand clamped to the screen window of my motel room. We stared at each other, both of us stuck there by the rain pouring off the eaves in a straight silver curtain onto the broken cement walk. It seems silly somehow to trust all our futures in those hands, I think as I tighten the clamp and test the net again and again. After a few laps today he'll get racy like all the youngsters do, but he mustn't get hurt, he must ride as safe as we can make him.

It's true that in racing you either win or you lose. Usually you don't think of the third thing, but there is one. An excluded middle. It's Omaha, where you don't go racing, where you do nothing but wait and work and wait while it rains and dries and rains some more. It's what you do in between times that takes up most of your life.

The Trouble with the Truth

I married a man who loves weddings and all I have to show for it is the gold stub of an Elvis Tour bus ticket. He'd just lost his job changing tires with the race team after he cracked a ball joint dropping the car from the jack. It fell off as the driver headed for the track. Lucky, was what they said. Could've cost us the race, maybe the car and driver too. This was the very sad story he told that night a year ago in Billy's Bar getting drunk and watching video replays of old races on the TV mounted in the corner with the sound turned off and the handicapped words printed in white across the bottom. When did they decide people need to watch TV while they drink? I asked him. We nursed our seven and sevens till closing time and haven't been separated since. Until now, that is. I pick up the Elvis Tour bus ticket and put it in the same box as the plastic bride and groom from the cake my cousin Mavis baked.

Five years ago Mavis went all the way to Saint Paul, Minnesota for the Vo Tech cooking course, but quit after ice sculptures and wedding cakes, her two specialties which supplement Lonnie's income as an over the road trucker. He's such a good Christian he won't take hauling jobs that don't serve the Lord, so he spends a lot of time at home watching the *700 Club* and eating pretzels in a slow, almost demented way. And drinking water. You'd think he was an Arab, Mavis complains. Mavis is also Christian and tucks little crosses into her creations, regardless of how the customer feels about it. It's become a game at receptions to find the crosses on the ice swans and sailfish, or the three tiered cakes bogged down by clumps of bright unidentifiable flowers. Mavis only got a c- on the cake section, she told me one day, but that was prejudiced on the part of the instructor who was a man. What did he know about cake baking? What Mavis is good at is texture and flavor. My own secret ingredients, she smiles whenever anyone comments. My cake was cranberry-apple flavored and the crosses sat deep inside the red and yellow clumps supposed to be roses, but resembling oranges instead. The crosses themselves were hard white sugar creations made in molds Lonnie ordered off a Christian shopping channel as a surprise when Mavis opened her business. For Easter and Christmas, Mavis makes cross cakes with three of those little sugar crosses standing in a row along the crossbeam and gives them to all her family and friends. Sometimes it feels more like a burden than a gift.

The man who loves weddings acted like Dracula when he saw the first cross cake and refused to enter the kitchen again until I hid it. He's as bad as our dog, Frank, who is so afraid of pigs that the day I brought home the big black plastic pig bank I'd won at the auto parts store where I work, he scurried out of the house and hid under the porch. I've had to hide the pig just like I hide the cross cakes when they arrive.

Maybe it's a guilty conscience, I decide after I meet his other wife Doris in Osceola a month ago. How many wives does a man need? I yell and he tells me the other one is an accident. Accident? No, a car hitting a tree is an accident, I correct him. That actually sends him out to look for a job, something no amount of nagging has been able to do. Working at the garage, he'll be able to file for divorce from his other wife and me both. We're going to get married again as soon as he's done with all the legal work, he's promised. That will give him three weddings in a row, I calculate. But there lurks in my imagination the idea that other wives could pop up, other women and weddings he's forgotten about as well.

I suppose you were drinking that time too, I ask sarcastically as we sit in the booth of the Big Chef waiting for our burgers. He gets that pig worried dog expression on his face and shrugs. He is a small, compact man, almost good at a lot of things, Doris and I have discovered. Maybe he did marry her in the accidental mood of the moment. He has a lot of those. In the garage, they can barely trust him to change the oil, patch a flat. He only keeps the job because I give them discounts on their parts at the auto store now. On our honeymoon to Graceland, he somehow broke the light fixture in the tour bus bathroom, and the rest of the way people could be heard thumping and cursing in the dark as they peed.

He started bigger in life than where he is now, that much Doris and I do know. But his story is as much a history of mistakes as weddings.

Once, when he made it all the way to Busch Grand National cars, he reversed the camber on the tires at Martinsville. Instead of getting full layover on the corners, the car slid up into the wall. Well, anyone can make a mistake, he says. Doris and I know there is nothing like a man in trouble to win a woman's heart. Look at Mavis and Lonnie. Look at Jesus. Look at Doris and me.

It might be better if he took up religion, I tell Doris when we meet at Billy's Bar. Turner's garage is born again. I guess it wouldn't be the worst thing that could happen. We both stare at our rum and Cokes with the little bubbles strung like beads up the sides of the glasses.

Doris is my height, five-five, and medium build like me. We could be cousins sooner than Mavis, who is a too tall blonde with none of the fun in her angles. We're serviceable types, Doris and me. We're the women pushing kids into cars, shoving grocery carts down aisles, working behind counters. We don't ask, how could I be so blind? Our vocabulary is limited to things like: what shall I do with the wedding photo, when do I change my driver's license, how do I tell my family? Looking at the two of us, no wonder he made a mistake, forgot he already had a wife. Like buying a second bag of flour or a book you've already read. People forget. And he loves weddings. Desire like that can override just about anything, I guess. Doesn't necessarily make you a bad person.

Someone punches in some George Strait, who I have never particularly liked, his songs having the same qualities as his face: good-looking and bland. What we need here is some outlaw music, some Steve Earle with his junked-up drunk voice chasing the words that come stumbling along a little too fast for him. Even in the sad songs he sounds both mad and about to burst out laughing. And there's something about right now that makes me feel the same way. Doris and I heard about each other by accident from Mavis who got an order for the same cake I had at my wedding. Seems Doris's four-year anniversary is coming up and he'd fallen in love with that cranberry-apple flavor from our cake. He gave her Mavis's number. So we're meeting for the first time here.

I thought he was at the track those weekends, I say.

Doris looks at me with these blue eyes that say rain is coming down inside here, honey.

Do you think there are others? Wives, I mean.

She has been so surprised by the first second wife that I don't think her mind has traveled to that next rest stop yet. Neither of us has children. Neither of us smokes, though all around us the air is cloudy from the drinkers lighting up and blowing their exhausted day into the dark room. Billy's has knotty pine walls so old the varnish is orange and a brown linoleum floor so dotted with black cigarette burns it looks like the original pattern. Set off the road, there's a sprawl of gravel parking lot in front so everyone can see who's here. I personally know four or five different guys who park their pickups at the used car lot a block away and walk over so their wives don't find them here. It's late afternoon, and outside the sun is shining like some holy war is about to begin, and the way it stabs through the holes where the black paint has peeled off the front windows, you'd think it was the Almighty Himself pointing fingers at all of us crouched down in dark safety here. I try to imagine the cake Doris orders showing up tiered with crosses marching to the top like tiny soldiers. Scare the bejesus out of him.

You remember that time he worked as the gas man at Watkins Glen? Doris stops and takes a drink.

I nod. That wasn't his fault either. They told him to get every drop in and it splashed back into his eyes.

She looks at the table, brushes the scarred green Formica with her hand, then looks at the jukebox. Wonder who he married that time?

There is this instant picture of the race at Daytona where he lost the thread chaser and they couldn't fix the stud while the other cars raced around and around like sonic zippers. I drain my rum and Coke and raise two fingers. We're both going to need more.

I guess we should be mad or something. But I'm not pissed off. Not at you, anyway. I guess I'm not mad at him either. What do you suppose that means?

She shrugs and finishes her drink, using the tip of her tongue to lick the ice cubes clean. I'd done that same thing a moment before. When you get down to it we're all pretty much alike, it seems, and that makes the hair-thin differences important. Maybe that's what he notices, and while it looks like what he's doing is buying the same shirt over and over, what he's really doing is falling in love with these tiny differences. I could probably pick us out of any crowd, we'd be so alike, but he'd know the truth, how each of us has come to stand in the sorrow of time.

So Doris and I sit here a while longer, watching the sun go down through the holes in the painted window, the fingers of light slowly pulling back until all that is left is spread on the gravel parking lot—pink, then gray, then the yellow green of the fluorescents coming on. On the jukebox a CD sticks, making a snap snap like a bug zapper for half an hour before someone notices. Doris and I watch the endless negotiations of the men and women at the surrounding tables and the bar. After a few more drinks, they begin to remind me of cars racing around a track, bumping and pushing, running close enough side by side they could carry on a conversation if not for the roaring engines. There is so much noise here tonight, Doris and I have to repeat each word in a shout and find our sentences getting shorter and shorter until finally we only gesture and nod. We get grace this way, for a few minutes, the perfect understanding that can come briefly when two people are drawn and held with enough force to a single place. I figure the man who loves weddings must recognize how irresistible we all seem to each other at moments like this, just before our world dissolves again with another crashing disaster. He never says mistakes were made. He calls them accidents, and it's hard to hate a man like that. That's the trouble with the truth.

Losing Downforce

He felt his car wash up the track again, the tires going away some more. Louise was the first woman crew chief he'd ever had, and he was so bound and determined to have his say, he'd made the mistake of not taking on new tires last pit stop. He fought the front end, then the back wobbling toward the wall, and inched back down to the groove the other cars were driving in.

Jimmie appeared in his side mirror trying to nudge on by. Jimmie was the leader and if he lapped him, he'd have to work that much harder to get back, so he moved down, running side by side toward the corner. "Shit, oh shit," he muttered to the silence of the radio. Louise wasn't reassuring him the way she should be. Damn women. He felt the car slow with Jimmie tucked right up next to him, close enough to french kiss.

"Jimmie's on your left side trying to get by," the spotter crackled over the radio so loudly it made his ears ring even with the roar of engine and track noise numbing his head. "No shit, Sherlock." He fought the wheel, glancing over at the flash of black he caught on the right. Perfect, Lane's black car was inching up trying to pass high where he'd been running all day, to capture the lead from Jimmie. He could feel the car really starting to go away, the aerodynamics messed up with the side-by-side racing.

"Better get outta there," the spotter said as the corner loomed ahead.

"Come on, come on," he urged, but the car didn't have anything more to give him. Jimmie's nose edged in front and Lane was coming down on him.

"Watch it—"

Jimmie's bump sent the car shivering in front. Shit—he wasn't going to make the corner as he nudged up toward Lane who tried to get out of the way and couldn't when the rear end let go and they both ploughed right up the track into the wall, once, then spun, then down and around, hit again by another car, then into the inside barrier, hit again, spinning until the sheared metal came to a shattered stop nosing the concrete.

"You OK? You OK?" the radio kept squawking, but he was too pissed to answer. He ripped the net off the window and started to climb out into the arms yanking at him. He was going to kick the shit out of that Lane kid, then get Jimmie after the race. The arms kept arguing with him as he struggled toward the other car smoking a few yards away.

Later, when he'd been released by the medical team and driven back to the garage, Louise just looked at him and shook her head. "Perfectly good car," was all she said.

"It had a push," he insisted.

She eyed him in a way that reminded him of a lot of women he'd lied to—his mom, his teachers, and lately his wife. What the hell gave women the right to know when a man wasn't telling the truth? Another man would give him that, know he was lying, but give it to him for the excuse he needed. A person needed some pride.

"You could've won that race," she said. "The setup was perfect. Best it's run all season." She was his age, early forties, and looking at her jaw was like looking in the mirror when he shaved. The thing that irritated him most was that the dark roots of her blonde hair always showed. Like she didn't think it worth the bother. His wife always looked nice. She made it a practice now that the television people were around all the time. With the gimme cap on, Louise's hair sticking out the sides, you couldn't see the roots, but in the garage you could and it bothered him.

"She's the best we can get and lucky to have her," the team owner had told him. "She's taken Carl's team to the top five year ends in the Busch Lights ten times. Now you need to settle down and drive, let us worry about the rest." But it worried him. First the old crew chief's let go, now a woman. Next thing, they'd be looking for a new driver.

He waited while she consulted the printouts on the race, running the columns of numbers with that short, thick, no-nonsense finger of hers. Suddenly, he wished she smoked. Something. His wife had told him not to cause trouble, they needed the job to finish putting the kids through college. They'd been a young, hot couple in bed, popping out the five kids one-two-three like marbles on a plate, racing featherlites and outlaws on dirt tracks, running from one place to another in their camper. Those were good, crazy times, not like today. Hell, they used to duct tape the cars together to keep 'em going, and they listened to him, did what he said because he was the driver and trying to win, and he did, that was how he got to Winston Cup and was Rookie of the Year, and then won a race or two a season. Now he was down to praying for a top twenty finish. They were going to dump him. He could feel it. This Louise, she was the beginning of the end.

"Probably my fault the tires went away right after the pit," he offered, willing to concede a little.

"Uh huh," she grunted and turned over a sheet. The skin at her throat was crepey too. Freckled and angry looking from all the days at the tracks in the hot sun. What made a woman want to give up her beauty like that?

"We were running so good, I wanted to get the bonus points for leading a few laps, put in a strong top ten finish. That's why I asked for the short pit. Car was really hooked up there for a while," he tried, "you all did a good job."

She put the sheets down on the shiny hood of the backup car. "Think the car had a push coming into turn two?" Those faded blue-white eyes stared right back at him, trying to get something out of him. He'd as soon talk to the clothes on the line as her right now. Her eyes about the color of his favorite pair of jeans, the holey ones he'd brought with him from the dirt track days, couldn't get one leg in 'em now. There were months when they were all he had to put on and he wanted to remember that. Once he caught his wife dressing the Halloween scarecrow on the front yard in those jeans and he'd thrown a regular fit. Where'd a person get eyes the color of old Levi's anyway?

He shrugged.

"What do you think—broken shock mount, maybe?" She tilted her head at him in a way he couldn't imagine any man finding endearing. Not that she was bad-looking, she was OK. She was just, well, truth be told, he never liked any of his crew chiefs, not really.

He shrugged again.

"Set of bad tires then?" She gestured toward the heap of metal behind her. "Hard to say now."

He felt something in him let go. OK, OK, have it your own way, he heard a voice sigh. His chest got smaller and he almost hoped it was some kind of injury so she'd feel a little sorry, but he'd checked out fine. Couple of bruises coming on his legs and arms, but nothing. He was damn lucky. Did she know how lucky it was out there today? He might have been killed—

"Doc says you're fine. Too shaken up to do a few test runs on the backup car after the race?" She looked him over like one of her damn cars, biting the edge of her lower lip in a callused spot that looked red and chapped. "We get the setup right, we can use it next time. And we can check for that push—"

"I should've listened." He couldn't say, "to you."

She picked up the telemetry sheets and started to roll them in a thick circle, her knuckles red and weathered-looking.

"The tires went away. Then Jimmie tapped me and that was all she wrote." He felt his face flush and burn as she looked out the big open doors of the garage toward the roar and whine of the cars on the track followed by the wake of crowd noise that came as an after echo of each lap.

"We're not getting any younger, you and me." She looked back at him with a slight curve of smile on her lips which surprised him. "Can't afford disorganized thinking."

"No," he admitted.

"Well, an old dog can still hunt. Just needs a few more tricks to keep up. Think about it." She pulled her hat off and he could see the lines on her forehead, the commas beside her mouth, and the patchy net on her cheeks. "We're bringing up that kid from the truck circuit next season. Running two cars. You can help."

There it was. Maybe better to kiss the wall goodnight. He pictured the final slamming force, the fiery flip in the air, the magnificent fireball tumble down the track, the collapsing chest, windpipe, face. No—he still had kids to put through college, the mortgage to finish paying off on their house in Holcomb so his wife could be comfortable. Insurance wouldn't cover all that. What would she do then? She was his age, five kids out of that body had taken its toll, too. He tried to picture her working like Louise. No, she'd worked her last day, he'd told her when he finally started making some money. The day he signed with the team, he'd picked her up at the supper club where she tended bar and given her the keys to a new car.

That was the dream, not this other thing, the stubborn I'm-right-about-it-all thing he'd been racing on lately. Like some dirt track kid, full of attitude, not caring how many times you wrecked 'cause you always walked away. Those days were going away now too. There was the bad crash at Talladega three years ago, another at Rockingham nine months later when he'd finally come back from his injuries. Darlington was lucky, and today—

"I was lucky today," he said softly, looking out at the bright blur of cars.

"That you were, my friend," she put a hand on his shoulder. "But I have a feeling things can get real interesting—once you stop running off your balls and let your brains do some work for a change."

He laughed. "Maybe a combination?"

"I'll leave that ratio up to you," she said. "By the way, Lane's been medivacked and Jimmie's engine let go while you were being checked over."

"Hell of a day." He looked around the garage at the tools strewn everywhere, half-empty cans of pop sitting on every flat surface, and the racecars resting bright and hopeful as young tropical birds on their racks.

You Know I Am Lying

 As my mother says, cattle have a good life, but they pay for it in the end. But then, she was always at sixes and sevens. What does that mean? I used to ask her, but she'd go on pulling the cucumbers off the vines with that little tug and twist and placing them careful as eggs in the basket she carried. I don't see those anymore, the rectangular farm baskets that fit over your arm with the deep sides. Not an Easter basket kind of affair. The slats were wide and sturdy enough to carry quart jars of stewed tomatoes or pickles. Out in the garden with the long rows separating the vegetables, she'd remind me not to plant the cukes near the cantaloupe if I wanted to keep their flavors apart.

All summer, I'd watch the cuke and squash and melon vines to make sure they stayed segregated to their own sections along the fence bordering the cattle pen so it was only a short throw in the winter tossing the manure over the fence to make the soil rich and worm-thick in the spring. My job was hoeing and it is a job I hope never to repeat now that so much has changed. I will miss those pickles though. I still have the Heinz pickle pin Mom's great-grandma got as a child at the first World's Fair in Chicago in 1893. Not many people knew about the exhibit, but I come from a long line of avid picklers and it was in the genes to track down that booth and come home with the prized pin that's been handed down with the family Bible through the women until Mom had only me, and that meant a male getting possession of things he shouldn't, I guess. Mr. Heinz was a man, I reassure myself. He thought up the card enticing fairgoers to his booth for a free gift—the pin. It was that one brush with fame—Mr. Heinz himself handing my great-grandmother the pickle pin she wore first as a brooch and later on a thin gold chain like a locket—that remains our family story. Until now that is.

The auctioneer has packed his truck and left. The yard is cluttered with flyers, paper napkins from the food table, and pop cans, and inside the house here, well, each room has one little thing left over to remind me—things nobody wanted. The half barn door we used as a coffee table after Dad and Uncle Harry had the argument arm-wrestling. As a bald-headed man said when I told him the price, "For seven bucks, I could buy me some chickens." I know, it still looks exactly like what it was: the barn stall door Mom had me lift off its hinges and haul to the house. The manure stains are so deep, no amount of scrubbing could pull them out of the wood. Kneeling, I run my hand over the edge worn smooth and shiny brown by years of hands pushing and pulling it. My father's and his father's and his father's hands, and then last of all mine. Maybe it was taking the door down, bringing it in the house that made things begin to fail in general, like Mom used to hint. I've wondered about that.

Hoeing the garden meant chasing the bull snakes that liked to sun themselves in the hot dirt waiting for mice and toads and small rabbits. They were never in a good mood, but then neither was I, out there in the heat of the day, my shirt tossed over the chicken wire fence, jeans sticking to the backs of my legs, my skin pringly tight with sun baking itself into me. And my hands, no matter if I wore gloves or not, my hands would blister before they callused. Adding more to the history of that damn hoe than I ever wanted, I think I wore that handle smooth in the years I spent out there. Now some woman took it home to paint it red and use it for her rose garden. She probably only has to deal with garter snakes and they're quick to get out of your way.

Bull snakes, they'll bite, you bother them. It hurts like getting stung by a handful of bees. And the way they lie there, so big and thick, like rattlers, every time I came on one of those critters I had to remind myself we didn't have poisonous snakes here in Iowa. They'd rear up and open their jaws and act mad as all get out, trying to convince me I didn't need to hoe out that ragweed with such a good start in the bean patch. It was all I could do not to bring that sharp edge down on their heads, but Mom thought it bad luck and worse to kill a snake in the garden. I'd of liked her to get out there and have to chop weeds around those pissy old men. That's what I decided one day, they were lying around like they were retired old farmers, my grandfather up to the house those couple of years before he died. They probably had all kinds of youngsters out there working themselves to death too.

Dad was on that tractor from dawn till dark a lot of days. Seems like we were always haying or getting ready to hay. He'd go to town and hire some day workers, bring 'em out and we'd work like sons of bitches until noon, the hired men doing half of what I could do since they weren't used to the heat and pure drudgery of lifting bale after bale and throwing it on the wagon and then having to stack them in the barn when the wagon got full. They got a taste of what I did and you could tell how grateful they were for the day money as they piled into the truck for the ride back to town at dark, despite the good food Mom fixed and the jar of pickles she sent home with each of them. I tried to tell her these men were not going to want those pickles, but she thought it was my usual selfish nature and ignored me. But I'll tell you, about the saddest thing a person could see is finding the sweet pickles you have helped your own mother make swimming in broken glass down the end of the road in the deep weeds by the mailbox.

After she filled the basket with cukes, she'd bring them in and dump them in the sink, and for some reason, there was always some stupid grasshopper trying to spring out but sliding down the slick porcelain sides instead. It was my job to catch it and throw it back outside, though why in the world we would be adding grasshoppers to the world, I couldn't say. It was like the snake deal though, you weren't allowed to kill bugs while she was making her pickles. Pickle day wasn't quite like other canning days. Grapes she harvested late summer, making thick sweet juice and jelly when the mood struck her of a morning before it got hot. Jellies got made all the time, in fact. Tomatoes were a nasty time, taking all day for days, the steam boiling up in clouds that coated the cabinets with sweat that dripped back down in brown streaks, and my mother's face and hands looking scalded themselves as she slipped the skins off the tomatoes, hot from the water, and pushed the red flesh whole into jars or smashed them into the sieve for the juice. Her hands would be raw looking until well into October from canning, and I'd shy from her touch on my cheek which I see now was not the right thing to do.

Pickle days she'd hum to herself as she took the clean cukes wrapped in a clean dishtowel she made from flour sacks and went down to the basement, leaving me standing at the top of the stairs to turn off the light when she had landed safely. She was ever an economical person. And particularly guarded about those pickles. No man in our family had ever had the recipe and she wasn't about to share it with me. Being her only child, I used to wonder, but didn't dare raise the issue. So each summer she would make her pickles, enter them in the county and state fairs, and always win a prize. I'm making it sound a lot easier than it was. Sometimes in the middle of the night, I'd hear her creeping down those stairs to check her pickles, muttering to herself and banging around in the kitchen if things weren't going right, or humming back up to bed if they were fine. I should've known how important they were to her. I mean, it doesn't take a genius to see that.

I go into the kitchen to see what's left. One can of Miller and a rumpled piece of old lettuce on the counter next to where the fridge stood. There's a black square of dirt, dust, and insect bodies in its place, and I drop the lettuce in the middle like topping because that's about what this feels like: a dirt sandwich. I pop the beer and take a quick swig, swallowing before I can really taste the warm grainy suds. Outside, the sun is dropping back behind the hay barn, hanging a moment there like a red-orange balloon caught in the trees of the windbreak on the hill at the edge of the eighty-acre pasture. There was a time when I studied the sky. As a boy growing up alone on a small southern Iowa farm, I had to invent a lot when I wasn't working. About this time in August, for instance, Venus is very low and brilliant in the sky after sunset. Then gradually you'll find Spica and Mars left of it. Procyon in Canis Minor, the little dog, will be the brightest star in the constellation. The heads of Castor and Pollux, the Gemini twins, will be to the moon's left. And reddish Betelgeuse, the shoulder of Orion, with Procyon and Sirius form the nearly equilateral Winter Triangle. When I made that discovery, it was as if winter was always out there, all the time, just waiting for its turn. The year got a lot shorter after that.

I salute the sun's last red lip at the horizon with the can of warm beer and put it down. Around me the house ticks and creaks as if it's restless now that the floors and walls are freed of our clutter. One of my mother's old dishtowels sits wadded up on the counter which looks dirty for the first time that I can remember. Automatically, I swipe at the black dots of bug carcasses and crumbs and sweep them into the sink, turning on the water to wash them away. There is a big mauve stain in the middle of the towel when I flap it open and shake it. Straining wild plum pulp for jelly. That summer Dad offered to pay me a nickel a sparrow to clear the thicket so there'd be enough plums for her jelly. But he told me not to mention it to her. Every morning she'd ask me what I was doing down there when I came back to the house scratched and sweaty, my hands dotted with blood. I'd lie and smile mysteriously, counting the profit silently. After the first day, I negotiated the deal to include the eggs whose smashed shells I would present for verification along with the dead bodies. Sparrows were a nuisance around the farm, dirtying the grain, eating fruit and vegetables intended for us, and creating such a clatter, it drove my father wild.

After the first couple of days it seemed like a simple job. I dug out the catalog Dad got from something called "u.s. Cavalry, World's Finest Military and Adventure Equipment" to prepare my assault, and marked several items that might be useful in addition to my BB gun. What I wanted was a knife, something to lop the sparrow heads off so I wouldn't be stuck with the whole body which ended up stinking and sometimes maggoty by the end of the hot day when my dad would come out to the tool shed with me to make the count. The Seal Team Knife was over a hundred dollars, but it was at the top of my list. I'd settle for the World War II Commemorative Knife, which I thought my dad would like since he'd been there, but I put the German-style Paratrooper Knife with the side saw-edge for versatility at $12.99 as a realistic choice. And I needed a scope and a mount. The 4 x 25 Assault was waterproof and fogproof which would allow me to kill in the rain too. Checking the prices though, I knew my chances of getting either were pretty slim unless I saved for them myself. Which I could do if I made enough off these sparrows. Then with the scope, I could make even more and save for something else.

By the end of the first week, the sparrows were so suspicious of me that they raised a panicked cry and flew frantically in and out and over the thicket every time I appeared. Since I'd raided all the nests within reach, I faced the problem of climbing the thorny trees for those higher up with the sparrows now dive-bombing me the way they did crows and hawks in their territory. It hurt, too. Those tiny sharp-pointed beaks left dots of blood that dried to sore scabs on my scalp which I didn't dare show my mother. Then there were the eggs. At first it was fun throwing them as hard as I could on the ground or heaving them at the steers when they pushed up to feed. It always seemed so hilarious to watch the expression on their dumb white faces when the egg popped open on their heads and dripped down. I liked getting paid every day too. Then one afternoon I noticed something. Some of the eggs were going to hatch, and instead of a nice clean little yolk, there was this pink wet thing dripping bloody yellow. Instead of lifting my foot to squash it, I turned away, keeping track of these things out of the corner of my eye. By the next morning some of them were gone, slurped up by the barn cats or raccoons or snakes, but one was still there, the form in motion as if it were trying to wriggle back into life, until I leaned close enough to see the insects and maggots replacing it.

My father called me lazy when I told him most of the sparrows were gone and the rest were too smart now. My mother was shelling peas every morning to be put in the pressure cooker before they were canned that week. One morning while I sat with her, trying to keep up with her quick fingers, she nodded toward the gun in the corner and said, "I know what you were doing out there." I felt as if I'd thrown a jar of her precious pickles in the ditch myself.

It was a bumper plum crop my father and I harvested in twenty-gallon buckets. My mother made the jelly dutifully, but not very joyfully while my father helped. He was his usual laughing self, drinking beer and kidding around. That towel though, I remember how she took a brand new one she'd just made to strain the pulp because it kept clogging the wire sieve, and how the strands of pulp had that red-blue cast that looked so like old rotting muscles and nerves, and how my father dragged two fingers through it and leaned his head back and dropped that mess in his mouth and somehow that reminded me of the sparrows. I have no stomach for plums anymore.

My father's troubles came later, from the stomach problems he'd been having since the war. Short-gut syndrome, they called it. His intestine was partially destroyed by the time I was well into high school, and they were trying to figure out if he needed a new liver too. The VA wasn't particularly helpful until they heard about a study being conducted with experimental drugs for transplants that would be paid for by the drug company. Well, that was not such a good thing, as it turned out.

With my boyhood military career cut short, I took a brief run at raising steers for 4-H, but my heart wasn't in four-leggeds. I still worked haying and hoeing and painting and cutting weeds and grass and helping Mom, but I didn't feel as connected to the farm. One day I was poking around back of the old hog barn when I found a car chassis. The sheet metal body had long since been dismantled piece by piece for repairing the hog fence and barn roof which was tin. I knew this because Dad and I had put in the replacements. Hooking up the small Ford tractor, I pulled the chassis free and hauled it up to rest near the tool shed where I began to work on something I could ride around in after the cows or over the fields when I had to take lemonade to Dad. Those were my selfless plans in the beginning. I think my mom was happy to see me spending my time on construction rather than destruction, and she was busy making pickles anyway. I salvaged a motor off the abandoned Allis-Chalmers that could still hump along like a spider on a mirror if you babied it, but lacked the strength for real work. It was the first motor I took apart and got back together with most of the pieces in the right places. Just puttering around the barnyard, maneuvering around the chicken coop and cistern back up between the mulberry trees—what a proud day. I'd cut the chassis down and rewelded it. I'd known enough to do that since I was eight. For safety, I had to know how to help Dad if anything went wrong. I learned to drive early and could go anywhere, even the highway down to the hay and cornfields, on the tractor.

I was so thrilled that first week, I left the hose running in the garden and flooded the cukes so bad several vines washed out and I had to kneel there with my knees and toes sinking in the mud trying to rebuild the mounds before Mom came out and saw the destruction. The next day when the mud baked dry, it looked like I'd been trying to leave casts of my hands and feet all over her cuke bed. She only looked heartbroken and didn't say anything when she saw it.

That wasn't the worst thing I did, I think now, as the yard turns violet with evening and the barn swallows stab in and out of the dark entrance feeding. From somewhere east, a swoop of bats comes in that too quick way that says they're not birds, flying flawlessly between wires, trees, barns, and sheds, to disappear across the field.

By high school I was building and modifying engines and cars for other kids who wanted to show off or go racing around. I wasn't home much, or rather I was here, but I was out in the shed where I worked, having reclaimed it from the debris of three generations of farmers, pouring a good concrete floor myself and hooking up the wiring despite Dad's predictions that I was going to burn the whole place down. Thinking back on it, I didn't hoe much anymore, didn't pick vegetables either. I guess Mom was on her own the way I was. I never gave it much thought. That's the way kids are, the volume in your own world turns up so loud you can't see or hear anybody else. Then when I had one semester to go, a call came from Mom's cousin Albert down in North Carolina asking if I would be interested in coming to work for him. I'd written him a few times after she told me who he was, and he'd never answered, but I never gave up. I just couldn't. Albert built racecars and said he had an opening, one of the guys up and quit on him. I wasn't going to get rich, but I'd learn a heck of a lot.

Mom and Dad were both against it, Dad partly because he was worried about Mom since he was so weak with diarrhea and dehydration from the intestinal failure. He'd lost a lot of weight and took a lot longer to get chores done, but he still wouldn't let me do much. He'd put the fields in the soil bank and hadn't planted for three years so by the time the offer came up our fields were filled with weeds we'd turn over for green manure each fall. He'd given up all but a couple of steers for beef and a single hog to butcher in the fall, which was like killing a family member. Mom told me not to worry, but said I couldn't leave until I graduated high school. Two nights later I left, driving the Chevy with the rebuilt motor that was barely legal in anybody's book in Iowa. I was hoping those southerners would be more tolerant of loud engines and speed.

I haven't been a bad son. My parents were just a little old-fashioned. When they tried the transplant, Dad lingered for a while, always on the verge of rejection until the infection swept in and took him away. Mom, well, her heart was weak, it turns out. She didn't last the winter, living out here with her sister. I came back some, when I could, in between races, and then a bit longer in winter these past three years. It wasn't until I was getting ready for the sale here, two days ago, when I went to the basement to drag stuff upstairs, that I realized what had happened.

See, I'd avoided the fruit cellar, as we called the little room lined with floor-to-ceiling pine plank shelves for canned fruit and vegetables. I'd already hauled the big, thick, gray sauerkraut tub upstairs, the old iron bedstead I slept in once I started high school, all the grease stiff Carhartts and caps and moth eaten wool coats and rotting rubber boots, and the mangle Mom used to iron the sheets and pillowcases so they were smooth and perfect, which was a bastard to wrangle up those stairs with the turn at the landing. The last thing left to do down there was the fruit cellar, so I went up and got a cold beer and a flashlight and went back down. I'd never liked that room as a kid, dreaded opening the door on the quick scurry and the air like a breath just let out and about to be taken in again. Although we set mousetraps, there would always be mice in there, trying to figure a way through glass and metal. They were fatally optimistic. There were huge spiders too, with nests I'd have to break apart to retrieve whatever Mom wanted for dinner. Seemed like she never sent me there in the morning—no, it was always late afternoon, I remember, early evening in winter when the sun was set and the basement was that too quiet dark. Even later, when I began to sleep down there, I avoided the fruit cellar if I could. Usually I was too tired from school and farm work and work on the cars to do anything but fall straight across the bed into a dead sleep by then. Now I opened the door, giving the room plenty of advance notice, saying, "OK, all right, here I come—" as I pulled the light cord to the burned-out bulb and had to turn on the flashlight to sweep along the shelves.

I guess I expected the shelves to be full from last summer's crop. Instead the boards were empty except for dust and a couple of sprung mousetraps with the mouse so long dead it was flat and brittle as old paper when I shoved at it with the flashlight. Even the spiders had abandoned the place, their torn webs hanging in gray dusty strands below which were the anonymous bits of insect pieces. Then I noticed up on the top shelf a row of jars which required a ladder to reach. I had to go back upstairs to bring down the stepladder and replace the burned-out bulb before I could examine the jars closely.

Each jar was filled with pickles, whose oblong bodies rested like deformed fetuses in the cloudy liquid, with a label stating as always the type and the year and the award they had won. Jars for every year I could remember, in precise order, which came abruptly to an end two years before I left for Albert's. I turned the flashlight on and examined the pine board, brushing the dust away, hoping for the ring that would say the missing jars had once rested there. Then I rechecked the other dates, squinting there in the twilight of the sixty-watt bulb. It was true, of course, she'd stopped and I hadn't even noticed. Hell, I hadn't noticed she wasn't serving them at meals either. I probably couldn't tell you what meals I'd had with my parents those last few years. In fact, I'd be lying if I said I thought about anything but myself during the past six years. I'd come home and see how thin and frail Dad was, how tired Mom was, but I couldn't, you see, I just couldn't come back here and take up where I left off the day I found that chassis.

I look around the kitchen one last time, trying to memorize the stained sink, where the stove and refrigerator and table and chairs stood, the cabinets, and the view out the window which looks right at the shed I spent all those nights in. She must have stood here like I am now, watching the yard light come on, the barn cats tiptoe out into the pasture, my form bent over the engine concentrating so completely on my betrayal.

So here I am, the proud possessor of a Heinz pickle pin and the check from a farm we'd been able to keep in our family for three generations. Not much of a check at that, not anywhere near enough. You know I'd be lying if I said that it was.

The Luck of Junior Strong

 "Can't escape necessity," Uncle Marv announced as he propped the broom and dustpan in the corner where Junior could reach it and waved in the direction of the bathroom.

"I wouldn't think of it." Junior used the toe of the boot cast on his left leg to push the table far enough away so he could unjam the wheel that had caught and caused the mess to begin with. The walk-out basement of Marv's house was fixed up like a family room with a gas grate in the fireplace and a brown-and-yellow linoleum block floor in a shuffleboard pattern, though nobody remembered how to play the game. The bar was a red Naugahyde and rust dotted chrome affair with a dripping water faucet in the half-sink, a tiny built-in fridge that wouldn't freeze ice, and cloudy mirrors behind the empty shelves that held bottles of liquor until Marv quit drinking after the airplane crash coming home from the Iowa State/University of Iowa football game four years ago.

It was the black-and-gold foam Hawkeye headpiece that saved Marv, they said, when the other fellas in the small plane died at the site. Marv took up his life with greater seriousness after that, ignoring the national media and going to the philosophy and religion section of their town's little public library instead. A year later he discovered Buddhism and it had been downhill ever since. It had gotten so the family avoided him at holiday dinners unless they were armed with drinks and other people. He was their favorite person to sic on newcomers to the family. On the other hand, Marv was the only person who offered to take Junior in after the hospital released him.

"Well, this couch folds out just like this—" Marv reached behind the black leather back and pulled a lever and the front unfolded with an awkward sigh like a fat woman dropping her drawers. He straightened and looked at Junior in the wheelchair, his broken legs splayed in their heavy casts. "Maybe we should just leave it open."

"Long as I can get around it." Junior pushed the wheels forward to see if he could edge between the chrome barstools and the bed.

"No reason to go back there anyway." Marv tilted his head toward the knotty pine cabinets on the back wall in the corner that held games and puzzles.

"OK, leave it then. I can get through the doorway for the bathroom and the patio this way." Junior backed the chair up and wheeled himself toward the unfinished part of the basement which held the toolbench, furnace, and concrete floored bathroom with the rust-stained sink and shower. He didn't know how he was supposed to take a shower, but he was too tired and pissed off to mention that fact.

"I'll be going pretty soon, so if you need anything—" Marv headed for the stairs. "Have to be there early tonight." He paused, his thick-fingered hand on the knotty pine door frame. He almost smiled and Junior knew he was supposed to show some interest.

"Why's that?"

"Teaching a new class—Guilt: Let it go, Let it go, Let it go." Marv smiled for real and Junior obliged with a shake of his head and a hand wave.

Marv had told him there'd be no Christmas here, not since he was a Buddhist now. And that he'd be gone every evening to the Center to meditate and give classes. He never got paid for these, but he acted like he did. During the day, he worked as packaging supervisor at the small bottling plant on the outskirts of town. Junior looked around at the various framed certificates and photos over the mantel. According to these, Marv had a college degree in packaging and was a certified Packaging Management Institute Graduate. Although he'd made a lot more money at his previous job with a big manufacturing firm in Cedar Rapids, Marv had quit to have more time to open the Center with two other Buddhists after the plane wreck and reading had taken him to this higher consciousness.

Before the crash, people used to say that Marv was the kind of guy who knew when to buy you a beer. After the crash, he'd acted pissed as hell until his birthday dinner four months later when his wife announced that he had webbed toes and she felt like she was in Jurassic Park every time he climbed in bed. After that she up and left him for good.

Later, when he first started in on the Buddhism, he'd say things like, "Did you ever see a hearse with a trailer hitch? You need celestial pull not tractor pull." That was when the relatives started acting shy.

While Marv was helping him get settled, Junior hadn't thought about food, but now his stomach grumbled as the light began to fail outside, sheeting the windows and glass patio doors with dark gray. As they drove back from the hospital in Iowa City where they'd air-lifted him after the crash, the winter sky had worn that thick felt overcast all afternoon. Now it seemed to squat down, obliterating the huge old cottonwoods outlining the backyard, turning the icy snow flat and dull. The wind died and a silence took over that made him nervous and too alert. Even the crows that usually collected in the treetops squawking and flapping about this time of day failed to make an appearance.

Junior wheeled himself over to the phone on the fieldstone mantel and pulled the cord so it flopped down in his lap, banging his little finger against the chair arm. He still had enough painkiller in him it didn't bother him that much though. He couldn't remember the number for pizza, but after wrangling with information, he captured it and called. Lucky he had had some cash when Marv showed up at the hospital to take him home. No telling when he'd get to a bank. Actually, the money wasn't technically his. Not yet at least. Well, maybe. Junior tried to brush the facts aside, as he'd done for the past week lying in bed after they'd operated on his legs and feet, putting the screws and plates in and keeping him on a nice float of drugs.

"You're lucky," they said, but he figured they told everyone that. What did they know about cars and racing, especially about hoping to make it as a driver with two bum legs? One turn around the track when he was supposed to be taking the damn car to the other garage with the cash in his pocket to pay for the blower they were going to install. He didn't think it would matter, he'd done it before, snuck a car out for a quick turn around the track so he could practice.

"Levon?" The yellow and red pizza box came down the stairs followed by a pair of jean clad legs and finally the shoulders and blonde head of a girl. In the odd lighting, he couldn't see who it was at first, not until she put the pizza on the bar and unzipped her black ski jacket.

"Sharee—" he said, reaching for the dollars stacked on the bed beside his chair.

ACTS OF LOVE ON INDIGO ROAD ~ *183*

"My dad said it was you who called, so I figured I'd come over and see how you're doing." She pulled her jacket off and slung it over the bar.

"So how ya doing?" Her frank blue eyes made him want to lie, to make her look beyond what he appeared like at this moment.

"Had some luck, I guess. I'm OK, how about you?"

She smiled, keeping her lips pressed together, and sat down on the bed. That's when he remembered why he'd only gone out with her a couple of times, long enough to get her to sleep with him, then stopped. She never talked. Almost never. Great, the one person comes to visit him besides his crazy uncle is a mute girl who called him by his old high school name, Levon. A name he'd changed to Junior for his budding career in racing.

"How's that pizza?" He nodded toward the box and she jumped up and brought it over, placing it on the bed next to his chair. Flipping the lid, she looked at him and smiled again, teeth carefully covered. He remembered those buck teeth that made her look like a rabbit with a cause. The top of the pizza was coated with a jumble of colors and shapes of items he hadn't ordered. "What's this?"

"I told Dad to make it special." She blushed and picked at the fuzzy balls on the faded pink blanket covering the foldout mattress.

He pried a piece up and took a big dripping bite. "Not bad. You want some?"

She shook her head.

When he'd demolished half the pizza, he folded the lid down and leaned back and closed his eyes wishing for something to drink. He was really really thirsty, the way he'd been the whole time since the accident. The pain medication, they told him.

"Think you could get me a glass of water?" he asked without opening his eyes. He heard her get up and leave the room. A minute later she was back, the glass dripping on his hand.

Sharee showed up every day for two weeks bringing him pizza and buffalo wings and cheese breadsticks from her dad's place until he was getting pretty sick of it, even Christmas Eve and Day when his uncle was meditating for twenty hours straight. Marv was too busy to cast more than an occasional thought toward Junior's well-being, so if it weren't for Sharee he'd probably starve, he figured, even though he rarely got more than a couple of words out of her. Maybe she was studying with Marv, he joked to himself in the long afternoons watching the red squirrels chase each other up one dark green clothes pole, along the wire, then down the other, over and over.

He spent a lot of his time reading and watching the weather out the back windows. Marv subscribed to several newspapers and magazines although he never seemed to have time to do more than leaf through them and grunt or let out a hoot at something dumb another person was doing with their life. Junior tried watching television but with racing in rerun, he was left with talk shows. Jenny Jones reminded him of some of his high school teachers, dressed a little out of style and full of mocking opinions usually only mothers could agree with. He imagined his mother in the living room of her little farmhouse seventy-five miles away cheering Jenny Jones for her good sense, while he only felt depressed by the constant parade of people with incredibly bad judgment. When the strippers came on and needed makeovers just to grocery shop, it seemed so obvious that they were just cheap, low-rent girls with no taste.

As the painkillers slowly ran out and he began to feel the first stabs of healing, he began to identify with Montel. Montel was serious trouble. No smirking or giggling at these people. Montel stood up and told it like it was. Montel was the man. "Look right in that camera there," he instructed one guest. "I want all the women in your town to know what a dirty, lying dog you are. I want them to see you coming so we don't have to have you on another show like this one." Junior agreed one hundred percent.

Sitting in Marv's basement watching talk shows and waiting for his legs to heal so he could get his racing career started, Junior was beginning to take on more of a global perspective. He needed evidence of something, luck maybe, that's what he told himself anyway. He had a whole shirt box full of clippings from around the world, and not one of them was from the *National Enquirer*. After the movie *Anaconda*, he found a report that an eighteen-foot serpent had killed three little kids in the Peruvian jungle by toppling their fishing boat and crushing them. In another story, forty-three people were devoured by piranha when the bus carrying them along rain flooded roads to vote in local elections fell into a river in the Amazon. Not all the stories were this drastic, but they did share some element of surprise that had surprised him. Like the man who held up a coffee shop with a live goose that he threatened to strangle, if someone didn't produce some cash. Three people ran for the ATM!

When Sharee came clumping down the stairs carrying a plastic box of salad and some slightly stale garlic bread, he had today's story ready to share. The lettuce was a little discouraged looking, the edges trimmed in brown and the tomatoes turning that peculiar deep mealy rose, but he dutifully squirted the tube of Caesar dressing out and ate as quickly as he could. The only thing fresh she'd brought was a bottle of Mountain Dew, his favorite since she told him he looked like one of the guys in the ad leaping out of the airplane on a snowboard. She'd glanced at his casts and got embarrassed then, but he hadn't taken offense.

"Sharee," he said after he'd finished eating. They were propped up on the sofa bed, side by side, fully clothed. It didn't even scare him. He could feel the first surge of caffeine from the Dew and it made him like her more. He leaned over and kissed her lips, trying not to press too hard since he'd discovered the braces she now wore over those rabbit teeth. So far she hadn't been willing to open her mouth to him, but he figured it was only a matter of time. Anything can be done in time, he was learning. Montel spent a lot of his shows trying to convince weak people of this fact while Jenny just seemed to laugh at them. That's the difference he had tried to explain to Marv late one night as they watched a rerun of Jenny after Jay Leno was done. Marv almost never stayed up to watch TV and almost never did more than poke his head down the stairs to check on Junior once or twice a day, sometimes now only hollering from the top of the stairs. It made Junior appreciate Sharee all the more. He was taking his time with her, trying not to scare her off. He would put his arm around her and let his fingertips rest right on the side of her breast. He never moved them up to the nipple, but he would glance down and see it harden at his nearness. He tried to remember what it had been like that time before, but since the accident, his earlier life seemed to have happened to someone else maybe, because he sure didn't feel like those were things he'd think or do.

"Sharee." He pulled away and picked up the latest clipping he had for her. She quickly covered her mouth with her hand, but he could tell from the shining in her eyes that she was eager to hear what he had to tell her. In fact, her eyes were a particularly nice blue today, like the January sky out there in the backyard, high and blue, so blue you knew it had to be cold because any heat would take away some of the shimmer. A blue-eyed blonde—he'd slept with her the first time to find out if she was a real blonde. That's what he'd wanted to brag. But he hadn't told anyone because, truth be told, Junior had to admit that he really didn't have any friends. He knew guys at the garage, at the track, men he worked with, but he didn't go to their houses, meet their wives or girlfriends. And it hadn't mattered much until these past few weeks sitting around waiting for someone to show up, send flowers or cards. Only people he'd heard from were the insurance agents for the track, the car owner, and the garage. They were all trying to figure out what to do with him. He could sympathize—he was trying to figure out the same thing.

"Levon," Sharee surprised him.

"Yeah?" He had the clipping right in his hand, the one about John Livermore who started a gold rush in Nevada, one of five major gold discoveries he'd made in his life. "The Babe Ruth of Gold Mining." The picture of Livermore showed a sly man who kept everything to himself as he looked up at the camera, that Sharee-like smile on his thin lips. Levon wasn't sure why he wanted to give this story to her, but it had to do with luck. Maybe something he was trying to explain to her about his future, but not in so many words. Bad luck for the prospector who lived in a shack and panned for gold until his death. Bad luck for the "trespassers" who were thrown off the property after Livermore showed up with his bulldozer. Livermore's good luck seemed to cost everybody else something.

"Come on." She stood up and pulled the wheelchair close so he could climb in. Then she went to the furnace room for his coat. The past few days she'd insisted they go out on the patio while the sun was bright even though it was freezing ass cold. He'd done it because it was easier than hassling with her about it.

But once outside, Sharee started pushing his chair off the patio and around the corner of the house, up the little hill where he worried they'd slip on the icy snow, and finally to the pizza van in the driveway. "We're going for a ride." She opened the door and started lifting under his arms until he waved her off and bracing himself half-hopped, half-climbed up onto the seat, pulling his bum legs in after him with his hands.

It was OK riding along although he found his feet seeking brake pedals and his hands reaching to brace against the dash of the van more than he liked. It wasn't even that Sharee was a bad driver. Maybe the empty boxes and cans sloshing around behind them made him nervous, he decided, but he couldn't ignore the way the other cars seemed to leap out of the distance at him, and the poles and fences, especially the stone walls, seemed to cut too close to the van.

That day in the car, he'd wound it up to the top in every gear, stretching her, feeling the nose tug at the white line, the rear end threatening to skip out with every shift. At 150 m.p.h., the G-forces began to push him away from the wheel, trying to pull him out the far side window, and he had to fight his body until his elbows ached with the struggle and his eyes teared. At 180 he thought his neck was going to come apart, and his ears suddenly plugged with a fierce ringing. His lungs felt smaller too, like the palm of a hand was pressing down too hard and he couldn't catch enough air. Still he hung on out of the third corner and bumped it up to 190, and that's when the engine let go and the rear end got loose and he took the wall. That's what he told them. "You're lucky," they said as they cut the car apart to get him out. Crying silently from the shattered bones, he could tell they were really pissed about the car.

Sharee took the turn onto the dirt road a little fast, sliding him toward her, then back against the door. "Sorry," she murmured and picked up the dark glasses off the dash and put them on. She had a nice profile, he noticed. A chin that didn't go too far in any one direction. In cars, she'd be something not too fast, good enough to learn on. Hit the low divisions where speed and cost were still under control before making the big time with Winston Cup. Maybe Busch Grand National but not quite. She sneezed and rubbed the bottom of her nose with her hand. "Dust—" she said.

The dirt road was bare and rose behind them in dusty clouds that drifted up and across the fields on either side, coating the snow tan. This was a frontage road that ran parallel to the interstate visible between the dips and rises of farmland. He hadn't been along here in years, if ever. He couldn't remember. What was it Uncle Marv said this morning? Something about needing to remember to discover and to discover to remember. The man was an almanac of bad philosophy, about as accurate as that one the farmers around here used for the weather. Look at today—perfectly good out there when the whole week was supposed to be clobbered with storms and arctic winds.

"We're here." Sharee nosed the van up to the wire gate with the For Sale sign on it, threw her sunglasses back on the dash as she got out, and played with the lock until it swung open. The sign overhead said Pleasure Island and in the distance beyond the acres of buckled asphalt parking lot, Levon could see the towers, loops, and hoops of an amusement park. Driving slowly over the humps and holes of the parking lot, Sharee nudged between the sand filled orange plastic pylons and wove around the Twister water slide, the Black Hole, and the Lazy River, all stranded and empty forms that showed themselves to be pathetic blue plastic and cheap metal constructions, fragile enough to be blown over by a good wind. They paused in front of a huge stack of inner tubes, apparently for the Lazy River, which were now glazed with ice and handfuls of snow caught in the crevices. The top of the stack was splattered with white clumps and streams of bird shit. Next to the inner tubes, along the fence for keeping nonpaying people out of the water rides, were a row of peeling kayaks standing on their ends, some ten or twelve slowly deflating bumper boats, a slew of paddleboats, and some water cannons. All bore similar marks of bird occupation, and when he looked at the ground, he could see the large prints of crows circling the piles as if they were inspecting the goods for auction.

Driving around the grounds, they found long rows of octagonal picnic tables, chaise lounges, table umbrellas, lawn mowers, and tools behind the several locked white metal utility sheds, which sat at some distance from the main one-story building that was really a long pole barn with lots of windows and the front cut out for easy access to the booths of food, drinks, and souvenirs. On the far side of the building, next to the merry-go-round, Ferris wheel, roller coaster, and tilt-a-whirl, rested a thirty-foot parade float with last summer's crepe paper flowers bleeding black and gold, the Hawkeye colors, and still bright neon blue onto the snow. The chicken wire shape of the giant bird on skis, one wing flung into the air while the other attached itself to what was probably a tow rope of flowers from the tiny boat plowing through chicken wire water, seemed to wave directly at them.

"Come on." Sharee parked beside the float and was out the door before he could say anything. By the time she had his chair assembled and waiting, he had resigned himself. After a series of awkward and painful maneuvers they were seated side by side on a long bench sealed inside the driver's compartment. It was dry, almost cozy with the hot sunlight coming through the scratched plexiglass windshield positioned between the legs of the hawk.

"Here we go," she said and peeled off her down ski jacket which she shoved into the corner behind him before tugging at his jacket. He submitted since he was already beginning to feel too warm. His legs ached pretty good from all the moving around, and he wanted to keep the rest of his body as comfortable as possible. Marv's advice for dealing with pain. "The mind is the last faculty to submit," he'd added last night when Levon complained about the casts getting wet when he tried to bathe by lying down on the moldy concrete floor, half-in, half-out of the shower stall.

"What do you think?" She smiled, letting the corners of her lips spread wide enough to show her braces without clamping her hand over them for the first time. "Neat, huh?"

He looked out the window and at the plywood ceiling and the dashboard with nothing but an ignition and steering wheel with a two slot shifter on the column in front of her. Made sense, you only needed one or two gears for a parade. "Nice—"

They both laughed and she slid forward so he was forced to lean back into the corner to give her more room. She lifted his left, then his right leg up onto the bench and squirmed around so she was kneeling on the floor beside him, with her hands on his thigh.

"My dad's maybe gonna buy this place." She rested her cheek on her hands, her yellow hair spilling across his knees in such a way that the sun caught and burnished it with a sudden gesture that made his hand reach and without intending to begin to stroke her head.

"Sharee—"

"Shhh—" She raised herself and pulled his head down until their mouths met, her lips drawn back while his lips caught the metal wires and cut themselves. As the first salty blood seeped into his mouth, the shrill alarm rose up his legs, spread across his stomach, numbing his chest and shoulders till his arms turned leaden, just like that afternoon at the track when he'd seen the needle climbing toward 200 m.p.h. and panicked, letting go of the steering wheel. And now with Sharee holding his face tight against hers and the taste of his own blood on his tongue, Junior began to feel a weight tugging at his soul, a weight that said it was skill and luck that helped you find the line on the track, that tucked you safely into the groove where suddenly anything was possible.

Mystery of Numbers

Tom was having that emergency recall of the conscience he always got Christmas Eve, but the car was due at the track two days from now for testing, and there wasn't a damn thing he could do about it. He tried to fit the headers back on the engine, still not right. He sighed and rubbed his face on his sleeve. Sometimes he wondered if he'd ever get the hang of it here. His last job, several years ago now, had been at Larold Martin's Chix-N-Stuff which everyone thought was a topless place until they got inside and saw the sign—Chicken Fingers! The Real Choice!—and smelled the deep fryers which were what eventually got them closed because Quinta, Larold's sister and general manager, refused to change the grease more than once a month and first that nice black couple from Des Moines and then Larold's baby girl and then the town alderman all got sick. Not close-to-death sick, but pretty darn sick considering all they were trying to do was fries and fingers and a Coca-Cola, which should be by God safe in this day and age. That's what Larold told them as he fired the lot, Tom ducking through the door under Speed Maxwell's crane coming to take down the sign and hoist up another for Larold's new place called Come N Git It! All in all, he guessed this job working for his dad's garage was a heck of a lot steadier, even if the hours were out-of-this-world long.

Tom still wouldn't go to Larold's again, not even if it was the only place open on a Sunday night when he was done working sixteen hours straight with only vending-machine candy bars and soda pop till his stomach was shaking hands with his backbone. Some nights he could feel the burning cramp all the way up his shoulders, as he tried to force stale bread with the cold sleeve of the refrigerator on it down his throat between gulps of water before he climbed tired as death into bed next to Marie who was, all in all, a good woman, if a bit vengeful. She didn't mind him putting his cold butt up next to her stomach and always clamped that one leg over his like now she had him she wasn't going to let him go, even though his feet were two icy bricks.

He was the one needed warming in bed, and she was the one to do it. Marie was a big woman, tall and thick-boned as an ax handle, his daddy Red had said when Tom showed up at the garage with her. Red Yearly'd looked eye to eye with Marie and said something—it was lost now with a lot of other useless items—but what Marie had said always stuck in Tom's mind of a morning when he combed his hair carefully forward and then back, looking for the telltale pink between the heavy brown waves. "Bald can take you someplace," she'd replied and Red smiled, lifting the side of his lip so those pick-sharp canines showed.

Red thought he looked like Elvis when he did that, but Tom thought his daddy really looked more like Scout, their skinny brown bird dog. Although he was tied by a long rope attaching him most days and nights of his life to the cottonwood out front of the garage, the dog never bothered trying to chew his way loose. It was the same tree with the block and tackle suspended overhead from the thickest limb ready to noose an engine up and out of a car. Tom figured maybe the dog had watched that enough times to imagine its brown useless body going up too because Scout was the least trouble a dog could be in the world and in the emergency recall of his conscience this Christmas Eve, Tom could see how that was a wrong thing. That dog living its quiet, terrified life under the chain of its demise. He should at least bark. Tom argued the dog's case with Red this morning, but his father was incapable of seeing how the humped back and curled head were the signs of something deeper than a bad gene pool. He'd gotten Scout from a pig farmer in trade for the salvage carburetor on an '86 Olds Ciera whose black finish was sanded salt-gray before the farmer got the car from his cousin in trade for Scout's mother and two pigs, Scout's mother being one of the best bird dogs this side of the Mississippi, according to everyone in the county. No reason that pig farmer should have a dog that nice, Red commented as the Olds drove off and left the puppy cowering flat at their feet.

But truth be told, Scout was afraid of loud noises from the git-go, hated so when his feet got even a hint of damp that he learned to climb trees just to stay out of the weather. The rope was long enough to let him up into the crotch of the cottonwood where he'd wait out just about any sort of change, and the dog had long ago learned not to tangle himself going up and down. "Maybe he should be a coon dog," Red remarked about once a week when he noticed the milk-brown eyes in the tree staring down at them as Tom came to work of a morning. "I got him that perfectly good doghouse too," Red would gesture toward the fifty-gallon drum on its side, streaked with rust and the tiny dents from that hailstorm last summer which had done a job on one of the racecars too. Fred Creed had shown up with all the bad luck of that summer right after the storm let up and had one of his royal fits. "As in fit to be tied, and about to be fired," Red called it.

Creed's kid Bobby was trying to be a race driver and Creed's Ford Lincoln Mercury dealership was one of his sponsors, along with his vacuum cleaner repair business which was a front for God knew what, but Tom figured there couldn't be that many bum vacuums in the entire county or nobody would have a clean house. "It's nothing." Red would pat his son on the back when he saw him getting those suspicions on his face in little lines around his mouth and between his eyes. "Tom, you worry about all the wrong things," his father would explain and nod toward the engine they were rebuilding. "Now mill that deck so we can squeeze another mile or two out of this thing. I think I figured this thing with the cylinder heads we can get away with."

It was Red's little innovations kept them in the racing engine business while Tom did the everyday car repair work. "Father and son," Red would announce every year when they posed arm in arm for their Christmas card with the shop as the backdrop, a racecar gleaming beside them and the dog peering out of the tree at them like a demented squirrel. They always looked exactly like father and son, Tom noted as soon as the cards arrived from the print shop. Red, the tall father, Marie's size really, and Tom, the short, compact son. It wasn't easy being a small man, but he didn't discuss it. Marie found him satisfactory in that way that women find a man more or less, but some days he felt like that dog, like maybe he needed to climb a tree to get a better view of things, because right now he felt like a stump in the woods.

Christmas Eve, even the Wal-Mart closed at six, Larold's at eight. Bobby wanted a car could run both the high side and the white line on the bottom of the track. Red had picked up the magnesium housing for the transmission shipped in from Richmond yesterday, same as

Winston Cup cars used, and said they could find the horsepower. "Maybe the spring rate's wrong." Tom had tried to convince Red of something hours ago so they could go home and have a decent Christmas Eve, but Red had reminded him they were engine men— their first job was engine, not chassis. "Bobby's living in a fantasy world," Tom had muttered, "so's the old man. Kid couldn't drive a mail truck let alone a racecar."

"Last race the power-steering belt came off and took the oil belt," Red reminded him and went to the workbench where he sat for hours writing numbers and making little drawings on graph paper while Tom started grinding the head deck. Late summer when Dale Earnhardt had driven into the wall at the start of the Mountain Dew Southern 500, they said he experienced "a transient alteration of his consciousness." Tom was thinking he needed one of those, but hoped it wouldn't take a smack in the wall to do it. When he called her at eight to say he was going to be a little bit longer before he'd be home to play Santa Claus, Marie had hissed, "I want a man in an Elvis suit," and slammed down the phone.

"Need to adjust that compression ratio and keep some fuel mileage," Red announced after the phone call. "I'm going out for a bit. Want anything? I'll think better with some fresh coffee." Red had wet what remained of his hair and combed it flat against the back of his skull. "Sex on the hoof," Marie had called him.

It wasn't long after Marie showed up, Red quit trying to fool anybody about his hair. Now she was cutting it once a month along with Tom's, her long white fingers pulling the thin strands away from the scalp, holding them there for a moment, the scissors poised, then the snip in a clean line that left Tom a little breathless. Sometimes lately, he didn't know why it bothered him to see her standing behind the chair with her hands resting on his father's shoulders for that brief time while the old man looked at himself in the mirror. Marie changed when she cut hair. Grew distance like grass, a whole yard-full he couldn't quite get across, like in a dream where your legs wouldn't stand up for themselves, or like Red when he was at his graphs and numbers. There wasn't anything Tom did he couldn't feel or think to himself, here I am, here I am.

Every time that damn Bobby Creed blew the engine from running the r.p.m.s too high too long, Tom took it personally. While his heart thumped and the first stink of sweat rose off the son trying to control his anger, Red would be walking around the engine block tapping his short fingers with the thick orange hairs against his wide grizzled jaw. While Red started making notes with the yellow pencil corrugated with teeth marks up and down the shaft, Tom had to be careful not to pick up a sledgehammer and smash the engine. Marie was like Red. Tom was the one weeping and confused when he was tired from twenty hours and no food, while Marie could always say what she wanted. And she had.

Tom looked over at Red with his head resting in his arms, snoring loudly now. He tightened the last bolt and straightened his back which hurt like a bastard from the hours of concentrated leaning over the motor. There was always something pure about the engine at this moment. He pulled the rag out of his back pocket and wiped a smudge from the valve cover. Maybe this would be the one, an engine the kid couldn't hurt, one that would take him sailing around the track as fast and as safe as his heart desired. See, he rubbed at another spot until he realized it was a shadow cast by the angle of light from the overhead fluorescents, it was the same as a new car or new house or even a new job or wife when he finished an engine. All promise, all hopefulness. He felt what he thought a person must feel for their child when he looked at the engine, though he knew other people like Marie only saw a chunk of metal. He swiped at it again and was going to stick the rag in his pocket when Red snorkeled a little and moved his hand, tipping over the styrofoam cup and spilling the last drops of coffee on the papers.

Without disturbing his father, Tom picked up the cup and dabbed at the spill with his rag until only a few dark bits of grounds remained. He thought about waking Red or pulling the damp papers away from the arm anchoring them to the bench, but did neither. Although the coffee had blurred them somewhat, the fractions and ratios seemed at first to move in a kind of church processional across the pages, then they seemed to clump and fuse, collect and gather, before releasing as random as water down the page. Tom carefully pulled the papers from under Red's arms without waking him and held them more directly under the light. In some weird dance they partnered with sketches of cylinders and carburetors, pistons and spark plugs, the engine taken to pieces, shaved by fractions until they found the exact degree where the metal could be thinnest and most whole, reconfigured to produce and sustain the most horsepower.

"It's Christmas," he muttered half loud enough for Red to maybe hear. The snoring paused, took a deep honk, then proceeded in a new key. Tom had this urge to touch his father's shoulder, to run his hand along the orange-white hairs of his arm, to see if he could feel the thousands of freckles stranded on the yellow-pink skin like tiny planets in a reverse sky. Replacing the papers on the bench, he held his hand over his father's, wanting to slide fingers in between fingers, while his shadow hovered larger in blunt definition, cuffing veins and pores with darkness. They weren't the same hands, father to son, Tom recognized. He had his mother's hands, her coloring and size. There was almost nothing of his father stamped on him except the shape of his head and his eyes maybe, the brown eyes that in his father seemed to pick up the orange-red glow of his skin and hair, while in Tom they remained the truer brown of brown. That's how he thought of it. Marie had said it so it must be true.

For almost the first time, looking at the tired slump of his father's back, Tom wondered about Red living alone out back in the trailer he'd bought after his wife died. Before that, it was Tom living in the basement of the house half a mile down the road from the garage with his parents thumping around upstairs while he worked at one job or another and finally Larold's. When his mother died of cancer, the two men seemed to run from the place, which was now rented to a young couple from the Teaching Corps who helped out at the rural school fifteen miles away. Although they had an old Chevy, they usually rode their bikes back and forth to work when it wasn't raining or snowing, with so many books stuck in the saddlebag baskets behind, Tom could see the muscles in the woman's calves straining with the load up the hill from the house. Once they'd had trouble starting their car, and Tom had driven them to work in the rain and come back and changed the plugs and oil, adjusted the timing, and cleaned things up in general. He knew the Chevy Cavalier never liked to work in the rain because Powell had owned it until he donated it to the County Vo Tech for rehabilitation. Now Tom got to keep working on it every time the season changed. He hadn't the heart to stay in the house after his mother died or to tell that young couple the truth about their car either.

He met Marie the day after the funeral when he and Red went out to Axel's to have a couple of mournful drinks and he moved in with her the next night. Red had gone off on his own somewhere with Mrs. Rankin, the widow from Oskaloosa who came to visit her sister Meryl on weekends so she could raise a little hell away from her neighbors. It had only seemed fitting for the two of them to find solace in their mutual grief, Marie had remarked, as she emptied her screwdriver, sucked the ice, and held up the glass for another. She was just back from beauty college in Des Moines and opening her own place in the basement of the walk-out her dad had left her when he died a year before. Marie found a place for Tom in her life about 1 A.M. that night when the lights came up and they staggered out the door together. He was even better-looking in the daylight, she announced the next morning and got up to cook him eggs over-easy and fresh thick country bacon from her uncle's pig farm. It was her uncle who had owned Scout's mother and left the dog with them a few weeks later. The whole family had been worried to death about Marie until Tom came along, he said.

Nobody mentioned marriage, but it happened right along with everything else. Within a year of burying his mother and meeting Marie in the bar, Tom walked down the aisle of the Christ Community Church and said he did to her I do and had a big meal and a car trip to Chicago for the weekend. He hadn't thought directly about his father living in the trailer for four years until now. Hadn't worried. Red was in better physical shape than Tom most days, and Marie always mentioned how good he looked when she cut his hair, so there hadn't been the need for concern. His father showed up clean and ready to work every morning, commenting only on Scout or the engines they worked on, while the days and months flooded by, notable only for the need to open or close the big front garage doors and turn on or off fans and heaters.

So now it was Christmas Eve, no, Tom corrected himself, early Christmas Day. The twenty-fifth. Should he wake Red and take him back to the trailer, or leave him here to wake himself? He hadn't been inside his father's place in over a year, maybe two years now. They met in the garage or Red came to the house to eat a meal when Marie invited him or to get his hair cut. What was back there anymore? He hadn't ever remembered Red cooking when his mom was alive . . . did he cook now? All he knew about the man were the scrawls on the papers in front of him. Hell, he didn't even know if the widow from Oskaloosa was still coming down to see him on Saturday nights.

What did he know, what did he really know about anybody else? His wife wanted a man in an Elvis suit and the stores were closed. He'd gotten her a new dishwasher for Christmas and at 9 A.M., only a matter of hours from now, Floyd from Seiffert's Appliance was going to deliver it with a big smile and red paper bow. And Red, well, he'd gotten him a new toolchest from Sears, the big dresser size to replace the one Bobby had backed the car into last month. But that wasn't the same, was it? The same as what, Tom couldn't say, but he knew he was somehow in trouble here. Recently he was coming to see that maybe Marie was right when she said desire was an educational process. Since Marie showed up four years ago, his mind was irrigated by possibility. Like those numbers his father arranged and rearranged, something sang to him while he spun shreds of metal with the grinder or checked the cathode color of the spark plugs, something whispered and promised him more than memories, more than he could understand, something which Marie saw when he called a little while ago again to tell her he was coming home soon, only a matter of minutes, he promised, and she told him he was eternally and fatally optimistic.

The clock over the workbench said 2 A.M. He turned up the heat and draped a coat over Red's shoulders. His father, nested down in those numbers, was probably going to be stiff in the morning, but he'd make it to their house for Christmas dinner like always. There'd be the usual distraction as Marie gave Red extra nice cuts of meat and made sure his coffee was hot the way he liked it, but Tom would try to ignore that business like always.

Outside, the dog lay shivering on the frozen ground in front of the oil drum, his eyes watery with moonlight as Tom started past, then noticed that the rope was wrapped around the tree trunk so Scout was held to the ground for a change. "Here," he said, and unsnapped the dog's collar.

For a moment, the dog waited, then stood cautiously, stretching in front with his head up and teeth bared in a grin, then behind with his head down so far his neck bones crunched and he shook himself all over before he took a couple of prancing steps forward, collecting his body like a horse.

"Good boy," Tom said and clapped his hands, but the dog ignored him and trotted around the driveway and tree a couple of times, sniffing and peeing on any object over a foot high, until finally he went to the garage and stood whining at the door. While Tom watched, the dog got more anxious, wagging his tail, jittering on his feet, until he jumped up and barked with a surprising high, loud voice, letting his claws squeal all the way down the metal door. In a moment, the door opened, and a pale hand came out and motioned for the dog to come in, then the door closed. It didn't surprise Tom as much as it might have a few hours ago, seeing his father take that dog inside which he must have been doing all along judging from the little ritual. Then it dawned on him that they might have been waiting for Tom to leave all those nights he worked late on the motors. That Red wouldn't want his son to know how he'd taken to babying the dog. And the dog especially waiting out here in the cold must have hoped the son would go home to his young wife sooner than he frequently did.

Tom folded his arms, tucking his hands into his pits to keep them warm while he stood beside the tree watching the garage for any other sign of activity, but there was only the silence of a deep winter night, frost clinging to car windows and fuzzing the sheet metal walls and roof of the garage. He thought about his father in there working the numbers again, divining, imagining them into new relationships. Twenty-four, that's how old Tom was, four years with Marie, three years married, four years and change working at the garage here, ten years since he could drive, four since he could drink legally, 10/23 his birthday, 5/30 Marie's, 7/11 Red's. These were the only numbers he cared about—the rest belonged to his father or anyone else who wanted to claim them, like that lady out east who saw the winning lottery numbers in her sleep. He figured they were hung low like clouds for some people to grab, and high as stars for people like him.

He stood there watching the yellow-white light of the garage, his breath a slow stream as he felt his toes grow cold as if the frozen dirt gripped up at him. Occasionally something would sigh or creak with that high squeak of the very cold, but the stillness was absolute and pure, as if Tom himself had willed it so, and in this moment anything at all could come true, and all he could think of was that it be this, this very world at his feet, all around him, and then he hoped that somehow, when he finally crawled into bed tonight, he could think of a way to convince Marie that he was as much Elvis as she might want or need on Christmas Day.

FROM

~A .38 Special & a Broken Heart~

My Mother's Hands

I didn't marry nearly as many of them as I could have. That's what I tell people. Some I just lived with, others I passed on by. *How do you know which to do?* they ask.

I come from a family of witches, women who see things. It was my dead sister, who continues to talk, who first called us that. It disturbed her, being able to predict things like who was on the phone before she picked it up, who would be senator or president, who would be doing her dirt next.

My mother's magic was in her hands, her big beautiful fingers that could ease the pain up and out of my father's spine, and snap green beans one two three like that. Sometimes they flew out at your face like angry birds and you ducked. It was a habit I kept for years. My mother's vision was long-term, the kind that saw the no-good of a person's life, that washed its hands of you too quickly. We all fled from her truth as fast as we could, hacking at the tendrils trailing us, like some widespread crabgrass across the geography.

Still, we saw the men she never liked fail, our lives shift under us like tectonic plates, as if she were sinking those strong fingers into the earth and stirring. My father said it came through the female line, such skill. The boys had nothing. Once though, my brother told me how he could feel the sight coming on him when he gambled, and when it left he had to stop too. One time he waited three days, holed up in a cheap hotel in Deadwood, South Dakota, his wife and kids tiring of McDonald's, the only food they could afford, until it returned. When it came, he walked down the street and played poker for four hours straight, came back with eight hundred dollars so they could get out of Deadwood. *All I could do was wait*, he'd said wistfully, tapping the cigarette against the saucer and taking a sip of coffee.

My younger sister claims she has it, but I wonder. No one brags as much as she does. And every time something happens, she says, *Oh, I knew that*. I wonder how come she makes so many bad decisions then. She's the one our dead parents come to though, so I don't ignore her. I'm a little jealous about all the attention they give her, walking up and down the halls at night, messing with the plumbing. I'm the one who finally told her to just ask them what they want. What they showed her was a jar of marbles, a mason jar full of old-fashioned marbles, rolling away from her. It made sense, but I didn't tell her that. She's a little crazy already. She never knows who to marry, so she marries everyone. She's flooded by men and decisions, and needs my mother's fingers to shape her, hold her like a fish petrified in limestone. When she breaks free, it's into modern waters too long past her to understand. She keeps trying to fit back into that molding stone but can't. My mother is the only one who can press her into shape.

Tonight my other sister calls to say that it's back. A few months ago she was walking down the hall at the hospital and saw a doctor she'd known years ago coming toward her. She said hello, but he didn't speak, and that was when she noticed the darkness in his face, his body. He wasn't even taking up the space he was supposed to, he was already dissolving into molecules. Her chest hurt. She worried for two days until the announcement of his death. Today it happened in the jewelry store around the corner. She feels lucky to have kept her sunglasses on. The jeweler is a friend of her husband's, but he was so dark and mean she began to feel bad. His face and fat body were singed, as if death and dying were angry activities. When she tells her husband, he gets mad, says to stop it, stop killing people. *It's not as soon as the other one*, she confides. We'll wait and see.

The night we buried our father three years ago, she laid in bed listening to Mother's chest heave with coughing, her strong hands pressed against the breastbone, as if she could force her own breath out once and for all to join her husband. They'd been together for seventy years. My sister's chest began to tighten painfully as she struggled for each breath in time with Mother. She knows where it comes from. She says, *It's Mother's, she bequeathed it the night she died.*

I remember once as a child sleeping beside our mother, waking up in the middle of the night and trying to breathe along with her but always getting out of sync, sometimes going so fast I was panting, other times so slow I was gasping. But I'm not envious of my sister's breathing.

The last thing she tells me on the phone is about my husband, who has taken up sailing and a single mother and moved to the suburbs. *He was dark,* she says, *at Thanksgiving. He was so angry at all of us I could see he was going to be leaving soon. When you said he was going to be in boats, I thought, no, not water.*

Now she wants a look at my lover too. *Just a glimpse down a hallway,* she insists, *nothing face to face.* I'm tempted, but I know that a man who could drop his seventy-five-year-old father who doesn't speak English at Target for three hours alone, just to get a break, isn't going to die soon. That kind of justice is a fantasy.

And I know he isn't going to be a husband, though he's muttered about it. I know we'll never live together, though he wants to. I saw the end as soon as I saw the beginning. That's my gift. I know men. I can feel a husband five states away, moving toward me. I know a letter is on the way a week before it arrives. All I have to do is think of a person and they get in touch with me as if my mother's hands had found them and were leading them to me.

Tonight the thunder walks among the trees in the backyard, the lightning hits close by and blinks the lights. I wonder if I should call my husband, see if he's off the water, out of the boat, make sure he's alive, that his darkness hasn't taken him further than it should, to a place we can't retrieve him from. This week they announced that, yes, black holes do exist in the constellation of Virgo. They suck all matter into them and compress it into super energized molecules, crushing and jamming them together so nothing can survive in its old form. *I knew that,* I want to tell them. My husband's a Virgo. Even my sister has seen how that darkness needs more and more to keep it going. It's just irresistible, once you touch the fringes, once you come within its emptiness.

Sometimes I know to marry them, and we're safe for a little while, before I turn them loose again, before they careen into their own blackness. Sometimes I know they're already at the edge, like my lover, and I have to pass by, taking what pain comes of such separation. Always in my heart, there's this squeezing, like my mother's hand, holding it in her big fist, sending me messages, this one, no, yes, like some signal at sea, and I can do nothing but obey her.

There Has to Be a Beginning

She thought that going back wasn't the answer, not anymore. She'd been a Cadillac kind of girl for a while, then she was just any kind of girl. She'd go here and there in the cars they drove because walking was something she only did before she learned to get in with the boys who leaned out of windows and called to her. She didn't get in with the loud ones, they were as scared as she was. It was the older ones who knew to drop their voices and speak softly so she'd pause, like answering old people who wanted directions.

The first one took her to the park across the street from her house, sitting her down in the shoulder of the bank where her mom and dad couldn't watch her while he put his arm around her. He wanted something, she knew, the way his fingers tried places, softly, like the words he kept saying, *honey, baby, don't worry I won't hurt you,* and she half-believed him when his hand cupped her down there quickly through her shorts and she got that hot feeling like she'd bumped herself on her bike and couldn't move. He kissed her ear, making it wet, and she wanted to laugh, but his lips kept crying on her skin, trying to wake something up that would run back at him, like a dog let outdoors. She thought about how their dog nobody liked sometimes whined and wet itself with joy when she stooped to pet its licking face, and it made her pull the boy's fingers from the side of her breast. It didn't matter, the hand went right back, like a dog to an accident.

Was this the accident waiting for her? she wondered. She knew the future was coming in a fast car to knock her down, like a dream in the hot sweat night. She was just trying to stay out of the way as long as possible. That's what she knew without saying such words to herself because she was still young and knew things like that in the true way before they get sentences and die with you. So the truth was she liked the way his hot breath and slick tongue kept trying to make a place in her, but she kept her mouth closed. Didn't even open to say no. She knew that was just another way of letting them talk her into something. As long as she stayed still and fought their hands quietly, she could keep them patient. The boy went away, and they could both taste the grassy beginning with some kind of satisfaction.

What she remembered all those years was the iron bar of his arm across her shoulders that said, *You're mine, now you're mine*, and how she'd chased that warmth for the weight it gave her heart, for the way it took her head away and said, *All right, it was safe*. He'd hold her close to the ground, she'd never fly back to her family's arguing faces.

There was a roaring cave they took her to, those boys in cars, with faces like question marks she couldn't remember answering. When the noise came on, she pulled the dirt up over her head and closed her eyes, she didn't want to know who was opening her shirt, her bra, her heart. It was years before she knew what he looked like down there, as if she were a blind girl who had to feel her way through the anatomy of the world. Sometimes she's squint to catch the dark curl of ear, dull white knife of teeth, pulse bob like a finger caught in the throat. It was like a voice speaking words out loud in a dream. *Now you are at ground zero*, it said, and she'd fall away from the world again. She didn't want to wake up a criminal with bloody arms the police were waiting for. She didn't want her picture in the paper while everyone wondered who wired the bomb that blew her parents' house apart. She just wanted to disappear into the good light nerve her flesh turned when a boy got satin smooth and begging hands, and she never had to say no if they never asked.

Politics

I wasn't political, I was pregnant. So was my roommate, a tiny belle from Alabama, who wore a two-carat diamond slipping around on her finger from a dead mother and a beaver coat from a live drunken stepfather. We took turns puking in the bathroom of our suite.

The light in the antebellum-mansion-turned-dormitory was always gray and cool those November days. The sun didn't shine once, as if it had gotten itself in trouble too. We hibernated our hurt under layers of blankets and tried not to look at each other. We knew what we'd been doing. There wasn't any use in pretending now. It was like looking in a mirror to see the stringy hair, the pale sick faces, the noses wrinkling at smells and sounds of food that'd send us scurrying back to the toilet.

When the announcement came in French class, I had a hard time even remembering who the president was. We never used his name at home. He wasn't a Republican. Some girls burst into tears, but the teacher held the class anyway. It was the last, no, maybe the only one I remember. I stopped going after that. People came from lunch with food smells hanging like dew on their clothes, and I left each session on the run for the dormitory.

The radio stopped its music and only talked about it. I wondered if I could get upset enough to miscarry. They talked about Jackie's trials and tribulations having babies, and I wanted to be that fragile. My roommate and I locked ourselves in, a box of saltines and a quart of 7-Up on a chair between our beds. Two groaning, bloated corpses with breasts so sore we secretly hated each other for the modesty that forced us into clothes.

Once we tried the dining hall, but the school had mounted huge TVs around the room so we could watch the funeral procession. To this day, I can't see that black riderless horse in yellow bile sunlight without wanting to puke. It had nothing to do with the president. His troubles were over; mine, you know, were just beginning.

The Family of Death

 We were a couple in a house the dead bought. We moved in on Halloween, inviting the shipwreck of the gods with a new king-sized bed. Right away, things began to die. When we didn't inaugurate the bed our first night, its gold satin-covered buttons punctured our kidneys, caromed off the spine's ladder, embedded their plastic teeth in the small trampoline of our inner ears. From then on, we mistook each other's words for argument.

A week later, the showerhead dispersed water evenly through the kitchen ceiling, bringing pinholes of plaster to the floor in white, iridescent stars sown the way one makes dissatisfaction clear after a while.

And every six months someone died.

Sister, grandfather, friend, grandmother, brother, father, mother, grandmother, friend. It was only a matter of time, we assured each other, before we ran out of relatives and friends.

That summer the basement grew wet. Water percolated through the concrete, outlining the linoleum squares. Then the porch roof rattled and shook and finally jumped ship. The next night while we slept, the storm window in our bedroom pushed away from its frame, leaned back and took to the wind, crashing below.

In the house of the dead, it wasn't any spirit business when the electricity clogged, switches balked and fuses came chirping to their smoky halt.

So we learned to point the TV remote at the ceiling to make it work, our arms above our heads in constant supplication, and wrote dialogue during the day to keep ourselves company.

My Last Try

 It was January, not a pretty month no matter how you shake it down. I thought when I left Yance that day, well, I thought that's that. I can see handwriting on the walls as well as the next person. It's the kind that makes that little sinky feeling under your ribs and puts its sharp blade down your throat to lick your breath.

We'd been drinking wine, or rather I had, because Yance was crazy enough without it. I was the one who needed that little booster rocket for what we were doing, what I was doing. He'd already declared himself free and independent, sliding out from under his wife to a downtown studio apartment. Nestled safely among the office buildings, where he could flash the workers in the late afternoon failing light, he didn't hand out his phone number to his wife or friends. He acted like he was so far ahead of the game he was playing the next one, and I was back there trying to bat that thing across the net all by myself.

It wasn't true, it turned out, when we came back one Sunday evening and found her note stuck in his door. By the time he'd hustled me into the elevator, checking both ways down the hall in case she was lurking, he was looking up at me. We used to see eye to eye.

That day the sun shone mean and glittery as a knife in my throat. Like a Broadway musical of my life, *The Phantom of the Opera* gone bad, and I was expected on stage any minute, with the mask covering whatever ugliness I'd been up to. It was that hard white and silver light on everything that says, *Redemption is just around the corner and, honey, you ain't coming.* It was Thursday and I faced another long weekend of my husband burrowed in the sofa like he was hibernating, with that long wounded expression as if we both knew I'd never be able to apologize enough for what I was doing. He just switched channels and got smaller when I tried to talk. I never saw two men so prone to disappearing. It worried me.

And there was the wine. A light, cool place, fruity with grapes in rain and green, oh it was so green there I took off my clothes just to be close to it, just to let that green soak my skin good and clean. I'd like to say that Yance was a good lover, really, because in this kind of story you need to say things like that, but I can't lie about it, not now, not after all this kind of failing. He was a hard man, a hard lover. Everything he did was just the other side of gentle. *Slow down, take it easy, not so hard,* I whispered, and sometimes just pulled his hands off me to make a point, but he was like a kitten fighting for milk, he wouldn't let go, not really, and I always gave in and tried to think good, light green things with the wine. It helped, it really did.

You know, being unfaithful isn't all that easy. In stories it is, but in life, it's as hard as being married. I felt tired that month, going from one to the other, like a mother with two sick children or a person with two jobs. I never slept. Someone was always upset, in trouble, needing me. I got worn out, grocery shopping for two households, taking so many phone calls I could've been a bookie, and all the time dissatisfaction growing moldy in the closets and corners like it's my fault the three of us are living in this ice and snow without proper arms around us twenty-four hours a day.

Where are the love notes, the flowers, the secret meetings full of music? I kept asking. How come I bring the wine, the bagels, the presents and talk Yance out of his depression? *Get some of those grow lights,* I told him. *Take some pills.* By the time I had him cheered up, I was depressed, and isn't that always the way? The most compelling reasons to stay alive really sound stupid when you say them out loud. That's what I began to notice.

No one noticed how run-down I was getting. They both thought I wasn't running hard enough. I went out and bought some of that under-eye concealer, the extra-thick-for-getting-old-and-wrinkled stuff, and tried it on the darkness. My wedding rings began to slide on and off too easily. One day I left them on the dresser at home. My husband got sick and moved to the other room, and stayed. There's a lot of true things that happen in our life. I think we see them at the very moment they happen too, then we try to forget about them. I know I did.

The house started creaking, like the joints above us were pulling apart, that squeaking thing when you wrestle a nail out of a board after it's been locked there for years, the claw of the hammer catching it, threatening to pull the rusty head off. That was the noise over my head alone in my bed at night after I'd hung up from Yance and waited for sleep like a big hand to come and close my mouth. I try to remember if I prayed then for anything, like let me die in my sleep, but I don't think I did. I was way past God, way beyond hope. I wasn't even in despair, not that you'd notice. I mean, now I had two men. *You're so lucky*, my friends were saying. *You've always had all the luck.* What do they know, I mean, really, what does anyone know when they can't lift the flap of your heart and read that secret print there? I tried to let them hear it in my voice, my jokes, but they were busy being thrilled, the way friends are, by good luck that rides right over age and circumstance. *At your age*, they kept saying, *imagine.*

The crows paced the snow in the backyard looking for food I threw out. Once I watched a crow hide a crust of bread in a snowbank and come back two days later to eat it. There was still a lot to learn, I knew that. I had just had about enough. Can't a person say that to themselves. I did.

That Thursday with the light mean enough to make it all clear, how this was going to come apart on me, and already was, I drove into the garage and closed the door. I mean, I got out and shut it with the button on the wall and forgot, no, I didn't want to turn the engine off. I left it running. It'd been that kind of day. I was pushing something. I admit it. I climbed back in my Oldsmobile, a car my father had preferred before he got money for a Cadillac. I think he always missed his Oldsmobiles, at least I like that think that, now that he's gone and can't dispute the fact, which he would, being stubborn and more married to mystery than truth.

I leaned back, closed my eyes. I can't remember if I had music on. It was in my head anyway. Some music of the wine and rough screwing, and the words which were off just enough to let me feel the trembling overhead that was my house with the nails pulled out, the joints spreading, my husband's uneasy sleep in the room down the hall. I rolled down the windows, wondering if the smell would drive me inside the house. I thought about things. I didn't have anything more to say to the world though. I didn't feel like leaving a note or anything. I was tired, anyone should be able to see that.

Waiting to die didn't take much. I tried to cry, couldn't, thinking as I grew drowsy, good, now I won't have to wake up. Then I did. I looked at the clock, half an hour, any moron could die in half an hour inhaling car fumes. I got out and looked around. Sure enough, the Olds was pumping good solid gray into the twilight of the garage, but there was a space under the back door and the big garage door didn't fit at all. Overhead, on all sides, and along the bottom, you could see daylight cracking in. What kind of cheap trick was that? No wonder I couldn't die. I'd have to spend the rest of the afternoon plugging holes. Just more work. I turned off the engine and went inside. See, in stories people can succeed with love and death. In my life I've just found a lot of things that fail. But it's one thing to fail at love—you see a lot of that— it's another to be such a failure at death. I wanted to call my parents, wake them from their eternal sleep and yell at them, *How come you didn't arm me with everyday know-how?* Now I've embarrassed myself to myself. I'm so ridiculous, even death won't have me.

I never really knew about despair until that moment. I knew about being tired. I knew about disappointing people around you and how you take your little breadcrumb soul and give it a good thrashing. But I never understood what it meant to be sentenced. I figured it was a special kind of failure, because you couldn't very well call your friends and tell them. It would never be shared, it would never be anything but another secret on your heart, another reason someone wouldn't get to know you.

The Gun

 A gun is a simple machine. The bullets go in the chamber easily, one through six, and if you're not careful, they slide back out just as quickly. You have to hold it barrel down or at least level. And snap the cylinder back. Cock it if you want or not—it's not that hard to just pull the trigger. On the .38 special, there's nice brown wood handgrips. It's a little heavy, but not bad overall. Easier than a rifle, which also is a pretty simple machine. Trouble is, simple machines are so easy to use. Nothing computerized that can jam or go bad. If you obey the laws of keeping things clean and neat, the gun can serve a lifetime.

That's what Mister always told us kids, when we came old enough to be taken out into the woods and shown how to use such things. And later when we were given our own gun. A .22 in my case. *Shoot all the rabbits and squirrels you want,* he'd said, *they make good eatin'. But never the songbirds.* So we always did just once to see what happened—nothing except a little empty thing in my chest when the damn robin fell off the limb.

We come from a long line of murderers, committers of mayhem, trouble, violence. There are car crashes and assaults, brawls and batteries, and just the general upside-downs of our world that always lead someone in the family to kill or be killed. And it's always some kind of love trouble. *We're the black eyes of the black-eyed peas,* Aunt Walker always says.

So when the report came about Caleb, it didn't surprise me as much as you'd think. One way or another, the family blood comes out, no matter how far north you go, I guess, no matter how hard you run, no matter how good you try to get. He'd left me that night, just drove away, the garage door gaping like a big black mouth hollering at the whole damn neighborhood that he wasn't coming back, no matter what. I shut it, listening to the final clank and sigh as it touched bottom and settled into place like a big old mechanical dog, whooshing down in front of the fire.

The surprise is that it took so darn long for that blood to catch up with me, like somehow I'm not even a full member of my family and it got all thinned out and maybe in a generation or two they won't even claim us as kin. I don't know what to feel about that. Honest I don't. I just wish Kit could understand that I surely did not mean for his father to go out there and get himself killed sleeping in some old abandoned warehouse in Minneapolis, Minnesota. No one can say that. He'd given up on himself, and then on me. You could see it. Hadn't worked in six months. Wouldn't take just any job. Every day a little something more leaked out of him, like he was just this little ol' mouse balloon the kids used to get at the state fair and drag home.

I just didn't have any more comfort to offer after we sold my horse and the cabin, cashed in the life insurance. I would have worked. If it had been me, if he hadn't gone on about women never working in his family. It was no big treat to sit home in that empty house with the kids gone and him moping like some teenage girl stood up for a dance. Maybe I should of taken the gun to him myself. Freshen up the blood. What else is there to pass along anymore, I ask you. What claim to fame do your families offer you?

The only worry I have is that this murder doesn't count—because it wasn't love that did it. I didn't love him, not for a long time, I think. I liked him. I took care of him. I felt a little safe with him in the parking lot after the movies late at night. Does that count? But love. I didn't feel anything when he left but relief, the way you do when your grandma in the nursing home dies after she hasn't recognized you for five years already. The last thing she did before she turned out the lights was crochet covers for a bunch of hangers and tell you that's what ladies should put their nice things on. What—flannel shirts, cotton tees? Or that polyester number you could keep under a pile of wood and still yank out and wear to church? Just another useless piece of advice, I thought, and stashed them in back of the closet until she died, when I remembered her and dragged them back out and started using them because, really, they were her last words to the world.

When they called about Caleb, I couldn't remember anything except the Oreo cookies he'd been eating when I came home that last night. There was this big pile of fronts and backs separated, neatly, as he went through the package licking the middles out. He was just finishing up when I walked in, and he had that look on his face that said this was just about the last thing he intended to do. He tried a couple of tops and a couple of bottoms while I sat there, but you could tell it wasn't the same without the middle, and we both knew it. He slugged a can of Leinie's and stood up and walked out the door. I let that pile sit there till morning, and then I cleaned it up because of the mice. We get a lot of field mice in the winter, and I just didn't want them eating all that chocolate. It's poisonous for most animals.

At the funeral with the closed casket, I tried to remember what Caleb looked like when he was young, when we first started in. He was clean. His clothes were clean and cotton and pressed. They were never wrinkled in our Southern way, never sweaty or hot like they'd been worn all day. I liked that. Even later, ironing those shirts and chinos, I didn't mind. It reminded me of how far I'd run from the Ozarks, from Little Dixie, from Mister Always and Iberia, my parents. My life got clean. I knew who I was for days on end. I was just this person who kept things simple. Like a gun.

Sometimes I wonder if he'd be alive if we'd gone to bed that night. I mean, if I'd broken the silence that way, would he have straightened up and tried again? It'd been years. I slept in my own room, the guest room. Maybe in that way, it was love trouble that drove him to meet his fate. Maybe it's in the blood, like I said, and you just can't tell how it's going to work its way out into the muscle of things, lay eggs and start hatching. You just don't know which arms will have strength and which won't when that trouble starts in.

I'm heading south now, home to Missouri. "Misery," Caleb and I used to call it. Home to tell whoever's left that they were right, you can't escape this thing. It's in the blood. I've got it on my hands now. Now I can join the family parade. Now I can finally find my place in town. I've got the .38 special on the seat next to me, under my Dwight Yoakam and Steve Earle tapes. I figure if the cops stop me, they won't care. I'm a woman traveling alone day and night. I'm not safe. I don't have to tell them about a dead husband, two kids who ran off, or a whole family of bad waiting for me with love trouble.

The Jesus Barber Shop

Main Street is closed tighter than a Sunday fist on a ten-dollar bill. Even the Rains Hotel looks oddly abandoned, forlorn, as if there'd been an air-raid drill and everyone streamed out and headed for the underground shelters and just forgot to come back up. There's a yellow dog sitting on the corner across from the courthouse, waiting on the light that's blinking orange in all directions.

"That's useful," I say and drive past the Dixie Donuts, which is closed except for the dim light in the rear over the ovens that aren't hot yet, past Hair Benders, the New Age concession to a beauty parlor, past even the Dairy Daddy that's deserted despite its yellow fluorescent light.

The Jesus Barber Shop's red pole spins slowly, looking lopsided where the paint has chipped, like an over-the-hill skater. Inside the shop, the head of Jesus with long curls and smiling beard glows white and brown from its plastic backlit circle. Maybe he's waiting for a perm, I decide, and remember those Friday-after-school sessions in there when Iberia would take us all for our hair croppings every few months. She did it in between times.

At the Jesus Barber Shop we'd get a good dose of Christ and cutting and come out feeling ashamed of the white line around our scalp like a halo and our ears ringing red as if they'd been boxed, not preached at. *Does you good*, was all Iberia said. She went to church as she saw fit, but Grandmother Estes made sure we got dragged out every Sunday morning and night. Mister Always just sat around, reading the *Kansas City Star* because the *St. Louis Globe Democrat* was run by communists, and waited for us to come home so he could put us to work. The day of rest never meant us.

I think about stopping and putting a note under the door of the barber shop to point out that Jesus never cut his hair or anyone else's, that actually long hair is meant as a sign of humility in many cultures, but I don't bother. It's too late for that kind of action. Probably give old Jack Ashley a heart attack, and his fat belly would burst through that baby blue smock. Jack's hair has been white since he was thirteen and the Lord saw fit to touch him with lightning, killing his sister and his good hunting dog, Rufus, as they all stood under a big old sugar maple on the family farm twenty miles outside town.

The dog lived a few minutes longer than the sister, and Jack always swore the Lord Jesus Christ spoke to him in those minutes, coming through the dying groans of his beloved dog, promising Paradise if Jack would devote himself to spreading the word and cutting hair in the way Jesus told him. No one could remember Jack being interested in hair before that time, but we never question the authority of true vision here, especially when it's meant to further the good-sidedness of the general population, and there's only been that one time that anyone could remember when Jack faltered on his path and that was when this bald-headed hippie girl came through town and settled down in the Rains Hotel for a few months.

It was the tattoo of the bleeding heart of Jesus that confused him. It was right on her chest, and although he knew it was the work of the pagan-worshiping Catholics, he was still struck dumb every time he went to shave her head and caught sight of its red pain-filled expression under the thin gauzy shirt she wore.

That was when I was in fifth grade, and it was a very big topic of conversation at supper, especially after it became clear that as soon as Jack closed up the Jesus Barber Shop for the day, he went to eat at the hotel café, which was still serving supper then, and was observed on more than one occasion to be climbing the backstairs of said hotel to the second floor, where that hippie girl, Bathsheba she called herself, had taken up residence in a splendor of candles, incense, and cheap scarves she bought at the five-and-dime.

That lasted right up to the eve of a Sunday sermon the Methodist minister was going to preach in which he addressed the problems of temptation and falling by the wayside but ended up preaching the Good Samaritan again for the hundredth time instead, by my calculation.

Bathsheba was last seen on the back of a motorcycle, clinging to a man in black leather and a World War I German helmet, which wasn't all that disturbing since there were still an awful lot of Germans around here and they had never really formally declared their allegiance one way or the other, preferring to keep their mouths shut and their pride and friendships intact. The scarves had been tied together and streamed out behind Bathsheba like a wonderful rainbow rope that somehow Jack had failed to hang onto, we all realized later as we watched him grow old and nastily Christian before our eyes.

Love had failed and with it most of the New Testament. Jack switched churches to a Pentecostal that made its members spend Saturday nights on their knees being beaten with fresh willow whips while they hollered out their sins and ate handfuls of bitter leaves. Once in a while someone died from getting poisonous ones by mistake, but Jack survived and only grew a little more green and bitter himself each year. His haircuts became the main punishment parents could hold over their children for poor behavior and lack of proper devotion. Even the Methodist minister was seen on occasion dragging one of the younger children entrusted to his care for catechism up to the door of the Jesus Barber Shop.

Invisible

 The pity party was over. Daralynn was just going to have to go back to work. She'd seen what she'd seen this morning. Now it was time to do something about it. She still had five rooms to clean and no matter how she cut it, there was pigbreath Taxer waiting for her to finish so he could ream her out for that bitch in twelve who said there was cigarette smoke in the towels. *This ain't no goddamn Holiday Inn, honey.* That's what she'd say if she was Taxer, but it wasn't in his nature to do more than stick his big old snoot up people's skirts and yell at the help to please the customer. She gave the room a last shot of lemon pine freshener that made everything reek like the toilets in the cheap bars out by the old highway. Same distributor for both places, this salesman who came through Spartus once a month and left his smelly sprays and cleaners like droppings in his trail. *It's all those goddamn salespeople,* she muttered, *goddamn them, god god god damn them.*

She stuffed the last of his underwear in her trash bag, sprayed the pillow case and tucked the red and brown flower print spread over it carefully. With any luck that stuff would make his damn hair fall out. Had too much anyways, the thick wavy kind that made you want to stick your fingers in it. Kept it like a woman. Hair products all over the place. Natural this and that and even some stuff that guaranteed to keep the black shiny and sure. *Did that mean it was dyed?* she wondered as she emptied a third off the top and poured some of the powdered cleaner in and then shook it gently to mix it good.

He always claimed to have such good luck. Now what kind of a thing was that for a person to do, wasn't that just asking for it? Didn't that make you think you were better than everyone else at thinking and fooling? She pulled out the little stick of super glue she kept for emergencies in her apron pocket. Rita had taught her that trick. No point in getting charged for things you didn't do, like breaking lamps and ash-trays. Taxer was awful quick with his calculator and blame. Hard enough to get a whole week's pay out of him.

It didn't take her but a few minutes to seal the zippers down on his pants. He wasn't as smart as he thought he was, buying all his fancy label clothes from the other reps or down at the outlet store off the interstate. Sure he looked good, that's what had attracted her to begin with, she liked a pretty man. *Why take an ugly one when you can have a pretty one*, she always told Rita and Sugar Jo. She poured a little roach killer into the toes of his shoes, the stuff he claimed would eat the rust off a hundred-year-old hoe. Use it at home, he'd urged, pressing a handful of sample packets into her palm as he kissed her neck good-bye last month.

She hadn't ever told him where she worked. Well, she'd worked at the motel on the other side of town then and felt a little ashamed because it wasn't as nice as this one. At least on the surface. The floors were linoleum and the sinks all had rust stains even if they were the old-fashioned kind it took two grown men to haul around. Things were newer at Taxer's, but the plastic was starting to brown and crack on the vanity counters, and the rugs had a permanent damp beer and foot smell a person couldn't fight. Even with that damn deodorizer, it smelled just like the big old sweaty butt of Loyal D. Rock every time the window air conditioner pooled out some of its sickly cool air at you. Loyal D.'s butt was famous in Spartus among those who had to go to school with him, ride around in his car cause they didn't have trans-portation, and sit in the booth at the Peach House Restaurant and Bar after he'd gotten up. It was the alphabet's fault, really, that her last name, Rodgers, came right after Rock in school, and that'd sealed his smell in her nose forever.

Loyal D. should of kept his homely little wife closer to home last night. Inna Rock was no more visiting her sister in Greenwood than Daralynn was. Not unless her sister had a sex-change operation and looked drop dead good as a man. Not unless he knew how to put her on her knees and poke it in from behind like some animal would do. *Animals is people too*, Rita said when Daralynn went weeping into the linens room, wetting down a stack of stiff white sheets.

It was Rita stopped her from calling Loyal D. to get his big fat butt over and watch his wife taking it where the sun didn't shine. She even did the first clean on the room, watching so Taxer wouldn't catch them trading. The people in Rita's room had been asshole fishermen who left beer cans and cigarette butts all over like the whole damn world was an ashtray. They'd dumped their shitty fish water in the tub so they could refill the cooler, even though the ice machine had a big sign on it saying NO ICE FOR COOLERS with the PLEASE left off because Taxer was sick of people using up all the ice and then complaining when there wasn't any for their drinks.

Fish scales stuck to the tub like silver sequins and about as hard to pick off. But she did, every last one of them, even those that spilled onto the fake marble linoleum floor and dried there. She did it because every bruising ache on the knobs of her knees reminded her of what she'd seen in that room Rita was cleaning, and she wanted to remember it, wanted to stay both mad and sorrowful long enough to go back there and finish. *You only have so much time to clean things up*, Rita always said, *and you'd better do it right the first time, regardless of how you're feeling*.

Rita was right, even though she took some shortcuts, like vacuuming the sheets for hair if she didn't feel like changing them, and wiping the sink with the bath towel so she didn't have to scrub it. That paper strip Taxer wanted them to put over the toilet, well she just flushed and put it there without cleaning whatsoever, unless there was something real visible to the naked eye. The naked eye was what she always used as her standard. *And some people's are more naked than others*, Rita said. Most rooms you can get by just picking up the big stuff. People assume you're on your hands and knees scrubbing and inspecting like you're in your own house, but it's the naked eye that counts.

Daralynn thought about having what her girlfriends called a come-to-Jesus meeting with him, but then she thought about Taxer and how he'd fire her butt for sure and keep the whole three days she'd put in to boot. So tonight when he came to meet her at the Peach House, Daralynn promised herself, she was going to act like he was just something she could kick under the bed, turn out the lights, and leave behind as she moved on to the next room.

The Change Jar

"You can't understand or represent the 4th Dimension—
but you can take a cross-section of it."

Saul keeps a jar of change, mostly pennies, in his bedroom. Right where he undresses. When the coins start to tumble off the shelf, when their moist faces stick to his bare feet, when his wife tries to vacuum and must pick them up on her hands and knees, muttering, she dumps them in the jar. He used to do it himself.

He feels like the brown extension cord, underpowered, unable to carry the really big microwave load, plugged in and getting hot. Someday, Saul thinks he's going to melt, frizzle and spark, burn the rubber and plastic, send a thread of noxious smoke into the room and be left there, a black char on the floor.

When he dresses in his suit each day for work, his wife smells hopelessness, or its cousin, fear. She dry-cleans his clothes weekly, launders and bleaches his shirts and underwear so that he is spotless. She can't figure out where that dirt is coming from.

Saul keeps a secret, the thinness of his shoe soles, the aura of a hole that is beginning. He stores his shoes carefully after work so they won't call her attention. He wants that hole. It's something he figures he can escape through when the time comes.

His wife has a face like God, angled and blunt, changing like pond water with the surface of the sun and the sky. He can't tell who she is most days, so he's stopped looking. He sees parts of her, like an apple pared for a pie. Everywhere he stares though, he notices her stiffness. As if the mere act of looking were turning her brittle, crabbed, her movements crustacean. She certainly is the girl he married, he just isn't sure whether she's Cinderella or the stepsister.

Out the window he watches the leaves fall down and the trees grow up. He checks the roof shingles of all the neighborhood houses in case an arm, a head has sprouted, but no one is escaping. At night, in bed, he calms the panic like a low machine hum, thinking of the years to come, when she'll appear in the doorway, making him start over with himself, making him a half instead of a whole.

When he encounters a toad in the garden, he examines the sky, but finds only a neighborhood friendliness. They are at peace. No question of what to do.

In the backyard the black ropes of powerlines bisect the green and end abruptly at the pole. He notices this and has no explanation. He wishes there were something to be said. He wishes he could fly himself into their touch, tangle like a kite, crucified, feel the balsa of his bones snap and burn, he wants his skin flapping in the wind like paper.

He'd really like something to happen. Help me, he calls out to the wind quietly as he gets dressed for work. Fasting until 10 A.M., he takes the coffee and donut reluctantly, catching the failed face the glass and stainless steel counter reflect back at him. He thinks something is happening when he sees his skin mottle, spot, but then realizes it's only the fingerprints of people before him, smudged on the surface. Beneath the deep aroma of coffee and sugary palm of donut, he catches the first whiff of himself, of the day, the sweat of his despair. Saul pays for the snack with a dollar bill, like always, smoothing its surface with the side of his hand before he gives it to the cashier. He pockets the change. You know where that's going.

What It Means

The dead have privileges. They can shop at Target or K-Mart, places they'd never dream of going before. They can twirl the racks of cheap dresses and shirts and never worry about paying for anything.

They can wait sleepy in parking lots while a granddaughter directs cars to their proper slots until the beauty parlor is ready to do their hair. The dead have all the time in the world, and they're still drowsy. They have to be coaxed and dragged sometimes to their appointments. Sometimes they're so quiet you could slap them, and do. The dead can be beaten and they come back for more, every time. And they forget. They're like pop-up toys: smash 'em down, up they come. They only bear malice when it pleases them.

The dead never come around in a storm. They hang onto their old fear of lightning. The dead don't mind being indoors in the rain, they don't ask for much when the windows are open and the air cools the room so you dive under the covers. They're not trying to crowd you then.

But when you make love, the dead stay close, fill the bed, lie along the bodies in tiers, sandwiching all their lives with yours. It's embarrassing to be naked with the dead. They're all eyes and hands. Their mouths are caves of dark desire you get lost in, never come home from. There's more dead inside than out, you discover. The dead panting. The dead moaning to get loose. The dead wanting to spill, to pour out of those mouths onto your skin, the sheets, the ruining sweat. The dead come alive in our kisses, our fluids. They drink us like blood and rise to the ceilings of rooms, hanging there limp and satisfied as leaves. There's no air when the dead take the room, the love. There's no way out when they seal the walls with their skin and make it drum tight. Your lungs, your heart suffocate for the dead.

Dead Space

There is a funeral you imagine—the one where they roll your sister efficiently toward the hole. None of this effort of straining men. They have done everything they can or know how to do already. Father's in a wheelchair. He can't lift a hand again. Ex-husband has taken his cynical smile to the cruel motel and waits. Maybe he has another bride. Who knows, maybe he's in the part of the cemetery dissolving into the overgrown hollow and abandoned cars beyond.

You know this because this is the funeral of November. So let's put him on the other side of the hollow, his careful pant legs stickered and ragged with weeds. He's been caught and rumpled in the bush. He's been stumbled and fallen in the dry creek. Morgan Creek. All the creeks have been drier since the great drought. This one is no exception. He caught a Gucci in between two rocks and went down on the mossy stones. His knees are wet—darkly wet. There's hope of blood, maybe mud. One of them would be worse. You want them to be muddy so he doesn't get the valor of wounds in the shower inspection. No, you just want him stranded in a knee-high thicket of ragweed and blackberry and burrs. You want him in the possession of something with enough power to ignore and nag him. An irritation like a splinter on his attention.

OK. This is the funeral. The air is slight and cold with wet, though it is not raining. Brothers who would be strong enough for coffin lifting have put themselves elsewhere. They're worried about what they'll have to steal to get home again. There's almost nothing in the cemetery of value—though in a wild moment they imagine backing a van to the slabs at night and stealing the very old Civil War ones. The weather has made them light enough to carry, and the faded spires with elaborate dull print might appeal to someone seeking a really unique object.

They try to think if they know anyone like that. They glance at the bald head of her ex-husband, it's finally lost its shine. He looks poor today, he can't even afford to stand with the family.

When the coffin comes rolling onto the gurney, you're struck by the way the legs flop down and stand up under her. *There*, you want to say, *that's what she needed—four long steel rods and wheels.* You notice the brothers peeking in cars as the procession works its way along the roads.

At each family plot you must ask, "Will you have her?"

"We're crowded," they complain. "We don't remember her. Where's *her* family?"

It takes an hour and a half of struggling the coffin over rocks and ruts to come to the lowest part of the cemetery. The oldest part sits on a small rise at the center, inaccessible by roads, so you must walk on the heads and shoulders of the dead to speak to them. The coffin rocks perilously at the Bellocks but their silence keeps her away. The newer members spread away from the old heart, gradually working their way to the road, the hollow, the little houses, and the poor.

Mother walks behind, the chief mourner, though she wants to gallop ahead, lead the wagons. She's known where you're headed all along. There was never any question, but she's been told to stay behind, so she does. This is one time your sister gets to lead the way, and she's not giving up the authority of death. Not even to the powerful figure of her mother in black—a dark hum, a sound held and gutturalized. You have dressed her in galoshes—the old-fashioned heavy black rubber kind with metal gripper fasteners that flop and clank with each step. She keeps wanting to kill the corpse again so the hair and fingernails don't grow. Someone has to be sure.

The father, miles behind, is going to ashes, so his wife doesn't have a chance at him. He wants a sure end to things—no growing out of control after the breath flattens and the tongue stills and softens, the first thing to rot, he once believed, until his wife told him of the cells whose job it was to keep living, growing, the dead rising again. Either you sat up with the body, waiting for the clack of teeth, the snort of breath, or you embalmed, killing again, or you burned, killing again, every cell crackling and popping in the choking fire.

Grandmother Neallie's stone lies flat with her friend at her feet. They've got two trees to themselves. Keep the men at a distance. When you reach her, she won't recognize anyone—not even her son. She doesn't approve of this ragged lot. That's why she took her place here with someone who isn't even family.

Father pretends he doesn't notice, his knuckles yellow-white on the chair arms.

In the middle of the group your sister's daughter staggers under the load of jewelry, clothes, furniture, paintings, and silver she carries. This is what envy brings her. She is a series of half-successful gestures. She was born old and has been catching up all her life. If there is grief pocketed in her, you can't see it beneath the accumulation of her mother's wealth. She thinks of putting something down, but can't make decisions like that. Not since her mother, you know—

Behind her daughter come the sisters. Dressed in bright blues and greens, bejeweled like queens or circus stars. You are afraid to touch anything. You're thinking of the bathroom at the motel, pure water with no aftertaste, no stink to soap your hands again and again to wash off. You'll never wear those clothes again. You'll discard the shoes edged with red clay, a tiny pebble caught between sole and stitching. This business is all physical—it makes you want to brush your teeth, like an embarrassing smell has caught on the back of your tongue, along the rim of your gums. You can't admit you've never been in a graveyard. You don't have a fallback like the bandit brothers. Looking pretty is your only option. Each of you wears a rainbow of face makeup, greens and blues and pinks and yellows. It makes your faces look surprised, hopeful, an expression you have learned so that you won't be mistaken, hurt. The three of you, like harpies tamed to the hand, husbands trudging behind on little leashes, tinkling chains in the gray dull light. Their faces are scrubbed clean of features.

Finally, when the weight of refusals from the occupied stones shoves your little procession to the fringe, the edge where newly dead stretch rawly in the yellow grass, your eye notes how embarrassing it is, without trees, within clear view of the blacktop traffic and tumbledown shacks whose porches hold the overflow couches, appliances, boxes, an open-air closet, something defiantly intimate that makes you turn your eyes away when you want to stare.

That's where the ground stops talking and the men stop the gurney. You'd like to say a hole appeared, that no one was asked to lend a hand. When it happens though, you only have to scoop a bit, your high heels sinking so you're rocked back, tilting away from the shovels of dirt.

It doesn't take long. The rain has helped. The rocks grind like molars on the metal blade, but it's not unpleasant. It feels good to be doing something, and soon even the brothers put their backs into it—though later they'll steal the shovel. Ex-husband is panting like a dog on the other side of the culvert. He drops to all fours, the Harris tweed filling quickly until he's bushy with the bald spot like a bolus of tree fungus. "Don't worry," you say, "he can't get across."

Even Mother gets into the act, happy she's worn galoshes after all since she won't throw anything away. She gives the shovel a hefty dig and pulls great mounds of dirt out, heaving them easily over her shoulder. Some of the dirt crumbles over her as it flies through the air. Good thing she wore black, you think.

Father won't get out of his chair. He shouts directions and caustic remarks everyone ignores. After all, what does he know, he's afraid of fingernails, hair, and his own cells.

By the time the chain gang husbands are done, the hole is as big as a house foundation and the men easily drive the gurney in, press a button, and leave the coffin squatting bewildered in the middle of the scraped red earth.

Now this is something, you think, as you all look around. At this funeral, there is no minister, no stranger to the wills and wiles of the family. The coffin transport workers have faded from sight. In a minute you hear the backfire of the old hearse, which doubles as ambulance and scout expedition bus for the tiny town.

The brothers haven't stolen the shovel yet, but no one makes a move. You can wait a long time between efforts. The ex-husband's soft whimpers and growls get blown to pieces by the swooping caws of the blackbirds who arrive like visiting gods and walk among the headstones behind you. Every motion elongated, slowed, deliberate until they resemble the grace of elephants, giraffes, draft horses—something bigger than possible.

It takes a while for you to recognize the clinking and clanking and turn your head to the figure of her daughter, a tumbledown tower of stuff shuffling to the hole. Descending the dirt ramp in the gurney tracks, the weight sinks her deeper and deeper. Each time she yanks a leg out, it leaves a pock surrounded by a puddle of colors and forms. She resembles a dinosaur making its gradual progress into the tar pit. By the time she reaches her mother's coffin, she is waist-deep in muck and only her final shove of goods from her shoulders, back, and head keeps her from sinking out of sight. Miraculously, when the noise of metal and glass and cloth hits the bright anodized aluminum canister of coffin, it doesn't sink.

Her daughter stands bare except for a simple black dress like her grandmother. Levering herself on the coffin, she pulls her legs and stands naturally but doesn't bother pushing at the mud caking her from the waist down. Instead, she is the one who begins to fill the hole. Using her hands, she digs ferociously at the sides, pulling the dirt down around her, then climbing out again, over and over.

You watch this. Then you look at Mother, who stands on the rim. One of the sisters hands her the shovel, but she has lost her strength now. The bandit brothers take the shovel and work hard—really hard, for the first time in years. They have things to do now. They need to finish before dark. Next, the chain gang husbands, let off their leashes, get their backs into it, but the hole is taking much longer to fill than to dig. By the time the sisters have to dirty their hands, you need to borrow dirt from surrounding graves. There just isn't enough to go around. Even Father gets out of his wheelchair. He's so annoyed he can walk again, but he finds out what his advising voice didn't know: the coffin keeps rising foot by dirt-filling foot until the hole is gone and the place is marked by the giant bright cigar in anodized red. Your sister's grave.

After you're gone, her ex-husband comes sniffing by, lifts a leg to pee and gets an electric shock when the yellow stream hits the burnished red. He runs away howling.

In the motel room, you bathe her daughter, wash her hair, clean her fingernails, and give her a plain practical life without tragedy and drama. Father gets lost in the corridors and whimpers until he hears the galoshes slurping and clacking toward him. Mother has decided to wear them always.

The husbands are in the bar getting drunk, trying to get some expressions back in their faces.

Out at the cemetery, the brothers have possession of the shovel and are passing it back and forth, estimating its weight and the price it will bring.

And your sister finally has what she wants.

The Specific Dreams of Our Republic

First let me remind you of a few facts, and then I'll answer questions. The knives are long, some of them, or short and curved for a specific purpose, like rooting out all that is in there, the sore spots, the bloodied and bruised places, the ones where some splinter has gotten under the skin. Maybe for those you'd choose the needle-nose knife, the one so thin it disappears in the sun and you have to look everywhere for it, afraid you've left it in the grass for someone's foot.

And keep in mind too: the purpose of a knife is always obvious. I mean, there's never any doubt about its formal training, its degree of commitment, its ability to get the job done, say, when it's right at your heart, right there, being pressed through each layer of hide and fat, muscle and bone, so there's a little pause as it saws through. A knife is made for such uses, and this one probably has the special serrated edge just for carving through mammalian meat, pointed teeth like robot animals we've drawn and then created. That's how it goes with knives. They're all ours. They're really something we can claim here, aren't they?

All of you in the audience tonight, you each have one. Don't even try to deny it.

You there, yes, sir, pull your knife out. Why, it's as big as a machete, and how the blade bellies out there, the handle as curved as a swan's neck. You'd never imagine it'd fit right under your arm that way, so the head nestles into the warmth of your hand as you walk along. You seem to have quite a relationship with that machete, you've taken such care of it, the way it shines, even the nicked edge of the blade. I see where you've honed it, the bright scrapes of the whetstone, such a fine netting it seems intentional like pavé or patina. And the handle has been polished and rubbed with affection but enough authority to make it behave.

That's important for keeping a knife. The dark wood, rubbed and stained, it makes a real statement, like the bronzed shoulder of a boxer. Have you ever cut yourself on its sharpness?

And you there, miss, I see the knife without you even opening your purse. It's a nice long triangle of kitchen use. Something to bring along at the last minute to meetings like this. Eleven inches of high carbon steel, it's right there on the blade. Pull it out and look. The point sparkles like a diamond, it does, hold it up to the light. There's a bit of bloody rust or stain just above the handle on the reverse side, but you just ignore that. The knife does its job, you're not going to baby it along or anything. It stays sharp on its own. That's why you bought that German steel. They advertise it that way, though lately you suspect they might have exaggerated their claims. People do that a lot to you.

When you come home at night, you only have to pull it out of your purse and hack up a few bits of fruit and vegetable and voilà—dinner. Then you take it in to watch TV with you, but you're still not going to baby it, it doesn't get a special cushion or anything. It has to sit there right alongside and not complain. It never gets to change the channel or fall asleep. And when you're tired, it has to go right upstairs with you, doesn't it, and stay on its own side of the bed, tip gleaming dully in the streetlight casting through the window, so you always know where it is when you wake up from a bad dream and need the comfort.

Hey you, buddy. Yes, you slouching there in the third row. Listen up now. You thought I wouldn't stop for you, I can tell. You've been getting away with everything, your knife and you. I saw the names you carved on the pillar of the porch outside, the dates, the act of numbers you can't not be attracted to. Your mind must run like tumblers in a lock when you try to dial the telephone. There's evidence, you know, lots of it. You're as easy to follow as a bird in the snow—sprays of prints, tiny toed corrosions. You know what I'm saying here. Don't look away, out that window. You have knives on you. There, that one chained like a vicious animal, beside the flat docile billfold, that's just the one you need for your nails and teeth, for opening things, for small telegraphs, and under your coat, there, see, I knew it, that's the friend you never have, isn't it, that's the one watching your back, because you can't not go into dark places alone.

Now slide that sleeve up. There's the switchblade breathless as a young girl when you touch it, the soft snap and almost a sigh as it slides into view and slices. I know about that knife, we all know about that one. And don't forget the hunting knife strapped to your leg. I could make you drop your jeans so we could all see, but I won't. You're always being made to do things, I can tell, just the leather straps clasping your calf like little hands, so many depending on you. It must make you tired and ornery, at the end of the day, prying the buckles open. In their little sockets, the bright blades are like hungry mouths you just can't face in the failing light of your room. You feed them once and they all want more. I understand, I know how it goes. They clamor, don't they, creak restlessly in their cases, twist and mutter, try to organize against you, until you turn up the music and put a pillow over your head, another over them, laying the big fat blade from your boot on top in case they get any ideas. You're a man so protected no one can touch you. On the surfaces of your room, you have carved their runes: STAY AWAY, DON'T COME ANY CLOSER.

You out there, you're smiling at all this, aren't you? Such caution and excess you're not prone to, that's what you think. You with your silver elegance disguising two inches of sharpness in the pocket of your suit pants. Don't deny it, don't say it's just a penknife, a gentleman's knife. Every man must have a knife, even the lethal diminishment, ornamented with initials, scrolled, doesn't obscure this. You feel naked without it, don't you? It waits silently with the coins on your dresser at night, secure that in the morning you will palm its violence and tuck it neatly into the thin fabric of your pants pocket where it will be warmed by your thigh all day, waiting for your hand to close on its pleasantness, the act of unexpected usefulness, a clever cut, just so everyone's eyes open a little wider and sparkle, the way they do when a man brings out his knife. As intimate as any undressing, the knife says it all. It's full of promises. It says, *I can afford to*, because the miniature is always expensive. There, you're laughing now and slipping your hand into your pocket to make sure it's there. Your fingers rub the smooth silver surface and it just makes you feel better, doesn't it, all that polish and promise.

And the rest of you, I see your knives. The Swiss Army knives you women are buying now. They're so fat and funny, you can't resist them, carry them with you and whip them out to trim paper with the scissors, open wine bottles and tighten screws. You like how competent you look when you do these things, how efficient, but you don't do anything with that big fat blade in public, do you? The razory one, I'm talking about, not the fingernail file you offer, but the wide one, with no use at all except to be a knife, the real thing you handle only in the privacy of your own car or house, the one that slices your finger as neatly as a line drawn on paper when you test the edge. Sometimes you dream about it, not even asleep, you get the scenes in focus, the one, the only one there is for a blade like this, where he comes for you, as you've always known he was going to, and you're ready. You have the knife hidden in your hand somehow and he doesn't see it, but you feel confident as he comes, and when he's there, doing whatever he is going to start doing, you let him have it, sticking that blade in and ripping it upward, outward, again and again, because that's what's missing in all the stories. Afterward, you wash it carefully, drying it on the same towel you bathe with, or maybe you even take it into the shower with you, watching the pink swirl and puddle at your feet together, never letting go of it and keeping your eyes open, ready in case the curtain moves, or a dark shadow appears, because that's what's missing in the stories. Pretty soon, you two are so close you forget you never had one and slip it up inside yourself, because everyone needs a knife.

Asparagus

My father won't look at the fish finder his father is holding as we walk through the asparagus patch by the house because he's never believed in such things. *It catches eight-pounders,* Grandfather insists, *and it's only slightly more bulky than your regular rod and reel.* There are rules for fishing that a son shouldn't have to remind his father of, that's what my father's face says as I bend to slice the white green bottoms of stalks. They are so ready the knife slides easily and the asparagus topples and I can't cut enough to keep up. *Come on,* they urge, *your bowl will be full before we get to the patch down yonder.*

My father has a big round wooden bowl dangling from his hand, and I've got the dented aluminum one, its side caved in like a head. I notice my head isn't feeling too symmetrical either. My landlord showed up this morning to carpet the narrow rooms upstairs, and after I yelled at him, I could tell I'd be moving soon. *What about the carpet I bought? What about how I'm fixing this place up?* I said in a not nice way. His bland fat face ignored me with the kind of shrug that doesn't have to be made to let you know you don't count. His assistant giggled on his knees at the baseboard, they were dripping paint everywhere, a couple of doofuses. I wanted them out, but how do you kick a person off the land he owns? The Wild West show was over and I just went downstairs to the shove of their laughter.

I don't tell the men in my family that I have no place to live with my children and that the asparagus is a memory I've come back for, like the horse that gallops away from us in the big green pastures unrolling like wallpaper. They're in a dream with the small tensions of the returned. They have their own issues to settle as father and son. I'm just along for the same reason I was ever there—being related, they had to put me someplace. No wonder I want to ride away on that horse, make concentric circles like a good explorer mapping the land around the farm. Daily, the circles grow larger until pretty soon I have to take my lunch and don't return until nightfall. No one asked where I went. They approved of the tired brown on my face and arms when I did the dishes and went to bed.

Small failures have begun to appear on my skin. My father and his father don't notice, of course. We never make it to the asparagus patch. The fish finder argument hangs in the hands of my grandfather with the gray metal box that sends his line singing through the air so he never fails to catch something. He's waited all his life for this kind of break, and now it comes in a dream. My head feels boggy, and there's a sharp pain cracking the side, like a tell-tale split in an overripe melon. It was only a fork he tapped me with, whoever that man was in my house all those years, a fork to the side, and my head, as thin-skinned ripe as could be, just cracked. *It happens*, he told me, *just a lucky hit*. You won't die, you won't die, they all tell me. Sure, there'll be some blood, a clot maybe, headache, nausea. When I fell forward, unable to move my limbs, I wasn't surprised, I knew things could be worse.

That's why I went back there with my bowl for the asparagus, for the disagreement that was so slight it made the world safe again, gathering the sure stalks that would taste like a buttered green sun at supper. This was before my house was reclaimed by its landlord, before I was reminded of how temporary I am at living. We don't make it to the patch down the hill in the horse pasture, however, because I realize I can go back, I can go back to the house before. I can buy a house and live in it with my children or whoever cares to follow a life laid out in dreams before and after it is being lived. This isn't an intentional thing, they have to understand. I order carpet for the bedrooms without notifying the landlord because I forget that being comfortable doesn't mean you own the place.

I miss those men, the farm, the horse that took me on his broad brown back so fast sometimes through the tearing weeds and sticker bushes and who ate bologna and lettuce on Wonder Bread secretly because it was lunch and there was no one there to witness how he could step out of his hide and stand beside me in the old cemetery, the graves sunken so low I thought they'd been robbed until I realized no one would want those old German farmer bodies so used up they couldn't hold the pressure of earth back when it started to push down.

I don't ask my father for money. Housing is a personal matter, a kind of failure and success we create and destroy on our own. It's enough he lets me go along for asparagus, that he lets me hear Grandfather again explaining the fish finder and says, *I was out here just this morning and I swear it's shot up since then. Have to cut them before they get woody or pulpy, I guess, but don't take too much, don't fill your bowl too early. We still have to go down to the other patch.* On my knees in the hot dirt, it's his knife I use for slicing, thankful and only a little anxious in this place I can dream us back to again.

❖ ❖

FROM

~Bend This Heart~

❖ ❖

I Can't Stop Loving You

For two years I lived in a neighborhood of lovers. You could tell love was everywhere. Matching sixties Cadillac convertibles arrived and mated every spring beside the tiny corner house. Each one claimed by a short fat member of the husband-wife team who built the swimming pool, which consumed the backyard, and the stockade fence, which hid their cooing and the tanning of sausage-round limbs. Only the ballpark-size floodlight was shared, like a full moon on dark nights

In my house we were having none of that. I had retired from love, from friends. I was busy eating, being alone with the television's sympathetic light bathing me blue and more as I slept on the sofa. Once I left the door unlocked, and as if it spread its arms to the sidewalk like a net, it caught a man, whose clumping steps announced him. A mistake. Even the six-pack under his arm. "It's not my fault," he declared. "You should keep your door locked." I agreed as I let him out, hoping he'd find the woman he was after.

Next door, Patrick kept the gardens just the way she had, although he gave all the vegetables away and spent weekends with a former wife. There was her memory to be serviced like a lawn being kept neat. After a while he shoveled my snow too, even advancing to sweep the porch when I wasn't around. I bought chocolate chips and made cookies for him, over and over, eating them every time in a fit of shyness. Now I can't remember delivering a single plate to his door, though I might have taken one—the scene is so clear the way I knew it would be.

Across the street real love took place. Cyndie made men swoon from her second-story balcony. Left the lights on all night long, came home when it pleased her. Sunbathed all summer day and drove off at dusk in her little red sports car. When we woke up at dawn, there was always a strange car parked for her—electricians, carpenters, salesmen, a few times even a chauffeur whose long black limo crowded our tiny curbs and old cars like a bully newly moved in. Cyndie's soft Czech limbs and wild honey hair wound the male dreams of our neighborhood onto a tight spool and saved them from the temptations of the massage parlor three blocks away.

One night when storm sirens brought us all to our front porches, I saw Cyndie's lover wheel his motorcycle into the shelter of the garage, his black leather pants bleeding dark into the shadows of the house as his white back and shaved skull blinked, "Touch me, take me." Later they grilled steaks under the shelter of her second-story porch and left the light on all night long. Inside my house I watched storm warnings roll like credits along the bottom of the television screen.

Directly across from me lived one of the true lovers of this story. His love streamed out of his garage, on forties music: an aging Frank Sinatra with a drink-ballooned body, tousled black hair—it was never quite the day he'd washed it—and desire he wore like a tattoo for everyone to see. I met him at the corner store in my riding boots. He never forgot. It became a bond between us, a secret—what I knew he knew. At night I undressed in the windows facing his, with the lights on. Summers the trees might screen me, winters, the frost. We never spoke directly, except for the times late at night he called me. I was alone. I should have been asleep. I had left the lights on, the door locked. That stopped when he got a girlfriend.

How do we know?

It was his violence of loving. When they fought, he threw her clothes into the alley and lit them on fire, emptied the contents of the house and his heart on the tiny lawn at three o'clock in the morning, then rode his bicycle like a drunken acrobat up and down the alleys until dawn. Once I almost hit him. And like our neighbors it was the gift of locomotion that betrayed him: the beat-up Datsun he bestowed on the woman's daughter. It lurked like a bird by the curb in repair, rusted, unhinged, pounded with luck and love. It received his attention almost daily.

Down the block, Huey and his mother waged the wars of love too, in a house dislocated from time, the Fourth of July flag leaning crazily against the plastic jack-o'-lantern on the front porch all year long. Inside, there were paths like jungle trails through the shoulder-high newspapers. Huey sold drugs, and his mother gathered the neighbor-hood gossip, until her body went bad and she had to be carried around like a bag-lady version of Cleopatra on the arms of Huey and his freaked-out motorcycle friends. When the bars closed, Huey opened his doors. Later he cursed his love to the moon and stars, cursed the Vietnamese, the United States government, and someone trying to OD in his front yard. It did no good to call the police. They'd known Huey all their lives. "He's crazy. He's always been crazy." They drove away. On Sundays, Huey and his mother fought all day long.

Finally she firebombed his motorcycle, parked under a tree out front. The stain of black remained on the leaves and bark until winter. Huey stayed put, though, his transportation gone. He used his mother's car. Driving her on her daily rounds, he was clearly in love, as he peered crazily ahead and didn't quite brake for the stop signs that patrolled our tiny block at either end.

An apprentice at love in that neighborhood, I went on a diet. I talked to no one I used to know. When my car was wrecked, I figured it was a good sign, an act of love, a promise of more to come. And when I met someone finally, I trapped his heart like a small animal and held it, held it, held it.

And Blue

Downstairs Reba's ex-husband is watching soap operas. He's been at it for two hours. Doesn't bother to apologize when she walks in the door. His favorite is *One Life to Live*. He's a Buddhist. Going to be a monk, he says, when he's too old for sex. Some of the far-out ones still screw around, he adds. It's no use trying to figure out if he means himself, Reba decides and walks through the neat piles of bedding and clothes he sandbags along the walls and bookcases as if there's going to be a flood. She doesn't like it about herself that she finds his things a little nasty.

Reba is lying in bed watching blue cabbages of light bombard the dark field that appears when she closes her eyes. Maybe they're asteroids. She hears creaking in the hallway but ignores it. She'll find out soon enough.

"I'm coming through there on my way east," he'd said. "I'm going into real estate, going to sell."

"Get a haircut," she'd advised. Reba wonders if Buddhists sell only to each other. A secret network or something.

Her new husband doesn't mind the ex on the sofa. Does this mean the romance is over? she wonders.

Twenty-five years ago, when she was pregnant, Reba would stay up all night, go to sleep at dawn, wake up just when the heat began to close its hand around the apartment. She'd eat Jell-O and turn on the television for the afternoon soaps. Every day the same thing. It hurt her when the weekend came and the day stretched like a yawn she couldn't close her mouth against. Her ex was a Baptist then. When he voted for Barry Goldwater and lost, she felt triumph and pity. He didn't know what was good for him.

Upstairs Reba thinks everyone is tucked in an envelope, waiting for the tongue that licks the edges and seals the letter. His daughter watches soaps in her room, but they're different ones, so she can't watch with her father in the living room. She likes *The Young and the Restless*. They all have good hairdos on that one.

"I hope she finds out where she's going," Reba's ex says. "I'm forty-five, and I still don't know."

As Reba drives him to the grocery store, he asks, "Do you ever think about the void, nothingness?"

She concentrates on her driving—stop at the light, move over one lane to avoid the turning truck, pull around on the green, swing back into the lane, and turn into the parking lot.

"No," she says. "I'm too busy."

He's careful just to eat leftovers. Won't start a meal of fresh food on his own. "Where's the asparagus from last night?" he asks her three times one morning. There's panic in his voice.

"Make yourself some bacon and eggs," she tells him.

"Is it OK if I eat that leftover hamburger?" he asks.

Reba catches her name on a page he is writing in his cramped, childish handwriting, as though a right-handed person was forced to do it left, though he *is* left-handed. She feels him disapproving of her.

"Can we have vegetables tonight?" he asks.

"We had them last night. Artichokes, remember?"

He nods, unconvinced, then goes back to writing. Later she catches her new husband's name on the page too. He thinks they spend too much money. She knows he's read the bills, her mail. She doesn't know how to tell him it's OK.

When the painters come one day, her ex is full of advice. He sneaks inspections and pulls her from her work to discipline the men in the basement for not doing the job the way they should.

"There's no reason why they can't do it right," he says. He is sitting on the living-room floor combing out the gray rug fuzz packed in the vacuum-cleaner attachment. She notices that he's using his own little black pocket comb. He does this for an hour. "I bet no one's ever done this, have they?" he says.

"No, but it hasn't hurt it. Ten years and it still works fine. What difference does it make?"

"It makes a difference," he assures her. "Ten years, huh?"

"We've never done it," she tells him. "Why don't you just vacuum?" The pile of fuzz grows slowly beside him. It is so small she would have missed it on the mottled tan rug if it weren't outlined against his leg.

An hour later when he vacuums, he does such a poor job Reba can hardly tell it's been done.

At noon when she comes back from work, she asks him if he's eaten. "Ice cream, brownies, cake," he tells her. Leftovers.

When Reba can't sleep at dawn, sneaking downstairs to grab a cup of tea, he is awake, dressed. This happens every morning, although the hour varies wildly. His bed is neatly folded, and he is sitting cross-legged in the living room, facing the floor-to-ceiling draw drapes in the gloom. She wonders if this is a trick he is learning. Or if he's like a household dog, always awake a minute before the master.

On Saturday night they order Vietnamese food. The ex doesn't know any of the dishes on the take-out menu and asks for their help. He eats judiciously, saving the stuff at the bottom of his cartons for the next day.

In three days her ex does not use the towel or the washcloth Reba's set out for him. She notices that he doesn't smell. She worries that maybe he is using her towel. She tests it for dampness each time she goes to the bathroom, hesitating a moment before she holds the towel up to her face. She doesn't want the odor of him in her mouth—the gray metal slice of sweat souring like wet diapers with Dial soap rubbed dry over it. Even now as she tests the towel, she is afraid of pressing its big body against her face. She waits for him to take a bath and leave the room steamy and sour for hours after.

There was only one year when Reba liked his smell. They would bathe together, him in front, her in back, the reverse of her husband now. She would groom the blackheads from his back, washing each red pinched spot carefully with soap and hot water. In this way she cleared up the last of his adolescent skin troubles.

The smell hadn't appeared really until their divorce, when he spent three months in a windowless room in the basement of a house, after she'd kicked him out. First he shaved his head, then put on his wool sweaters, although it was late spring and hot. Then madness appeared in his eyes and on his skin. He chased her on his bike all over town, in and out of the beds of other men, until they were both exhausted and she let him back in the house for the summer. It was then that Reba noticed he wore the smell like a permanent stain on his clothes or like a birthmark, glass of wine spilled across his skin.

For twenty years he has been coming to visit Reba this way. She is beginning to feel sorry for him. The way his hair and beard hang ragged around his worn collar. The way he neatly folds his wide workman's leather belt. The way his work boots have begun to split and crack along the sole lines. The way he hunches over, his hands clenched as he watches the progress of the couples on his favorite soap.

Cupid

Leslie and Frank are parked right outside the museum. The air and the streets are moist and dark, springlike, although it is too early for winter to be over. All day the change in weather has pulled people from their houses onto the sidewalks, bewildered, their jackets open. At dusk it has begun to drizzle lightly, just enough to bring the good dirt smell up out of the ground temporarily.

Leslie knows. She spent the afternoon with Frank, walking around, talking about books and his life. He is a famous poet visiting, the star. Though now his hair is gray, his face lined, he is still a beautiful boy. The early clear looks that drew men and women alike to him are lingering there, smudging his face with a sense of what is gone. To see him now, Leslie thinks, is to feel loss, regret.

Frank is saying, "And Amal gave me this—pure stuff. He always has good drugs." She watches as he pries the lid of the medicine vial off.

"Tennessee Williams," Leslie says, and he laughs. He is feeling loose now.

They have stopped at a liquor store in a poorer neighborhood where he felt confident he could get a pint of Jack Daniels in a paper bag. He wanted the bag to fit exactly with just enough to twist around the top. He wanted it to look right when he drank on stage that night. He'd insisted she go with him.

She felt his eyes splash like oil on her legs as he walked in behind her. She watched him lick his lips as the drunks around them savored her short tight black leather skirt, studded belt, blouse open to show she had no bra on. She felt Frank's step lighten and rise as he searched the store longer than he had to, while she was positioned like a package he'd checked at the counter. She felt the bee hum of the men as they pulled wadded dollars from their filthy jeans and followed her gold chain all the way down the dark crevice where it disappeared between the curves of her breasts. She brushed their sound away from her face with the back of her hand.

On the way to the car, Frank had hugged her. Inside, they each took a quick hit from the bottle. Leslie knew he was going to kiss her. It was only a matter of time. She'd felt slightly betrayed when she found herself pulling the black leather out of the closet, slipping on the dark stockings, the black spike heels, as if they'd always had this appointment. She was too old to feel safe in this outfit anymore. She wasn't afraid enough when he looked at her.

Instead, Leslie watches the theatergoers, hand in hand, walking up the steps and entering the church-huge glass doors. The museum, which only saves twentieth-century art, shares the structure, which, like municipal buildings, jails, courthouses, and libraries, seems designed to make people seem small, transient.

Next to her in the car, Frank is busy doing mysterious things. Once he reaches over and changes the radio station to hard rock. Leslie remembers his role with some of the popular bands of the sixties. He was a presence—beautiful, additional. Everyone had wanted him then. She remembers seeing him in a film, how he took your breath away, then gave it back in a new language. It hurt to see him leave the stage— a real physical thing she stored inside until this moment of him next to her in the dark of the car as he prepares his drugs.

"Have you ever tried this?" Frank asks.

When Leslie shakes her head, he takes the rolled dollar bill and places it a hair above the white powder in the vial cap. The only noise is a long breathy sigh. Then he does the other nostril and leans back, closing his eyes for a minute while his head rests on the seat. "Amal's right. S'good. Perfect."

She doesn't want to appear too eager, so she waits until he opens his eyes and offers her the rolled dollar. She knows how to do it. She's seen it in movies over and over. She's even been offered some before. But she's never done it, never trusted herself. Tonight with the whisper of leather on her arms and thighs, with the damp before-spring air and the coming lights and performance she'll watch, she feels the old ground inside of her breaking up.

At first Leslie feels nothing. She's done it slowly so as not to make a mistake and blow the powder into the car or knock it over.

She's seen that in a movie too and heard the advice that if you go slow with something new, you'll look as if you know what you're doing. She believes it.

Then it hits her. Not like a train, not as she expects, but as if a platform she's been standing on is slowly rising. And the dark ground inside her that she's always afraid of softening, crumbling, becomes a sheet of marble. The world gets flat and interesting, very bright and pure. She knows almost everything.

When they get out of the car, they hold hands until the steps. Then he adjusts the scarf he wears around the collar of his upturned sports coat, checks the weight of the pint in his pocket, and fixes the leather case of poems under his arm. "How do I look?" Frank asks.

Leslie smiles and nods. He smiles and says, "Later. Oh, and don't say anything to Amal. I was supposed to save him some." All her friends like her confidence, admire the black leather, her legs. In the bathroom in front of the mirror she opens her blouse another button.

After Frank's performance they get lost trying to find his hotel. When his hand first slides inside her blouse, she slows down and laughs uncomfortably. It should feel good.

Leslie rubs his thigh tentatively, thinking that some response is required. It would seem rude of her, otherwise. He feels encouraged and sticks his hand up her skirt. She squirms as his fingernails scratch at her panty hose.

When they find the hotel room, Frank immediately strips. Leslie sits on the bed. It is such a small room, and when he turns on the television without sound so they'll have some light, she feels disappointed.

She doesn't want him to kiss her. The drug makes that much clear. What he wants is her sucking on him and, more important, him sucking on her. He rummages through her clothes like a bear in garbage, testing pieces and places for sweetness, for appealing tastes. Then he spreads her legs so far they ache, and he shoves his face in her. Later Leslie sucks on him for an hour, while Frank moans and never comes.

While she dresses, he keeps telling her, "Find someone who loves you. Find someone tomorrow who loves you."

She can't see how to tell him that's impossible, so she just keeps agreeing. Actually, on her way home she does try to think of someone to love her, but it doesn't seem as though there's anyone around. She goes through everyone, including married friends. "I'm going to call and check on you in the morning, OK?" he'd said. "I want to get a progress report."

When Frank calls the next day, it is early afternoon. "Did you do what I told you to do?"

"I'm looking," Leslie tells him, as she adds the drug to the list of things she can't do again. It makes everything too possible. She has to.

Later she receives a book of Frank's poems, like the one she already has. He has inscribed it to her. Leslie thinks of how at one point in their sex, he had rushed to the bathroom and she could hear him groaning in pain as he urinated. "I have a problem," he'd said when he returned. "It hurts. It's not contagious—don't worry."

Time Only Adds to the Blame

See, the problem starts with the body. There isn't one. Not that we can see. So how can it be any different? Like James Dean or Jim Morrison. They must still be alive somewhere. Mother arrives from South Carolina retirement. First thing she asks, "Where is it?" We'd been all through that on the phone. But she's still asking two days later as she boards the plane back South.

"It's gone," we say. "You wouldn't have liked it anyway." The stewardess glances at us like *we* killed her. I shake my head and buckle mother in, noticing the drip of lunch. Was it there before the service? I can't remember and try to pick its scab off her good black linen. The dress looks suspiciously like part of the yellow and black mother'd worn to my wedding a month before. A giant bumblebee in distress.

The body hadn't been there either. "Don't tell Mother I'm broke," the body had urged.

"Well, it's pretty obvious you're not here." I'd been miffed, with the flowers she was supposed to carry down the aisle stinking up the house already. It was four hours till the church, and for once I was supposed to be the star attraction.

"I can't help it. You understand." I didn't.

"And then when he had to drop out of the campaign—and those crazy LaRouche people—I didn't get my money. Do you see?"

"OK." It was the only thing I could think of—that and a heavy sigh to let her know where things really stood. We never told the truth. That was the big thing for us. "You can do anything you want, but don't you step on my blue suede shoes." Lying had become the only way we could all be nice to one another anymore.

Then there was the unmistakable clink of glass against the receiver. Later I would see that it could have been the whole bottle too. She bulk-ordered them from the liquor store down the street. And like an apology for the sound—another lie we laid like a piece of railroad track all the way between her town and mine with a contract stating, No one rides this train—she said, "Oh, and your present's coming."

It was always coming. I wanted to tell her that the only resurrection happened in April, and you had to go to church for that one. But the present was a lie we knew so well it had come to stand as a code: Saying it makes it true. I've given you the antique garnets my husband got from a client, a hand-knitted sweater from Ireland, the silver bracelet my artist friend made.

I even thanked her.

"If I'd only see the body . . . " Mother smooths the black linen, and I try to imagine the yellow striped jacket it should have over it. A highway sign: DANGER. I want to take those big hands with the big oval fingernails someone has painted a bloody red and squeeze them too tightly. Even with the knobs and turns of arthritis, they hold power and cruelty. They can hurt us again.

"There is *no* body," I say.

Her fingers test the metal buckle of the seat belt for sharpness like a knife blade. The rims of her eyes moisten, and her pupils harden against it. "Of course there is."

She's fading into a better place, I realize, as I put my cheek dutifully against hers. To touch her bare skin gives me a shock, like the numbing buzz on the electric fence on the day the plastic grip split and current leaked into my closed hand. The body had laughed. My arm had savored the sting all afternoon. Neither of us told that the fence was broken.

"OK, Mother," I say, backing down the aisle. She looks at me with sudden hate, as if she's sorry that I'm not the body.

Once in the terminal, I want to run back through the boarding gate and tell her it wasn't my idea. I wasn't even going to invite her to the wedding. The body made me do it.

In the following weeks, we all came to see what a mistake it was, not to have tried harder for it. We are like the losing team who has to face the home crowd. We came back without a body, nothing to put in the showcase. Although we'd brought cameras, no one had the heart for pictures. What would we say—"Here we are at her funeral, but since we couldn't come up with a body, we had a memorial service instead, so here we are"?

First we went to the funeral home and got in the coffin elevator. We had to stand in a row. It took five of us upright to equal one body flat.

I'm always the joker. My father's the same way. He had a laughing fit right in the middle of my baptism. I had to think of bad things. It was his idea to begin with: "Just to keep Mother quiet." She'd had an attack of religion and had seen to it that I went through confirmation in the Methodist church. As a senior in high school, I was the oldest kid there. The minister got tired of my questions, but he let me finish anyway. He must've known I didn't believe in God. But it turned out they'd never had me baptized. The body had been. She joined the church on time too. She was like that—a step ahead of me.

As we stand on the third floor of that Chicago mansion turned funeral home, looking at the boxes and urns on the gray metal shelving, I want to make a joke. I work at pulling the corners of my mouth down although they lift like helium balloons as soon as they can. Like the day Mother told me that Gram had cancer. I had to turn my back so she couldn't see the dazzle of teeth. She must've thought I was going to cry. In our family, another part of the code: You cry, you cry alone. It's like a lie, I guess. But I'm not in danger usually.

Mostly I'm curious. I can hardly concentrate on the containers tricked up to look like something ordinary you'd use to store cigars or jewelry or flour. In the gloom around us sit the coffins. They hunch like dogs waiting on the porch for the master to come home. They sparkle like rows of new cars in those vast suburban dealerships. I want to walk up and down the rows, rubbing my hand over all the shiny surfaces. Here is something that says death. I feel cheated by the stupid canisters.

The body's daughter will have to come back and choose, we decide. For all our casualness, we are too shocked to pin it down. Burned. "We don't even have a body," we each protest silently. "Ashes" doesn't come up. We can't make that conversion. It's like a problem in metrics.

The body's ex-husband drives us from building to building, to pick up forms and releases, yet she isn't ever seen anywhere. Finally, on the street in front of a Travelodge he drops his teenaged daughter who is wearing a shabby blue-gray knit top and skirt, dirty, sizes too big for her. I want to yell at him, "What's this?" But we just go inside and get her a room.

All afternoon he has chain-smoked, the car's air conditioning barely huffing to cool the caustic summer heat. I crank open a window and look at the buildings he likes or doesn't like. Chicago architecture has become personal—he owns it somehow. I find myself liking the ones he hates, violently liking them. I could kill him I like them so much.

We eat because we have nothing to do. We're afraid to drink, which is what we should do. Whenever we lift a glass or imagine the familiar bite of liquor on our tongues, we glance guiltily around at the others. We have to do this. We're afraid of the body.

That's what we should tell Mother: "You're so brave, you go find it." She doesn't have to stop herself from wanting a drink. Secretly, when we've exhausted each other and are back in our separate rooms, I want to order liquor, all kinds. I want to drown in it. Get singing-loud drunk, go rouse them up, and have a good look at it. The body. We could all sit close, eat popcorn, and slouch low in our seats when the scary parts come on. As it is, we lie sober and alone in our beds. I leave the light on, though my new husband sleeps like a hand along the edge of my body. "What does he know?" I ask the face in the television I watch without sound. Motions. That's all I want. Not the voices. There's too much to say already.

Sometime in the night, whether asleep or awake—what difference does it make?—I decide two things:

1. My sister is not dead.

2. If she is, he killed her.

What would you do? Mother knows. She almost says it out loud. I think I can see her jail-stripe yellow and black jacket peeking out of her suitcase like a trapped animal, when I pick her up for the service.

As we drive over, she asks, "Is the body going to be at the church?"

Taxi rides for three blocks. They think we're crazy, so we overtip them as an admission of guilt. "Yes, it's true," our fingers clutching the extra bills say. "You guessed it, bud."

Inside, there's the usual: architecture we can all agree on. Tastefully, baroquely ornate. How could she leave this? I ask myself. She couldn't. See, the answer is simple. Irresistible.

Somebody's dead, I caution myself. We rise and kneel and rise and kneel. But I'm lucky. I just had a wedding with this religion, so I know how to pull the kneeler out, get up and down without snagging stockings or tumbling headlong into the pew in front of me.

Abraham Lincoln used to come here to worship. Just the place for the body. Probably way out of our league. I glance both ways down the row of us. We're dressed all wrong. Too grim. Black. You don't wear black anymore. I've got blue on. Doesn't that count for something?

Mother looks around her, skepticism in those hard blue eyes. Her hands tremble with anger as she grabs a hymnal, as if to say, "That same damn song." She thinks we've hidden her daughter, that she's away with a man secretly. "How do you know it's her?" she asked on the phone.

"He identified her."

"Oh, him," she scoffed.

While the minister, who is too young, talks about things, I have a disturbing sight: the body is going up the heavenly stairs. She wouldn't do anything unladylike, so the ladder'd be out. And leading her is Our Lord Jesus Christ. She looks pretty good, I notice, for someone who's just starved to death. "That's what happens when you drink instead of eat," I want to yell at her. But she looks fine, so who am I to talk? Then she glances over her shoulder with this smug look—self-satisfied, that's it— a smirk. "I'm still way ahead of you," it says. Right there she turns, and, without tripping on the sheer robes of grace, she is gone, waving good-bye once, like Miss America opening a shopping mall.

Does that mean there's a body? I cry harder, knowing she's got something I don't.

There are times at the reception tea, with the real china cups, pâté, and cucumber canapés, when I wish real hard for that body. Oh, I do wish. I want it there just the way they found it: shrunken pygmy-small and naked. I want it to look like an Egyptian mummy fresh out of storage. I want all those women who want the body to get it. I want to grab their restless, greedy hands and shove them into her skeleton-hard skin. "Here it is," I want to say to them. "Now you know."

Instead, we comfort them. I even promise to return the crystal bowl one lady loaned the body two years before. She's so drunk, she won't remember. The man who gives the eulogy is drunk too. And the ex-governor and her ex-husband. Everyone has had a drink but us. How fair can this be?

Only Mother, in her black dress like a lethal can of spray paint, receives comfort from her own words. No one asks her a thing. She gets to talk undisturbed, while the rest of us look at the pickets of lies growing around the table she sits at.

I notice a pattern in our conversations:

1. They ask how I'm feeling. "You know . . . " I say.

2. They want the body, the chalk mark on the rug like in the movies.

3. They want to tell how long it's been since they said or did something with her. A badge of honesty. Their Girl Scout eyes say, "This is an apology."

4. Like amateur coroners, they come back to the body. Cause of death. Exact. C of D. I find myself smiling too often now, my mouth like a person belching.

There is the matter of her Lake Shore condo. The windows overlooking the basin, where the moored sailboats bob and tug like geese, are so clouded with dirt, even the sunlight filters brown over the wrecked living room. But I don't tell them details: the feces stuck to the sink, toilet, floor, cabinet, sheet, wall, rug, because she forgets how to take care of herself. Or won't.

I give them *Camille, Portia Faces Life, Madame Bovary*—"I have always depended on the kindness of strangers." "You can't even trust your own family," my eyes tell them, as my mouth rides up and down. I can't give them a body, and that's what they came for. They'll leave something behind, a donation to the church, but first they have to be sure there's been a crime. Murder. Suicide. Death.

Instead, they leave hours later, pausing to look around the bare linoleum floor of the church parlor with dissatisfaction on their faces.

"I didn't even like her," says a woman who is the last to leave. She is lingering by an embarrassingly large bouquet of orange flowers in the center of the room. "This is mine." She points at the silver bowl and the loud arrangement. "I want it back. I only did it because his new wife's my friend. Like I said, I couldn't stand her. She cursed me all the way across a restaurant one night."

The orange stands out because the body hated it. We order white flowers for the reception. White is correct. We know that. White calla lilies. And we order: *no* new wife. But she comes anyway, with her caterer and orange-flower friend.

I find myself saying a little prayer, asking only that the fetid breath of the body loose itself on any orange flowers in the room. Just once. Just once. But there's no miracle.

After the reception the sisters go to the bathroom to repair makeup. I am talking to them through the gray metal door of the stall. When I come out, though, I'm alone. They've all left, forgotten me. It's the loneliest feeling, see. Though I can hear their voices in the hall outside, I know they've forgotten me. I stand and stare into the mirror mounted on the gray tile wall. Under the fluorescent light I look old enough to be the oldest now.

"Goddamn it," I whisper to the mirror. She can't get away with this. But I just stand there, tears crowding out of my eyes, feeling sorry for me, because now I've got to be oldest and alone. This is worse than being tricked by those three husbands or having to earn my own living. I want to slap her face. "So where's the goddamn body," I whisper to her. "Bring that goddamn body back here."

After the service the sisters take a taxi to the east-side police station to retrieve the body's jewelry. The station is new, clean, and efficient. The help is courteous. Things I notice about this excursion:

1. The trouble I have signing my name for the goods. We have agreed. I am the oldest. They step back for me when the desk person asks for a signature. Already they are pushing me out and ahead. From now on they'll be behind me. Well, good. Outside, I pull the taxi door open and climb in first. I thank her for that, wherever she is hiding.

2. We laugh all the way back to the hotel. Each of us wanting a drink to get the taste of jewelry or ash off our lips.

3. The satisfaction on her daughter's face when she opens the manila envelope with her mother's name on it and pulls out the gold bracelet set with sapphires and clips it on her own arm.

"It's just another lie," I tell my heart, as I watch Mother's plane rise out of the dull yellow Chicago sky. She'll be South in two hours. She can put her gangster clothes away.

Two years later we have almost stopped thinking about the clever marble jewel box the body's daughter picked out. As far as we know, it's waiting for us at the funeral home. There are a dozen excuses here. At first we torture each other weekly about it.

Father refuses to pay for anything. "When I die, throw my body in a ditch. I'm not spending a dime."

We think of buying land in a state none of us live in, keeping her on someone's mantel, in an attic or basement, on a lawn, in the lake, out to sea. Leaving her at the funeral home is a solution none of us imagines. That makes it the best one. The funeral home never contacts us. We don't contact them. It works out. Besides, they're the only ones who claim to have seen a body.

Each Time We Meet

 It's like driving into the hot damp mouth of a dog, when the lawyer sister and I walk out of the airport terminal in South Carolina. At the ranch Father says, "It's no laughing matter. She keeps locking me out of the house. Says I killed your sister, but you know I haven't stepped foot out of here in months." His face is a puzzle of feelings.

"I told you not to come." Mother gestures with the tin box of candy. "I don't want you here, you understand? I don't want to see you." She gets up and walks past us into the kitchen, which opens into the living and dining areas in one of those floor plans that takes the secrets out of your life. We put our bags down. We haven't expected this. Although we knew she wouldn't like it, we aren't ready for the directness.

"There's no reason for you to be here. I didn't invite you." She slams the tin box down on the inlaid-tile counter, shades of brown and tan as always. "I'm not cooking, there's not enough food for you here. Don't expect anything. I didn't invite you." Although it is still early evening, she is dressed in a long nylon gown, stains of coffee marching up it as determined as mice. When she shakes her head and lights another cigarette, her eyes spark unnaturally, and her hair, which hasn't been combed in days, stands up around her face in a halo of orange clumps thick as snakes. She hasn't been keeping the color, I notice.

"Hide the knives," the doctor sister urges long distance. "She could get more violent." She hasn't been able to come. Now she can be the voice of authority, the rest of us just the incidence of her voice in action. "You know I'd be there if I could. Just be careful." She calls the hospital and gets references for rural South Carolina care.

Mother picks up the phone while I'm talking, yells, "How dare you tell them that." The floor plan of the house is not arranged for such events. We're too close to each other, even locked in the bedroom. Her hearing has become preternaturally powerful—the unhinging of the phone from its cradle, the *click-click* as the dial rounds its route. We barely start a conversation before she is on us.

At three o'clock in the morning, the door to our room smashes into the bed we have shoved against it, like a bomb in the hallway. Her body is lethal, and we push back with all our might. The frogs have not silenced the Southern night. July breathes hot and insistent into the room, and the fan pushes air away from itself in the dainty motion of a lady waving a hand in front of her face.

At that moment I believe that the only person who could make her behave is her ninety-nine-year-old mother, blind and bedridden in southern Missouri. Her sharp Methodist words could still straighten her daughter.

I spend the night dreaming of sieges. When I wake up, I search all the drawers and closet shelves for photos. I clean the house of myself, as best I can. I take my smiling baby and hide it carefully in my purse where she can't get at it.

"He's an evil man. He killed her," she warns. "You know that. I just want to get away." I want to let her, but this has gone on too long. Maybe she has to be punished too.

"Don't believe anything she says," the doctor sister warns. "Check her medication. Has she been taking her pills?"

Father shows me the dogwoods he planted for the dead sisters, mother's and then mine. The trees are both dead now because Mother left them in her hot Southern car trunk while she played bridge all afternoon. "They were dead when she brought them home, but I planted them anyway." He is wheezing beside the fence around the house, needed to keep the animals out. Not snakes. It doesn't work for them.

"She won't let me tell our friends that your sister died." I own her, in death, I see. The insects' raw hum seems to turn the heat up. We go back inside, the sound scraping the inside of my ears, scouring. Father spreads his hands helplessly. "I keep watering them anyway." Later he leans across the kitchen table. "Did you see the body?"

She watches one television preacher after another—all morning, the healings, prayers, and pleas for money. Her gown grows dingier as she paces, sitting only to eat more candy from the almost empty ten-pound tin, smoke cigarettes, and drain another cup of the coffee she is brewing constantly, like some mad version of a good wife. She keeps the television turned up so loud that it is impossible to speak without shouting.

The youngest sister, the lawyer, argues with her, threatens to cry. Mother wisely ignores, stopping only to pour an acid remark here or there. But by noon it is arranged. "Wish I could be there." The doctor sister has convinced a hospital forty-five minutes away to take her.

I know we're in for it when Mother chooses the black and yellow outfit for her ride to the mental hospital. It's her traveling costume. She doesn't go along easily. We threaten her, and the collective will wins out, although Father, the joker, tries to back down at the last minute. "Maybe she's not as bad as I thought." I shove him aside and open the door to the back seat for her. He sits in front because she won't let him in back.

In the car she begins to despair. Refuses to touch the dog. Talks about the Gestapo search of her house, her purse, her friends. She is on her way to the camps, on the move again. She opens her fears like a suitcase and begins unpacking. Father taunts her. I silently urge her on. Lawyer drives the boat-big Continental down the interstate, empty except for the occasional family returning from church. I notice that everyone else on the road looks normal. We must look normal too. Except for the rag of feeling we tie to the antenna that we keep raising and lowering electronically like a signal of distress at sea. The air conditioning can barely keep up with the heat, and she opens a window to let out the cigarette smoke.

"Do you have any money?" he asks her.

"You can't have it," she replies.

"Do you want more?" he asks.

"No, just put me in the welfare ward. Tell them that I don't have anything anymore." She unwraps a mint she has pulled from her purse. "I wore the wrong thing. Too bright. Yellow and black are too strident." She is on the verge of tears, and for the first time I want to reach out and touch her hand, but I don't.

"And tell them I didn't choose the colors in the house. They'll ask about that. Tell them I didn't buy those paintings. People gave them to me. They're not mine. They'll check on that—they always do. But I don't know—I don't know what colors are good. Something quiet. Not loud. I always choose the wrong colors."

We're silent in the car, which holds the speed limit and floats above the road, registering nothing of bumps and tiny waves in the new concrete.

We're all pretty drowned by the time we reach the hospital, despite the car's air conditioning.

"Do you know your daughter's dead?" They ask her at the hospital.

"Of course." Her mouth snaps shut like a purse. Lies—I send the look to the young doctor with a Southern accent and a sympathy for my father.

It's tough convincing them to keep her for a few days, but it's a hundred and five degrees, and father's too old to stand out on that shadeless cement walk pleading to get into the house all day.

As we wait for the processing, she says to me, "This is good-bye. I never want to see you again."

"That's fine, Mother."

"I mean it. This is the last time I ever want to see you."

"I know," I tell her. "Every time I see you, I say good-bye for good."

We have finally reached an understanding. She is done with me. My older sister died, I am living. She won't see either of us.

We leave her sitting in the chrome and orange vinyl chairs of the modern patient lounge, marooned in her angry colors, Southern Methodist womanhood in the midst of everything she disapproves of: a cop show banging away on the large television, teenaged patients flopped in other chairs or pacing and arguing, snapping gum. The cajoling voice of the black social worker who is the final sign of family injustice. "Rose, you want to come with me? Rose, may I call you Rose?"

"No," my mother replies, in her angry-bee dress, "you may call me Mrs. Taylor." She plants her purse more firmly on her lap and tightens her knees, pretending not to notice us walking through the double glass doors into the late afternoon humidity.

The Only Thing Different

Every time his voice tumbles down the hall and around the corner into the bathroom at her, she takes another swipe. The hair sprinkles the sink like pine needles, curved slivers of heart.

When the sink is filled with red brown, she gathers up the hair and puts handfuls of it in the blue plastic wastebasket. "You just don't realize that you're being selfish. That's the problem." He calls from the bedroom, where he is getting ready.

Selfish? she thinks, as she pulls out a curly lock and straightens it between her fingers. Stand up and be counted. The scissors cut deeply, and her hair remains stiff with its top lopped off and falling silently in slow motion. Selfish, selfish—it flashes in red highlights.

"What are you doing in there? You know I have to dry my hair." She can picture him bending down to pull on his black socks and remembers the dream she has just had while napping—a dream in which her hands and then her arms up to her elbows were coated with soot. She kept trying to get to the sink to wash it off. She was worried in the dream that it wouldn't wash off, but then it had. Everything else in the dream was going wrong. There were dirty dishes in the sink, the walls needed painting, and the party would begin soon. A trouble-in-mind kind of dream, she calls it, as she peers closely at the shape of her head, which is changing with the haircut.

Before they'd met, he'd seen a picture of her in a book of poetry she'd written. He'd fallen for her, he told her later, because of her words and the wistful, Victorian look on her face. Hollow cheeks and eyes. And why had she cut her hair? After his comment she'd gone in and examined her boy-short cropped look—what women were doing then. It was ten years later. What did he expect? She's been wearing a nightgown in the picture. She had a hangover. A lover had snapped it as a joke. For years men had declared love for that Victorian suffering. She'd been getting ready to brush her teeth, she protested. Those dark circles? Eye makeup that smeared. Drinking can do that for you. He'd just ignored her, laughing in disbelief and closing his eyes again to find her.

She'd tried to grow it out for the wedding. What she achieved was an aging wood nymph. Her hair had suddenly turned curly again. After all those years, a betrayal like this. She knew then she was lost. It didn't drop limp and tragic looking. It wound in knots and wood-shaving big loops around her face. It grew out, not down. She dyed it red and ordered a wreath of flowers, a crown of charm, to distract him. He forgave her. He wasn't a bad person. He just couldn't understand how her hair happened this way.

"I'm writing fiction," she told him.

"Besides," he calls to her, "it's a matter of being responsible, that's all." She can feel him getting closer and hurries her scissors on the path around the top of her head. A little off each side and the back, where she never looks because when she does, she sees how the hair falls away from the cowlicks exposing the nude scalp. She'll just cut a row along the back there, and maybe it will bend to hide the holes.

When her hair was long, it split like a fork in the road over those places. The curls nestled like forest undergrowth with an occasional peek of ground beneath. Or a head of snakes. The scissors glitter with possibility for a moment.

"Come on, I'm not trying to be hard on you." His voice arrives before he does.

She gives a couple of blind clips to the front, leaving half the curly bangs for a jaunty effect, and gathers two more fistfuls of hair from the sink, as he fills the doorway.

"Can I get in here now?" He looks handsome in his suit. With his boyish good looks he always looks like a kid dressed up for church.

"Do you like my hair?" she asks, as she always does. He nods and unhooks the hair dryer from the back of the door without looking at her. "No really, do you like it? I gave myself a haircut."

He looks at the telltale worms of hair in the sink. "I wondered what this was." Then he plugs in the dryer and turns on its noise.

She waits, standing in his way in front of the mirror while she tries to get the top, an inch long now, to behave like hair, not a crew cut.

"It makes your face rounder, you know," he says.

She smiles and nods. "I know." She's left the curly length in back and along the sides. It is an altogether satisfactory haircut. He shrugs.

The Magician's Assistant

After the first week he shoved his card in her hand. He had crossed out Lois and printed Marla above it in black ink. She wished he'd used ballpoint so it wouldn't run when they did the milk-in-the-pocket trick.

Later people would ask her if they were married, wonder if they were lovers. Marla would only look puzzled when the subject came up. Was that a trick she would be learning?

Benefits and birthday parties were their mainstay. She told him she wouldn't dress in any goofy costumes, though. Nothing with sequins or sweetheart necklines. He bought her a tuxedo like his, only the pant legs were cut off at mid-thigh. The first time she wore it, she felt his eyes travel up her legs like a road to the tunnel of love.

Her friends wanted to know two things: Did he saw her in half? Did he make her disappear?

She watched him handle the rabbits and pigeons matter-of-factly, but when his hand touched her bare skin, it shook for minutes afterward, as if he had held the heart of an elephant.

The main problem was television conjurers who made expensive cars and camels disappear. No one cared about the flick of the wrist, the scarves that came magically to bloom in the palm of the hand.

When she finally asked him where Lois had gone, he stared at her. His face clouded with pain, and his fingers worked the magic on her.

❖ ❖

You Belong to Me

 There is nothing like the act of watching yourself doing something, he decides as he ducks another armful of clothes from above. It isn't even a question of the neighbors seeing him dressed in his wife's flannel nightgown in the backyard at midnight. Above him the sky rains water and his clothes from the bedroom window.

When something whizzes past his head and lands *thunk* in the dead grass behind him, he ducks instinctively, then looks. In the army they told you, "Never look, for Christ's sake," but he does anyway. His shaving stuff. The electric razor plows a little hole for itself like an undetonated bomb. His hand catches for a moment, then finishes reaching for its chrome brightness, and drops it into a pile beside him.

What puzzles him isn't the bombardment of clothes. He probably deserves that. When he said there wasn't room for his stuff, his life, because she took up all the room, she replied, "Fine, move out back. There's all the space in the world." He'd barely had time to duck and grab the first piece of clothing he could find on the floor beside the bed. Of course, he'd hoped for his pants, not her nightgown. Now he knows he looks like the wolf in "Little Red Riding Hood" dressed up as Granny.

He has to be fair, though. That wasn't all he said. They'd had a good enough time in bed. Sure, that's fine now. He doesn't make any of his usual earlier mistakes—telling her that she should hurry or that he's tired when he's finished. He's grown up there—not enough to brag to anyone, but she can't complain about that.

His attention is caught sharply by the record album slicing the air in front of his nose like a Frisbee. Shoot. He looks up and watches albums pour out of the window like paratroopers, then glide gracefully down to stumble and fall on the ground below. He starts to run around grabbing them up in his arms like a man chasing his hat on a windy day, but he stops. The rain is changing to snow, and globs of it begin to clump on the clothes and welt the cardboard record covers. "Good-bye, Willie Nelson," he mouths. "Good-bye, Bruce Springsteen."

"Honey," he calls. "Jo?" Above him her wild face appears, then is gone like the pulse of a neon sign. He waits below, hopeful for the next flash.

What he receives is the pottery pitcher, the first thing they bought together, which explodes at his feet. Bending down to examine it, he realizes that this is the first thing he can feel really sorry about. As he picks up the shards of blue glazed clay, he misses the bulkier things dropping onto the bushes: the framed reproductions of paintings they both liked, the plaster cast of a woman's torso, the pillows off the bed.

It was their courtship, and clumsy as he was at it, he had been sincere. Leaving the safety of his first wife for the breathlessness of this new woman had scared him. Sometimes he felt trapped in a forest fire that was whipping the waves of flame back around him, sucking the air into itself. He had to struggle just to walk upright in the house some days. How did he get here? he'd ask himself.

"I'll huff, and I'll puff, and I'll blow the house down," she'd tease him when he went quiet before going home to his wife those first months.

Tonight he feels an unraveling, almost the same as the unwrapping he'd experienced with her that had spun him like some mummy far out of his marriage into her life, unwinding, unwinding, the bandage wrappings held by her effortlessly as he spun like a top between the poles of the two houses, his wife's and hers. Finally, when he was bare again, he settled in with her, coming to her unexpectedly in the middle of the week, carrying a small gym bag with his toiletries and a change of underwear. Just when she'd given up, just when she was going out of town with friends, he arrived on her doorstep like a Girl Scout selling cookies.

Now the shards of pitcher glint and cut at something deeper: the invisible, binding, filament line that holds him perfectly and cruelly in his place. He wonders if he'll have to find someone else now.

No. The broken pitcher is a message he tries to read. What is it saying? What is she saying? He feels like a man stranded on the moon, space-wrecked. He shakes pieces of pottery in his hands like old bones, small rocks of soothsaying. What? What?

He doesn't know how long he sits there with the shards at his feet like archaeological remains. He stops wondering what to do. He stops worrying about the snow, which begins to crust him over, sticking coldly on her nightgown and his feet and hands sticking out of the cloth. He doesn't know his eyes are closed until her hand, brushing his face and hair, tells him.

"Are you OK?" she asks, as she tucks his overcoat around his shoulders.

"I guess you're not that hard to live with," he says, but all he can hear is the wind rising in the elm tree above them.

"Come on." She pulls at his arm, trying to get him up. He watches her do it. Maybe she's the tar baby he's stuck to. Please don't throw me in the brier patch, he thinks. Then he gets confused. What happens to the tar baby? Is the rabbit stuck with a friend for life?

"Don't," he says, meaning the brier patch.

"It's OK. I made some truth serum. We'll go in, get dry."

He is walking then, watching himself: a snowman moving on thick chunks of legs back into the house. He doesn't think about his things in the backyard, only the hot rum waiting in cups with a chunk of butter slicking the surface to make it go down more easily. "Truth serum"—they've named it for the way it makes their talks glide.

Toward morning they will return to the bedroom, where it started. And he will tell her of his relief now that all his things are gone. He can get a clean start, and he'll feel that something important is true here. When she offers to let him throw her stuff out the window to make it even, he smiles and holds her close, rubbing her skull with the gentle intentness of Aladdin polishing his lamp.

❖ ❖

FROM

~Pretend We've Never Met~

❖ ❖

Mercury

 At first it had gone relatively unnoticed, or perhaps they had done very little then—prying the letter *R* off—maybe the initial of one of the neighborhood kids, or just the loosest chrome on the car, an elegantly printed name, MERCURY, spread decorously across the wide wide front end, still intact after eleven years. Around the same time they had crushed some sort of fruit on one chrome bumper, it could have been thrown, it dried in orange pulpy strands like a larger species of some South American insect. Of course, the usual fingerprints and odd smearings left on the hood and trunk. They were never *seen*, these children, but their mark was always visible in some minor way. What could he expect—leaving it out in the alley behind his small house and yard. It was too large to fit in the single-car garage. He had forced it a couple of times, but had scraped the right side good in a long, even slice. No way to completely shut the garage door then. It always came to rest on the bumper, so what was the point?

There was no hiding the fact of its existence. There it was: long and wide and square. He had never even pushed the gas pedal to the floor, there was no need—it hunched at stoplights waiting to spring out.

He had to hold the power brake tightly then—a light tap on the gas and off he went—rocking around corners, floating down highways. A car much too big for a single person, he knew, and much too expensive to run, he knew.

Ten years ago he had marveled at such cars, sleek and luxurious, yet assertive in their taut linear design. Always present. Not a laughable vw toy or something modest, middle of the road, like a Chevy. It was consciously extravagant—a relic now of that time. There was no economy in that 390-horsepower engine, the six-way power seat that still worked. Who needed the embarrassing suggestiveness of reclining seats? Here was the vehicle as hotel, each seat comfortably taking the length, it seemed, of a human body.

At night in early fall, when he had first gotten the car, he would lie on the front seat, radio turned low to the back channels—no FM then, but not necessary either. It seemed right that this beauty should only have AM on its three-position sound system, good as the day it was built. FM had been phony symphonies, things a Parklane owner wouldn't be interested in. Then the neighbor kids were in bed, families settled in for the night, dogs taken indoors from the small fenced yards, and an odor of evening cooking still lingering in the air, mingled with the smell of dried leaves and drying grass. The metallic scent of hot summer gone. A light breeze brushing through the car once in a while. He was happy.

But now, something was happening. First the *R* had disappeared. He regretted it, but promised himself that someday he would go to a junkyard and get another or maybe even put an ad in one of those old car magazines.

Then they began to throw things at it: in the fall a rotting apple or two, but now he discovered small dents weekly, and another letter had disappeared—the *Y*—one of his favorites, spread wide with modern yet classical grace. He had been particularly pleased with it. He tried to think of the last names of all his neighbors—maybe that would be a clue. He even considered going to the city directory and checking the adjoining blocks, but he never did. By the time they had taken the *U*, he had given up on ever replacing the hood letters.

But it continued. He still imagined it was children, who would stop at the letters and rocks. He began again to try to put the car in the garage, but its rear end remained visible and vulnerable. How could their parents let them out at night? In addition, he caught one bumper against the metal garage door frame, and the car pulled the garage frame askew. The door no longer returned properly. His bumper, that lovely chrome expanse, had been pulled slightly off so that now it hung lower on one side, but not by much. Fortunately, it was again the right side, so he didn't have to look at it much. The Mercury was still in remarkable shape. No point to lament a few dents or scratches.

But it continued. Every morning, all summer, he woke to the fury of their small hands. Why did they pick on his car? Why not the neighbors' small sporty compacts—noses buried in the lilac bushes behind their garages? Was it because his car sat there, encroaching openly on their territory? Other cars did have to drive slowly, carefully around it, edging inches away from its pale, metallic-green sides.

In addition to the front letters, someone had diligently removed—he didn't know how—the Parklane plate on the left side. Now he had to face the empty holes and darker, unfaded paint beneath it each day. It had been an excellent design: neat, sharp, no-nonsense letters framed in a field of red reflector-speckled paint. He couldn't understand their obsession with the names and words on his car. Why not rip off the aerial or slash the tires or smash the windows, why this slow and painful dismemberment, as if denaming it were in a way disarming its power? What next?

It remained. He still drove it. Of course, their constant attack was beginning to tell now. The paint, once nearly flawless and certainly extraordinary on a car this old, was dented and nicked, fading and darkening in spots. He couldn't imagine why small flecks of rust began to appear. A larger dent in the right rear end, where they had thrown something the shape of a field stone against the car, began to rust out. At first the old paint had cracked but clung, then finally it had fallen in the summer heat and rain. He had promised himself that he would go to the Mercury dealer nearby, purchase the paint, and at least repaint the spot. But now it was too late for that.

At that time the Mercury lay like a boat shivering in rough waters each night, and he awoke each morning to new storm damage. They seemed intent on prying off, unbolting, unscrewing, breaking (but only at last resort) each and every detachable or chrome item on the car. He knew they were working on the bumpers. He pledged he would stay up on guard all night to catch them at it; but he didn't. As if some agreement had tacitly grown up between them, he continued to love and grieve over his car; but he also continued to sacrifice it, unwilling to protect it. As if it had a hard lesson coming from the world, like a mother sending her sons off to the war, certain they would be wounded or killed, but certain it was necessary and right, he could not, would not, move the car. Yes, he had thought of renting garage space, looked up a few numbers in the Sunday papers, had never, though, gotten around to calling.

When they were nearly finished with the outside, and it had taken them a while, several weeks to get the bumpers (he had had to take sleeping pills a few nights to get through the racket of their work in the alley), he began to leave the Mercury unlocked. Whereas the car had earlier seemed haughty in its grandeur, with an old-world embellished flavor, now it seemed proud in its new naked aspect, less imposing but more moving in its tragic, ridiculous appearance. A car meant to be decorated, to be fawned over, now like a general without medals and ribbons. The artistic chrome moldings were gone from the sides, as were wire grills, big plated hubcaps, side mirrors adjustable with levers from the *inside* (a feature just then appearing on the new cars). They had even managed to remove the little levers themselves from their slots, and the metal frames of the slots—everything, in fact.

By fall he could only drive the car during the day because the head-lights and taillights had been neatly extracted: lenses, bulbs, glass covers, chrome holders, the works—even his wiring. At times he marveled at their thoroughness. Wondered, too, where the hell the stuff was going. Should he discreetly check the neighborhood garages? What if he came upon one of the six-foot bumpers shining in the darkness—what would he do? No, he'd best leave it alone.

Then, too, he speculated about the workers. They couldn't be the kids he saw around the neighborhood during the day; those were just children, eight, ten years old. No. It seemed to be more carefully orchestrated work than fifteen- or sixteen-year-olds could manage, this dismantling of the car—as if hands that yearly took down the Christmas tree now set to work, maybe in a tired but patient fashion, to remove the car from itself. Yes, it looked like adult work. Not malicious at all. This thought comforted him.

In October he again lay out in the car at night in the alley, listening to the radio, local music stations, occasionally a signal from further out—Nebraska or Canada—but mostly just local DJs. Request-night songs, girls to boys, all traveling in their imaginary cars out of their houses and down the streets with the music to sail them along, happy and excited by the songs they gave each other. He was glad for them, smiling as he lay on his back, arms crossed over his chest, feet crossed and propped on the windowsill of the car. Occasionally he would play with one of the three switches for the power seat, adjusting to an inch higher or lower, tilting back or up, the middle of the seat rotating slightly, like a human pelvis. The disc jockeys pleased him, too. Their patter had remained the same over the years: a little bawdier, more explicit perhaps, like the music, but still fast and clever, full of incredible energy, even late at night. And a sameness he enjoyed, a continuity, nothing really new to get used to, to jar him into a different place, the same songs over and over, introduced by a thousand inventions, he enjoyed it all. On those clear October nights in his car (he really didn't need to drive at night, after all, the pleasure was still there, just to be in it, folded resting in its comfort and weight, it was more *there* than anything he had ever known, he felt), he could see the stars if he looked out the window. He could smell the world. He could know it all.

And then in November, when it was too cold to spend his evenings out there, they began to work on the inside. The outside of the car was now the stripped shell he often saw in pictures of assembly lines in automobile factories—the busy men with torches and wrenches, just on the verge of applying all the superficial aspects of the car. He saw it in that light now. He realized that it was something he had not known before, what was really there. The car seemed then more compact, more self-centered than ever, yet also larger and more sprawling. It seemed to take up more room. He marveled at its growth, at its new potential and stature. It appeared to be growing younger, but hadn't assumed the uncertainty of youth. It was stronger.

Of course, he could no longer drive the Mercury, though they considerately left the license plates on—see they weren't irresponsible teenagers, he argued. They had taken the windows though, first the side ones, not so bad, but cold. Then when the door handles and gear shift and pedals had been stripped, they somehow removed the windshield. They hadn't broken it, he knew, no glass littering the ground around the car. Next, all the dash dials. He didn't regret the clock, the one thing that has never worked in the car, it stopped and started by some mysterious process of its own. He rather missed the oil, gas, and temperature dials though, little round agents metering his performance. He liked to watch their red arrows jump up when he started the car, which, of course, he couldn't do now. The steering wheel was gone by late November. He continued to be amazed by their efficiency, they took *everything*. Still the car persisted, without brakes, ashtrays, dials, overhead dome light, glove compartment, armrests, lighters, flow-through ventilators, the works. He never looked under the hood these days, but assumed that the engine would be intact until the interior was finished.

His one moment of regret, to be expected, was the morning he noticed that the radio was gone. They had done it neatly, humanely, he realized. No dangling wires, thick black cords, truncating sounds, missing connections remained behind. No. There was simply a hole. A neat incision. There was nothing to see. He felt that finally the car had been gutted like an animal. He was certain that the parts were carefully husbanded for later use. Nothing left, but still it bothered him. He could see that this was the end of something now. Again he considered putting a stop to it—but how? He probably couldn't. Where would he start? What if he recovered the radio—even the other parts which surely lurked in the neighboring garages and basements—what then? The mystery of the car would never be disclosed to him. He could hardly put it back together. No, this process, which had suddenly, abruptly reached a painful place for him—and it was *real* pain now, he knew that, and *real* longing, he knew that too, no, this process could not stop now. Maybe they had waited that long for the radio because they knew, somehow, what it would mean to him, the crisis and pain. Maybe they had tried to hold it off, as he must have, too. And maybe they had his point of view, that the *radio* was the *center* of the car.

When they took the six-way power seat control and later the front seat itself, he felt resignation tinged with sadness, not despair actually. In fact, it was also relief, he thought. Now it was over. As if he had held his breath for a long time, maybe since the radio had gone, now it was really over. He thought he wouldn't care anymore, tried to convince himself that since he couldn't sit in the damn thing, why bother caring about it. But he couldn't stop himself, it turned out, from visiting what was the essence of the car—a heavy steel frame enclosed with panels of sheet metal. They were working on the insulation and padding these days, like insects picking flesh from a carcass; there was nothing wasted. The doors and trunk were soon gone, too.

In mid-December the snow began, often drifting high against the backyard fence and the car parked right outside it. There was no question of protecting it now. He noticed that the engine was gone during a thaw after Christmas. Once in a while he sighted the car from his back windows, its color gone now, too, as if the paint had been carefully cleansed. A light coat of rust covered the car body. Finally, he couldn't see the car. It was a terrible winter, more blizzards than anyone—even older farmers who should know better than the rest—could remember. He quit using his back door; the snow drifted it shut. He now concentrated on the front of the house, spending hours digging himself out each day. It took all his energy; he forgot about the car in back. For days, weeks, it didn't exist, until something would remind him of it: a letter *R* in a form similar to the perfect row which once crossed the front end, or the glint of chrome on his toaster—the peculiar distortion of his face in its mirror would remind him of the magnificent bumpers or hubcaps. He couldn't stand anything the color of pale green now. It brought a fit of remorse which was only dispelled by much snow shoveling.

Generally, however, he forgot about the car. If it existed, it was his memory of it only—the length and luxury of its body, the crafting of the details, the ultimate thoughtfulness of its design. He didn't recall its destruction—neither the early random violence against it, nor the later careful execution.

When spring finally came, late and long-awaited with the great piles of snow melting into liquid ground, he was once again able to use the back door. On the first day of his return to the alley, he was not surprised to see that the Mercury was gone. He had forgotten about it entirely over the past month, and now there was nothing to ensure its memory—not a bolt, not a shred of glass or metal, not even grooves where the weight of its bulk had settled into the ground. It was gone. He was certain it had been there once, but it was clearly not there now. It seemed better that way.

Stiller's Pond

Look, I just want to tell you what it's like out there, what the wind and the river do. How still. How I am walking by the pond in Stiller's cow pasture. It was January, like now, and twenty below zero, before the light comes up. I can't sleep. I want to be somewhere.

The pond is frozen into these little waves the wind puts there, starched on the top. The kids won't be skating there anyway, not since a long time ago. The pond doesn't have to freeze sheet clean, because none of us would ever be skating there again. As if it knew, the pond always froze in peculiar shapes, as if someone was still under there trying to get out.

If you stood over those places where the water bobbed dark, speckled with stuff churning up from the bottom, you'd think you could see a face pressed and distorted against that little skim of ice, like something from dinner your mom put plastic over and plopped in the fridge, until later when you looked, it was unfamiliar again through the moisture-beaded wrap. At one end the cattails stood at attention, still as boys in ROTC, backs swayed in a pose you knew they'd never be able to walk out of, and little tatters of dried leaves waved like flags from the stalks. Around them lay the litter of last summer.

It was in those left, standing the way they are now, that they found her, hair tangled around. They had to chop part of it off to get her out. That's what the adults told us, and if that quick thaw hadn't come up, it would've been April before she was noticed. He was a different matter, bobbing like a cork in the hole that stayed over the spring. Still, it was hard to tell the difference between him and the water at a distance; you couldn't really get very close. But the thaw sent him skimming over the edge so that his tuber-white face rose up like a signal at sea, and someone finally saw it. I suppose it was lucky that the thaw came—and the kids. Though they knew they wouldn't be skating with the ice that way, they came down to the pond as always, just to fool around. Throw rocks. Build a fire. They weren't permitted to build fires anywhere else. But somehow, it was OK if you had a legitimate winter excuse like skating. Sledding was marginal, but skating was OK for fire building. Being kids, they figured the permission was for location rather than activity, so they went to Stiller's pond whenever the arson rose up in their hearts.

To this day, I can't look at those cattails without thinking of the way they told the little ones to pull the dried leaves and stalks for kindling—and the confusion they must have felt when the lady's hair wouldn't let go of them. She was face up, too, like she was sleeping in bed at home, watching the stars through her little attic window before nodding off. She'd seen a lot more since then, every night anchored there like a boat, her arms treading water gently like oars holding her steady. And the hard part was when they finally dragged her in, men in hip boots with hay hooks and ropes so they could get a grip on her, her eyes plucked out by the turtles, removed with the skill of surgeons so the lids fell gracefully, sunken over the holes.

Surprised they had left the rest of her, the men said, knowing the winter hunger of turtles drifting sleepily to the surface for oxygen before they dropped back like stones to the bottom mud. And strange, how the water had filled in the scars on her face, softened the bones until she became sweet and round and beautiful to the men, who recognized her only from the long blonde hair—and from the broken front teeth. And I think that was what bothered them the most—that she came out of the water better than she went in, that they were able to see her firsthand the way he must have, in his heart, when he would meet her at Stiller's pond after her parents were long asleep, and after her sisters and brothers were long asleep, and after the cows were long settled and the pigs and the horses heavy in sleep from their day's work, even the poultry sleeping on one leg in the roosts, as passive as camels in the dark stench of the henhouse.

And old man Stiller, refusing to help pull her out, refusing the use of his team, his wagon, his ropes, refusing the use of his blankets to wrap her in, and finally refusing her body in his house, even in his barn, where she might have lain like an animal in a stall until the fires softened the ground enough to dig even a shallow hole for her. And the mother, as hard as the father, and the children staring out the windows like portholes at the distant ocean of events they couldn't begin to understand. Incurious as the buildings that held them, they never asked, even later, for the grave of their sister. And only the fact that the children weren't allowed to come again to the pond to skate or build their fires ever served notice to them that their sister had floated like a log for a month in their cow pond, had been dragged out like a burlap bag of drowned cats behind Rofer's buggy horse and been wrapped in his wife's quilt, never to be used again, and stayed wrapped like that until put in a homemade box with the dull nickel nails winking out of the mismatched corners, and been dropped with a clattering bang into the shallow hole of frozen dirt and covered once more into darkness, only to resurface in May, when the ground heaved her up again, like the pond before it, as if something in her must have the light of day, the light of night, and been buried once more, a final time, with huge stones placed on the coffin to hold it down the nine feet they had dug to be certain this time the body, holding its quilt around it like a cape, would not wriggle its way back into their lives.

Grandmother told the children that she was coming back for her eyes. Parents told the children to ignore what Granny said, she was just trying to scare them. But they told the children never to skate on Stiller's pond again, never. And the one time they tried—and each of them did—they got whipped, hard enough to make an impression. So when they became our parents, they told us never to go to Stiller's pond, as it was still called, and we got whipped hard enough to make the same impression. At least we never skated there. That was as specific as they had made it, and we were specific in our obedience. What we did was spend summer afternoons there, hooking turtles and dragging them up on shore, turning them over with sticks, because some of them were snappers and we couldn't tell which, so they all got treated to our punishment—beaten and prodded with sticks the big ones could snap in two. We would watch, thrilled at the sight of the pointed beak, which we knew had plucked an eyeball out of its socket with the ease of pulling a grape from the arbor vines. Though some insisted their parents had told them to look on the bellies of the old turtles to find which ones had taken her eyes because we would find their image there still, we never found such a thing and soon enough stopped believing we would discover a transparent hole where she could look out, still trying to see things she shouldn't. But for a while it had worked, and I remember our fear when we turned each turtle over onto its back, the claws waving helplessly in the paddling feet as we took turns checking the underside. The younger children, overcome, would go screaming and crashing through the cattails and weeds up the banks until we told them it was all right.

The Stiller children moved away, died, fought in wars, and came home. Always someone survived to work the farm, though in the community heart, they were stained with this memory. They followed a pattern, too, the old ones would hint, only to be shushed by the parents. The darker gleam of interest would lead us aside one time, finally when we were old enough, and the rest of the story would follow. How when they dragged the man out, unlike the Stiller girl, he had been eaten at, like a piece of suet hung on a tree for birds. There were peck marks all over the front of his face and body, the clothes ripped to threads on the front, intact on the back. This was what they discovered when they rolled him over. The whiteness that had revealed him was the remaining uneaten chunk of cheek and the milk-white bone, polished by the silky bodies of small fish swimming in and out of the face. The men, in particular, couldn't stand this story, because *everything*, the old women would insist and look long and hard at the boys, *everything* was chewed on. And when they were finished with that, the turtles turned him over and gnawed on the rest.

That was bad enough, but the worst part was that no one could identify him. Stiller wouldn't come near him, and rumors had it that both the hired man and the oldest boy had disappeared that night. Mrs. Stiller never spoke a word about it. She might have identified the rags left on the body at least, but no—so he was buried in another shallow grave next to the girl's, only he didn't come up in the spring. In fact, by the time they began digging the hole to proper depth in May, the box had sunk another two feet and filled with water. When they tried to move it, the seams burst and the thing fell apart in their hands. Inside there was even less of the man than before. Almost a skeleton, the men told people. As if he couldn't wait. That was handy though, because when they made a new box, they could make it half the regular size, just dump the bones in, and save a lot of work digging the deeper hole, too.

As I'm walking out here by Stiller's pond, I remember the old mystery and fear that always mingled in the air around the place. Now, of course, I understand that it was not knowing—the obscenity of the two missing men—that made it impossible for our parents and grandparents to tell us the truth, and therefore, to let us continue at Stiller's pond. The other man was never heard from again, whichever he was. Maybe he was at the bottom of Stiller's pond, weighted with the heavy sleeping bodies of turtles. During the summer, the cows still walk in their ritual paths to the pond, still muddy the edges, plowing the ground with their hooves, leaving pocks that freeze in uneven holes to trip small feet in winter. The cattails still grow at that one end, waving graceful and lithe as women. Sometimes I almost imagine I see the hair they chopped off so many years ago to pull her out, still woven like a basket to trap the silvery fish that lurk in the cool, dark shallows we can't quite reach when we hunt here as children. And out in the middle there's the tree limb that broke off long ago, and then the tree itself dropped to the ground and was sawed up and hauled away, leaving only the limb humped up like a sea serpent, dark and sinewy, along whose length ride the turtles that rise like ancient people from ancient sleep every spring and crawl up the back of the limb to sun, their necks stretching the tenderness where the skin is paper-thin and throbbing with a heart that once fed on the eyes of a woman who tried to cross the pond one winter.

As I start across the pond under the sliver of moon that lies like a knife in the night sky, I remember the last thing our grandmothers told us, the last whispered secret that leaked out of those lips withered by year after year of disappointment and concealment: They weren't wearing skates. And that's why, they always declared with malicious joy, you can't go there—ever, you hear—ever. Thus sealing forever in our hearts the desire for the place, a desire that can never be satisfied, a desire we give to our children for Stiller's pond.

This Is a Love Story

A man and his dog. In the wag of a tail he found the missing piece of an equation, the answer to the Sunday crossword. After obedience school, they were perfect for each other. He could have checked into the bridal suite at the ski lodge up the road. He kept the dog in the car though, and ordered two dinners, one to go. You know where it went.

When the morning failed to burn the mist off the hillside soon enough, the dog would go barking up the pasture, tearing it away with its body and voice, a hole in the white the man could walk through on his way into morning. At night he dreamed of the pressing hotness of dog fur and wrapped his arms around his wife's cool, hairless skin.

At the diner he told his friends he'd give his bed to his dog. This embarrassed them, but he was sincere and stared them down. A meal without the warm nudge of its body against his knee made the man nervous. He expected the failing blue of sunset to fall through the roof of the café, splintering like glass as it arrived. When he looked out the diner window, he could watch it watching him from the car. Balanced perfectly on haunches and front legs, it could have been his wife in the front seat. He forgot where he'd left her. The perfect, moist circle of its breath on the windshield, the hieroglyph of pad and toes on the glass was something he had to stare through to drive. He saw the last red sun rays come at him like a fist his dog was riding on top of—in command—the tongue a spray of gladiola pink.

Was it unusual to find love at his age? To admit the strangeness of his wife? To find himself repeating the gestures he'd recently learned: throwing his head back and smelling the air as it came alive miles around him, noisy with scent, closing his eyes in the rainbow of smell that crowded him out of his skin? When they traveled, they always left the tent of human enterprise so far behind them. A man and his dog, on an invisible track that moved the dirt aside, pulled the birds down, swam them into the water and out again.

As the man smoked in the living room late at night, he watched the dark turn gray through the swirls, turn shapes, turn dog and lie down at his feet.

A Pleasant Story

 It had happened quite by accident the Saturday Lucille was planting the geraniums. And she hadn't really missed it until a few days later, when it was too late to retrace her steps. Well, she thought to herself, there I go again, losing another one. No telling where this one might turn up, like the last time, in the washing machine, bedded like a lover with one of Arnold's socks. She had just sighed though, and reached into the drawer for another larger, less suitable one. Why was it always the smaller, handier ones that got lost first? You'd think I was tossing them out the windows here or something.

But she had continued fixing dinner that day, letting her mind turn to other things, planning the garden in back of the house, almost tasting the hot, salty tomatoes in her mouth come August. Sometimes she felt like her whole body would like nothing better than to stretch out there in the back like a vine and grow tomato-red, little beads of dew glistening on her every morning.

Wouldn't Arnold be surprised at his tomato wife the first time he came to bed and she wasn't there? Then he'd call all over the house, even down to the laundry room to see if she wasn't catching up on some washing or ironing, but not a sight of her. (She chuckled to herself as she sliced some cucumber for the salad.) And then he'd probably wander out back, stumbling a little in his bare feet and pajamas. Why, he'd look like a drunk, she thought, chuckling again, with his head thrust forward like a parrot, a nearsighted parrot, peering into the dark with his eyes all squinty. He wouldn't want the neighbors to hear, so he'd be half whispering, half calling, and his voice would go hoarse with the effort. "Lucille," he'd call, "Lucille are you out here?"

She'd catch a little twinge of anger in his voice because he wouldn't be able to find her, and then she'd have to roll around a little, make a rustling noise in her vine shape so he could. Pretty soon he'd be standing right over her, seeing her for the first time, demanding that she get right out of that garden and come inside before the neighbors saw her and called the police. Maybe she'd pop a hard green tomato at him then, just a joke, pop it like a button into his face, then laugh at his surprise as he rubbed the spot on his cheek.

"Now that's enough, Lucille. You come in here right now, get out of those tomatoes. I've had enough of this . . ."

But she'd roll around a bit more and he'd realize that she wasn't coming in to bed that night, and go off, panting to himself, walking gingerly, not wanting to hurt his bare feet.

"Lucille, is dinner ready?" She could hear Arnold's voice from the other room, where he was reading the paper.

"Yes, dear, in a few minutes." That sure would be a joke on him—make him sit up and think, to have her become a tomato vine.

A few days later she noticed a new plant among the geraniums and nettles in the garden. It didn't look familiar, and at first she was inclined to weed it out, but then she thought to herself, why not give it a week or so longer, it wasn't hurting anything and it might turn out nice. She was always taking chances with the garden. She lacked the organization of her neighbor, who knew what everything looked like, knew exactly where weeds and flowers grew. In fact, her neighbor always leaned over the redwood fence that separated their yards and gave her advice until Lucille wished that fence would suddenly give way and her neighbor would land like a fat squirrel in the wild mustard she was letting dominate the garden. (Then Lucille could chase it around with her rake, give it a good scare.) "The wild mustard has nice yellow flowers," she told her neighbor's humpf. Lucille was a gambler in the garden. She bet on every hand, every weed. It was roulette and there was always a chance—the slightest one at that—that the plant would unfold itself into something wonderful, beautiful, mutated even with the others, an emissary between flower, vegetable, and weed worlds.

Arnold just shook his head when she pointed out the strange plant among the geraniums. "You know I don't know anything about this stuff. Grow vegetables, I told you before, something practical."

When Lucille finally pointed it out to her neighbor, the woman's high, cracked laugh let her know immediately that it was another failure.

She looked with disgust and longing at the neatly ordered dahlias, iris, gloxinias across the fence, then to the patchy scene in front of her—bits of weeds and a couple of elm seedlings struggling up the middle of daisies, columbine, geraniums, all too close together, underwatered, underfed. She was of a mind to let everything go to seed this year, blow across the fence and teach her neighbor a lesson.

"I don't care. I think I'll see what it turns out to be. No harm in that—I like surprises." Lucille had answered the laugh with a resolute stab of her hand spade into the dirt. When it struck something, she kept digging, then pulled out a bit of metal—something broken off of a machine, a cog or wheel, thick with rust. "What's this doing here?"

"Oh, people used to plant those in the garden, anything metal, to provide minerals for the soil. I find things like that all the time . . . when I'm cultivating." She said this last with a particular tone that implied something more like "when you're not cultivating," but Lucille let it go. She had something in store for the neighbor later that day. A friend of hers from the country was bringing in a truckload of horse manure for her gardens. It would smell to high heaven, and her neighbor would have to wear a scarf over her nose to do any gardening for the next two weeks. It delighted Lucille.

A month later the plant had assumed the straight, hard stalk of a tree and begun to leaf out. Lucille was content to let it be. It didn't hurt anything except her neighbor, who glanced at it maliciously each time she tended the garden on her side of the fence. And when Lucille was outside, the neighbor would usually hustle out the back door, wiping her hands on the apron she always wore as she came to the fence, almost breathless with advice. "That's a tree you know, a tree!"

"What kind do you think it is?" Lucille knew this would stump her. She had been through all her books on trees and gardening for the Western United States, and she couldn't find it. Maybe a tree seed from the Eastern United States had accidentally blown over the Mississippi and landed here. It was hard to know what to do about those books when you lived on the dividing line the way she did. You couldn't buy both sections, it was too expensive, yet it did make sense that some seeds could migrate or that birds could drop them off. She had heard of that. Birds as seeders—it was a nice idea and she quit disliking the bird droppings on the garage roof after she had thought about it.

The neighbor put her finger to her cheek, cradled her elbow with her other hand and took a long, withering look at the plant. It almost rustled under her hard gaze. "A Japanese mock orange . . . no, a false widow's willow . . . or a prickly striped basswood." She paused, then nodded her head wisely, "Take my word, it's one of those and it will make a mess out of this . . . this garden if you leave it here. Trees are a nuisance. We took the birch out because it was only supposed to grow to five feet, a miniature they told us, then it shot right up to eight feet and started shading everything in sight. So I had my husband take it right out of there. 'No more trees,' I told him, 'enough is enough.' You'd better have Arnold dig that out right away or it will take over everything."

Lucille remembered the birch. First they had tried topping it off so that it stood like a decapitated body for a few months, thick and oozing life out the stumps, until, finally, its ugliness brought it to the end and she had awoken at eight o'clock one Saturday morning to the buzz of the saw. The neighbors always did major work as early as possible.

Lucille tossed some more horse manure on the tree; it seemed to like the care it was getting because it was growing faster than anything else in the garden. She had even replanted the rusted cog beside the tree and, since, had added other bits of broken metal.

When it reached four feet in August, it began to bud out, like a fruit tree in April. Again the growth seemed remarkable, but Lucille put it down to the extra care, the horse manure and the metal pieces. It was comforting to see it rising above the fence line, waving gently in the summer breezes, and once in a while she caught a glint of something silvery in its leaves, which were long and dagger-shaped. The tree pleased her. Arnold, of course, had taken the neighbor's side of it. "Cut it down," he ordered.

"I don't think so," she replied, tossing an extra dash of pepper into the mashed potatoes.

"Watch what you're doing there."

"Then don't distract me while I'm cooking—go read the paper, or take a walk. The tree stays." Arnold was surprised by Lucille's tone, but obeyed her. Sometimes Lucille was very surprising.

One morning Lucille was startled out of bed by the phone. She had gone back to sleep after Arnold left and now felt clumsy with tiredness as she fumbled for the receiver.

"I tried to trim that part that's reaching over the fence to my side, but I can't. What is that thing?" It was her neighbor's indignant voice.

"What?"

"What is that tree? It broke the shears and cut my fingers trying to pull off the leaves. I told you so—it's starting to shade my garden and I can't get it to stop!" The neighbor's voice was rising hysterically, like a mother pig's squeal, Lucille thought, running in circles that voice.

She yawned and answered, "I'll be out in a few minutes to see what I can do." Honestly, that woman needed to get a job, a hobby, children.

Looking out the window as she dressed, Lucille could see the friendly wave of the tree as it dipped across the fence, its fruit now long green stems about as thick as her fingers. They looked like tadpoles, taking on more and more definition as they ripened. It looked so restful down there among the squash in her garden this time of year. She often wanted to curl up under the broad leaves, snuggle into the warm, moist shade beside the zucchini and crooknecks, and take a nap. Imagine Arnold finding her there, head resting comfortably in the curved cushion of the squash, a yellow blossom at her throat, dinner forgotten. He'd know she was there by her feet sticking out from the patch, the shoes resting at the edge of the garden. Now that would be fun, she giggled—Arnold demanding that she get out of the squash immediately. The neighbor lady looking arch and knowing from her kitchen window. When she woke up, she knew she'd start laughing at the sight of Arnold, the leaves over her face would bounce up and down with the gasping. Lucille almost laughed out loud as she pulled on her shoes.

Outside, her neighbor waited, angrily tapping her foot, arms on her hips. This is serious, Lucille thought. When the woman saw Lucille, she started waving a bandaged hand at her. "See, see what that tree did to me? Worse than barberry—worse than anything. Cut right into my fingers, sliced them neat as you please."

Lucille apologized for the tree and looked at the cuts when the neighbor exposed them. Really, it was a bit much for first thing in the morning. They reminded her of the sort she got fixing dinner. Walking around the tree for a few minutes, she thought how nicely it was coming along. And it only reached across the fence a little bit. She didn't want to spoil its shape by lopping off one side. She'd have to placate the neighbor. "It's not really shading your side yet. Let it go until fall and I'll have Arnold get to it. You can have a cutting off my President Lincoln lilac if you want." The neighbor and the tree nodded simultaneously.

A week later she discovered the first one. It was a bright morning in late August. The neighbor must have been gone, because she didn't come out of the house to bother Lucille as she worked in the garden. Arnold was at work. The tree's fruit was clearly beginning to mature, and when she had examined the tree that day, she had found it on the ground at its base. A paring knife. Just like the one she had left in the ground when she had planted geraniums way back in May. She remembered it then. Of course, that was where the knife had gone to; she had used it to cut back the long stems as she transplanted. Although she knew she should use her pruning shears, she always just picked up a paring knife from the kitchen to work with the plants. Now wasn't that something! She had turned it over in her palm and noted how nicely the metal glinted in the light and how fresh the wood handle looked. You'd never know it had spent all those months underground. She ran right into the house then and tried it out. It worked beautifully, just like its old self.

A few mornings later, when Lucille was weeding the begonias, her neighbor stepped around to the fence with an object clutched in her extended hand. "Here, you must have left this on the post there, where the wind could blow it over. It was in my garden by the coralbells this morning." It looked like the knife Lucille had lost and found earlier, only she didn't remember using it the day before.

Startled, she took the knife without protest. "Yes, uh, thanks. I've been missing that," she lied. Lucille was pretty sure she knew where it had come from. Later that same day, she spotted another with its tip neatly buried like an ostrich head in the iris, only the brown wooden handle gave it away. It was handy finding them this way, she reflected; summers were usually her worst season for losing paring knives.

On the following day she woke up early and went out to inspect the yard carefully. Sure enough. There were paring knives in other places, lying carelessly in shrubs or sticking out of deep grasses in shady corners, as if all the knives she had ever lost were now turning up at once. All day she thought about it, the surprise of it. When Arnold came home she would pull him, eyes closed, to the backyard. Once in front of the tree, she would command him to open his eyes. "What do you see?" she'd ask him.

"The same tree that has been driving us all nuts this summer."

"Look closer," she'd urge him, "what do you see?"

With this, he would lean closer and examine the fruit; some others were beginning to ripen. "No, no, this is one of your games, isn't it, this couldn't be . . ." He would protest, but she would insist.

"Yes, it is. It's a knife tree! I accidentally buried the paring knife here last spring and it sprouted. Isn't that great?" In her fantasy, Lucille could see that it wasn't great to Arnold; he just shook his head. She'd never be able to convince him.

Lucille's knife tree grew with phenomenal speed, and by the next year its branches were tapping metallically against the dining-room windows. Lucille didn't mind though, because although it was spreading out to cover the whole yard and garden, its silvery thin leaves didn't really shade anything. Even the neighbor couldn't complain, except when the fruit ripened and the clatter on her sidewalk kept her awake at night and made her afraid to walk outside during the day. But Lucille took the initiative and went around with bushel baskets and gloves and picked them all up so that no one would get hurt. The neighbor's husband would get up each morning to inspect the backyard for the alleged attack of noise the night before and find nothing. He began to worry about his wife's sleeplessness.

Arnold, on the other hand, was pleased that Lucille was finally showing some energy by getting up early each day to work in the garden. The only thing that bothered him was that by the third year, the tree was peeking in the upstairs bedroom window and he worried that one of the sharp limbs would poke through the screens. There was this other problem, too, but he had decided not to speak to Lucille just yet. It seemed that over the past few years she had started collecting paring knives, and now they filled all the drawers in the kitchen, and boxes of them had started appearing in the hall closet, the attic, and the basement. He was afraid to look under the bed, because he thought he had seen the metallic wink of a blade the other day when he had been looking for a lost shoe there. A few months ago when he had casually mentioned the fact that instead of losing them now, she seemed to be finding them—more than her share to be sure—Lucille had just laughed and tossed her head. "It's the knife tree out back," she had smiled mysteriously as she peeled a radish into a perfect little rose. Well, it was just another surprise in Lucille, Arnold thought. It seemed harmless enough. A knife tree indeed.

On the other hand, he probably would have to chop it down one of these days. A few weeks ago he had noticed that there were holes in the roof caused by limbs dragging across it during storms. And lately he had noticed some seedlings starting up around the yard from fruit she had missed; at least she claimed she had missed them, but you couldn't tell about Lucille all the time—after all, she had said that she was growing a knife tree. But he would explain it all to her, and she'd be reasonable. The lawnmower couldn't cut through those seedlings, and the roof—well, they just couldn't afford to get a whole new roof for the sake of one tree. She'd understand.

During the winter everything went along fine because the knife tree was dormant. Oh, once in a while Lucille would pick out the silvery glint of a residual fruit in the thin wintry light, but generally things were pretty calm. The backyard looked like anyone else's on their street. Even the neighbor's.

Then the next summer, the fourth year, things started to take off in a little different direction. Lucille, for her part, was as happy as ever, gardening, putting out little pieces of metal to fertilize the tree and little bits of seed for the birds that hopped around the yard. She was aware, though, that her neighbor eyed her angrily from her kitchen window, afraid of her own backyard these days, what with the tree and all. Her garden was a mess, too. She just couldn't work up enough courage to get out there and go at it with all that commotion overhead. Who could blame her, she muttered to herself. At night when her husband came home, tired and worried from work, she threatened him with lawsuits and divorce unless he did something about that tree next door. It was a public menace—who knew where it would end? And now they couldn't even have people over because their yard was such a wreck, the perennial beds a mass of waving grasses, nightshade twining around peonies, roping them to the ground almost, and she wasn't going to take her life in her hands and go out there. No sir, she still had a scar on her palm from the last time. Her husband just eyed her with quiet resignation and wondered if it would be worth it to sneak across the fence some night, chop down the tree, and get some peace and quiet for a change.

But nothing really happened until August, when the neighbor finally found a course of action. Lucille had spent the morning in the garden, enjoying the solitude without her neighbor's advice, digging and fertilizing before it got too hot. She liked the way she had to dress now that harvest time was here again—a pith helmet she had gotten at a yard sale protecting her head, a short fur coat (figuring that the animal hide would resist better than cloth), and a flak jacket she had saved up to buy out of the grocery money last year (wouldn't Arnold be surprised!). On her legs she wore goalie pads she had picked up second-hand from an ex-hockey star turned advertising executive. Whenever Lucille gardened in this outfit, she imagined her neighbors warning their children to stay away from her—she *was* an odd one.

She'd like to keep bees in this outfit, she thought—drop a piece of netting over her head, pull on the goalie mitts she'd gotten with the leg protectors, and lift the cores of the hives out. Soaking with honey, they would glisten and tumble over her hands clumsy in the gloves studded on the back with sharp metal stars. The bees, furry with sleep and work, would crawl up her arms, and she'd get right into the hive with them, bury herself in the sweet thickness of their hum. And Arnold would come home that night, tired from work, impatient for dinner, and, unable to find her anywhere in the house amidst the still-growing collection of knives, he would come stumbling out into the dazzling late sun in the backyard. "Lucille, Lucille, you come out of there now— I'm afraid of the bees," he'd call to her from the safety of several yards away. Her laughing would erupt as an angry buzz of startled bees. "Oh, Arnold, you should try this once," she'd want to call to him, but her throat so thick with honey . . .

In the afternoon, when Lucille was taking her nap, a big storm started building, the way they do in that part of the country, the air swirling with dust and leaves tearing from trees. What awakened her, though, wasn't the sound of the wind or the tree limbs that had begun digging into the roof. It was the grinding buzz of an electric drill or saw, something that was coming from somewhere behind her house. She paused in her drowsiness for a few minutes, the way she always did, to locate the noise, to reassure herself that it was in the outside world and not coming from some dream. Then suddenly she knew. Leaping out of bed with nothing but the sheet clutched around her bare body, she ran to the window looking out over the backyard. Yes, there it was—a truck whose motor ran roughly under the whine and grind of the saw that the man was pressing directly against a larger limb of her knife tree that stretched out to her neighbor's lawn through the overhead wires. She gasped as she watched the saw sink dramatically all at once up to its edge, the limb giving way suddenly to its bite. Then the man, middle-aged, balding, dressed in some sort of tan uniform or utility clothes, pulled the saw away. Next he attacked a small limb hanging out over the alley where his truck was parked. That limb, too, gave way easily. When he noticed Lucille watching him, he waved, pointed to the sign on the side of his truck, turned and got in behind the wheel, and drove away. The sign had said Northern States Power Company.

Despite the thunder and lightning that now started booming across the neighborhood, Lucille quickly dressed and ran downstairs and out-doors to check on the tree. It creaked and groaned overhead, as she inspected the wound on the trunk, the gap in the branches; and when she turned to look at her neighbor's house for a moment, she thought she heard a crack of wood giving way, just as she caught a glimpse of her neighbor's figure moving away from the window.

It was awfully upsetting for Lucille. The doctor had to be called, and Arnold couldn't do much but sit around holding her limp hand, his face all white and soggy with worry. It was only a mild concussion and she'd have to take it easy for a few weeks; she'd be OK, he reassured Arnold. The next morning when Arnold called Northern States Power, they told him there had been a report that the tree was rubbing power lines and that the inspector had just been checking to see if there was a danger of it taking down any wires. In fact, it turned out that the tree was rotting from the inside out. Unusual, yes, but not unheard of in trees that reached maturity rapidly. By the way, the person had asked Arnold, what kind of tree was it, just for the record. Arnold thought for a minute, then answered, "A Knife Tree."

The Dead of July

 I go all day wearing Mama's face. I feel it sliding over mine in that tight rubber-glove way as I drive to work. I know it the instant I finish talking to someone I haven't met before, but disapprove of . . . not because of anything they've done or said, but just because. Mama always disapproved of something about almost everyone.

This is the way the face looks: the skin pulls over your bones like thin rubber stretched tight—the rubber glove. It's that way so the mouth can't do anything drastic, like smile. It can only get thin as paper. And with some effort, the corners pull in and down. That's what Mama got from her mother—that's the Methodist in them. And the eyes, well, they're blank, neutral as flour. And the brow, it pulls up a little, into the scalp, so it would look surprised if the eyes had any light in them. But all you get is the Methodist again.

Well, this is the story of the dead of July—the air so still you hate to disturb it breathing. The cat runs off. She's had enough to last a lifetime of my kicking covers off and pulling them back on. The fan's noisy rattle runs my sleep from midnight to dawn, then light breaks through and captures the room anyway. The fan seems useless against the heat crouched outside the front door. I get up to let it in.

Overhead the noisy growl of approaching planes, and outside the stillness of things too hot to move or grow. This is how we reach into August, and later September, but for now, it seems impossible that anything will change again. This is the middle of July.

In the paper the accidents start. The boy and his girl turn mad as dogs, running loose through the middle states, killing and stealing, not paying much attention to which they do. And a nun from two towns over hangs herself in the attic of our old Catholic church. Just visiting her folks. We knew something was up when the bell started ringing on a Tuesday. But it was too late. Cancer. Despair. We all know enough, even the Methodists, to understand how bad it is with her—cast down to hell and shame. Her family walking around like they're embarrassed to shop at the A&P anymore. I can understand their worry. Now I feel Mama's face glitter like clear nail polish when I see them on the street.

This is a mean time. Birds squabbling in the bush outside the trailer, rising like cinders and burnt scraps of paper from a fire, tossing them above the trees then dropping back. In the morning, all they've got in them is a couple of chirps before the sun gets up good, then it's back to sitting where it's cool.

Lazy. That's what Mama's face says. Lazy as dogs. The cat didn't run off, she'd tell me, it got tired of having to work. Left a drift of black fur on the counter with its dirty paw prints and took off. Good riddance, Mama's face says.

But I don't listen to this face all the time, after all, she said that when Jake took off, too. Methodists like to keep things neat, I have to remind myself. Especially the old kind. They don't hold with things that can get sloppy on you—dancing, playing cards, smoking, and drinking. Especially drinking. You should've seen Mama's face the day Jake brought home his first case of beer and stacked it neatly, all of it, in twelve-ounce cans, in the bottom of the fridge. Like we were taking a trip to the moon and he was stocking provisions.

There is a lot that makes me wear that face in the middle of July though. This is the face I wear for the summer heat, for the disapproval that lets me sleep alone.

Yesterday I was at the laundromat. No place hotter in July, the clothes thumping hot against the hot dryer walls, when you pull them out, they grab hold of you like they're going to keep thumping. I come out needing a bath after every weekly trip. Anyway, I heard these ladies talking about the nun—said she'd had cancer in her face, it'd eaten her sinuses away so she couldn't bear the weather. The worst thing was to get a cold and have to sneeze, like acid was being run through her head. Then it went for her eyes. She started trying all these cures—positive thinking, natural foods, she even went to Texas, where some guy claimed he could arrest your cancer with marigold pollen. It made her allergic. She came home puffed up like a pumpkin and had to take drugs and eat out of a straw for the rest of her time. Finally it got so bad that she was seeing double all the time, and every little sound rang in her head so loud she couldn't think straight. Like the cancer'd made a clear channel in there, like a sea shell, and she couldn't take the roar of the ocean anymore.

They figure she was only praying at first, but it must've been pretty tempting to climb the stairs to the old bell tower. Her head as round and carved as metal by the time the cancer was through, just her brain hanging there like an oyster surprised when the blade slits open the shell. I maintain that that's July for you. When nothing seems to grow and you begin to believe you'll never get cool again. Never sleep a whole night again. Never have your own face back.

July. This is the time when you try to keep things the way they always are. You know better than to introduce a change, like putting different horses together in a pasture. The kicks connect in July, they break jaws and legs. Horses down, horses rolling in pain, horses on three legs, that's July.

When I dream, it's of big, too-big houses, wrapped in white cotton and it's getting cold out. All through the dream the temperature drops like someone's sucking at it from outside the picture, and when I go to sleep, the blanket's too thin and worn to keep me warm. But all that space, I figure I can make it through the winter.

I suppose it would be the normal thing for the divorce rate to go up then, for people to turn tail and head for Nebraska, Missouri, ports east, but that's not usual. When the weather turns on us, we like the comfort of someone to fight with, someone to be the soft connector to the arm, the fist slashed out, the anger bubbling under the skin that's cooking in the heat. No, they leave later when the heat breaks, when it looks like a chance for a fresh start, not now, when there's nowhere to go anyway, when the physical effort of having emotions is too much. When the indifference makes falling into bed with someone an act of infidelity, even if you're married to them.

That's probably why I ended up sleeping with Jerry. It was probably easier than going home to my own bed with Jake. I just couldn't face the drive in that heat.

I don't even think I bothered taking Mama's face off before he was on top of me. It wouldn't have mattered. I was too hot to be disapproving, even of myself. All I remember is the suck of our chests together, a sound like something breathing in that nun's head, and his hands rolling my nipples like they were balls of beer-soaked napkin on the table back at Sleepy's, where we'd been drinking. His hair and skin weren't any worse than mine, soaked in smoke and beer and dull conversation, floating on the green breath of July heat.

Later, we lay panting side by side, trying not to touch, in the wet sheets, while the sun finally plopped down like a fat lady on a couch and fell backwards over the hill. The mosquito, almost too lazy to strike, walked deliberately up my arm and with the precision of a surgeon began to sting. I had to debate whether it was worth the effort to slap it.

What the Fall Brings

The fall here in Divinity, Iowa, always brings back such memories that I almost go running home with a sack over my head so I don't have to watch them come ghosting up high over the buildings, or leaking out of doorways like someone's washer running crazy and crazy.

Some days, I feel my body with my own hands, you know, just to make sure I'm here and not evaporating like some of the people I've known. But I've seen the way bones break, and the way they resist and grow back, so I figure they can stand a lot. I also figure that maybe they aren't so different—the folks around here—from anyplace else. I mean, we got a certain number that end up in Anamosa, the state penitentiary, not much more or less than anywhere else. We got the same regular numbers being trucked over to Independence (the mental hospital's there) by their families, or occasionally by the deputy, the squad car light whirring most of the way, just to impress everyone with the importance of his errand. And yearly, the same number more or less heads on out to the cemetery, usually carried along in the big black hearse belonging to Thompson's Mortuary, but occasionally arriving from out of town in someone else's. We get used to it. All our friends and family are there after a while.

I like to think about all of us years from now, where we'll be, how many of us will still be going to the same jobs, the same daily routines, say, twenty or thirty years from now. Since I'm just turning thirty now, hell, I could live to be a hundred, but I don't think many others will. It might be awfully lonely then. I might end up like Miss Ethel's mother—all bones and a bag of skin. What I'm afraid of, is that maybe as you get older, things start falling out of place. Maybe a rib could detach, maybe your shoulder blades could start traveling around. It's a funny idea, I know, but after the way I've watched things start to loosen in people, it's something to think about.

Like every fall, I can't help thinking about that one time after the state fair, just when everything was beginning to color up nice, early October. I was still in high school, just my first year, I think—yes, that'd be right, because that's how I still knew him. We'd gone through grade school once I'd moved up here, and he was the second boy I kissed. The first one didn't work, so it took me a long time to work up nerve again. But Billy Bond was sure a lot nicer about it. We were in seventh grade. Billy lived on a farm outside of town, and although the school bus took him back and forth, often as not he'd walk me home, then go on and walk all the way, five miles out, just so he'd be able to spend a little more time with me. I know his daddy must have given it to him for always being late for chores, but Billy worked pretty hard, so no one could complain too much. Everyone in my family just pretended like Billy Bond wasn't there—that was their way usually. And I do recall that in the next year, the eighth grade, when Billy decided to like LuAnn Menderson instead of me, it did come as a blow. But then, LuAnn lived on the farm next to his, and I guess they could take the bus home together and see each other more, so it made sense, sort of. Better sense than walking five miles just to see me.

And they were both in 4-H, I remember that. It's a big deal for kids out here, 4-H and Future Farmers of America when they got a little older. They'd all walk around in their shiny satin jackets with the fancy stitching along over the front pocket—their nicknames—and in the back, the big round symbol and title—Future Farmers of America. It was like a fraternity. When they went to college, they studied agriculture and animal husbandry and came home and took over the farms, going through the usual fights with dads and older relatives about new ideas the ag school was pumping out in its monthly bulletins. Like how many cows a man without a hired help could maintain efficiently versus the farmer with help. And whether the hay was better baled and stacked, rolled in giant rounds and left in the field, or racked into long cylinders like old-fashioned curls and then bound with twine and put up in the barn. Every farmer had his pet theories, and every farmer fought with his kids from ag school about the changes.

I know, because you used to have to listen to it everywhere you went. In school the boys would get into fistfights about whose dad knew the most, and whether you want China blacks or Polands in hogs, and which wintered best—the shelled corn or the unshelled. And there was a hierarchy, too, depending on what you raised—cattle at the top, hogs in the middle, and poultry at the bottom. Billy explained it once when we went to the county fair. We spent most of the day in the animal 4-H exhibits, while I just wanted to ride the Ferris wheel and have Billy win me a big panda bear. But Billy was a serious person; he had a big stake in doing a good job with his pig growing and didn't want to mess up by letting anything go. So we spent most of the time checking on this big old mama hog, fat as a piece of butter and smelling pretty good, with just the hint of piggy odor about her. Billy told me that he used Wella Balsam Creme Rinse on her hair to get it to lie flat and smell good. He liked the piney smell of it. Then he made me put my face down into the pen, with my nose almost touching her pink skin. He was right—piney, with just an edge of hog underneath.

God, the things he showed me to do to a pig. He'd stolen some of his mama's clear fingernail polish, and after rasping his hog's little hoofs rounded and smooth, he painted them up with the polish. Boy, did they shine. Since the animals were kept bedded in clean, sweet straw, they didn't have a chance to go out and act like pigs, get dirty again. It was just like an animal palace at those fairs, the animals just lounging around, nothing to do but lie there or stand and have some person spend hours picking their ears or getting every last crumb out of their coat. Why, if you forgot these were farm animals, you'd think you were at one of those dog-grooming parlors watching fancy little poodles getting bows put in their hair or something. When I tried a joke with Billy, asking him why he'd neglected putting some eye make-up on his pig, he gave me a strange look, reddened, then opened his trunk sitting just outside the pen, and pulled out some Maybelline eye-liner and mascara. "I thought about it . . ." I didn't have the heart to laugh, so I just nodded serious-like and let it go.

I don't want you to get me wrong here though, Billy Bond wasn't the only one. These kids ate, slept, dreamed their animals. There wasn't a one of them wouldn't do what Billy was doing. It was a strange sight, believe me, to look down the rows and rows of those 4-H barns and see kids with their animals, some of them sleeping in the stall, some of them outside it. Some of them bent over as they handpicked each particle of manure out, and some of them looking like little mamas, dressing their babies with a tenderness and consideration that only comes from a genuine love.

I suppose that if Billy hadn't been so careful, so meticulous about his hog raising—if he'd let something slip by, if he'd gotten interested in girls more, or horsing around with his friends when he should have been handfeeding and grooming—then things would have turned out different in the long run. But you don't get anywhere thinking like that, I guess. The facts are what they are. Like bones—there one day, and then who knows, maybe it's the skin that lets go of them somehow.

But I remember that the fall of our freshman year in high school, Billy Bond's hog, Bluebell, won the grand championship at the Iowa State Fair. She was the biggest and the best. There were pictures of Billy and his hog in newspapers all over Iowa. They were a winning couple, and besides, the pig was the biggest ever to win the 4-H, and you knew that was going to set Billy up for good as a hog grower. People remembered those things, and if Billy's pigs could turn that size and quality, then Billy wouldn't have a thing to worry about. Everyone was proud of him, I recall, his dad and brothers strutting around town like they were behind the whole thing. There was even a little parade the day Billy and Bluebell came home when the fair was done. They drove real slow down Main Street, and the high school band played some snappy songs, and the hog looked out the grates of the little trailer, sniffing suspiciously like she knew just what was going to happen next.

Because it was part of it that Bluebell had been auctioned and bought by Reese's A&P and would spend a couple of weeks on display for everyone to see right in front of the store, to honor Billy and the pig and the 4-H. Half the proceeds were to go to the club in town, to build future 4-Hers like Billy, and Reese could take the tax write-off and sell or donate the meat as the highest grade pork around. But Billy looked pretty miserable through the whole thing, even while he was squatting down, posing with his arm thrown around Bluebell's shoulder for the newspaper photographs. And I remember how when the picture came out a few days later, it reminded me of a boy and his girl watching a movie, the same intent distracted look on each of their faces.

I've never much liked to see animals on display, like at zoos, or at fairs and carnivals, and I think Billy's hog just reinforced that for me. It was sad to walk by her every time you wanted to get a loaf of bread at the A&P. Bluebell always came trotting up to the little portable fence, sniffing like you'd brought her a treat, like Billy probably taught her to do, then when you didn't have anything for her, she would shuffle back to the far corner and stand with her back to you, dejected. And while their mamas shopped the little kids were spending too much time tormenting her, throwing little rocks and clods of dirt to watch her stampede around, then they'd have a laughing fit seeing all that wobbly fat. I think it'd been Reese's idea to build some publicity for the hog slaughter, and put even more fat on her by keeping her confined and stuffing her good for a couple of weeks. I don't think he intended more than that. Reese is pretty harmless. He just wants to make his money and let it go at that.

Every afternoon after school, those two weeks, Billy Bond would come over, snap a little collar and lead line on the pig, and take her out back to the vacant lot to eat grass and get some exercise. He was careful, though, not to let her run much since they wanted to keep the fat on and Reese had warned him about it. And I swear, the time or two I caught sight of it, Billy and that hog looked just like a boy romping with his dog at a distance.

In Divinity, the homecoming game on Saturday afternoon is the biggest celebration of the fall, and since we knew we'd win that year, everyone was real built-up. You could feel it all week as you walked down the street, in and out of stores, people a bit more pumped up than usual, joshing the football players they saw, or the families of the players. As part of the celebration afterwards, Reese had decided to butcher the hog and have a big pig roast. To help things along, some of the merchants had gotten together and decided to buy a couple of kegs of beer for the adults and pop for the kids. So all morning before the game that started at one in the afternoon, the A&P had been busy with folks coming and going, buying food to fix, and taking things down to the little park beside the river a couple of blocks away. The hardware store had donated some strings of lights and the men were busy with those, putting them into the trees overhead, setting up tables and chairs, and cleaning up the little bandstand.

I don't think anyone thought much about the empty pen outside the store. People were used to the animals that came and went from season to season. Farm kids learned early that that was the way things were. I guess I didn't keep track either. It was the first high school homecoming I was actually going to be a part of, like I belonged instead of some dumb kid running around. And I had a date, my first, although I had to take my sister Baby along, so nothing could happen. Kenton Maxwell, the boy, told me not to worry though, he was a year older than me and knew how to get around big obstacles like Baby. Just before one that afternoon, we'd walked up to the game, the three of us from my house, where Kenton's brother had let him out. None of us but Baby were old enough to drive yet, and Baby was too big to fit behind a normal steering wheel, so she still couldn't. EuGene, as usual, wouldn't have a thing to do with any of us, and just drove off in his empty car to pick up his date. I was so excited, I guess I didn't think much about the aroma of roasting pig that drifted through that afternoon, it was all part of the excitement—the game, the picnic and dance later. And I was going to all of it. Probably no one even missed Billy Bond, not even his family, because everything was focused on his brothers, who were on the varsity string playing that afternoon.

Of course, our small towns always choose to play the smallest, weakest team they can find for their homecoming, and I don't know who this team could play since it came from such a small community that they were barely fielding the two lines. To no one's surprise, we trounced them good and sent them brokenhearted and broken headed onto their buses at four, for the long ride back home, while we all came busting out of the field, running for our cars and the victory parade down Main Street afterwards.

Some of the high school clubs had fixed up floats, and the candidates for homecoming queen were all dressed up, sitting on the backs of honking convertibles. It was the sort of thing that is still going on each October in this town. But the reason I remember this one so well is Billy Bond, who had climbed on top of the four-story bank building, the tallest we have, right in the center of town while everyone was at the game, and who was, apparently, driven crazy by the sight and smell of the beloved Bluebell turning slowly over the coals in the late afternoon sun, because by the time the parade was halfway through town, he had picked up the BB gun he'd climbed up to the roof with and started shooting at things in the street below him, hollering.

I can still remember how loud his voice was. You could hear it clearly, plainly, above the marching band even. Although the range was too much for the BB gun most of the time, he managed to pop one under the skin of Reese's forearm before everyone took cover. Reese was plenty mad when that happened, and after a moment of shock, then realization that it was Billy Bond up on the bank roof taking pot shots and messing up the parade, he sneaked into the drugstore and called the sheriff's office, which was stupid, since the sheriff and his deputy were both on their posse quarter horses leading the parade like always. When Reese realized this, he went ducking and sneaking down the street to where the two men sat on their horses, taking stock of the situation, well out of the range of the BB gun.

Reese demanded that they do something, "take the little bugger off of there," calling Billy every name in the book and waving his forearm with the welt from the BB rising red and angry, looking like a big spider had bit him or something. The sheriff was trying hard to hold off a smile—you could see that a mile away—and whether Reese could or not, I don't know, but he could sure tell he wasn't getting anywhere, because in a few minutes he stomped his feet and started walking straight back to his place in the parade, forgetting about Billy for a moment until a BB ticked the top of his head, ruffling the hair enough to send him cursing and sliding into the corner of the hardware store. Then he started yelling right up at Billy, saying, "Goddamn you, Billy Bond, I'm gonna get you for this. You're going to Anamosa, you goddamn juvenile delinquent," and stuff like this. Billy just answered by showering the street below with more BBs—he had a Daisy Repeating Rifle, must have gotten it when he was eight or nine years old, like most of us kids. The BBs keep bouncing around, like someone was throwing little pebbles down from the sky, most of them harmless, but an occasional one getting enough velocity that they'd stick in something. Meanwhile, folks started getting tired of holding the parade up, and began drifting away, with the deputy directing traffic down to the park.

When Billy realized that the parade was breaking up, he stood up and started calling for Reese, "the Nazi butcher," to come back. Finally, he was so mad, he started threatening everyone in sight, saying he was going home for a real gun, his dad's .22, if they didn't listen, and warning them not to eat Bluebell. His parents, everyone noticed, had kept out of sight, because on a day when their other two sons had done such a fine job, Billy had to go and embarrass everyone, so they were trying to ignore him like a whiny child, I guess. By the time the sheriff and deputy had put their horses away and gotten back, a group of local men had gathered a block away to discuss what to do with Billy. Everyone else was down at the river having a drink and savoring the smell of the nearly done, crisping pork they would soon be eating.

Some of the younger men wanted Mr. Bond and his sons to climb up there and take Billy down forcibly, and kept muttering about what a disgrace it was to have a kid making such a big fuss in front of the whole town. Mr. Bond looked pretty uncomfortable, but kept his silence. I don't think he trusted Billy not to shoot him with the BB gun as he came over the top. Besides, he was sick of Billy's moping around about the damn hog anyway. "I'll leave it up to the sheriff," was all he'd say. Then the men turned to the sheriff and asked what he intended to do.

The sheriff looked around him, hooked his thumbs in his belt, and announced, "Nothing. I'm going to get a beer and some food now, and if Billy Bond wants to sit on that roof for the rest of his life, he can." Then as he moved through the group, he added, "But I bet he'll be down by the time snow falls." And true to his word, he went to the park, got himself a beer, and started flirting with the younger women, like he always did. Some of the men tried to get up energy to go get Billy after that, but the heart was gone out of it, and the town just went on and celebrated the homecoming, drinking beer and eating roast pig.

I liked Billy, but I tried not to think about him up there alone on the bank roof, probably sobbing his heart out while the rest of the folks were down there eating his Bluebell. "Things have to go on in life," that's what people told each other that night. "You can't take on so about a mere animal; you have to know that they're here for people to eat. This is a good experience for him," they told each other, and his dad promised he'd get a good whipping once he got off that roof. So everyone felt pretty good, and I didn't even mind so much being with my sister Baby on my first date. She got so wrapped up in the food, like I knew she would, and Kenton was careful to get someone to keep supplying her with big full plates while he and I snuck off with some of the other kids our age to the dance. All in all, it was a fine homecoming, and even Reese got to laughing about the BB in his arm by the end of the evening.

No one gave Billy Bond a thought as we drifted back home around eleven that night. The big bonfire that'd been built down on the river-bank was starting to die down, but its aroma filled the cold fall air with a wonderful burning wood smell. And I guess we just assumed he'd gotten down and walked back to the farm—that is, if we thought about him at all.

The next day, when Billy hadn't shown up by one o'clock, after church services were out, and no one had heard a word from the roof, the sheriff and his deputy did go up there to see if they could find him. He was there all right, sitting in the corner, hugging himself like he was still cold from the hard frost we'd had overnight, but when the men tried to talk him into standing up and coming home, he'd looked up at them with a face as white as milk—that's what they'd said, he was just gone. There wasn't anything left in him, so they'd carried and dragged him down the ladder to the street below and carted him off home. But it didn't do any good. A few days later, as we were going to school one morning, there goes the deputy driving by the high school with Mr. Bond beside him in front, and Billy Bond sitting in the back still hugging himself, looking out the window with a face like an empty bowl. And when I waved, he looked at me like I was the man in the moon.

Aronson's Orchard

 And in the fall, it is being haunted by the dried vines that have left their darker mark along the wooden fence behind the house on the farm I remember as my first home. I think we were happy there. Now I don't know for sure. I'm haunted by the orange globes that dot the dying-out garden to the left of the biggest barn, the pumpkins that lie there in wait for us a week before Halloween when we'll be out to pull them in, carve them up and give the extras to the neighbors. We don't have to hide them the way we do the watermelon patch, which kids spend half their summer nights trying to discover, driving slowly along the little back roads hoping to spot a clearing, a scarecrow, the aluminum pie plates strung on a rope along the edge back near the woods. Sometimes they'll spend a week watching for the farmer to make his move toward the beloved watermelon patch. The next morning, the melons are gone—only the rinds of those eaten on the spot litter the area. But by October the kids have lost interest in the hunt. They're back at school, back at football, and back at each other.

In the fall here in Divinity, it is being haunted by the sight of those dark red, almost mahogany apples at Aronson's Orchard. Aronson's great-great-grandfather had brought the first seedlings over from the Old Country, wrapped in burlap and secreted among his belongings. Every day he'd unwrap them, slip them out for sun, cupping each in his hand like a kitten, so that by the time he'd landed, he was ready to start his apple orchard. He'd always told the other farmers that came out with him, "First you plant the trees. A tiny house for you to live in, then the trees. A man must leave his mark on the land so the future will know him." But the neighbors always figured they could get their apples from Aronson. Eventually he planted enough trees to keep the growing community, and opened his orchard officially. Although it had always been his intention to start dairy farming, not apple farming, he just never got around to doing more than slowly building one big barn and acquiring a single cow. Over the years his descendants carried on the same routine: trading apples and other fruit for the produce and meat they needed, then selling the surplus to the suppliers of large stores in the cities.

Curiously, they always kept just one cow, as if the old man, the first Aronson, had set a precedent they couldn't break. After a while the barn was put to use for storage and processing, and more recently, Aronson's cleaned it up inside for the customers he has coming from all over to buy apples and see his little "apple museum." During the apple season, from late August to January, older women come in to bake their best apple pies. Usually these are women whose husbands are retired or dead, and they can use the extra work and cash. At first it was just a couple, like Tom Tooley's mom, but after a while it became such a popular thing, those pies—and you can buy them fresh, baked, or frozen, they're all good—that people would stop and buy one at the drop of a hat all fall, just for dinner. Then last year he added homemade cinnamon ice cream, and that's real good, too, on hot pie. This year he's making donuts and trying out apple muffins.

Each year, Aronson feels like he has to improve something. "It's part of the old-world tradition," he tells folks. "You have to keep working on it, making it a little better year after year."

Aronson once came to our high school for career lectures and explained how the apple trees are only productive for a certain amount of time, then you have to have another batch of trees coming up alongside so when you dig out the old tree, the new tree is ready to go. Aronson swears by the strain his great-great-grandfather brought over. Still uses it. He's worried that all the dinking around they do to dwarf trees, to make them higher yield and blight, insect, and weather resistant is ruining the flavor of the apple. Aronson keeps trying to do it the old way, but he's having trouble getting people to help him, he says; young people don't want to work that hard. But he's not down on us like other folks around here. He still feels awful, you know, after what happened to his son Reinhardt.

Everyone has a theory in Divinity. They always have and always will. Theories and opinions and dreams. With a few historical facts thrown in. And lots of memories. Reinhardt Aronson is one of those people who produced more than his share of all of these. Twyla makes a face and orders another drink whenever his name comes up, and it never does unless we're in a bar. That's one thing about Reinhardt: you don't mention him at the dining room table or in the presence of small children. Twyla's encounter with him wasn't as bad as it could have been—that's what everyone says. She says she could have lived without any of it, wished she had, too. Another thing about Reinhardt is that no one mentions his name to old man Aronson, and if his wife had lived, to her either. Although the old man makes a trip to Anamosa to see Reinhardt once a year, it just doesn't do much good. I don't know who he'll leave that orchard to—Reinhardt won't come back here afterwards, that's for sure.

Some of the opinions around here hold that Aronson worked Reinhardt too much, too early—and that's unusual, coming from a farming community where as soon as you're old enough to walk, you start getting your chores. People can understand farmwork, that's one thing, but tree work, that's another. Picking the apples, backbreaking work, is something you should hire out to migrants, but Aronson would never do that, didn't believe the apples would be treated right.

Other people say that it was in the genes—that's the genealogists, of course, Baby and her crowd. Too much inbreeding. Reinhardt was bound to come along sooner or later. They're worried. Maybe they'll get a Reinhardt of their own one of these days. Maybe some of them already have. Like my brother EuGene maybe. Some of them luckily got killed in Vietnam, where the families sent them to grow up or die. Of course, no one would ever say that out loud. But there seems to be a good chance that growing up can kill you the way it's done around here.

Whatever the cause, old man Aronson lets the kids who work for him get away with murder. Maybe that's since Reinhardt, or maybe he was always too nice to his son. Should have cracked him, instead of trying to be understanding all the time. The problem was that no one seemed to let Reinhardt know that he wasn't doing everything just right. Even the teachers at school tended to let Reinhardt get away with things. There was something that made him get a talking-to, while someone like Clinton got the ruler across his butt. I think Clinton knew pretty much that Reinhardt was going to get away with everything in life, because he didn't spend much time with him after a while, although they were cousins.

Reinhardt Aronson looked like a god, or better yet, like a prince. That's what a teacher told him once—like a Bavarian prince. It stuck, and we called him Prince, like he was someone's pet horse. He took to believing it after a while, too, pushing what he'd always done anyway a little more. Taking his turn first, taking advantage, but always with that clear, bold way that reminded you of someone in the movies, playing royalty, always shoving in front of everyone else and not even looking around to see if everyone fell back the way they should. And we did. It seemed natural to give way before Prince Reinhardt with his golden hair and hard, handsome face. There were moments that reinforced it too: like the times Reinhardt had to beat someone up and would do it in a particularly vicious fashion, continuing to punch and kick long after the other boy had clearly finished. It left a little pinched place in your memory to watch that, and after a couple of times, nobody bothered him.

Although there were lots of rumors about him by the time we were in junior high, the story about Reinhardt and the cat was the first thing that made us really wonder about him. Clinton said Reinhardt had showed the boys how to stick their finger up a cat in heat to relieve it. It was Jimmy got caught doing it and slapped around pretty good by his father. But you know, the cats would take to following a boy who tried it. They'd know whoever had done that to them, they'd want more. Maybe that's what gave Reinhardt encouragement, because the next thing he tried was chickens. It just went on from there. In high school he started in with anything he could put himself inside, according to Clinton. While his dad was out working in the orchard, he'd be in the little stall with the cow, showing the other boys how to do it. It was enough to make me sick, let me tell you. They say some of those boys giggled and made jokes with the Prince. After a while, when animals weren't enough, he started on girls.

Most of us girls had gotten wind of what Reinhardt did, and wouldn't go near him. Handsome and having all the spending money he wanted, he'd still have to recruit girls from other towns or go with the wild ones. Either way, it'd always end up the same. He was a little too rough, a little too demanding, and they'd drop him after a date or two and go around wearing this little hurt expression, feeling sorry about something—maybe themselves. Once during a dance in our junior year there was a big fuss in the parking lot outside the high school because Reinhardt had dragged Babette Ponder into the back of his father's big Oldsmobile Ninety-Eight and torn off half her clothes. She'd had a few drinks and her guard was down. Probably thought it'd be a good trick to pull on her boyfriend she was having a fight with or something. But Reinhardt wasn't satisfied with making out and tore her blouse trying to get at her, and if she hadn't developed a healthy set of lungs, he probably would have torn off the rest of her clothes.

All hell broke loose, and Reinhardt finally just shoved Babette out of the car to the waiting arms of her boyfriend and a gathering crowd, then jumped in the front seat, started the car, and rammed it through the lot before anyone figured out that they should pound him into the pavement. I remember the way everyone stood there, mouths dropping, frozen in the receding red of the taillights, with Babette still crouching where he'd thrown her, the knees of her nylons torn out, the skin bloody raw from being scraped on the concrete, and her red silk blouse hanging by a couple of threads from its collar, with one arm poking out naked and tender. You could almost see the imprint of his fingers on the flesh, the way they would be when she showed everyone in the bathroom on Monday morning at school. And we all wore that same dumb look you saw on the villagers' faces in a Dracula movie.

I don't know why we never said anything to our parents. We just didn't. Maybe we were ashamed, like being caught in a situation with Reinhardt was our own fault. There were always wild girls to go out with him though, to match him—or to try to match him—at whatever he wanted to do. People at school said that he'd already knocked up a girl in Osceola, but that was just rumor. It was always someone's cousin who heard it, or it happened to, but never really a related person. And for some reason, there were always girls who took chances with Reinhardt, as if it were some kind of test they wanted very badly to pass—going out with Reinhardt and coming back unscathed, hot and bold with their bragging that they'd put him in his place, he hadn't got to base one with them. Everyone wants to walk into the mouth of the lion and back out. Some of them even made it. I know that our boyfriends used to tease and threaten us with Reinhardt, and sometimes we'd both pretend and let ourselves go. It was fun once in a while that way, like all the controls were gone.

When we graduated from high school, Reinhardt went away for a while, first to college, but we heard that he left there, then to Vietnam, but he didn't stay there long either. We couldn't imagine him taking orders. Anyway, he was one of the first back, and by then his father couldn't do anything about him. Reinhardt just took over the family car until the old man bought him his own, and spent the nights and days when he wasn't sleeping out on the roads looking for women, drinking, and fighting. It's not like there was any direct proof for a long time. I mean, no one charged him with any of it. He was careful, too. He didn't touch children. I think women had become his meat finally.

At first he operated well outside of here, and since most of them were too embarrassed to report it even, he was free to do it again. Before long, though, the stories about people's cousins, then sisters and wives were piling up so high that we had to start believing them. About that time he was getting lazy, staying closer to home. I think, in fact, that Twyla was about the first he tried right here in town. She was lucky. When he popped up out of the back seat on the outskirts of town late one fall afternoon, holding a knife to her neck and telling her he'd "kill her if she didn't stop the car and fuck him," she told him to go ahead—she'd had a lousy day anyway. This surprised him so much that he jumped out when she slowed down for a stop sign at Highway 11 and the entrance to our road.

Twyla sat there for a few minutes laughing her guts out, then panicked and drove to my place. By the time she stepped out of the car, she was shaking all over and bawling her head off. Jake was out of town and Tom was out and about, so we just sat there at my little kitchen table, the door locked and a chair shoved under the knob to make us feel more secure, in case he'd followed her.

At first we were going to tell the sheriff, call him right up, but then the more we talked about it, the more we realized that he'd probably think she was lying, because everyone thought Twyla and I were the biggest runarounds in town. Reinhardt would just deny it, of course, then wait to catch her alone again. After we'd come to that, we started drinking, and by ten o'clock we were so drunk we could almost laugh about it. That's what we did that night: made jokes and passed out at midnight.

They found Carla's body about six A.M., when Bevington went to milk his cows. She was tied to one of the stanchions, carved up good, and dead. They found the knife outside the barn in some dried weeds that had been trampled down, and the tire tracks up the back way through his pasture. The rest was simple. Reinhardt was sleeping it off at home, and the old man didn't put up so much as a single word. I think he'd known all along something was going to happen. Mrs.

Aronson collapsed silently and died the next day. According to Mel Weller, the deputy, the Prince didn't even want to go to the funeral. I don't think he bothered much with family feeling.

When Twyla had to go in and testify about the knife, I went with her. It was something. The description of the body was enough to make you sick. The sheriff said she looked like a piece of fresh veal after the job Reinhardt had done. Reinhardt still looked like a prince at the trial, we were just the dumb villagers who would be tended to later. Old man Aronson looked a lot older, his face engraved with worry that never went away after that. The last thing Reinhardt sneered to him was, "Go fuck yourself."

Tom made a big deal of swaggering around the bars after that, claiming that he was going to get Reinhardt if he wasn't sent up for good. Finally he quieted down when Twyla reminded him that he'd been out screwing around when he should have been home to protect her that night. Reinhardt got sixty years in Anamosa for killing Carla Ross, and he's up for parole in twenty, but I doubt he'll get it. When the trial came up, the sheriff started getting a lot of phone calls from all over the place, telling him things Reinhardt had done. Most of them were anonymous, but they were enough to make him have a talk in private with the judge about the Prince, and I guess the judge had a talk with the prison, so he's not getting out till he's seventy at least. Deputy Weller made sure everyone knew that, and you know, it was comforting, for a change, to hear his gossip.

It took old man Aronson a few years to get over losing his wife and son, to get over feeling like we all thought *he'd* done it, not Reinhardt. I think what convinced him, finally, was that people showed up the next fall for the apples, just like always. But the following year, you could see his whole body lift up and his face get a little brighter when he realized that we weren't just coming back there for the curiosity, but that we really wanted the apples we had come to depend on him growing. The best, the sweetest, the deepest-blood-red apples you can find. At Aronson's Orchard, down Old Quarry Road, right off Highway 11. And every year there's something added, like another apology to us all. Apple dumplings, apple cider, apple donuts, apple dolls, and always and always, apples. The hardest and juiciest of which he saves back each fall for the truckload he'll bring up to Anamosa at Christmastime for Prince Reinhardt, who never sees him.

At Last

And then the day came when there was no more. First the grasses yellowed in places, stopped growing. There was no need to cut the lawns after that, until all of them lay flat and brown as in February. But it was June now. We watched the garden flowers begin to wilt—the blooms came slow and dusty, small fists of effort, then the buds merely burned on their drying stems. The tomato and bean plants dried from the bottom up: each week another layer of leaves dangled limp and yellow from the vine. The hollyhocks bursting tall like long fingers into the sky, six or seven feet, frozen in the heat. Later they waved in the wind, dead sticks, nearly empty seed-pods rattling on the stalks. We expected rain each week, as we always did in this place, thought it would come, piling dark on the eastern sky or blowing up from the gulf—but each day passed and then another.

The five-lined skink laid more and more often where we could see him out in the shade of the woodpile. There were no cups of moisture in the vines about the stone foundation of the house. More and more the trees and bushes sought their own economy—dropping leaves to protect themselves from the vast drying air.

Even the birds, previously only heard with a musical chirruping in the woods, began to move closer to us: a hummingbird searching for the flowers of our bushes, which would not come now, a downy wood-pecker, the wrens hopping along the porch, all looking for the least drops of moisture. Not even a night dew now.

Every day the sky, a blue. Nothing more. Nothing less. Then we began to find the turtles: the large ones, two or three times bigger than a hand with spread fingers. In the drying woods we could stumble over their shells, humped like rocks among the dead leaves, discover their decaying bodies inside. We found five of them that way before we realized what was happening—an omen we felt; though not by nature superstitious, we knew this to be a sign. The turtles, even the terrestrial ones, living on the moisture from the foliage and insect bodies, lost, lost in some amazement—the surprise of a forest turning desert. Even the water holes long sucked dry by thirsty air.

It was then, too, that we noticed the insects, their unusual voraciousness, their hunger for sweat and blood, some liquid, of our animals, of ourselves. At night they netted our bodies with their constant motion, the continual seeking for pores like tiny pools where their drinking could take place. But often they lacked the strength. Bobbing along the ceiling, they would suddenly drop—by morning the beds were dotted with their black and gray forms. We noticed, too, that the spiders, especially the larger ones, began to spin webs in strange and erratic patterns. A certain disorientation seemed to occur. And the webs themselves, filling with the weaker moths and flies, often went unattended. Later when we searched the nest, we would find the spider, brittle legs bent stiffly or outspread in an awkward position, its body sunken and papery.

We would find even the larger moths each morning, the pale luna and the polyphemus, the sphinx—all the magical ones—dead on the porches and windowsills. Drawn by our lights through the dark, they spent their last energy beating large, delicate wings slowly against the screens.

There were no butterflies to speak of, and after a while, even the tree frogs were silent in the long night heat. We did not examine the trees then. Although it was the time for seven-year locusts to come mottling out of the ground, we no longer heard their harsh whistle. The birds, too, grew more sluggish. It was possible, finally, to walk within a few inches of a cardinal perched on the wilted bushes along the drive. Speckled thrashers continued to hunt for grapes in the arbor, unable to understand, it seemed, that those hard, nutty berries clustered in the drying vines were the only crop now.

It was not that we became friends then—the animals and the humans—but that we were no longer independent of each other.

After we had begun to urinate in the woods (the toilets no longer usable, only a trickle of water plumbed through the pipes from the emptying well), we realized that our body excrement could nurture some of the smaller insects and plants—those surviving in the acidic burns. At this point, it had been so long after all, we were aware that while we had always taken the animal noises and their presence, as well, for granted, still the absence of that variety of whistles and hutterings left us with a kind of blankness, a silence full of longing and fear. At times, we would have willingly opened a vein to feed these creatures. Surrounded by their death and by the relentless heat, we entered a new stage of mourning. Somehow it mattered less that we were alive, so haunted were we by the silence. We knew that when the wind stopped—as we also knew it must, even the blistering one that threw waves of glowing hot air over our bodies until we almost drowned in it—we knew that when the trees stopped rustling and rattling, and the houses stopped creaking as of under great strain, then that would be the last of it. To have the only sound a human one of body against bush, of self clapping onto self, the only sound an extension of ourselves, would be our death. Perfect stillness. The dream of our life, would kill us.

FUNDER ACKNOWLEDGMENTS

Coffee House Press is an independent nonprofit literary publisher. Our books are made possible through the generous support of grants and gifts from many foundations, corporate giving programs, individuals, and through state and federal support. This project received major funding from the National Endowment for the Arts, a federal agency. Coffee House Press also received support from the Minnesota State Arts Board, through an appropriation by the Minnesota State Legislature; and from grants from the Elmer and Eleanor Andersen Foundation; the Beim Foundation; Buuck Family Foundation; the Bush Foundation; the Butler Family Foundation; Lerner Family Foundation; the McKnight Foundation; the law firm of Schwegman, Lundberg, Woessner & Kluth, P.A.; St. Paul Companies; Target, Marshall Field's, and Mervyn's with support from the Target Foundation; James R. Thorpe Foundation; the Walker Foundation; Wells Fargo Foundation Minnesota; West Group; the Woessner Freeman Foundation; and many individual donors.

This activity is made possible in part by a grant from the Minnesota State Arts Board, through an appropriation by the Minnesota State Legislature and a grant from the National Endowment for the Arts.

MINNESOTA
STATE ARTS BOARD

NATIONAL
ENDOWMENT
FOR THE ARTS

To you and our many readers across the country,
we send our thanks for your continuing support.

Good books are brewing
at coffeehousepress.org